PRAISE FOR

"Beautiful writing makes way for a [...] by Tea Cooper. With the same care a paleontologist unearths a fossil, Cooper has crafted a historical mystery that reveals itself layer by layer, piece by piece, and secret by secret. Highly entertaining and much recommended!"
—JENNI L. WALSH, AUTHOR OF *BECOMING BONNIE* AND *THE CALL OF THE WRENS*

"Cooper paints a fascinating portrait of two women rebelling against the expectations society and their family has for them. Historical fiction fans will delight in this romantic tale of family and long-held secrets."
—*BOOKLIST* FOR *THE CARTOGRAPHER'S SECRET*

"Cooper gets to the heart of a family's old wounds, puzzles, and obsessions, while providing a luscious historical rendering of the landscape. This layered family saga will keep readers turning the pages."
—*PUBLISHERS WEEKLY* FOR *THE CARTOGRAPHER'S SECRET*

"Tea Cooper's meticulous prose and deft phrasing delight the reader. Her storytelling weaves the places on Evie's map in tandem with the search Lettie makes so that the reader becomes immersed in a distant world. This fascinating novel informs the reader about Australia's storied past."
—HISTORICAL NOVEL SOCIETY FOR *THE CARTOGRAPHER'S SECRET*

"*The Cartographer's Secret* is a galvanizing, immersive adventure following a family's entanglement with a vanished Australian explorer through the lush Hunter Valley at the turn of the twentieth century."
—JOY CALLAWAY, INTERNATIONAL BESTSELLING AUTHOR OF *THE FIFTH AVENUE ARTISTS SOCIETY* AND *THE GREENBRIER RESORT*

"In *The Cartographer's Secret*, Cooper invites readers into another sweeping tale full of mystery, history, romance, and family secrets."
—KATHERINE REAY, BESTSELLING AUTHOR OF *THE LONDON HOUSE* AND *THE PRINTED LETTER BOOKSHOP*

"Deeply researched. Emotional. Atmospheric and alive. Combining characters that are wonderfully complex with a story spanning decades of their lives, *The Girl in the Painting* is a triumph of family, faith, and long-awaited forgiveness. I was swept away!"

—KRISTY CAMBRON, AWARD-WINNING AUTHOR OF *THE PARIS DRESSMAKER* AND THE HIDDEN MASTERPIECE NOVELS

"A stunning historical timepiece . . . With a touch of mystery and an air of romance, this new novel from one of Australia's leading historical fiction specialists will leave you amazed."

—*MRS B'S BOOK REVIEWS*, AUSTRALIA, FOR *THE GIRL IN THE PAINTING*

"Cooper has fashioned a richly intriguing tale."

—*BOOKLIST*, FOR *THE WOMAN IN THE GREEN DRESS*

"Refreshing and unique, *The Woman in the Green Dress* sweeps you across the wild lands of Australia in a thrilling whirl of mystery, romance, and danger."

—J'NELL CIESIELSKI, AUTHOR OF *THE ICE SWAN*

"Readers of Kate Morton and Beatriz Williams will be dazzled. *The Woman in the Green Dress* spins readers into an evocative world of mystery and romance in this deeply researched book by Tea Cooper."

—RACHEL MCMILLAN, AUTHOR OF *THE MOZART CODE*

"Boast[s] strong female protagonists, an infectious fascination with the past, and the narrative skill to weave multiple timelines into a satisfying whole . . . fast paced and involving storytelling . . . smartly edited, cleanly written . . . easy to devour."

—*SYDNEY MORNING HERALD*, FOR *THE WOMAN IN THE GREEN DRESS*

"A freshly drawn, bittersweet saga that draws nuggets of 'truth' with timeless magic and might-have-beens."

—*NORTH & SOUTH* MAGAZINE, NEW ZEALAND, FOR *THE WOMAN IN THE GREEN DRESS*

THE
FOSSIL
HUNTER

THE FOSSIL HUNTER

TEA COOPER

HARPER MUSE

Library of Congress Cataloging-in-Publication Data

Names: Cooper, Tea, author.
Title: The fossil hunter / Tea Cooper.
Description: First Australian Paperback Edition. | [Nashville] : Harper Muse, 2021.
    | Summary: "From USA TODAY bestselling author Tea Cooper comes the story
    of how a fossil discovered at London's Natural History Museum leads one woman
    back in time to nineteenth-century Australia and a world of scientific discovery and
    buried secrets"-- Provided by publisher.
Identifiers: LCCN 2021059020 (print) | LCCN 2021059021 (ebook) | ISBN
    9781400237968 (paperback) | ISBN 9781400237975 (epub) | ISBN 9781400237982
Subjects: BISAC: FICTION / Mystery & Detective / Historical | FICTION / Romance
    / Historical / 20th Century
Classification: LCC PR9619.4.C659 F67 2021 (print) | LCC PR9619.4.C659 (ebook) |
    DDC 823/.92--dc23
LC record available at https://lccn.loc.gov/2021059020
LC ebook record available at https://lccn.loc.gov/2021059021

Printed in the United States of America

22 23 24 25 26 LSC 5 4 3 2 1

This book is dedicated to my oldest friends, henceforth to be known as The Fossil Girls. Vanessa, Carla, Jane, and Annie . . . Where has the time gone?

CHAPTER 1

———◆◆———

1847

WOLLOMBI, NEW SOUTH WALES, AUSTRALIA

"It's blood—bad blood—that's causing it. A new pinafore and some education ain't going to change nothing. Still the same soul tucked beneath. You can teach a wild dog to come when it's called, but you wouldn't turn your back on it, not once it's bloodied."

Mellie sat hot and cross-legged on the dirt of the scullery floor wedged between the washboard and the mangle, hands over her ears, trying to block out Cook's words. Why she kept finding herself on the edge of the millpond at sunrise, with nothing for company but a blanket of mist and the cries of the curlews, she didn't understand.

Twisting this way and that, she plucked at her soggy nightgown, searching for the bad blood Cook kept ranting about. No sign of any stains on her skin or her nightgown, bad or otherwise.

"Why does she keep going down there? That's what I'd like to know." Fanny pushed up her sleeves and threw another bundle of kindling under the main copper.

"Only thing a scullery maid needs worry about is how to clean. Get to it."

"She ought to have learned her lesson by now."

"She's drawn to the place." Cook's beady eyes skewered Mellie. "If you keep going down there, you'll be taken. Small, plain, and bony, or large, round, and plump, he don't care so long as he gets tender young flesh."

Mellie crawled closer to the copper and rubbed at the goose bumps on her arms. The more she tried to remember how she ended up at the millpond, the more the nothingness grew, as though someone had singed a great hole in her memory. She'd tried to explain that she didn't do it on purpose, didn't know how she'd ended up there. But Cook never believed a word, called it a flight of fancy, whatever that was.

"Did you hear what I said?" Cook reefed Mellie to her feet and gave her a bone-rattling shake. "You'll be taken."

"Taken where?" Mellie's words squeaked, high-pitched and quivering.

"To his lair. He'll drag you down into the murky depths and . . ." Cook clapped her hands. "Gone." The loud, horrible slap bounced off the weatherboard walls. "Never to be seen again."

Mellie stuck her fingers in her ears and crawled back into the corner.

"You can't say that," Fanny hissed. "It's not true."

"True enough, if it keeps her out of the millpond. Saves her from drowning."

Cook reached under the mangle and hauled Mellie out of her hidey-hole. "Come on, missy. Go and get yourself dressed, then bring that gown back here. It needs to go in the copper."

All Mellie wanted was to go home. But she had no home. They'd burned all her clothes, all the furniture, the bedding, everything in the little slab cottage down by the brook. And she still couldn't get a straight answer from Mrs. Pearson or anyone else about Da.

She stomped through the kitchen to the sleep-out, the little room tucked into the corner of the veranda. The last thing she remembered before the fever got her was running through the bush, dogged by crashing footsteps, sweat blinding her eyes, her heart galloping. She'd dodged and weaved, then her feet went out from under her and her lungs filled with a gut-wrenching stench. Damp and rancid, with an underlying stink of moldering sludge.

She made it back home before the fever took hold, and then life became a horrible sweaty, itchy blur until two weeks later when she'd woken in the sleep-out with Mrs. Pearson daubing a foul chalky lotion all over her.

Turned out she'd caught the wretched chicken pox, though how she'd managed that she'd no idea. The chickens had gone long ago into the blank hole of nothingness along with Da and everything else. Mrs. Pearson blamed the fever, and said some things were best forgotten.

Mellie dragged her pinafore over her head, scooped up her night-gown, and tucked it under her arm. If she was careful, she could sneak through the back door, drop it outside the scullery, and disappear before she suffered another of Cook's rants.

She ducked underneath the wisteria cave, glanced through the yellowing leaves to the millpond, balled up her nightgown, lobbed it at the scullery door, and took off.

"Mellie! What are you doing out there? Come inside."

"I'm on my way to do my schoolwork, Mrs. Pearson." She crossed her fingers against the lie.

"In that case, show me how you're getting on."

"I'm going to practice in the copybook." No matter how hard she tried she'd never be able to imitate the perfect copperplate Lydia and Bea, the daughters of the house, produced with nothing more than a flick of their fine, thin wrists. And the chicken pox was no excuse; Mrs. Pearson said she had to do her schoolwork now the fever had gone because she was so far behind.

"Follow me." Mrs. Pearson led the way into the cool darkness of Dr. Pearson's study, the room where he talked to people who were sick, where he doled out foul-looking tonics from a squeaky cupboard crammed into the corner by the front door.

Now that she'd gotten over the towering piles of leather-bound books, the ghostly faded pictures, and the strange mixture of smells—carbolic, ink, dust, eucalyptus, and pipe tobacco—she quite liked the room. Especially the books, not that she'd discovered one she could read. She liked to rub her fingers over the soft leather covers and the bumpy gold letters. Lydia said they weren't fit for young girls so Mellie'd sneaked a peek when no one was looking. One book, by a man whose name she couldn't wrap her tongue around, was full of creatures and their skeletons. Worse still was another, packed with drawings of people's insides, of bits she didn't dare think about. Enough to make a person wonder what Dr. Pearson was up to.

"Sit down, Mellie. I wish to speak to you."

That didn't sound good. She rocked on the edge of the chair.

"Sit up straight, hands in your lap while I'm talking."

She shifted back, trying to escape Mrs. Pearson's probing stare, the spindles of the chair grating against her back.

"This wandering. It must stop. I realize it's difficult for you, forced to remain inside the house, but you've been sick, quite sick, and we don't want you to infect anyone else."

Her finger reached for the last remaining sore on her forehead, the only one that hadn't scabbed over. Mrs. Pearson promised that once the nasty crusty craters fell off, she wouldn't be a danger to anyone else. She picked at it; maybe if she pulled it off . . .

"Don't pick. Do you remember what I said?"

Mellie bobbed her head. "I can go outside when the scabs fall off."

"Then can you please tell me what you were doing down at the millpond?"

"Nothing." Her mouth dried. Nothing she remembered. Perhaps the black hole would lighten if she looked around in daylight.

"Don't lie, Mellie. Cook keeps finding you down there, and in your nightgown."

Mellie glanced around the room, her face getting hotter by the moment, not knowing what to say. She clenched her handkerchief in her fist.

"Do you remember being in the scullery?"

Mellie nodded again.

"So why do you keep going to the millpond?"

She lifted her shoulders. "I don't know." And then that flickering image drifted before her eyes. The mist creeping over the hills, the soggy grass beneath her feet, the glassy eyes of the old white mare watching her every move. "Oh!" She leaped up.

"What is it, dear?" Mrs. Pearson grasped at her hand. "Sit back down."

"I thought it was a dream. There's a white horse down there." She snorted into her handkerchief. "The millpond smells horrid. Damp and moldy. I don't mean to go down there."

"I'm sure there's a simple answer. I'll talk with Dr. Pearson again."

Not more poking and prodding—she couldn't still be sick, surely not. She raised the back of her hand to her forehead. No sign of a fever. "What's wrong with me?"

"Well, if you're not going there intentionally, Dr. Pearson believes you must be sleepwalking. It's understandable, after everything that's happened. It's your mind's way of working through the matters troubling you, but the water is deep and dangerous. We don't want you to come to any harm."

More like she'd come to harm at Cook's hand or from the horrible creature that lurked in the murky depths. "Cook's told me I'll be taken, snatched away."

"Poppycock and nonsense."

"I want Da." Her voice wobbled, then a great wave of sorrow stole her breath, almost drowning her. She covered her face to hide her trembling bottom lip. "Where's Da? Can I go home when I'm better?"

"Oh, my dear." Mrs. Pearson reached for her hand again, her gaze fixed on some spot beyond the window.

A griping took hold of Mellie and she jerked away, clutching at her stomach.

"Do you not remember anything before the chicken pox?"

She and Da in the little house down by the brook where they'd lived ever since Ma and baby John went. Not the best, but Da had plans, big plans. The picture flickered and faded, overtaken by a puddle of miserableness. "Is Da back yet?"

"No, my dear, he isn't."

Why? What had she done? Surely he wouldn't up and leave her.

Mrs. Pearson kept wringing her hands as though she needed to wash them. "I thought you understood. Dr. Pearson brought you here because no one would take you while you had the chicken pox."

She probably ought to thank the Pearsons, but she wasn't sure she was grateful. Bumping her feet against the rung of the chair, in time with the pendulum on the carriage clock, she tried again. "When's Da coming home?"

"I don't know, my dear." Mrs. Pearson straightened up, her eyes skittered back to the window, then her face brightened. "It might be better if you leave with the girls. I'll ask Dr. Pearson."

Leave? "You said I could stay." Her voice hitched embarrassingly on the words and her throat scratched. She couldn't go home. Everything had gone up in flames.

"This isn't a punishment. It's a holiday. Let me explain. I'm sure you're going to be very excited."

In all honesty, she couldn't think of anything that would make her excited unless someone stopped Cook's mouth and Fanny's slit-eyed glances and swept away the mess of the last weeks.

"Every Easter, Ella and Grace visit from Maitland and spend a few days here before they go off on a holiday with Lydia and Bea. Wouldn't you like to go with them? A holiday would be lovely."

A holiday. What was a holiday? And no. No, it wouldn't be lovely, whatever it was. Not if it meant going away. She was only beginning to get the hang of the doctor's house on the hill. "I want to stay here." Mostly. Cook's horrible mouth aside. "Da won't be able to find me if I go away, and what about my chicken poxes?"

"You won't be contagious for much longer, and those nasty sores will heal with fresh air and sunshine. Another upheaval in such a short time will be difficult, but it'll be for the best. You'll have a wonderful time with Anthea. She'll welcome you with open arms. Trust me."

Mellie hadn't much faith in trust. She smothered a scoff.

"Anthea lives at a place called Bow Wow, less than a day's ride from here. She's a fascinating woman, a paleontologist of some repute."

"A paleo what?"

"Someone who collects fossils."

Fossils? "What are they?"

"People call them curios—bones, shells, stone imprints of animals and plants."

The illustrations in Dr. Pearson's books reared before her eyes. Someone who collected bones. Da had a kangaroo skull tacked on the wall outside the cottage door where he hung his oilskin. Big holes where the eyes used to be and huge, horrible teeth. Where was Da? She covered her face with her hands, the pain too much to bear. She wanted to go home.

"Anthea is a scientist who tries to find out how things were in ancient times by studying the remains of the past."

This was getting worse by the moment. Da was the only remains of the past she'd like to see, but it didn't seem as though that was going to happen any time soon.

Mellie's eyes dived to the book on the shelf, the very one with the skeletons she'd taken down and studied. A shudder traced her shoulders and she shot to her feet. Perhaps that's what Cook meant when she said she'd be taken. "I don't want to go." The high-ceilinged room shrank around her. "I promise I'll behave. I won't be no trouble."

"Come along, Mellie. This isn't like you. Let me show you something." Mrs. Pearson walked over behind the desk and took down one of the pictures. "This is a daguerreotype. A new way to record images. It was taken a couple of years ago by a man named George Goodman. Here's Anthea, and her husband, Benjamin, Bea and Lydia, and Ella, and other visitors. They're having a lovely time."

A group of people stood in front of a huge rock face; in the middle were a man and a woman arm in arm, and two other people with a pack horse, and in between a group of girls, their long skirts brushing the grass and parasols held above their heads.

"Mellie, you're a brave girl. Lydia and Bea will be going, and Ella and Grace."

Ella. She shuddered. Lydia's best friend, all pink cheeks and airs and graces. She'd bossed her around ever since she'd arrived, and her younger sister, Grace, was even worse. Every time Grace caught sight of her, she stuck her hands in her armpits and danced around like a headless chook shrieking *bawk-bawk*. And now Bea had taken to doing it too. "You said this was my home. I won't wander, I promise. I don't want to be bloodied by the bunyip."

"Bunyip! Bloodied!" Mrs. Pearson leaped to her feet, her shadow towering over her like the giant beast Cook reckoned inhabited the millpond, waiting, just waiting, to snatch young girls away. "Go to your room and organize your belongings. I'm going to have words with Cook. This is the very reason you must go with the girls. There'll be no more nonsense." Mrs. Pearson threw open the study door. "Cook, Fanny, where are you? I want to talk to you."

"I won't go to the millpond again. I promise."

"It's got nothing to do with the millpond but everything to do with Cook's drivel and your overactive imagination."

Mellie gaped at Mrs. Pearson's disappearing back, taking long, cooling breaths until all the unanswered questions stopped bouncing around inside her head.

Bow Wow Gorge, New South Wales

Only at Bow Wow, beneath the dense canopy of the trees, did Anthea truly find peace. The place where the layers of life reached back to the beginning of time, before a single human had walked the land, before the earth solidified. From the towering sandstone cliffs to the meandering creek, which over millions of years had carved a narrow winding gorge, the landscape had slowly revealed its secrets.

Her foot, perhaps the first ever to disturb that specific spot, settled in the damp, moist undergrowth. This place once formed part of the coast, and embedded in the sandstone were marine fossils. A treasure trove of the past, which had lured both her and Benjamin from the outset with their dreams of discovering one of the larger marine reptiles that had fired the imagination of all of Europe.

But it was not to be. Despite every endeavor, their search proved fruitless. They'd discovered plenty of exquisitely preserved specimens of the smaller mollusks and shells but nothing resembling Hawkins's great sea-dragons—the ichthyosaur and the plesiosaur.

At sixty-two her time was limited—she no longer had the energy she'd once had when she and Benjamin would stride out happily and spend all day, even during the hottest summer, exploring the gorge. Now she rarely lasted more than a morning and would be home with a cup of tea on the veranda well before the sun dropped behind the surrounding hills.

She paddled down the creek lost in the memory of the wiry, weather-beaten man, seven years her senior, the man with the easy smile who'd made her heart sing and filled her mind with possibilities. Benjamin had brushed away the remnants of her strict religious upbringing and together they'd discovered Bow Wow Gorge and its hidden story.

She'd found her passion but she'd lost the man who'd inspired her to an agonizing case of pneumonia, and since his passing, like a weathered fossil her luster had faded. The thick, tawny hair Benjamin so loved reduced to a salt and pepper mess, leaving her old and crumpled. Not that she'd admit the fact to anyone, although Nette knew. It took one who'd survived the vagaries of time to understand.

The old sawpit marked the beginning of the snig trail to the house, and Anthea paused for a moment, seeing in her mind's eye the team of bullocks straining as they hauled timber up to the house.

The recent rain had washed away the heated remnants of summer and the ferns had flourished, creating vivid green curtains that draped the caves, the home of brooding shadows and leathery winged bats. She pushed through, her eyes, more from habit than anything else, raking the freshly revealed wall created by a small tumble of earth.

A glint of something dark against the crumbling sandstone brought her to a standstill. Fingers trembling, she brushed aside the loosened dirt. A small cylindrical-shaped stone tumbled into her cupped hand. Wiping back the strands of damp hair from her face, she stared down.

Her heart pounded.

Not much larger than a florin, it nestled in her palm, its center dented as though marked by the pad of an unknown thumb. There were no fractures, no cracks. Only a smooth, consistent surface worn by the movement of the layers over the ages. Pushing her way deeper into the cave, she ran her hands over the newly exposed wall and moments later a second stone tumbled free.

A wave of heat crept up her body and over her face. Not one of the dreadful hot flashes that so tormented her. Nothing like that. This was the pure thrill of a find. Something she'd seen before. Something from long ago, before she'd met Benjamin, before they'd escaped to Australia. She tucked the two stones into her collecting pouch and bounded up the trail.

Amazing what a find could do for her demeanor. What a mournful fool she was, wallowing in self-pity. Benjamin lived on in their combined interest. He would never lie forgotten as these pieces had.

"There're only two reasons you sing—so which one is it?" Nette tipped her head, rather like the resident willie wagtail who perched on the fence, waiting for a treat from the freshly turned soil, watching her every move with small, dark eyes.

Anthea trilled the final line of a song and allowed a smug smile to drift across her face. "You know me too well, but not quite well enough." A little bit of vanity, but she enjoyed keeping Nette guessing.

"Come on. Either you found something on that walk of yours or it's because the girls are coming."

"Both." She sat down and folded her arms across her ever-expanding girth: too much good food and not enough time spent outside. That would be rectified soon enough if today's discovery was what she imagined.

"When are the girls expected? There are beds to make up, supplies to be brought in, menus to organize. Jordan and I need dates and times and . . . What did you find?"

Anthea teased the side of her finger with her teeth, not because it needed chewing, but more because she wanted to string out the flood of pleasure and delight. Years of conjecture and hypothesizing, then, just like that, a simple mudslide after a few days' rain. "Two vertebrae."

Nette hooted, the sound an uncanny imitation of the powerful boobook that held sway over the gorge with its far-sighted scrutiny and swift raptorial claws. "You never did?"

"I might well have done."

"Don't just sit there, show me. Where are they?"

"How I wish Benjamin were here. We always hoped we might make such a find." She eased the stones from her pouch. Two vertebrae, if she was correct, but she hadn't had any tools with her, hadn't dared to run the risk of scratching with her fingers, spoiling what had laid waiting for more years than she could count. She held up one of the vertebrae, the central indentation from the marrow clearly visible, and as she studied it for the umpteenth time her conviction grew.

"It's from the base of the animal's neck. You can tell by the facets on the side."

Hooking her wire-rimmed spectacles over her ears, Nette moved closer. "Looks as though it might be."

"I have to compare it to the drawings I have in the workroom before I share it with the girls. Then they can help me in my search. This is Benjamin's dream come true. He always said the gorge had more to show us. We'll work slowly and carefully, see what else we can uncover. There's an illustration of Mary's ichthyosaur in one of the geological papers in the workroom. This will be so exciting for the girls. A real treasure hunt. I'll write tonight to Mitchell and send one of the specimens. Unless I'm mistaken there hasn't been a find like this in Australia."

"You won't be mistaken."

CHAPTER 2

1919
LONDON, ENGLAND

Penelope Jane Martindale strolled along the Cromwell Road, an agonizing mix of sorrow and regret congealing in her throat. Two years ago, she'd covered the same path, wedged safe between her twin brothers. They were on forty-eight hours' leave before they headed for France, thinking it would be nothing more than an adventure along their path to adulthood. She hadn't questioned their decision until it was too late. She should have known better.

The solidity and permanence of the Natural History Museum, set among incongruous wartime rows and rows of cabbages, potatoes, artichokes, and cauliflowers, drew her. It was a link to the past, to the last time she'd seen Dan and Riley, and she wanted to relive that day. There might not be another chance. She needed the memory clear in her mind. Pa would want to know about the last day they'd spent together.

In an hour or two she'd meet Sam and face another gut-wrenching farewell. She'd left him only the day before at Dieppe when she'd been one of the last to board ship. She'd wanted to stay in France, too, but he'd insisted she should go ahead, said he had a couple of matters to sort out. She'd agreed, loath to leave the man with whom she'd worked side by side for so long, but trusting in his promise that he would be right behind her and would meet her on the steps of the museum at four o'clock.

While she and Sam had ferried the wounded from the front lines to the doctors and nurses in the clearing stations, her thoughts had often returned to this cathedral of nature: initially as a way of escaping the acres of mud and misery, but later—after the telegrams arrived—as a reminder of the boys. They'd been lost too soon, along with millions of others, fighting a war Pa believed wasn't theirs to fight.

Buried in a profusion of memories, she made her way along the path where a mass of signs hung advising the public on wartime allotments and how to deal with insect infestation; there was a whole section devoted to the carrier pigeons, so important for relaying military communications and life-saving messages. She climbed the steps and wandered through the huge doors into the glorious concoction of space—the arches, sweeping staircases, and stained-glass windows dominated by the giant diplodocus.

One hundred and five feet of reconstructed history. *Diplodocus carnegii*, named for the man who had financed the acquisition of the skeleton found in a paddock somewhere in the middle of America. Andrew Carnegie had casts made of it and donated them to museums around the world in the hope science could transcend borders. Perhaps now the war was over his dream would be realized.

Dan and Riley had fallen in love with the dinosaur the moment they set foot in the museum. It hadn't mattered to them that Dippy was constructed entirely by human hand, the giant jigsaw sent across the ocean in thirty crates and assembled in the museum. They'd dreamed one day of finding one of their own, imagined it being named in their honor—*Diplodocus martindalii*, they'd joked.

She skirted the drooping tail and peered through the dinosaur's empty eye socket across the vaulted chamber, back into a past that made her eyes smart and her vision dim.

It had all begun with Dan and Riley's dusty old collection of fossils, which had provided them with hours of entertainment throughout the years. The boys taking the role of intrepid adventurers uncovering ancient bones while they'd relegated her to the less inspiring position of museum curator and sometime paleontologist. And right now, since she'd paid homage to Dippy, she intended to visit the paleontology collection.

Skirting a group of African elephants and numerous other giants, she made her way through to the back room where myriad glass specimen cases housed neatly labeled vertebrate, invertebrate, and plant fossils.

Holding her hair back, she leaned closer to the glass. A hastily scrawled sign read *An amphibian that lived in Australia over 200 million years ago.*

Home. How she longed for the Australian sun, the khaki-colored leaves outlined against a deep blue sky, and the song of the cicadas. A painful sigh whisked its way between her lips. It wouldn't be the same without Dan and Riley's boisterous buffeting and infectious good humor.

"Fascinating, isn't it?"

She lifted her head and came face-to-face with one of the wardens, his threadbare uniform a relic from an age long gone. No doubt he would have retired years ago but for the war.

"Are you interested in fossils?" His rheumy eyes, buried deep in wrinkled skin, twinkled.

"It's more my brothers' interest. I didn't know they'd found fossils like this in Australia."

"Apparently so. This is a new acquisition. Found in a brick pit in Sydney, Australia."

"What's it doing here?"

"Our collection holds quite a few specimens from Australia. Thought one day I might take a trip. They say the sun always shines."

"More often than England, but not always."

He threw her a puzzled look.

"I was born in Australia."

"And you've been doing your bit, I see." He gestured to the faded Red Cross armband on her coat. She'd worn it for so long she'd almost forgotten about it.

"As an ambulance driver. A very small bit."

"Not from what I've heard. Plenty a man owes his life to an ambulance driver. Could have done with a few more of them ambulances in the African War; we had horse-drawn carts but no motor vehicles. Still, this is my spot now. The paleontology collection is my responsibility." He straightened a little. "That doesn't mean I collect them or prepare them. I simply look after them. They're pretty quiet patients." He winked. "Not like you'd be used to."

She offered a half-hearted smile. She didn't want to talk about the war. Here with the past, she could forget the images that haunted her dreams. "You said you had other specimens from Australia. Could I see them?"

"You've found the star of the show. Hasn't been properly labeled yet." He pulled a large bunch of keys from his pocket, selected a small brass one, and slipped it into the lock on the frame of the display case, then extracted a piece of cardboard tucked under the jaw bone. *Paracyclotosaurus davidi, a new labyrinthodont (Paracyclotosaurus), Sydney, New South Wales, T. W. Edgeworth David.*

Penelope leaned closer, her fingers reaching for the wide jaw.

"No touching." He snapped the display case shut and locked it again. "Can't have greasy finger marks."

She shoved her hands into her pockets, her whole body responding to the information on the label. A flood of recollections of the place she hadn't seen for so long . . . the small town nestled between the arms of the waterways, the house overlooking the millpond, the sweeping hills and dappled valleys, Pa and Dan and Riley.

"Tricky things, fossils."

The images cleared and she followed the old man.

"You either get them or you don't. Some people can't see the significance; they write them off as a pile of old rocks. But they hold a wealth of secrets."

"I was born in New South Wales, a place called Wollombi. I had no idea . . ."

"So you know this man with his back-to-front name, this Edgeworth David?"

"No, no, not at all."

"Come with me." He flicked his head in the direction of a small door at the back of the room. "That's where we keep the other Australian specimens—maybe some were found in your back garden."

Highly unlikely. At least she couldn't think of anywhere in the little village there might be fossils. Drawings and carvings made by the Wonnarua, Awabakal, Worimi, and Darkinjung people up at Mount Yengo, even an ax head or two, but nothing resembling this crocodile-like monster. Dan and Riley would have swarmed over it like a plague of meat ants.

They bypassed numerous glass-fronted cabinets and more display cases until the light dimmed and the air thickened with dust.

"Some interesting stuff in here—the early specimens from Australia. A man named Thomas Mitchell, Australia's surveyor general, sent them to Sir Richard Owen—he's the one responsible for this wonderful museum. A paleontologist and superintendent of the museum years ago, before my time." He gave a breathless cough, maybe a laugh. "Transformed the place, he did, and opened everything up to the public. I can remember coming as a boy. Always a good place to spend a chilly afternoon. Never thought I'd end up working here, though."

His words washed over her, her mind reeling. She and the boys had talked about visiting fossil sites in America, the places Riley and Dan had spun their yarns around, and here was a specimen found less than a hundred miles from home.

"Follow me."

They squeezed into a smaller, badly lit room and she followed him through the maze of display cases until they came to a halt in front of a pair of glazed mahogany cabinets.

"Have a look at this."

She studied the giant skull. Two huge incisors protruded from the lower jaw.

"*Diprotodon australis.*"

"What's a diprotodon?"

"A giant wombat."

"A giant wombat. Good heavens." She smothered a laugh.

"Have you ever seen one?"

"I've seen plenty of wombats. They can be a bit of a nuisance. They dig their burrows and destroy the paddocks and tracks. But I've never seen one as big as this."

He nodded. "They reckon they weighed around three tons. Big as an omnibus."

"The wombats I've come across are nowhere near that big."

"So they're small? Like rabbits?"

"No, nothing like rabbits. About this height." She reached down and held her hand level with her calf. "Quite heavy and often slow. Where did this come from?"

"A place called Wellington, New South Wales too. Mitchell gave an address to the Geological Society." He rummaged through a pile of yellowing papers. "Here it is, in 1838. Wellington," he repeated. "There's a small town in the south of England called Wellington. Perhaps you Australians pinched the name." He paused for a moment, scratched his thinning hair. "Well, I'm a fool, aren't I? I should show you Mary Anning's specimens. She came from down south too. Not that she got any credit for her discoveries. The scientists of the day used her finds to establish their own reputation. Wasn't until she was fifty years dead they made her an honorary member of the Geological Society. Still, times are changing—they say women will get the vote before too long."

"Tell me a little bit more about these Australian specimens."

"Right you are." He locked the cabinet and moved on to the next. "Here are some more Mitchell sent Sir Richard." He lifted the lid of the unlocked cabinet and gave a dismissive huff. "Numerous marine fossils from the early Permian period." He flipped one of the labels. This one is from the Hunter Valley, a place called Harper's Hill. Does that ring a bell?"

"Hunter Valley does. I don't know Harper's Hill." What she wouldn't give for a map. "Can I pick this one up?" Her hand hovered over the small, polished rock, more like an ashtray than anything else.

"Guess it wouldn't hurt—looks like a vertebra to me, probably an ichthyosaur or a plesiosaur. Quite common down on the south coast of England, throughout Europe, in fact."

Cool to the touch, the polished stone nestled in her palm, the center indented as though molded by someone's thumb. She had an overwhelming urge to hold it tight. She clenched her fist and turned to the label. "Oh, this is interesting. Mitchell didn't find it. It was found by someone named A. Winstanley, in a place called . . . Bow Wow Gorge." As her lips formed the words a vision burst into her mind. Dan and Riley, freckles popping after another weekend with their bicycles. Mrs. Canning, hands on hips, demanding to know where they'd spent the night. *"At the gorge. Bow Wow Gorge."* And much cackling laughter and foolishness while they argued about the origins of the name. Something to do with a dog's hind leg.

He studied the label. "Hmm. The name Winstanley rings a bell. I'm sure there's something else. Come along."

She followed him across the main room, trying to hold tight to the poignant memory.

"I wanted to show you this." He threw open the door and her breath caught. Displayed on the wall was a huge, polished stone and in bas-relief a giant dragon-like creature. "Now that's what I call a fossil."

"It's amazing."

He gave a humph of satisfaction and grinned, his eyes disappearing into a bed of deeply etched wrinkles. "That's Mary Anning's treasure—*Ichthyosaurus anningae*. First full skeleton ever found."

"But not Australian."

He shook his head and tutted. "Told you. Down south. Dorset. Lyme Regis."

Her fingers smoothed the vertebra still clasped in her hand. "I'm not sure where that is."

"You've never heard of Lyme Regis? I thought you were interested in fossils. That's where Mary Anning lived. Her father taught her how to search for fossils when she was just a little child. She'd help him clean them and they'd sell them to visitors. After he died she took over the business and about a year later made her first big find. Not bad for a twelve-year-old girl. Scientists thought it was a crocodile; others called it a sea-dragon. Wasn't until years later they named it ichthyosaurus." He puttered along between the display cases. "That Winstanley. There's something here, too, from her." He flipped the label on another specimen. "There we are. Winstanley. Nice example of an ammonite. 1860. Ah. From Lyme." He traced the spiral form above the glass. "Perhaps the most widely known fossil, thanks to our Mary. We have some of Elizabeth Philpot's fish somewhere too. Beautiful examples, every scale in place."

"Mr. Ambrose. Mr. Ambrose." Strident tones echoed in the confines of the room, destroying the ancient ambience.

"That'd be me. Time to go. I've got to check everything's shipshape before we close for the afternoon. Can't trust anyone else. I've enjoyed our little talk, Miss . . ."

"Martindale. PJ—Penelope Jane." PJ was Sam's nickname for her; the mouthful Ma and Pa had landed her with had lasted less than five minutes the first time she and Sam crossed paths. He'd christened her PJ, said it suited her because she was one of the boys, and it had stuck. She liked the short, no-nonsense initials, a nod to the woman she'd become since she'd left Australia, but she felt Mr. Ambrose would appreciate her full name.

"Come back another day, Miss Penelope Jane." He gave her a crumpled wink. "Not often I have the attention of a pretty girl like you."

"I'd really like to." But her time was up. Sam would be sitting outside waiting. Drumming his fingers, wondering what had happened to her. "Thank you, Mr. Ambrose, I'll try. Thank you so much for your time. It's been fascinating. I'm going to see if I can find out anything more about this Winstanley person, and Mitchell, when I get home."

"Goodbye. And if I ever get to Australia I'll look you up."

She curbed a smile. No one quite understood the size of Australia. How many times had she had that conversation with an injured soldier?

With a final glance at Mary Anning's sea-dragon, she left, slipping a quick pat to Dippy's nose as she passed through the central hall and out into the street.

A seething mass of men in every different kind of uniform clustered around the courtyard, some with their faces aglow and their arms linked with smiling girls, others gray-skinned yet determined, the price they'd paid obvious in the array of bandages, limps, and missing limbs. But overall the atmosphere was one of enthusiasm and optimism. Finally, the war to end all wars had freed them from its clutches. All that remained now was finalizing the massive task of repatriation.

PJ stood at the top of the steps searching for Sam's shock of unruly hair and his upright stance, but no one made her heart jump. Nothing could have happened to him. He'd survived so much. Volunteered so early, months and months before America had entered the war. Argued long and hard with his father, broken his mother's heart, but convinced it was his duty, he'd traveled to London and a family friend had helped him organize everything. He'd bought the Wolseley, had it converted into an ambulance, and taken off to Paris. Once he'd got the idea in his head, he was unstoppable.

"Miss Martindale." She jumped as a hand grasped her arm. "I've called your name half a dozen times. Didn't you hear me?"

She scanned the face, not recognizing a single feature, but his slow drawl and elongated vowels would have given him away as an Australian even if he wasn't wearing a slouch hat and a cheeky grin.

"How do you know who I am?"

"I can spot an Aussie sheila from a hundred paces. Most beautiful girls in the world. Captain Groves sent me. Name's Ted. Ted Baker."

Color tinged her cheeks and her shoulders sagged. "Where's Sam?"

"I'm afraid he's not going to make it."

Her stomach took a dive, right down to her boots, and the air wavered.

"Blimey. Didn't do that well." Ted grabbed her arm. "He's fine, really fine. He's got caught up. Trouble getting Sid back. Asked me to tell you not to worry and he'll be here in a couple of days. He said same place, same time, but two days later."

"Why's he bringing the ambulance back?" Typical Sam. He loved that car, a Wolseley-Siddeley he'd christened Sid. Sam's only fault, if it could be counted as one, was his impulsiveness, but that was the characteristic that had brought them, and many others, through the war unscathed.

"Not real sure, but he seemed determined enough. Said a Sid Wolseley wasn't going to lie and rot on the battlefield no matter what the brass said. Sure you're okay? I gave you a bit of a shock. Let me see you back to your lodgings. The captain'll have me guts if anything happens to you."

"Thanks, it's not a long walk and I can find my own way."

"Right you are, then." He tipped the brim of his hat and bounded back down the steps to a group of Diggers sitting on the wall sharing a packet of cigarettes and what sounded like a ribald joke. They deserved their peace. The Australian Defence Force had earned a mighty reputation for bravery in the trenches.

She shrugged deeper into her coat and rammed her hands into her pockets. Her fingers tightened around the smooth polished surface of the vertebra. "Oh my goodness." She whipped around and bolted back up the steps where a warden sporting a faded frock coat similar to Mr. Ambrose's gave the doors a final slam and fastened the chain. She rapped her knuckles on the glass. He glanced up, shook his head, and mouthed the word *closed*.

She held up the fossil, but he had already turned his back and was walking away.

What to do? She'd had no intention of taking it, had forgotten all about it—what if Mr. Ambrose thought she'd stolen it? She tried the other doors, then finally admitted defeat and walked back down the steps. She'd bring it back first thing tomorrow morning. It sat snug and warm in the palm of her hand almost as though it were happy to be released from the confines of the museum.

For goodness' sake. What rubbish.

Good job Sam hadn't arrived when he'd said he would. She might have forgotten all about it, not found it for days.

A lilac glow illuminated the skyline as PJ trudged back down the Cromwell Road. Tempted by the scent of baking drifting from one of the tea shops, she shouldered open the door and found a table tucked into the corner by a window.

She placed the fossil carefully in front of her on the tablecloth and picked up the label, taking care not to dislodge the small glob of glue holding the string firm. *Winstanley.* Who was Winstanley? What had the man in the museum said? A group of people working in Lyme Regis, and he'd mentioned another name, Elizabeth someone. Philpot, that was it. Mary Anning, Elizabeth Philpot, and Winstanley. More to the point, Winstanley visited Bow Wow Gorge. Dan and Riley would have been beside themselves. They'd have turned the gorge upside down searching for their very own sea-dragon.

"What can I get you?"

"A pot of tea, please, and some cake. Have you got fruit cake or, better still, scones? A Bath bun?"

"Afternoon tea's over."

"A pot of tea will be fine." She sat staring at the fossil, turned the label once again. *Possible Ichthyosaur vertebra. A. Winstanley. March 1847. Bow Wow Gorge, Australia.* Suddenly the hum of the tea shop faded and she was back at Wollombi, crouched in the hallway, lining up the labeled fossils Dan and Riley had found in the attic, the writing faded and blurred by their sticky fingers. And dates, they'd all had dates on them because Dan and Riley were so unusually pedantic about labeling their own finds.

"Pot of tea, for one." It landed with a bit of a thump, pulling her back to the present. "Table's booked for six o'clock. Won't be long, will you? I have to change the cloth and clean up." The waitress gave the corner of the table a dramatic brush with a napkin, sniffed haughtily, and walked away.

PJ poured a cup of tea, milk, and sipped the thick, stewed brew. A good job Sam wasn't here. He detested tea with a vengeance most reserved for the Boche. Maintained the most important thing he'd discovered since he'd arrived in Europe was how to make a decent cup of coffee. He was right, but then Sam was right about a lot of things, and his innate sixth sense had saved her more times than she'd care to remember. Saying goodbye was going to be hard, but she had to go home.

Sam had become more than a friend. He'd become someone she relied on, and she knew he felt the same about her. They'd lived in each other's pockets for so long. She'd miss him. Miss his constant good humor, his ability to blend into any situation, his talent for making friends. And how she loved his old-fashioned manners and his accent, making even the most mundane of words sound exotic. But there was no point in moping. Family came first, and she hadn't heard from Pa since she'd written after she'd received the telegrams about the boys. Mrs. Canning had sent the odd, infrequent letter but nothing more.

She had to go home—she was all Pa had.

CHAPTER 3

1847
Bow Wow

"Bawk-bawk, smile. It won't crack your face."

Smile? Why smile? Mellie stuck out her tongue, then turned to Lydia and Ella, sitting there so composed, so at ease, as though the world knew how important they were with their all-too-perfect hats and lace-encased hands folded in their laps. Why couldn't they speak up? Rescue her from the horrible taunts. She was sick of it. Sick of the constant teasing. Anyone would think she'd caught chicken pox on purpose.

"Come on, Bawk-bawk, give us a smile." Bea stuck her hands under her armpits, drummed her boots on the carriage floor, and began squawking. "*Bawk-bawk*, Pox face. *Bawk-bawk*, Pox face."

Mellie turned aside, not wanting to be caught in the sticky web of catcalls as the open carriage lurched and swayed on the uneven track. How could Mrs. Pearson have done this to her? She'd pleaded, spent hours being on her very best behavior, begged not to be sent away. There were only so many times a girl could be uprooted like an unwanted weed, thrown into a new patch, and survive. Besides, how was she supposed to find Da this far from Wollombi?

Lydia reached out to clasp her hand but she shrugged her away. She didn't want any half-baked sympathy. "Everything will be fine, Mellie. You'll see. Aunt Anthea will be thrilled to meet you. And we always have a wonderful time. I promise you'll love it."

The carriage lurched again and turned into a damp, green tunnel of leaves. She hugged herself tight. Why was she shivering as though it were the middle of winter? "Are we nearly there?" she mumbled, her tongue refusing to let the words free.

"Not much farther, about a mile. You'll see the house once we go around the next bend. There's a bit of a climb because it's on the top of the hill."

Before Lydia's words seeped into her muddled brain, the carriage lurched, throwing Mellie back against the seat and Bea and Grace headfirst into her lap. Bracing her feet, she sat rigid, wishing they'd landed flat on their smirking faces. So much for the lovely time Mrs. Pearson promised, and they hadn't even arrived at Bow Wow.

It wasn't until the house came into view that the nasty tightness in Mellie's chest eased. Bathed in a pool of sunshine, it sat atop a small rise flanked by the tallest grass trees she'd ever seen.

"It's a lovely place. And Aunt Anthea is the kindest of women."

Lydia reached for her hand again and this time Mellie didn't pull away. Lydia was the only one who had been kind to her, the only one of the four girls Dr. Pearson had allowed to come anywhere near her while she was sick because she'd already had the chicken pox. His strict rules had worked. Bea, Grace, and Ella had been spared.

"I hope Aunt Anthea doesn't mind me coming."

"She's not *your* aunt, Bawk-bawk." Bea's jeering blew a waft of warm sugary breath into her face. "We're allowed to call her aunt because she's a friend of Mother's. You can't because you're not family."

Is that what friends did? Made themselves part of one another's families? A strange thought. She only had Da, and he still hadn't come home. "What should I call her?" After all, she wasn't a friend. Not anyone's friend, nothing but a charity case. Someone Dr. and Mrs. Pearson had taken under their wing, after everything had gone wrong. So very wrong.

Grace let out a sort of huff, rather as though Mellie didn't have the brains of the chickens Bea said infected her.

"Her full name is Mrs. Anthea Winstanley." Lydia glared at her younger sister. "Mellie should call her Mrs. Winstanley until she's told otherwise. It's good manners."

Manners again. Mellie groaned. She'd come to hate the word. It seemed to crop up all the time. *"Sit up straight. Keep your elbows off the table. Wash your hands. Don't speak until you're spoken to. Don't bite your nails. Smile. Be polite."* So many things had the stupid *manners* label. So many things she didn't understand and she'd never had to worry about when it had only been her and Da.

Anthea paced the veranda, eyes trained on the driveway that sloped up from the road. When Jordan left yesterday, he'd assured her they would be back before nightfall. Nette had the table laid, the beds made up, and a delicious smell of meatloaf wafted from the kitchen.

It was nigh on twelve months since the girls had last visited, and although Anthea'd kept in contact with Edna, she hadn't seen Lydia and Bea. The fact Edna would willingly relinquish charge of her precious daughters never ceased to amaze her. Benjamin had come up with the original idea, a tradition that now spanned several years, and various friends had accompanied the Pearson girls on their visits, although the Ketteringham sisters, Ella and Grace, had been a constant. She'd enjoyed watching them all grow and mature. Before long Lydia and Ella would bring their own children to visit. Edna already had her sights set on a suitable husband for Lydia, and Ella wouldn't be far behind. Still, there were Bea and Grace—they would turn twelve soon. She must ask them if they would like to bring a friend next year.

With a chorus of squawks, a flock of black cockatoos settled higher in the branches of the casuarinas, heralding Jordan's return and the possibility of rain. A smile broke out on Anthea's face. "Nette, they're here. Come quickly." She smoothed her skirt and patted down her hair, then raised her hand in anticipation.

"No point in waving yet. They can't see you for the trees."

"I am ridiculously pleased at the thought of their visit. I have some wonderful plans."

"And some of them will revolve around those vertebrae you found, I have no doubt."

Correct as always. She'd received a reply from Mitchell only yesterday, saying how interested he was in her find and that he intended to discuss it with other members of the society. However, he thought it most unlikely that it was a plesiosaur or an ichthyosaur because no one else had found any evidence of one in Australia. That was a load of nonsense—it didn't rule out the possibility. There was always a first. She would do her damnedest to find further evidence.

Having placed the vertebrae alongside the illustrations in the Geological Society papers and Mary's drawings, she was convinced she was right—ichthyosaurs and perhaps plesiosaurs had swum in the waters of the gorge. A curl of excitement fizzed through her. A dream come true. The girls would be thrilled by her discovery. It would give their visit an unaccustomed purpose, and with their help over the next ten days she could comb the area. Who knew what they would find? How wonderful would it be to discover more than the usual array of mollusks?

"Here they are." Anthea lifted her skirts, skipped from the veranda, and spread her arms wide. "Welcome, girls. Welcome to Bow Wow."

Faces wreathed in smiles, giggles breaking the silence that all too often cloaked the property, Bea and Grace, cheeks rosy, eyes alight, threw themselves into her embrace.

"Hello, Aunt Anthea. It took so long. We had to stop so many times for Jordan to secure Ella's trunk." Bea lifted her hand to her mouth, stretched up on tiptoes, and whispered, "She thinks she's a lady now. She's got a beau—his name's George, and Lydia is insanely jealous. They've done nothing but snarl at each other all the way here."

Bea and Grace squealed with laughter and rushed away to greet Nette.

Ella and Lydia, now grown into young ladies, allowed Jordan to hand them down from the carriage. "Aunt Anthea, it's delightful to see you." Lydia's clipped vowels spoke more of elocution lessons in Sydney than her Wollombi upbringing. Gone was the skinny girl with scratched knees and tousled hair; before Anthea stood a brightly polished young woman.

Anthea's hand slipped to the pendant she wore around her throat, and she slid her thumb over the lamp shell, the first winged brachiopod she and Benjamin had taken from the gorge. It was her most treasured possession. They'd cleaned and polished it to a lustrous hue, and he'd taken it to a jeweler in Sydney who'd fashioned a decorative silver bail clasp. What would Benjamin have thought of the girls he once led through the gorge with their collection pails?

"It's insufferably hot for April." Ella removed one glove and dabbed at her powdered face. "Mellie, can you hold this? Mellie, where are you?"

A scrawny young thing with unruly honey-colored hair dangling to her waist edged from behind Ella's well-padded rump, her huge eyes wide.

Lydia reached for the girl and tugged her forward. "This is Mellie. Ma suggested she come with us. She's at a bit of a loose end." The child's haunted gaze skittered from side to side as she scuffed her broken-down boots and clung to a battered carpetbag as if her life depended on it.

Anthea bent down and held out her hand, noting the riotous mixture of freckles and scabs adorning the child's forehead and cheeks. A recent dose of chicken pox, unless she was mistaken, and she was one of Edna's charity cases, judging by her bony wrists and the overlarge hands poking out from her sleeves. One extra would make little or no difference. No doubt Lydia would know the story—the poor little scrap hardly looked as though she'd make a dent in the mountain of food Nette had prepared.

The tall woman with dull gray hair eyed her with a look of distaste. All Mellie wanted to do was leap back into the carriage. Beady, currant-colored eyes bore into her, right through to her backbone. She glanced at Mrs. Winstanley's clawed fingers, looking for signs of her bone hunting, signs of blood.

With a rustle Lydia pulled a folded piece of paper from the little bag dangling off her wrist and waved it in the air. "Ma hopes you don't mind Mellie coming along. She's had chicken pox, but she's not contagious anymore. She's explained everything in this letter."

Heat rushed through Mellie's body—her face would be all mottled and her scars would pop like raspberries. Mrs. Pearson hadn't said anything about a letter. She didn't want the whole story pored over again and again. It was supposed to be forgotten. Not that she wanted to forget Da, but she was heartily sick of all the sideways glances and people muttering under their breath.

Mrs. Winstanley took no notice of Lydia, much to Mellie's surprise; instead, she reached for her hand. "Hello, Mellie. I'm Anthea Winstanley, but you can call me Aunt Anthea, like everyone else. Welcome to Bow Wow. I hope you enjoy your time here."

Whatever it was that had stolen Mellie's tongue gave it a further twist and her mouth dried. What was she meant to do? She let her carpetbag fall to the ground and tried to pull her hand away. Mrs. Pearson had told her it was bad manners to touch people uninvited, but this woman wouldn't let go.

"Jordan will see to everyone's bags. Come along, Mellie." With a smile Aunt Anthea towed her up the steps to the veranda. "Let's get you all settled."

Not daring to meet anyone's eyes, Mellie followed, her gaze pinned on the huge room ahead of her until her foot caught on the mat and she pitched forward.

Aunt Anthea steadied her. "Be careful. It's such a nuisance, but Nette insists we all wipe our feet so we don't trail mud through the house." She made a show of wiping both her boots like some dog kicking over its traces and then stepped inside. "Make yourself at home, girls."

Bea and Grace shoved past and galloped off across the room after Nette and Ella. Mellie hovered; she had no idea what to do or where to go.

"Aunt Anthea." Lydia brandished the letter in front of her. "I need to speak with you." Her muted tone kept Mellie rooted to the spot. "Privately, for a moment. Mother asked me to apologize, but she simply didn't have time to write beforehand." Lydia chewed on her lip, then lowered her voice to a whisper. "Mellie can be a bit of a handful. She tends to sleepwalk so we have to keep an eye on her."

Not the sleepwalking again. Why bring it up? Dr. Pearson had promised it would stop once she had a change of air.

Aunt Anthea patted Lydia on the arm. "I can remember someone else who needed an eye kept on them. Look at you. Quite the young lady about town."

Lydia peeled off her lace gloves. "Don't worry, I'm ready to get my hands dirty."

"That's good to hear. I've got some exciting news."

"First I must give you this. Mother thinks Mellie needs a fresh start. She said it's all in the letter."

Throwing Mellie a brief smile, Aunt Anthea led Lydia into another room and closed the door, leaving Mellie scuffing her feet. She stepped closer, pressed her ear against the smooth timber. Nothing but the rustle of paper and the sound of a snatched breath.

"Charged?"

"And taken to Newcastle."

Da was in Newcastle? Why hadn't anyone told her? He might be home any day and she wouldn't be there. It was all so horribly unfair. She knew Da wouldn't have shot the man on purpose. More likely Cogley, the oaf, had, or one of the other horrible men who'd hung around the house for weeks on end.

The door swung open and Mellie sprang back.

"Why don't you go through the walkway to the kitchen, Mellie? You'll find Nette there with the other girls. Lydia . . ." Aunt Anthea beckoned with her finger.

Once Mellie disappeared toward the kitchen, Anthea turned back to the letter. She unfolded it and reached for her pendant.

The skin-warmed treasure calmed her as it always did. Surely she would have heard if a local man had been found guilty of murder and executed at Newcastle.

I cannot find it in my heart to mourn his passing, as I fear poor Mellie has been most abominably treated by her father and his scurrilous band of bushrangers.

Her hand covered her mouth, stifling a low moan. It was simply dreadful—the poor, poor child.

Despite my best intentions, Cook and Fanny have gained knowledge of this awful occurrence and continue to hound Mellie. I am sending her to you in the hope she can recover in peace. She has no knowledge of her father's fate and is still expecting his return.

Anthea refolded the paper and tucked it into the waistband of her skirt. She'd read it again later; surely Edna wouldn't have discussed it in full with Lydia. Not the kind of thing any young girl should have to hear about, never mind live through.

"You said you had some exciting news." Lydia's voice broke into her thoughts. "Do tell."

She lifted her head and smiled. Oh, but it was good to have Lydia here, and the other girls, but Lydia especially. The children she'd never had. The children Edna lent her once a year and had done since Lydia was not much taller than Mellie. "How old is Mellie?"

"She's just turned twelve, but she doesn't look it or behave that way."

"In that case we better go and rescue Nette. Come along."

"There's one more thing, Aunt Anthea." Lydia's tone held a quaver, one Anthea hadn't heard in her voice before.

"What is it, my sweet? Is your mother well, your father? Not working too hard?"

"No, everyone is well." Dismay flickered across Lydia's face. "Ella and I aren't seeing eye to eye and I wondered . . ."

So that was the lay of the land. What had Bea said? A beau, and Lydia was insanely jealous—maybe more to it than she'd first thought. "And you don't want to share your usual room with Ella?"

"I knew you'd understand. Is there anything we can do?"

To keep the peace? Plenty. It wouldn't be the first time Ella and Lydia had squabbled. A few days outside in the sunshine and some decent exercise and their disagreement would be forgotten. "I expect so. Let me talk to Nette."

"I'd be quite happy to share a room with Mellie. It might be a good idea. I could keep an eye on her. Her sleepwalking is a bit of a problem."

Good heavens. Perhaps it was more than a tiff. "Come along. You must be parched. I'm sure it's nothing Bow Wow won't cure."

CHAPTER 4

1919
LONDON

The splatter of rain against the window woke PJ. She rolled out of bed and pushed aside the curtains to reveal a dull gray day. So much for summer. Perfect for another visit to the museum, though, and time to return the vertebra. She wandered over to the small table beneath the window to retrieve it . . . It was gone.

Not on the floor, not under the table. She checked the pockets of her coat. Not there, but then she knew it wasn't. She'd put it on the table last night before she'd climbed into bed. How could it have vanished? With a tug, she pulled back the bedclothes and let out a long breath of relief when she found it lying next to the pillow. She reached out and lifted it from the bedclothes, still warm from the heat of her body.

The vertebra sat in her palm, bringing her dream flooding back. A winding track lined with eucalypts, their scent heavy in the air, bright blue skies, and a creek—a fast-flowing creek carved through time between two towering rock faces. And then there was a sea-dragon peeking through the trees, a tag around its neck—*Ichthyosaurus martindalii*.

"For heaven's sake." Her words bounced from the walls of the small room. Dreaming of sea-dragons in Australia. What rubbish. The sooner she got the fossil back to the museum, the better.

Within ten minutes PJ stood outside the door of the boarding house, opening her brolly to shield herself from the incessant English drizzle. She strode off in the direction of the museum, hopeful she'd find Mr. Ambrose and return the fossil before anyone noticed it missing, and if he wasn't there, perhaps she'd be able to slip it back into the display case. The mere thought of having to explain herself made her face hot and her palms sticky.

Unlike yesterday afternoon, the courtyard outside the museum was empty. She ran up the steps and pushed against the door. What time was it? It was impossible to judge from the sky because, although the rain had stopped, the lowering clouds blocked out the light and made her feel as though she might graze her head on them at any moment. She passed the time by wandering around looking at the carvings on the outside of the building: birds and animals of all descriptions, some even more fantastic than the sea-dragon of her dream.

When the doors finally opened, she as good as barged past the warden, skirted Dippy, and ran down the stairs into the paleontology rooms without a backward glance. There was no sign of Mr. Ambrose, so she slipped into the back room, praying she'd find the display case unlocked.

Luck was on her side, and she slipped the fossil back and closed the lid with a pang of regret. She then edged along the jumble of cabinets with a vague hope of finding something else containing the name Winstanley.

What was a colleague of Mary Anning doing in Australia, at Bow

Wow Gorge? Perhaps visiting Mitchell, the surveyor general—hadn't Mr. Ambrose mentioned him? Or was Winstanley an Australian who'd visited England and met Mary Anning? She strolled around the collection but couldn't find another reference to either Winstanley or Australia on any of the labels. Only the story of Mary Anning and a drawing of her: a diminutive Victorian woman cradling a basket full of fossils, a small black-and-white dog curled at her feet.

"Didn't expect you back so soon."

PJ spun around half expecting to see the Victorian woman and her little dog.

Mr. Ambrose grinned delightedly and waggled a finger. "I've got a bone to pick with you . . ." He gave a spluttering laugh and his eyes disappeared into the mass of surrounding wrinkles. "Bad form laughing at your own jokes. Beg pardon. I spent half the night going through the records. I might have found something to help you. Winstanley did live in Lyme Regis, but I doubt she knew Mary Anning because we lost her in 1847 and the ammonite is dated 1860. I did, however, find something in Richard Owen's letters—a reference to Winstanley. Some correspondence with Mitchell about a plesiosaur or an ichthyosaur, in that Bow Wow place. The vertebra I showed you yesterday, I presume."

"I didn't realize that so many people were interested in fossils in those days."

"The perfect pastime for fashionable Georgians and Victorians seeking to add to their cabinets of curiosities."

"So you think Winstanley might have been part of a group in Lyme Regis?"

He shrugged his shoulders. "Lyme's as good a place as any to start. And it so happens I might know someone who could help you if you're interested."

Was she? Yes. Quite why, she didn't understand. Perhaps the connection, however intangible, with Dan and Riley. They wouldn't have thought twice, would have jumped at the opportunity. As children they'd spent hours and hours with the dusty collection of fossils they'd found up in the attic. They'd set up the cupboard in the hallway as their museum, convinced if they reassembled the pieces they'd have a dinosaur. She swallowed the lump in her throat and nodded. It was the very reason Dippy had appealed to them. And besides, what else was she going to do while she waited for Sam?

"I am interested."

"The man you're after is Dr. Wyatt Wingrave. Worked for years at the London School of Anatomy, then as a pathologist. Spent all his spare time here, though. More interested in the past than the present. Can't say I blame him. He's had a longtime dream to open a museum down at Lyme. He's made quite a collection of fossils of the district. He upped sticks and moved down the minute peace was declared. If anyone knows about Winstanley, he will. He's making a start; he's got a couple of rooms in the museum they've built on the site of Miss Anning's original home. If you walk out onto the Cobb and look back at the town, you'll pick it out."

"I'm sorry. The Cobb?"

"The harbor wall, curves out into the sea like a great arm. And have a look at what's under your feet while you're there—it's literally paved with fossils."

"And I'll see the museum from there?"

"Can't miss it. Looks like something out of a fairy tale."

PJ bit her lip, tasted the thrill of the unknown, and made up her mind. "How far away is Lyme Regis? Is it difficult to get there?"

"Train goes from Waterloo. You could be there in time for tea—providing you can get yourself a seat."

PJ couldn't get the thought of Winstanley out of her mind. If anyone had asked her to explain what it was that had piqued her curiosity, she'd have been unable to. And as she sat over a cup of tea and toast in the little tea shop she'd found the day before, she pondered her sudden interest.

Initially she'd returned to the museum simply to relive the past: the last time she, Dan, and Riley had been together—a tribute perhaps. In normal times, she would have visited their graves, placed flowers, and sat, musing on their loss; instead, she'd gone even further back in time, and in so doing she'd hit upon the perfect way to commemorate their short lives. What if Winstanley had found something significant at Bow Wow Gorge and the boys' collection held more evidence? *Ichthyosaurus martindalii*—perhaps their dream of having an ancient creature named after them wasn't so far-fetched. After all, Edgeworth David had found a new species in Sydney.

Sam would think her insane. In a fit of wishful thinking, they'd spoken of the future—a visit to his family in Philadelphia; he'd promised New York, too, with all its theaters and museums, skyscrapers and jazz clubs. The alternative she'd offered Sam was far more mundane: Sydney, Wollombi, the Australian bush. A new land, a country full of promise, she'd told him. But was it a new land? These fossils, the vertebra she'd held in her hand, spoke of an ancient past she'd never imagined. Was there more to Dan and Riley's obsession than she'd realized? Did Winstanley hold the key? No matter how foolish it sounded, she felt she owed it to her brothers to find out.

She had two days before Sam arrived, according to Ted, and she had to make a decision. She could hardly greet him with the news that holding a fossil in her hand—one, heaven forbid, she'd accidentally stolen—had made her rethink the future. Perhaps the old man at the museum didn't know what he was talking about. Surely Pa would have mentioned something about fossils so close to home. Not that she could remember him ever having much time for the boys' collection.

There was only one thing for it. And she had fewer than thirty-six hours remaining.

Leaving thruppence on the table for her now-cold pot of tea, she shot through the door and well before lunch was sitting on a train heading for Lyme Regis with a hefty translation of Eduard Suess's *The Face of the Earth* and two more books—one about sea-dragons, the other fossil identification—purchased on the spur of the moment at Foyles bookstore to keep her amused. Since she was off in search of Australian fossils, the least she could do was brush up on her knowledge of her country's origins.

Once the train left the outskirts of London, it picked up speed, clunking and clattering, spewing buckets of black grimy smoke and thick steam. PJ latched the window and disappeared into the past, to a time when the southern continents were one, covered by lush rainforests and vast seas—a supercontinent that Suess named Gondwanaland after the Gondwana region of central India, where geological formations matched those of similar ages in the Southern Hemisphere. By the time she changed trains at Axminster, her mind whirled, full of ideas and more facts than she could digest in a lifetime.

A mild golden light bathed the town and surrounding hills as the train descended toward Lyme, revealing a panoramic view of the rugged coastline. PJ packed up her books and, once the train came to a halt at the small station, she hefted her haversack onto her shoulder and set out down one of the narrow streets leading toward the shore where the river poured into the sea.

There seemed no plan to the town, simply a random wriggling of thoroughfares, none wide enough for a carriage or motor, but all leading down to the harbor. Clusters of houses clung like limpets to the steep hills, and before she reached the waterfront, she picked out a tall brick building complete with turrets and a cupola. Mr. Ambrose's description of the museum hadn't let her down. Hopefully the rest of his information would prove as accurate.

She trudged out onto the Cobb, the great gray stone wall paved in fossils as Mr. Ambrose had said. It curved out into the sea, creating a tranquil harbor for the fleet of small fishing boats. Once she reached the end, the wind picked up, whipping her hair free. Not a spot she'd relish in rough weather. She paused, inhaling the cool, fresh air before she set off to seek Dr. Wingrave at the museum.

Solid timber doors fronted the building, and she hammered hard, studying the turrets while she waited for a response. None was forthcoming, so she worked her way around to the back to the modest tradesman's entrance and looked through the dusty windows. The outline of jumbled furniture created what appeared to be a wall and beyond it a soft glow of a light radiated. She gave a sharp knock, then turned the handle and eased open the door. The soaring strains of "Ave Maria" greeted her. She stalled, lost in the recollection of the eerie sound of a lone German voice in the darkness over the trenches. Blinking the memory away, she called out, "Hello?" Her cry rang and the glorious singing dissolved into muffled curses and a *thump*.

"I'm sorry to interrupt. I'm looking for Dr. Wingrave." She shuffled her feet, uncertain whether to remain glued to the spot or flee.

Another curse and the scraping of a chair, then the tramp of heavy boots, and the outline of a small, stooped figure gradually materialized into a man with flyaway hair and huge ears, dressed in an old-fashioned tailed coat. "We're not open, and won't be for another six months at least. And if you're here to talk about the Lending Library, I'm not interested."

Not the welcome she'd hoped for. "Dr. Wingrave?"

"No. Not here."

"Do you know where I can find him? A London friend of his, Mr. Ambrose from the Natural History Museum, suggested I should speak to him."

"Ambrose? I thought he'd be pushing up daisies by now." He reached beneath the bench and pulled out a three-legged stool, sank down with a sigh, and scrubbed a large grimy handkerchief across his face.

"Oh no. He's very well." In fact, Mr. Ambrose was in a far better condition than this frail gnome of a man. "My name is Penelope Jane Martindale."

He squared his shoulders and heaved himself up a little straighter. "Well, Miss Penelope Jane Martindale, you've had a wasted trip. Wingrave's in London for the week."

PJ swallowed a wave of disappointment. If Mr. Ambrose was correct, Dr. Wingrave couldn't help her in London because his fossil collection was housed here. "I wondered if I could have a look at Dr. Wingrave's fossil collection."

"The museum's not open yet. So far it's a nucleus. Dr. Wingrave hopes in time, with the help of loans and gifts, it will become worthy of Lyme's great reputation, and of the building itself. I'm still dealing with the rubbish the Red Cross left lying around. Armistice is signed and everyone packs up and vanishes, never giving a thought to those who have to pick up the pieces."

One last try. "I'm returning to Australia soon, and I am trying to find out if Dr. Wingrave has any fossils in his collection found by someone called Winstanley."

"Winstanley?" He pocketed his handkerchief and scratched his head. "Memory's not what it used to be. Leave it with me."

Her heart picked up a beat.

"Come back in the morning and I'll see what I can do."

"I have to return to London on the last train this afternoon. I—"

He eased himself up from the stool and crossed to the window. "From the look of it, you're here for the night. Last train leaves at 4:35. Be nigh on that now."

The lengthening shadows out in the street proved him correct. "The Cups will have a room if you're not too fussy, then, like I said, come back in the morning. I'll be here at nine o'clock. Take it or leave it." He straightened the sides of his jacket and held open the door.

Not a lot of choice, and it seemed silly since she'd come all this way to give up now, and, besides, if there wasn't a train tonight the decision was made. "Thank you, Mr. . . . ."

"Woods." He held out a gnarled hand.

"Thank you, Mr. Woods. I'll see you in the morning."

"Up the road a bit. You'll find The Cups on your left. They do a nice stargazy pie. Tell Mrs. Garred I sent you."

With a smile, she closed the door behind her and took off up the steep slope. Stargazy pie? She'd eaten many meals she'd rather not remember, and she wasn't sure she fancied stargazy pie. At least not until she found out what it contained, although from the tangy breeze blowing up from the Cobb, she'd put money on fish being involved.

CHAPTER 5

1847
Bow Wow

Mellie trailed after Lydia, refusing to think about the letter Mrs. Pearson had sent Mrs. Winstanley and what it said. It can't have been anything too bad because Lydia seemed much more at ease than before. But then every time Mellie thought she understood what was happening, something changed. Right from the first moment she'd lost Da nothing had made any sense and no one had bothered to explain. It hadn't mattered how many questions she'd asked, she couldn't find out when he was coming home. It was all that mattered to her. Maybe Lydia would tell her what was in the letter.

"I hope you don't mind sharing a room with me, Mellie. Aunt Anthea wasn't expecting you so we have done a bit of shuffling around." Lydia opened the door and stepped aside.

Mellie gaped. The large bedroom full of afternoon sun overlooked a patch of cut grass with an enticing bench beneath a huge lemon tree, just waiting for her. Tucked to one side of the garden stood a small slab cottage very much like the one where she and Da had lived before Dr. Pearson took her away.

"Am I going to sleep here?"

"I hope you don't mind sharing, Mellie."

Mind? Until a few moments ago she hadn't given a thought to where she would sleep. She'd rather expected a sleep-out on the veranda like the room they'd given her at the Pearsons. She ran her hand over the slippery cover on the brass bed and shook her head.

"I think we can keep each other company very nicely, don't you?"

Dumbstruck, she grunted, then, fearful of upsetting Lydia, pointed to the slab hut in the backyard. "Who lives there?"

"Nobody. That's Aunt Anthea's workroom. She's very particular about cataloging her finds."

An unexpected tremor moved beneath her skin, hot and cold at the same time. "The place where she keeps her bones?"

"They're not really bones as much as rocks. Bones and bodies that have become rocks."

Bodies and bones.

"Come on. We have to unpack and then we'll go and have something to eat."

"Where are the others sleeping?"

"Bea and Grace always share the room next door, and I expect Aunt Anthea will let Ella have the stranger's room on the other side of the veranda."

"But she isn't a stranger. I am. Shouldn't I be there?"

"It's one of the rooms Aunt Anthea keeps for unexpected visitors. It has its own entrance."

"Where does Ella usually sleep?"

A hint of color stole across Lydia's cheeks. "Aunt Anthea thought it would be better if you and I shared, to help you feel at home. Come on, unpack your clothes. We'll have one top drawer each and one bigger one, and there's room in the wardrobe for your dresses." Lydia opened the very large trunk at the end of the bed and pulled out more clothes than anyone could wear in a lifetime, then started arranging them in the big cedar cupboard behind the door.

"I've only got what I'm wearing and my Sunday best." Mellie dragged her crumpled blue serge dress out of her bag.

"Plenty of room for that in the wardrobe. Let's tidy your hair and we'll be ready." Lydia reached for a brush and tugged it through the tangle of knots hanging down Mellie's back and then tied a ribbon around her head. "There you are. Pretty as a picture."

Mellie stretched onto tiptoes and studied her image in the looking glass hanging above the chest of drawers. She didn't see anything as pretty as a picture. In fact, she looked rather stupid with the big floppy bow hanging down over her forehead accentuating her pockmarks, rather as though she'd bumped her head and Da had bandaged it with his neckerchief.

"We mustn't be late." Lydia patted the top of her head and adjusted a couple of pins. "Come along."

The butterflies in Mellie's stomach took flight. "I'm not very hungry." She forced a yawn; she didn't want to leave the lovely room. "Can you tell Mrs. Winstanley I'm tired and I don't want anything to eat?"

"Come on, don't be silly. And it's Aunt Anthea, not Mrs. Winstanley. You heard what she said. She's got a surprise for us."

"What sort of a surprise?"

"Wait and see."

Mellie searched for another excuse, but when Lydia grasped her hand and gave it a gentle squeeze, the butterflies in her stomach settled and together they walked into the room where everyone sat around a huge table.

"Ah, there you are. All settled in?" Nette asked as she placed a bowl of steaming vegetables onto the table, then dolloped spoonfuls of gravy onto the thick slabs of meatloaf.

Mellie's stomach rumbled as the air thickened with tantalizing smells.

Lydia leaned over and whispered, "I thought you weren't hungry."

The delicious sight of the steaming plates piled high made her mouth water. "I've changed my mind."

After several minutes of silence as they all enjoyed the meal, Aunt Anthea's knife and fork clattered onto her plate. "Girls, I intended to wait until we reached the gorge before I told you this, but I can't keep it to myself a moment longer." She leaned forward, her eyes bright. "I have a secret to share."

Bea and Grace lifted their heads and Ella patted her mouth and rolled her eyes to the ceiling. Mellie slipped in a quick extra mouthful. A secret. How exciting. And then an awful thought snuck into her mind—perhaps Aunt Anthea was going to share the contents of Mrs. Pearson's letter. She looked down into her lap and tightly interlocked her fingers. She couldn't bear the thought of Bea's and Grace's taunts, or Ella's scathing looks.

"I've made a significant discovery." Aunt Anthea beamed down the table at everyone.

Mellie forced the chewed bits of her last mouthful down, prayed they wouldn't reappear, then wiped her sweaty palms on her pinafore.

"And I have already sent to Sydney for authentication."

Oh no. What did that mean? Was it something to do with Da? For a moment her heart lifted. Maybe Mrs. Pearson had discovered Da was in Sydney.

"And I would like your assistance, searching for any other remains."

Remains. What remains? Remains meant dead bodies. She cast

a quick look around the table. All eyes were fixed on Aunt Anthea, except for Nette, who dabbed at the last bit of gravy on her plate with a piece of bread and threw a knowing smile at Jordan.

"It cannot be left for long because if we have any more rain, the soil might crumble and it could be lost."

Whatever was she talking about?

Bea and Grace clapped their hands. "What have you found?" they chorused.

Aunt Anthea sucked in a deep breath. "I believe I may have found the bones of an extinct marine mammal. Possibly a plesiosaur or an ichthyosaur."

Everyone around the table gawped at Aunt Anthea. Mellie had no idea why, but it did seem for once it had nothing to do with her. "What's an itchyosaur?" The words tumbled out of her mouth and seven pairs of eyes stared at her.

"I'm sorry," she mumbled and resorted to picking at the seam on her pinafore.

"Excellent, Mellie. I like an inquiring mind." Aunt Anthea rummaged in her pocket and produced a piece of paper.

Mellie's heart sank again. Surely not Mrs. Pearson's letter. Aunt Anthea unfolded the paper and held it up. "I have a picture here."

Mellie's heartbeat changed to an excited pitter-patter as she stared at the simple line drawing. She could see all the bones, rather like one of the skeletons in Dr. Pearson's book. A pointed nose, a long line of sharp teeth, a huge eye socket, and small wings. "It's a dragon."

"A dragon." Bea and Grace collapsed all over each other, their laughter making her face burn and her pox scars itch and stick out like pimples on a baby's bottom. She curled forward, her head touching her knees. Perhaps she could slip under the table and crawl away without anyone noticing.

"Oh, Bawk-bawk. It can't be a dragon."

"Dragons aren't real."

Fat chance of any escape. Since she couldn't bolt, she'd have to fight. She straightened up and threw back her shoulders. "Yes, they are. I've seen them in books." Which wasn't strictly true, but everyone had heard the story of Saint George and the Dragon. Da liked to take a drink at the George and Dragon in Maitland when they went for supplies, and the old man in the emporium next door had taken pity on her one night when it was raining and let her wait inside his shop. He'd shown her a beautiful wooden box with a dragon carved on the top; he said it came from the Orient.

"Yes, they are." She thumped her fist on the table, making the plates rattle. "I've seen one." She slammed her lips tight. She didn't want to explain that it was only a carving.

"Girls, girls." The stern tone of Aunt Anthea's voice wiped the stupid grins off all their faces, even Ella's.

"Mellie is not far off the mark. Many people believed ichthyosaurs were related to dragons and that ancient discoveries of fossils might have inspired stories about them. Some of the more famous paleontologists called them sea-dragons. Almost like a pet name."

"I'd like a pet dragon." Mellie regretted her words straightaway. Whatever made her say that?

The tittering laughter and *bawk-bawk* noises began again, but Aunt Anthea took no notice.

"A very famous fossil hunter in England, who found the first entire ichthyosaur, wondered the very same thing when the bones were first uncovered over thirty-five years ago. Such a perfect specimen that someone offered one hundred pounds for it. So Mellie is right on the mark."

"That is tremendously exciting." Lydia leaned forward, her eyes trained on Aunt Anthea's face, and something in her tone changed the atmosphere around the table. "And you think there might be more to uncover in the gorge?"

"I very much hope so. I'd like your assistance, all of you. This could be a most exciting discovery."

For the first time since she'd arrived, the frown between Mellie's brows relaxed and her bones lost their tightness. No stories about Da, no stories about badly behaved girls being fed to monstrous creatures. Just the astonishing fact that Aunt Anthea believed she had found a dragon bone.

"I don't understand," Mellie burst out. "How can you tell from one bone that it belongs to a dragon?"

"*Bawk-bawk.*"

Aunt Anthea shot a glare at Bea and Grace, which again wiped the smirks from their faces quicker than a damp rag. "I can see we are going to get on very well, Mellie. Now, Bea and Grace, I'd like you to help Nette clear the plates. While you're doing that, I shall answer Mellie's question and any others she might think of. We don't want to uncover something significant and not recognize it." She tapped the picture resting beside her plate once again. "The reason I believe the fossil I found may belong to an ichthyosaur is because I have seen similar specimens."

Mellie craned forward to look closer at the picture. "Who is this person who found a dragon skeleton?"

"Her name is Mary Anning."

Her. A thrill of excitement coursed through Mellie. She'd rather thought Mrs. Pearson was being polite when she said that Mrs. Winstanley, Aunt Anthea, was a famous fossil hunter. She didn't know before this that women could be hunters, but now Aunt Anthea was talking about another woman who was one as well. "Are all dragon hunters women?"

"No, they're not, not by any means. Women, though, are not the empty-headed fools men take us for. We are quite capable of understanding science. The British Museum has recently accepted contributions from several women. One day scientific establishments will open their doors and we will have as much standing, if not more, than men because we take care and have patience, which is often so severely lacking in the males of our species."

"How do you know about this Mary Anning?"

"She lived with her family in a small village in southern England, not far from where I was born, and she collected fossils to sell to people. She called them curios. She was only twelve when she found the first ichthyosaur."

Mellie's spoon clattered to the table. "She's a girl?"

"Not anymore; she's a grown woman now, though younger than me. I met her on the beach one day and we became friends."

The hair on Mellie's skull prickled. Twelve. "I'm twelve."

"Before you met Uncle Benjamin and came to Australia," Ella interrupted. She put a large bowl of something sweet and sugary on the table and clasped her hands to her chest, a soppy smile drifting across her face as she hummed some tune. "Such a romantic story. And he gave you a beautiful necklace."

"A long time ago."

Ella tipped her head to one side and gave a coy smile. "Please show it to us."

Aunt Anthea unbuttoned the collar of her blouse and hooked her finger inside. Dangling from a long silver chain was the most beautiful winged stone Mellie had ever seen. Her heart thudded. "It's a dragon scale."

"This is the first brachiopod Benjamin found in the gorge. He had it made into a pendant for me." She dropped it into Mellie's hand. It sat warm in her palm. She picked it up by the chain and held it aloft. Three carved silver balls sat above the dragon scale holding it in place. It twisted slowly as though it had a life of its own, catching the candle-light, sending out glittering sparks.

A shadow hovered over her. Ella clawed the chain from her fingers and hung it around her neck, then patted it so it sat flat against the lace of her blouse. "I can wear it for a while, can't I?" Without waiting for a reply, Ella sat back in her chair and stuck out her fat bosom.

Mellie stifled the cry in her throat. She wanted to snatch it back, hold it tight, never let it go.

"You may wear it for the remainder of the evening, Ella. Please put it on my dresser before you go to bed." Aunt Anthea reached out and gave Mellie's hand a gentle pat. "I believe Nette has made bread and butter pudding, everyone's favorite. Now, Mellie, do you have any more questions?"

She had a thousand questions, but they were all swirling around, tripping over one another and tangling in the glittering dreams racing through her mind. "Can the dragons fly?"

Bea and Grace collapsed against each other, their raucous laughter filling the room. "Fly? Can they fly?" Bea stuck her hands into her armpits and clucked furiously. "They're not chickens and they're dead. Dead bones."

Aunt Anthea glared across the table at them. "Girls, if you can't be civil then please leave."

With matching smirks Bea and Grace dug their spoons into their pudding.

"No, Mellie, they couldn't fly, but they could swim. That's why they were called sea-dragons."

"But we are miles away from the sea. How could they leave their bones here? Did someone bury them?" Mellie's stomach griped as she waited for Bea and Grace to gloat and start their cackling again. Much to her surprise they remained silent, eyes trained on Aunt Anthea's beaming face.

"Hundreds of thousands of years ago a large sea covered the Hunter Valley. Over the years soil and other debris washed down from the surrounding hills and turned it into a swampland. A little like our bread and butter pudding." She lifted the top layer up, revealing the plump sultanas and custard beneath.

"And then more and more and the dragons became buried . . ."

"Quite right, Mellie, and their bones fossilized. Most ancient animals never became fossils. Their carcasses were eaten by other organisms, or worn away by wind or water. But sometimes the conditions were right and their remains were preserved, their bones protected by the layers of sand or silt. All the fleshy parts wear away and only the hard parts, like bones, teeth, and horns—"

"And their scales, dragons have scales . . ." Mellie snapped her mouth shut, her face coloring as Aunt Anthea pinned her with a searching gaze.

"Those hard parts are left behind, and over millions of years the minerals in the water fill them up, bit by bit, until all that is left is a solid rock copy of the original specimen."

"And that's what you have found?"

"That's what I think I might have found—a small part only. It needs to be verified. And now it's time we helped Nette and the girls clean up. We've got a busy day tomorrow."

Mellie leaped to her feet. "Hunting for dragons."

CHAPTER 6

⬩◆⬩

After a remarkably good night without any repercussions from the stargazy pie, which consisted of mackerel, heads and tails intact, floundering in a sea of pastry, PJ made her way down the hill to the museum. Although she wasn't expecting Sam until four in the afternoon, the thought that she might miss him made her twitchy. She needed to leave Lyme by lunchtime. Lyme. She chuckled. Already she was beginning to sound like one of the locals, shortening the town's name. Perhaps when Sam arrived they could come here, take a couple of days and do some fossil hunting of their own. She cast a wishful glance at the cliffs fringing the seashore.

A rousing rendition of "Ode to Joy" wafted out of the museum, so she walked in. The bright morning light gave her a much better view of the two rooms than the previous afternoon, although the jumble of heavy wooden crates, boxes, and furniture dominating the room didn't fill her with any great sense of hope.

Why was she so determined to find out more about Winstanley?

Ever since she'd held the vertebra in her hand, she'd had the feeling that it contained a message. Such fey nonsense.

"Good morning, Mr. Woods," she called, eliciting a mumble of curses that brought the song to a halt.

"Ah, there you are." He bounced out from behind a stack of crates with a broad grin on his face. "I might have something for you. After you left I packed up and took the long way home. I felt the need for some fresh air and it seemed it cleared my mind. I knew the name Winstanley rang a bell."

PJ plastered an encouraging smile on her face, hoping to disguise her impatience. Unable to control herself, she took a step closer. "And?"

"And I found exactly what I was looking for." He puffed out his frail chest. "I hold a very responsible position in the town and have done so for many years. It's a role I take extremely seriously, and as such—"

She gritted her teeth. "Museums are very important institutions—"

"No, no, you misunderstand me. St. Michael the Archangel is far more significant—Lyme's parish church—and has been since the early sixteenth century." He adjusted his waistcoat and stood a little taller. "I have been the church warden for many, many years. In fact, my association with the church goes back to my childhood. Initially I was one of the choristers and then rose to the position of choir master."

Which would account for his excellent singing, but what it had to do with fossil specimens or Winstanley, she couldn't fathom. "And Winstanley?" she prompted.

"The name had slipped my mind, but as I was walking home . . ."

Oh, for goodness' sake, they were back where they'd started. She should simply have kept her mouth shut and let him tell his story.

"I decided to stop and pay my respects to Mary Anning. She's buried in the churchyard. Along with her brother, Joseph, and the Philpot sisters. The Philpot family financed the building of this magnificent edifice. You do realize you are standing on hallowed ground here, don't you?"

Hallowed ground—surely he wasn't going to tell her someone was buried beneath the floor. She shook her head and sank down on the little three-legged stool Mr. Woods had occupied yesterday. "This is the very spot"—he formed a wide circle with his arms encompassing the entire room in an embrace—"where Mary Anning and her family lived. Her curio shop stood right here." He stamped his foot on the timber floor. "This is where she, and her father before her, sold fossils until she had the wherewithal to move to larger premises on Broad Street." He paused to snatch a breath, a saintly expression on his weathered features.

"And Winstanley?" PJ asked again.

Mr. Woods brought the palm of his hand to his forehead with a *thump*. "How silly of me. I got quite carried away. Winstanley is buried but a few feet from Mary Anning."

PJ shot to her feet. "So he lived in Lyme? I wondered if he was an Australian."

"She."

Her shoulders slumped. "I thought I had found a connection to the Hunter Valley. I live in the Hunter Valley in Aus—*She?*"

"Anthea Winstanley, buried alongside her friends Mary Anning and Elizabeth Philpot." His cheeks reddened. "They all knew one another; they'd search for curios and interact intellectually, learning from each other. My father used to tell the tale. As a boy, he would trail them along the beach, summer or winter, fair weather or foul, collecting their offcasts, rejected chunks of rock, broken bits of ammonites and belemnites, brittle stars, shells, and sundry other fossils. Some of those pieces are here in this collection. That's what I was looking for when you arrived. I have the distinct recollection of a piece Mrs. Winstanley gave him. He said she was a charming woman. Very interested in ichthyosaurs and plesiosaurs."

PJ blinked again. Winstanley, a woman. A surge of excitement raced through her. The *female* Australian fossil hunter who had visited Bow Wow Gorge was buried here, in Lyme. No. She was jumping to conclusions. Nothing to say she was Australian. She was most probably English and had simply visited Australia. "What does it say on her gravestone?"

"Not a lot. Sacred to the memory of Anthea Winstanley and a set of dates . . ." He scratched at his head again. "Seventeen ninety to eighteen seventy."

"Nothing else? Not loving mother of, or daughter of, or something like that?"

"No, nothing. Which is why I remembered . . . I believe she did have a daughter. They were as close as . . ." He crossed his fingers.

If nothing else, it proved that the specimen in the Natural History Museum was correctly dated. Anthea Winstanley had visited Australia, and by 1860, when she found the ammonite, she was in Lyme. "Can you show me her grave?"

"I haven't got all day to dedicate to this, you know. I have other responsibilities. You're going to have to make a choice—Wingrave's collection or Winstanley's gravestone."

He was right. And she had to be on the train by midday, otherwise she'd miss Sam. She'd simply have to take Mr. Woods's word for it. "I'd like to look at the specimens."

Imagine if she could speak to Anthea Winstanley's daughter. Would she know about Bow Wow? "Do you know what happened to Mrs. Winstanley's daughter? Is she still alive?"

Mr. Woods tapped at his forehead, then shrugged. "She'd be getting on a bit and she's certainly not in Lyme. I'd know." Color suffused his cheeks again. "Especially in my role as church warden."

"Maybe I can help?" And speed things up. "I have to catch the midday train."

"Then we'd better get a move on." He peeled off his jacket and rolled up his sleeves. "Dirty work. Are you ready?"

PJ followed him into the back of the shop, behind the rows of stacked furniture and cupboards, to a long bench lining the back wall littered with a huge variety of fossils, some cleaned and labeled and others still encased in the surrounding shale or rock, every one appearing to have been hurriedly thrown down with little regard to order or condition. "Where would you like me to start?"

"You'll need a pair of gloves, then go through what's on the table here. Anything that's labeled you need to check and put to one side. I'll go through the other crates. One of them contains paperwork."

The hour and a half passed in a flurry of dust, dirt, and disappointment. Neither PJ nor Mr. Woods managed to find anything bearing Anthea Winstanley's name and not a single sketch by her elusive daughter.

When the clock struck eleven, PJ pulled off her gloves with a sigh. "Thank you so much for your help, Mr. Woods. I have to leave, otherwise I will miss my train. May I give you my address and perhaps you'd be kind enough to let me know if you come across any further information?"

The moment the train drew into Waterloo Station, PJ threw herself out onto the platform and bolted for the gate.

The ticket collector blocked her way. "Slow down, lovey. I'm sure he'll wait for you."

PJ thrust the stub into his hand and drew in a shuddering breath. "Natural History Museum?"

"Take the Bakerloo line. Change at Green Park, first stop's Kensington." He pointed to the stairs weaving their way below the station. "Good luck. Tell him he's a lucky bloke."

Half an hour later PJ emerged into the sunshine and ran along the Cromwell Road to the museum. As before, people dressed in uniforms of every shape and hue thronged the forecourt.

She raced up the steps, searching for Sam and at the same time praying Mr. Ambrose would be in his usual spot guarding his specimens. She clutched the bar of Fry's Chocolate Cream she'd bought at Lyme Regis station, a thank-you present, tightly in her hand. His introduction to Dr. Wingrave hadn't eventuated, but Mr. Woods had fired her with such enthusiasm. Anthea Winstanley was buried next to her friends in Lyme, but what had happened to her daughter?

She couldn't wait to tell Sam all about the mysterious female paleontologist who'd visited Bow Wow Gorge and found a vertebra belonging to one of the great sea-dragons. There had to be more to Dan and Riley's theories than she'd given them credit for.

She scanned the courtyard searching for Sam's tall figure and bright hair, but he was nowhere to be seen. In moments the museum would close and she would miss Mr. Ambrose. Casting one final glance over the throng, she made her way up the steps, through the foyer, and slipped into the back room.

The closed blinds heralded the end of the day and there was no sign of Mr. Ambrose. Surely he hadn't gone home. He'd told her he always stayed to make sure everything was shipshape before closing because he didn't trust anyone else to look after his specimens.

With a huff of annoyance, she sneaked one more quick look at Anthea Winstanley's Australian fossil and shifted the bar of chocolate into her pocket. Perhaps she could leave it at the desk for him. As she turned to leave, the door at the back of the room squeaked open. She spun around. "Mr. Ambrose, thank goodness you're still here. I thought I might have missed you." She ran across the room.

"Slow down, slow down, we don't want any accidents."

She skidded to a halt. "I've just got back from Lyme. I wanted to say thank you so much for your help. Dr. Wingrave wasn't there, but his assistant, Mr. Woods, helped me. I'm determined to go back home and see what else I can find out about Bow Wow Gorge, and I've promised to keep in touch with Mr. Woods. It turns out that Winstanley was a woman and she had a daughter. I'm quite fascinated. And she's buried in the churchyard of St. Michael the Archangel, close to Mary Anning and Elizabeth Philpot." Her words dried as she snatched a quick breath. "I can't stay. I'm meeting—"

"A young man, if the stars in your eyes are anything to go by."

Heat bloomed on her cheeks, and she raised her palm to her face, unsure whether the thought of seeing Sam or the excitement of her trip to Lyme had caused her flurry of emotions.

"Well, then that's turned out for the best. And if you do find anything more, I'd be happy to receive a letter from Australia." He winked at her. "My great-grandson collects stamps."

"Oh, I'd almost forgotten." She held out the bar of Fry's Chocolate Cream. "This is to say thank you. Maybe you'd like to share it with your great-grandson."

He took the chocolate and held it up to his nose and sniffed. "Haven't seen one of these for a long time. Most of them got sent to the boys in the care packages. Might not be too much sharing going on."

PJ shuffled her feet. She didn't want to walk out, but she didn't want to keep Sam waiting. "I'm really sorry, I have to go. I'll let you know what I find out. Thank you so much for your help."

"My pleasure, lass. Take care now." He held out his hand and a pang of regret shot through her as she shook it. "Off you go—don't want to hold up that young man of yours."

By the time she'd crossed the central hall, the crowds had thinned and the wardens were closing the doors. She slipped out and stood overlooking the forecourt.

It wasn't until her gaze traveled beyond to the Cromwell Road that her heart lifted. Sam stood on Sid's hood, waving his hands in the air, grinning like a loon. He must have spotted her when she came through the doors.

Taking the steps two at a time, she flew toward him. He leaped from the hood and clasped her tight, lifted her off the ground, spun her around and around, then planted a resounding kiss on her lips. "First kiss on English soil. Can't let it be a dud."

And then and there, right in front of the Natural History Museum, with all the onlookers, noise, and traffic, he dropped to one knee.

"Sam, are you all right?"

"Penelope Jane Martindale . . ."

He never called her by her full name. Her breath caught. His dark eyes twinkled up at her. "Will you permit me to ask your father for your hand in marriage?"

"Do what?"

"PJ, I'm asking you for your hand in marriage. You're meant to swoon, flutter your eyelashes, stutter. Not stand there gaping like a stunned mullet."

"But . . . but we're mates. Friends. Not lovers."

He scrambled to his feet, planted his hands on his hips. "Well, could you at least show some enthusiasm so I don't look like such a fool in front of the entire world?"

Only then did she notice the crowd circled around them. The looks of joyful anticipation on their faces were almost worse than the creeping disappointment on Sam's. How could she have not known? "I don't know what to say."

"How about 'yes' or even 'I'll think about it'?"

She stood for a moment taking in his rugged good looks, wide strong shoulders, and mop of unruly hair, then locked her gaze on his warm brown eyes. With a wink, he threaded her arm through his, bumped her hip. "Come on. This isn't like you. I thought you'd like the idea. We talked about a trip to New York, meeting my parents."

"I just need some time to—You're going back to Philadelphia. I have to go back to Australia. Pa—"

"Don't you worry about that. I've got it all planned." His words tangled with her thoughts, wrapped around her heart, stilled her breathing. Marriage? Something she had never contemplated. Regulations prevented marriage—it would have resulted in her immediate dismissal, but not anymore . . .

"Come on. No time to waste. I'm asking you to marry me and I'm taking you home."

She tried in vain to swallow the lump in her throat. "Home?"

"Yes. Home to Australia, so I can ask your father for your hand in marriage. No hurried wartime wedding for my sweetheart."

He wanted to take her home, ask Pa's permission? Such a contradiction, this American man whom she'd felt a connection with the first moment she'd set eyes on his mud-splattered face and wide grin.

"But I thought you wanted to go home, to America."

"I do, but first things first. I need an answer. The ship leaves tomorrow from Tilbury."

"We've got a berth?"

"Yes, ma'am. And we need to be aboard tonight, before everyone else if we want to take Sid."

"How on earth did you manage that? I thought we had to wait until the last repat ship had left."

He tapped the side of his nose. "A question of knowing the right people. The HMT *Norman* leaves tomorrow morning, an auspicious date, the fourth of July. Not too sure what berths we'll be assigned, but if everything goes according to plan, I'll have you back in Australia in a matter of weeks."

CHAPTER 7

━━◆◆◆━━

1847
Bow Wow

The day dawned fresh and clear; however, it took longer than Anthea, or Nette, expected to round up the girls, get them suitably attired, and fed. The coolest part of the morning disappeared in a tangle of hats, boots, and picnic preparations. And perhaps more importantly, it became increasingly obvious this year's visit would be very different. Anthea squared her shoulders and prepared herself for what would be an interesting ten days.

"Are we ready?" She tried her best to hide the tinge of exasperation in her voice but failed. "Jordan is waiting outside with the pack horse. Grace and Bea, would you carry the picnic basket out? And, Ella and Lydia, perhaps you'd take care of the drinks."

"It's very hot." Ella wiped her fingers across her brow and uttered a languid sigh. "I might stay at the house. I have some letters to write and I need to practice my scales."

"But we're going to the gorge." Grace dropped the basket with a horrified gasp. Even Lydia's mouth gaped momentarily.

No one ever stayed behind. And Anthea had no intention of the day progressing in any manner other than the usual. "Are you unwell, Ella?"

"No, not at all."

"Then you can accompany us. If your letters are important, bring them with you and you can make a start on them when we break for lunch."

"Mother would be less than impressed if she knew I was hitching up my skirts and paddling around in the mud and slush in my new slippers."

What on earth had prompted this sudden change of attitude? In the past Ella had proved to be one of the most enthusiastic collectors. "Your mother is very much in favor of your trips here and knows exactly how much paddling you do. Besides, I was hoping you'd show Mellie some of our techniques." Surely Ella would react favorably to some praise; she always had in the past. "Where is Mellie? I haven't seen her."

"She probably doesn't want to go—all that talk about sea monsters last night must have terrified her. I'll stay here with her," Ella said.

Mellie appeared from behind the door, her face a picture of abject misery. "I want to go. If I'm going to be a dragon hunter when I grow up, I must. Da always said it's better to learn on the job."

The poor little mite blushed as red as a beet, the words out of her mouth before she'd realized what she'd said. Not wanting to show her surprise, Anthea schooled her expression. Hopefully only Lydia had any understanding of Mellie's situation. No matter what the circumstances, a child always loved unconditionally.

"I have a headache coming on. I don't want to spoil everyone's day." Ella moaned and lifted the back of her plump hand to her forehead.

"Lying bag of bones," Lydia muttered under her breath.

Lydia and Ella's falling-out appeared to be more than the squabble Anthea had first imagined. Possibly fortunate, as their sniping had detracted attention from Mellie's reference to her father. "Of course Mellie will be coming with us," she told the girls.

Mellie beamed and lifted the basket and marched to the door. "I'm going dragon hunting."

"Don't be such a child. There aren't any dragons. Just a bunch of old stones." Ella sank down into the chair and fanned her face with all the airs and graces of a society lass. "I am quite capable of surviving for a few hours on my own. I really don't want to go."

"Ella's right, Bawk-bawk. We won't find a dragon," Bea said.

Anthea caught the patronizing glance Bea tossed in Mellie's direction. She hadn't realized Edna had instilled such a colonial attitude in her children.

With a toss of her head, Mellie thumped her hands on her hips. "We might. How do you know we won't?"

Anthea restrained her desire to applaud. Mellie might well be the Pearsons' latest charity case, but she wasn't taking their taunts lying down.

"If you think on it too hard you might change your mind, Mellie. Do you really fancy holding a long-dead body in your hands?"

Ella's catty remark was the final straw. What was the matter with them all? Usually the girls were enthusiastic, keen to get out and find new treasures. Lydia and Ella's barely concealed antagonism toward each other seemed to have spread like a disease. She had to put a stop to it.

"Once again Mellie is partially correct." She fixed a stony glare on Bea and Grace. "I told you last night many people believe that stories of dragons were inspired by ancient discoveries of fossils. I have a copy of a book written by a man named Thomas Hawkins called *The*

Book of the Great Sea-dragons. Mellie is not alone in her theories. We shall study it tonight."

Unless Anthea was very much mistaken, Mellie directed the point of her tongue at Grace. She was pleased to see the child had some pluck. "There will be no more of this bickering. Ella, I insist you come with us. Some fresh air will clear your head and improve your demeanor."

In single file, they followed the snig trail down the hill, through the grasslands that alternated between patches of light and shade alive with bird calls and carpeted by tiny native orchids. Anthea left Nette and Jordan to bring up the rear with the pack horse while she shepherded the girls until they reached a drop-off where a waterfall plunged over an impressive fault line into the gorge. After a slithering descent, they came to the creek bed edged by solid sandstone cliffs and laced with overhanging ferns.

The flurry of activity lifted Anthea's mood. Still unsure of the exact details of the rift between Ella and Lydia, she was happy to see them all clustering around and to see Mellie, such a dear, so spirited and enthusiastic as she tethered the horse and unstrapped the timber box that contained the tools that Anthea had collected over the years. Purloined from all sorts of places, they made the most wonderful kit.

"No, Mellie, you can't manage that on your own." The child would break her back.

"I've got it. I can manage." With her sleeves rolled above her elbows, Mellie's well-muscled arms gave evidence to her claim. Despite her youth and small stature, she had the sculpted limbs of a girl used to hard work.

"Where are we going?" She stuck her head around the side of the box, her arms stretched to their extreme.

"Let me help." Before Mellie could drop the box, Anthea grasped one of the handles and took some of the weight.

"What's inside?"

"All the things we need to unearth the dragons we're going to find."

The look of pure pleasure on Mellie's face warmed her heart. "This way, girls; be careful. The edges of the rocks are slippery after the rain."

They picked their way along until they reached the flat grassy spot on the edge of the creek and set up the blanket and the picnic basket in the shade of the sprawling iron bark.

"Now, I want you to pay close attention to where you walk. Hitch up your skirts so they don't trail in the water. Before you go racing off, I'll show you where I found the vertebrae."

She led the way under the overhang and lifted the curtain of rock ferns, then stood back to reveal the site of her latest discovery.

"I came down here, after a rain, and there they were, waiting to be found." She couldn't mask the excitement in her voice. She unclasped her fingers, the florin-sized stone nestled in the palm of her hand.

"Oh my goodness." Lydia ran her finger over it. "It certainly is different from anything we've found before. You think it could belong to an ichthyosaur? It could be . . ."

"It doesn't look like part of a dragon to me." Mellie wrinkled her nose and edged closer.

"It's only one small part. I am convinced it is a vertebra."

"What's a vertebra?"

Anthea ran her finger down Mellie's back. The poor child flinched and jumped away. She must become more attuned to the girl's sensibilities. "What I found is, I think, part of the backbone of an ichthyosaur. Those bumps down your back are your vertebrae. This creature was no different. Remember the illustration I showed you last night? A series of these bones would have run from the top of its head to the end of its tail."

Mellie clasped her hands to her chest, closed her eyes, and lifted her head to the sky. "Oh, I would be so happy if I could find a dragon."

"We'd better get to work, then. I'm going to allocate you all tasks. Lydia, I'd like you to work over here, very carefully with the brush, and see what you can uncover. Mellie, I'm going to give you this tool." Anthea brought out the marlin spike she'd purloined from Jordan, a relic of his seafaring days. "I'd like you to move farther along here. Let me show you."

The spike, a little over a foot long, had a sharpened point with a wooden handle. It made the perfect tool for removing loose soil, and she had no doubt Mellie would be able to manage it. "What I need you to do is stick this in a little way and very gently ease out the dirt, a tiny piece at a time. We must be very, very careful. Do you think you can do that?"

Mellie nodded her head enthusiastically and examined the spike. "It looks dangerous."

"It is. Which is why you must take care. It is your special responsibility. Sailors use them for rope making, but I have repurposed it."

Mellie moved closer to the wall, her gaze riveted on the layers of soil and clay, and she jabbed the sharp point into the crumbling sandstone.

"Now, Bea and Grace, if you'd come along here, this is where we might find something. I need you to carefully remove the already loosened soil. The bellows should help you there and perhaps the larger brushes. Call if you need me. I am going to work with Lydia."

Anthea pushed up her sleeves and waded across the creek. Hopefully she'd have the chance to ask Lydia a few questions. See if she could find out more about this beau who had caused the rift between the two friends. Lydia and Ella had never had a cross word, were always closer than sisters. Especially since they spent so much time together at that girls' school in Sydney.

"How are you getting on?"

Lydia pushed a strand of hair back from her face. "It will be slow work. I don't want to disturb anything too much. Do you really think we'll find anything more?"

"Benjamin always said that he believed we would find an ichthyosaur. The fossils we have collected in the past match those found in other parts of the world. However, to date, ichthyosaurs have only been found in Europe: England and Germany and Switzerland and—"

"Belgium. I remember him telling us."

"I see no reason why they shouldn't be found in Australia. Mitchell fully supported Benjamin's theory; he found fossils right through the lower Hunter during his original expeditions, not long after Benjamin and I arrived. He sent them to England to Sowerby and Owen for description—"

Lydia rested her hand on Anthea's sleeve. "You've told us. You hold those men in very high regard."

"Indeed I do. Indeed I do." She wouldn't dwell on Sir Thomas Livingstone Mitchell, surveyor general, renowned explorer and man of science. As much as she'd loved Benjamin, she could still remember the way her heart fluttered when she'd first met Mitchell, in awe of his standing in the country and his fine mind. Where had the time gone? The years had disappeared in a flash. Picking casually at a loose thread on her cuff, she waited for the memory to fade.

"Are you going to tell me what has happened between you and Ella?" She cast a quick look at Ella, who had settled herself under the tree next to the picnic basket.

"Nothing. Nothing at all. We've simply grown apart."

"Balderdash. The two of you used to be thicker than thieves."

Two bright pink spots appeared on Lydia's cheeks and the shimmer of a tear in her eye. Regretting her harsh words, Anthea reached out and stilled Lydia's hand. "Often it's better to talk about these things. Is it something to do with Mellie?" Quite what made that spring into her mind, she had no idea.

Lydia sniffed and offered a rueful smile. "No, not at all. Poor Mellie got caught up in something she knows nothing about. And Ella has enjoyed encouraging Bea and Grace's taunting."

If she'd interpreted Edna's letter correctly, Cook and Fanny had also fostered that taunting and it had become a regular occurrence.

"Ella's changed." Lydia lifted her shoulders. "We've both changed. I didn't think she'd come with us this year. She has better friends in Sydney now."

More than a touch of jealousy raising its ugly head, unless she was mistaken.

"And they are not your friends?"

"He was." Lydia wiped the back of her hand under her nose, making Anthea's heart wrench. Despite her appearance, she was still no more than a young girl. "I don't see why we can't all be friends. George was quite happy to teach both of us."

"George?"

"Mr. Hudderson's son, our piano teacher. And now Ella is all airs and graces and says she's stepping out with him so it's not appropriate for us all to be together. She's sitting there composing poetry, which she intends to send to him. He's convinced her that one day she'll be a famous singer."

So that was the story. First love. Maybe some time away from Sydney would rectify matters. "I'm not sure I understand what it has to do with Mellie."

"Ella is so dreadful. So patronizing. She treats her like a serving girl, and now Bea and Grace are doing the same. That's not what Mother intended. We're supposed to be looking after Mellie, helping her recover."

And how much did they know of Mellie's circumstances? "Recover?"

"She has no family. Her mother and baby brother drowned, and her father was wrongfully accused of shooting a man. She had the most appalling case of chicken pox—that's why she came to us. No one would take her. And Ella's turned Bea and Grace against Mellie. She's so uncharitable."

Not the full extent of the scenario Edna had portrayed in her letter; however, it was not her place to enlighten Lydia. "We shall do the very best we can to make sure Mellie feels at home."

CHAPTER 8

1919
SYDNEY, NEW SOUTH WALES, AUSTRALIA

An intoxicating swirl of happiness radiated through PJ as the ship rounded the Heads and glided past the rocks and gum-clad promontories into Sydney Harbour. She closed her eyes and inhaled deeply, savoring the eucalyptus scent of home. Ever since Sam had arrived in England and made his impetuous and unexpected proposal, she'd waited for this very moment. She squeezed his warm hand and he beamed down at her.

"Told you the fourth of July was an auspicious day to leave England."

He had. With that boyish glint in his eye, he'd puffed out his chest and explained that his hometown, Philadelphia, was the first city to celebrate American Independence Day with a display of fireworks and that next year they would watch from the steps of the city hall. But first he was taking her home, as he'd promised.

The familiar nostalgic pang traced a path to her heart. For a long time she'd harbored the belief Dan and Riley would be standing beside her at this moment, but the huge and hungry war monster that had swept across Europe was as impartial to nationality as it was to rank. Now Sam would never have the opportunity to meet her brothers. He was such a strange mixture of the old world and the new, this American she'd fallen in love with.

The depth of her feelings for Sam had taken her by surprise, sneaked up on her once they were aboard ship, finally freed of the nightmare blur of war: those days and nights punctuated by madcap dashes through plumes of stagnant black air to hospitals filled with the nauseating stench of putrefying flesh and the iron tang of blood.

She'd known from the first moment they'd crossed paths—abusing each other over the cavernous hole a whistling shell had created when it tore the road apart—that this man was unlike any she'd ever met. That they had a future. She'd presumed it lay in the team they'd become after her crippled ambulance was consigned to the scrapheap. Somehow Sam had made it all so much more bearable. Working alone, peering into the darkness, frozen fingers clenched on the steering wheel, was a bleak existence. Two pairs of eyes and the comfort of another living, breathing being close beside her had given her the courage to face whatever fate hurled in her path.

She stretched up onto her tiptoes and planted a kiss on his smooth, tanned cheek. "You'll love Australia, I know you will. The beginning of spring is the perfect weather for fossil hunting."

"I love you. I must. Why else would I agree to take off into the outback in search of bleached bones?"

Why indeed, when he had so much to return to in America, but the quiet nights aboard ship after the weekly dances, fancy dress parties, and their five glorious days in Cape Town had convinced her that beneath his brash impulsiveness lay a heart that was hers.

"We're not taking off into the outback. The Hunter Valley is only a hundred miles north of Sydney, and you've got something to ask Pa."

"I have." He reached out and smoothed her windswept hair, then bent to kiss her cheek, but she turned her head and her mouth brushed against his. He framed her face with his hands and deepened the kiss until the whistles from the men on the deck made them pull apart. "Few things to get through first. And then I might get you on my own. We'll find out soon enough about this quarantine business."

With the last of the bright sun blazing on the sparkling water and the cluster of buildings surrounding the coves and inlets of the harbor, she found it difficult to believe anything as dreadful as the war or the Spanish flu could have touched Australia's shores. "It's beautiful. I'd forgotten how beautiful." But for the fleet of quarantined ships anchored off Watsons Bay and the hole in her heart where she'd buried Dan and Riley, it could be the day she'd left. She wanted to get ashore. "I don't think I can wait much longer."

"The medical officer has come aboard; we'll have to bide our time."

"What about the injured? They need hospital treatment, a change of environment. We're clean. We haven't had any cases of influenza."

"Even when we do get ashore, we'll probably be wearing masks, same as those guys in the boat down there." He pointed to one of the small boats drawing up alongside.

Much to PJ's relief they weren't quarantined, and a fleet of ferries arrived to take everyone ashore. They did issue masks, though, and took pains to explain they should be worn on the face and not kept in the pocket. Sam's travel documents were checked, his citizenship remarked upon and more questions asked, and then the clerk turned to PJ.

"And what about you?"

"I'm Australian. I'll be returning home as soon as we go ashore."

"And where's home?"

PJ stifled a groan, the incessant questioning and bureaucratic hair-splitting testing her patience. "Wollombi, Hunter Valley."

"And how're you going to get there?"

"We'll be driving." Sam lounged against the rail, face tilted to the sun.

PJ recognized his stance, had seen it a hundred times before. In the past she'd welcomed it. His relaxed, innocent manner had helped them through numerous checkpoints and sticky situations, but now she wanted to get on their way. "We have an ambulance in the hold."

The rather officious little clerk looked them up and down. "An ambulance?"

"Yes. We're both ambulance drivers."

"Well, why didn't you say so?"

Because you didn't ask—PJ swallowed her words, smiled sweetly, and straightened her sleeve so the faded Red Cross armband became visible.

"I'll do the best I can for you, but you'll have to wait until we dock at Woolloomooloo—no seat for an ambulance on a ferry." The clerk snorted at his wit and moved on.

"That was a stroke of genius. Seems being an ambulance driver carries some weight in Australia." Sam dropped another kiss on the top of her head. "Don't know why I didn't think to say the same."

Despite the clerk's best efforts, they had to wait until the very last of the passengers had disembarked before they could offload Sid, and when PJ finally planted her feet firmly on the land of her birth, the tears of frustration as good as choked her.

She climbed in behind the wheel while Sam gave their sparse luggage a final check. If she didn't know better, she'd believe he was a tad nervous.

"Kit bags, tick, water, tick, gasoline, tick . . . Can we get gasoline in the outback?" He cranked the engine and it fired first time.

"I keep telling you, it's not the outback, and yes, we can. Most blacksmiths in country towns carry motor spirit and there's a garage a couple of hundred yards down from our house, opposite the hotel."

"Hotel as in a hotel with a bar?"

"The very same."

"Perhaps this won't be so bad, then."

"I thought you were looking forward to meeting Pa."

In a remarkably old-fashioned gesture, Sam continued to insist that their relationship would remain uncompromised until he'd asked her father for her hand. As Sam had said, there would be no hurried wartime wedding.

"I am. I am. It's all this paperwork and nonsense that's got up my nose. Let's get a move on."

"My first-aid kit's there, isn't it? No point in doing without that."

"Not planning on any accidents now we're here."

She shot him a ferocious frown and revved the engine.

"Yeah, and all strapped down." He threw himself into the seat beside her, pecked her on the cheek, and unraveled the map Ted Baker had drawn for him while they were aboard the repatriation ship. "We've got to cross the Pyrmont Bridge and several others until we get to a place called Gladville."

"Gladesville. I know the way."

They'd had the conversation a hundred times. Poor Sam couldn't believe that once they left Sydney they could simply follow their noses to the Hunter.

"You've never driven it. Let's see how we go." He patted the dashboard affectionately. "We'll appreciate the freedom Sid gives us. Turn here. Shame we can't get over the harbor."

PJ cast a quick glance at the wide expanse of blue water and the bevy of ferries plying their way across. "They've been threatening to build a bridge for the last hundred years, but every time anyone comes up with a design there's either a change of government or an economic downturn. I can't imagine it ever happening. It's an awfully long span."

"They've done it in New York—the Brooklyn Bridge. I'll show it to you soon. Maybe you Australians need some help."

"We'll manage. You're biased. You think anything American is the best."

"I don't hear many complaints from you."

She tossed him a smile. She hadn't any, but the sheer magnitude and grandeur of Sam's descriptions of his homeland had swept her off her feet, pretty much the same way he had during their voyage. "This is an adventure." She eased into the line of traffic and headed out toward the suburbs.

"Will we get there before nightfall?"

"It's about ninety miles as the crow flies, although there's a lot more traffic on the road than I remember. We've got to cross the Hawkesbury River at Wisemans."

"And then we're in the outback according to this map."

"I'm sure Ted wouldn't have marked it as the outback. He's from the Hunter, and I'll have you know Wollombi was once the main town north of Sydney."

"I'm thinking more about this Bow Wow place."

"If Suess is correct, it could be one of the most ancient fossil sites in the world, dating back to the breakup of Gondwanaland." She could never tell with Sam whether he was being deliberately difficult or simply didn't take much notice. "I told you about Gondwanaland, on the ship."

"Mmm."

"Didn't you listen?"

A hint of color stole across his cheekbones, making him look a lot younger than his twenty-eight years. "You had your books. I had other things to keep me busy."

That was true enough. He'd spent a lot of his time with the men, apparently chatting about opportunities and keeping their spirits up, but she suspected the lure of the two-up games had more to do with it than anything. Sam liked to gamble. Perhaps that's why he'd proposed. Quite a gamble, really. An Australian girl, without any of the connections she'd imagined his wealthy parents would seek.

"Suess's concept is really quite fascinating. I find it hard to imagine a super continent. Australia, India, Antarctica, South America, and South Africa all joined together in one huge land mass. The area around Bow Wow dates back before the breakup. It could house a treasure trove, an incredible array of unexplored fossils." And, other than Dan and Riley's fossil collection, there seemed to be no reference to it after Winstanley's find. "I'm sure Winstanley didn't appreciate the significance of what she'd stumbled upon. Otherwise, why would she have gone to England?"

"We'll see. Let's get you home first. We need to make a turn here."

PJ eased the car out of the main flow of traffic and swung onto the main road north while Sam tilted his hat over his eyes and settled back, apparently ready for a long snooze. Maybe she should have felt offended, but in fact she relished the way their relationship had grown since he'd asked her to marry him. Told simply, it sounded like a romantic dream. Handsome American whisks colonial doctor's daughter away from ravaged Europe and together they embark on a trip in search of an undiscovered fossil bed that could hold the answer to the hidden mysteries of life on Earth.

He had been as keen as mustard, hanging on her every word as she told him about her trip to the Natural History Museum. She would have loved to have taken him down to Lyme to The Cups for stargazy pie and wandered the beaches hand in hand, in Anthea Winstanley's footsteps, but that was not to be.

Her heart gave the same lurch it always did when she thought of Anthea Winstanley's discovery. Imagine if she could fulfill Dan and Riley's dream of having a prehistoric creature named after them. What better memorial to her two brothers? She sneaked a look at Sam; the corner of his mouth twitched in recognition of her gaze, but his eyes remained closed, his long dark lashes half-moons against his cheeks.

The miles ticked by as Sam dozed until he suddenly jerked upright. "Any idea where we are?"

"While you were asleep we crossed the Pyrmont Bridge, Glebe Island Bridge, Iron Cove Bridge, and the Parramatta River. Now we're truly on our way out of Sydney."

"It looks to me as though we're in the middle of nowhere."

"Don't be silly. There are market gardens over there and dairy cows." As she spoke she swerved to avoid a pothole.

"Maybe I should drive." He threw her a look he'd perfected, one he knew would make her bristle.

"I'm quite capable. I can't imagine it would be any more difficult than an ambulance at the front."

Despite her best intentions, the words were out of her mouth before she could stop them. She flashed him a smile by way of apology. In this post-war world she'd have to lose her defensiveness about her rights. "We'll swap over when we get to Wisemans. There's a vehicular ferry that'll take us across the Hawkesbury River, then it's about fifteen miles into St. Albans. After that we pick up the old convict road into the Wollombi Valley."

"Convict road?"

"Better known as the Great North Road. It was built back in the 1820s, the first overland route between Sydney and the Hunter Valley. It runs rings around some of the tracks we came across in Belgium."

"So how much longer to Wollombi?"

"Another hour or so and we'll be there."

"The Doctor's House. It sounds pretty impressive."

"Not really. Wollombi has always had a doctor, though originally it was a surgeon, largely tasked with the job of pulling teeth and fixing broken bones. The house, our house, has always been known as The Doctor's House. When Pa returned from the African War, he swore he'd never wear a uniform again and that he and Ma would never be parted."

"So this. Us . . . ," he said, reaching for her hand on the steering wheel and giving it a squeeze, "is history repeating itself."

In some strange way she didn't want it to be that. She didn't want her life with Sam to be commonplace. They'd come through so much together; surely there was something more waiting for them on the horizon.

"Pa always says the stars must have aligned because when he arrived back in Sydney, he saw an advertisement in the first newspaper he picked up for a doctor in Wollombi and the house for sale. For years the same family, the Pearsons, had lived there, but they'd moved on." She wouldn't spoil the mood by mentioning the series of family tragedies that had plagued the Pearsons. "The house sat empty until Ma and Pa found it."

"And your father bought it?"

"He did. The locals wanted a doctor so they encouraged him to stay. He said he'd found home." Until Ma had died, and now they'd lost the boys. A shudder traced her shoulders.

After Wisemans, as the mid-afternoon sun began to slide toward the hills, they followed the twisting track around the hairpin bends and switchback turns of the old convict road.

"I don't know about you but I could do with a decent feed and a good night's sleep." Sam reached over and pecked her on the cheek. "It's been a long drive."

Not all that long—they'd swapped over after they crossed the Hawkesbury River and made the climb up from St. Albans, and he'd made the long, steep descent into the valley.

"We're almost there. We turn at the hotel. Keep your eyes peeled for the cemetery and the millpond." Despite her best intentions she couldn't control the smile twitching her lips.

Her comment had the desired effect. Sam shot her a disbelieving look and sat up straight, scrutinizing the view. Against the backdrop of the dark water, the rows of headstones stood out like ragged old men's teeth. "I think we've arrived."

Bittersweet memories of childhood echoed as PJ stared up at the single-story weatherboard house set amid the neatly manicured lawns. Long summer evenings of cricket, an immediate six if the ball landed in the millpond; tall glasses of lemonade; the scent of orange blossom wafting on the breeze; shrieks of laughter as the boys wrestled for supremacy.

The comfort of Sam's arm across her shoulder brought her back to the moment.

"It's not what I expected." He pulled her closer, dispersing the memories.

"What did you expect?"

"A ranch, I guess. Long and low, overlooking acres and acres of pasture, cattle—you know."

It hadn't occurred to her to describe the house, her home. She'd never known another.

"And the graveyard down there—it's a bit somber. Handy for a doctor, I suppose."

Not game to voice her disappointment at his criticism, she drew in a breath and ran up the familiar steps onto the veranda, longing for Pa's embrace.

CHAPTER 9

1847
Bow Wow

Much to Mellie's relief, the hem of her nightgown showed no signs of sleepwalking and not a speck of dirt marked her bare feet. She pulled the covers up on her bed and dressed as quietly as she could before tiptoeing out to the kitchen. The low-lying mist heralded another fine day and she simply couldn't wait to continue her search.

The mouthwatering scent of fresh bread filled the kitchen, and all kinds of delicious bits and pieces covered the table—a bowl of shiny red apples, fresh lettuce, hard-boiled eggs, thick slices of ham, and a jar of chutney.

"Good morning, Nette." Mellie dragged her hair back from her face and offered a tentative smile. "Can I help you?"

"You're up bright and early. All ready for another busy day?"

"I can hardly wait. I'm going to find a dragon, you know. I dreamed last night I spotted him, under the ferns. He had huge eyes and his body was covered with glittering scales. I climbed on his back and he flew me across the treetops." Her heart beat a little faster and she clasped her hands over her chest to still the thumping.

It was the first time for weeks she'd dreamed of anything other than being chased, and she was certain she hadn't sleepwalked.

Nette's finger tapped her head. "A very fine imagination you have. Would you like to put your mind to something more practical?"

"What?" Manners. She clapped her hand over her mouth. "I beg your pardon. I mean, what would you like me to do?"

"I need some help with the porridge and then the sandwiches."

That was something she didn't need to be taught and perhaps it would make up for her bad manners. Aunt Anthea and Nette's kindness had already made her feel so very welcome. "Shall I make the porridge?"

Nette's eyes widened. "Do you know how to do that?"

"Yes." She'd made it every morning for Da since she was tall enough to reach the stove. "I usually put the oats to soak overnight with a pinch of salt."

"Then lucky I did. There's fresh milk over there."

Mellie collected the saucepan, brought it onto the heat, and began stirring. The warmth of the stove and Nette's gentle humming soothed her, sending the horrors of the past weeks into the deep recesses of her mind, allowing the glittering dragon to take center stage.

None of the girls had appeared by the time the porridge was ready so she took the bowl Nette offered and ladled some into it straight from the pan.

"There's plenty of cream and a knob of butter in the middle makes all the difference." Nette pointed to a huge pat of butter in the middle of the table and a jug of cream. "Help yourself."

Before she'd finished eating, Aunt Anthea arrived in the kitchen, poured herself a cup of tea, and nibbled on the corner of a piece of bread. "No movement from the bedrooms?"

"None. Except young Mellie here; she's a dab hand with a wooden spoon. Would you like some porridge? Mellie made it."

"Clever girl. This'll do me fine." Aunt Anthea popped the last bit of bread into her mouth and washed it down with a mouthful of tea. "Mellie and I can't hang around all day waiting. Nette, if you and Jordan can see to everything here, we'll leave now."

In a flash Mellie finished her porridge and laced her boots. "I'll go and get the tool box, shall I?"

"Jordan can see to that."

She couldn't go down to the gorge without her spike; Aunt Anthea had told her it was her very own responsibility. "I'll go and get the marlin spike." She ran out of the kitchen before anyone could say otherwise, across to the workroom where she'd seen Jordan carrying the tool box last night, slipped inside, and ground to a halt. Long, waist-height benches coated with dust lined the inside of the room, and underneath was a series of crates. Rows of shelves attached by thick lengths of rope dangled from the ceiling, each one crammed with rocks and lumps of soil.

The tool box sat on the floor in the middle of the room next to a small wooden table and chair. Several inkwells, nibs, and sheets of paper littered the table top, all crammed with rambling handwriting. She bent closer to have a look, but the words merged and blurred. With a sigh, she straightened up. The writing in books was difficult enough; anything handwritten remained a mystery.

"Mellie, Mellie," Aunt Anthea called.

She spun around, released the clasp on the tool box, and slipped out her spike.

"The others are still sleeping. I'm far too impatient. I'll show you Benjamin's shortcut; I haven't used the path since he passed. Jordan and Nette can chase the girls up and follow with the horse down the main trail."

A quiver of excitement traced Mellie's skin. "Another secret?"

"It's not as clandestine as it sounds, simply a faster route, but impossible with the horse, and you must never venture that way unaccompanied."

Mellie squinted into the distance at the fingers of light splaying through the trees, pinpointing the secret track. The mere thought of it made her shiver with pleasure.

"Did you hear me? I need your promise that you'll keep this path to yourself. You are sufficiently sensible and sure-footed. I can't trust Bea and Grace. They are both accident-prone."

A wave of warmth flushed Mellie's body. A private secret. One not to share with Bea and Grace.

"And while we're here, if you're going to become a serious fossil hunter, you need to be dressed for the part."

Mellie lifted the hem of her skirt, damp and muddy to the knees. It hung heavy from traipsing through the creek yesterday. "I'm sorry, I didn't think."

"You had much more important work to do." Aunt Anthea bent down and foraged in one of the crates beneath the bench. "These should do the trick." She straightened up and dangled a pair of breeches from her fingers and measured them against Mellie. "Much more suitable for clambering. Happy to wear them?"

Happy? She could barely keep still; her legs kept jiggling. She reached for the breeches with shaking hands. "Thank you, thank you so much." Although she wouldn't tell Aunt Anthea, or anyone else for that matter, she'd always worn a pair of Da's cut-down breeches when she had work to do, but they'd gone in the fire along with all her other clothes when the Pearsons had taken her away.

"And you need these too." Aunt Anthea offered her a pair of thick leather gloves with the ends of the fingers cut off. "Now you're all ready. Miss Fossil Hunter of Bow Wow Gorge."

Aunt Anthea unbuttoned her coat, showing that she was dressed in a similar pair of breeches fastened around the waist with a thick leather belt.

Mellie shucked off her boots and dragged the breeches up under her skirt. "Dragon hunter," she corrected, the thrill of their quest warming her heart.

"Take off your skirt, tuck your blouse in. I'll have to find you a belt another day; in the meantime, this should do. Come here." Aunt Anthea hitched up Mellie's trousers and tied a frayed piece of rope around her waist, then stood back, her head tipped to one side. "Much more suitable for a dragon hunter. All you need now are these."

Mellie slipped her hands inside the gloves, interlocked her fingers, and tightened them.

"The ends are cut off so you can pick things up easily. Do up your laces and follow me." With that, Aunt Anthea grasped a long, polished grass-tree stem and strode off across the garden.

With a final glance around the workroom, Mellie closed the door, slipped the marlin spike into the rope at her waist, and galloped along the path, weaving through the scrub.

After a few minutes Aunt Anthea drew to a halt. "Look down here and you'll see why you must be careful."

Below their feet the land dropped away. Down, down into a deep gully, filled with nothing but the strange whistling from the swaying treetops, and beyond an outcrop of towering golden cliffs standing guard.

Aunt Anthea turned into the dense bush. "About ten yards and we'll find what we're looking for. A yard is one very long pace for me, so perhaps you need to take two."

Mellie followed, counting her steps. When she reached fifteen she found herself atop a rock platform jutting out into the chasm.

"Watch me." Aunt Anthea lowered herself onto the rock, dangled her legs over the edge, slithered forward on her bottom, and disappeared.

Mellie dropped to her knees and squinted down into the gaping void. Tucked under the overhang, Aunt Anthea stood gazing up at her, a wide smile lighting her face.

"Your turn. Exactly as I did. You'll have to let yourself fall the last few feet because you're shorter than I am."

She swiveled around and hung her legs over the edge, a delicious rush of fear making her pulse race. Private secrets and dragon hunting demanded more courage than she'd ever imagined. She closed her eyes, took a deep breath, and launched herself over the edge.

With a bone-jolting thud, she hit the ground, teetered for a moment, the air wavering, then Aunt Anthea reached out and steadied her.

"Well done. What a brave girl. I knew you'd be able to do it."

She could do anything Aunt Anthea asked. Of that Mellie was certain. Not only did they share a secret, but she was a brave dragon hunter.

"Now the rest is easier. Going back up is much harder. Benjamin and I used to keep a rope here for the return journey, but these days I prefer to use the snig trail, the way we went yesterday." She stuck her hand into a straggly bush clinging to the rocky soil and pulled out a thick, knotted rope. "Look at that. It's still here."

Mellie took the offered rope and tugged. It seemed quite strong, and with the neatly spaced knots it would be simple to climb. She gave it a tug and placed one foot on the bottom knot.

"Oh no you don't. Come down. We have no idea what condition that rope is in. Another relic of Jordan's seafaring days."

With a grin Mellie jumped down onto the rock and tucked the rope safely back in place.

"And from here on it's not so difficult. Benjamin carved out a series of steps in the rock. In some places they're a little high, in others narrow and often slippery, but I have no doubt you'll manage." Once again Aunt Anthea set off, her staff ringing on the sandstone.

Mellie bounded down behind her. "Does anyone else know about this path?"

Aunt Anthea stopped and turned, her eyes twinkling. "No one except Benjamin, and he's no longer here. I thought it would be lovely for us to share a special secret."

And Bea and Grace couldn't be trusted. They weren't sure-footed and brave. Mellie's heart swelled; she wanted to throw her arms around Aunt Anthea and hug her tight. "I will never, ever share our special path," she murmured, the words sounding like a prayer.

"Come along. Not far to go now."

Overgrown and shaded by tall, stringy box and red gums draped with beards of mistletoe and lichen, the path wound its way down, down, down until finally the track opened to reveal the high-sided creek bed.

"Here we are. Recognize the spot?"

The creek tinkled and babbled as it meandered over the large round boulders until it reached the drooping curtain of lacy ferns covering the overhang. "But it is so much quicker. Why don't you always come this way?"

"I told you. Too dangerous for young ladies who aren't nimble.

Edna would have my guts for garters if anything happened to either of her precious daughters."

For a moment Mellie stopped and thought about Aunt Anthea's remark. Was she paying her a compliment or didn't she matter? She pushed the thought aside. And the fact that she and Aunt Anthea shared a secret pathway still warmed her heart. It made her special. "Will they be here soon?"

"I'd say we've got an hour or so. Let's get started."

Mellie grasped the marlin spike in her fist and flexed her wrist, her heart beating so hard her hand shook. She stabbed it into the wall.

Aunt Anthea's gloved hand covered hers. "You must be a little more gentle, firm but gentle." Aunt Anthea guided the spike into the soil. "A light but sure hand." A few chunks of dirt slipped out. "Now you brush away the bits and pieces and if you see anything that looks unusual call me. Do you understand?"

Mellie nodded, scared to say anything that would make her seem foolish.

"As I told you, this whole area was once underwater, and there are layers and layers deposited over the years. Remember Nette's lovely bread and butter pudding?"

How could she forget?

"Look here. You can see where the layers folded and sank and twisted over time, and in some places the lower levels rose to the surface, which is why when it rains interesting curiosities are sometimes revealed."

Mellie jabbed into the soil again, more gently this time, and gave the marlin spike a bit of a wiggle. She wasn't sure how much she understood of what Aunt Anthea had said, but she nodded enthusiastically. A few lumps fell, leaving a small hole. She jiggled the spike a little harder and loosened some more dirt.

Nothing.

If only she could find something, even the tiniest part of a dragon, then she'd show Bea and Grace that she wasn't the fool they made her out to be. If this Mary Anning, whom Aunt Anthea seemed to hold in such high regard, thought that these itchysaurs were related to dragons, then who was to say she couldn't prove it? That would certainly wipe the smirk off Bea's and Grace's faces.

Mellie worked her way along the crack in the soil. Nothing but mud, stones, and sand, nothing the slightest bit interesting. She squatted down and rocked back on her heels. Perhaps she wasn't in the right place. Maybe she should move along a bit closer to Aunt Anthea, who stood running her hand backward and forward over what looked like a totally flat and uninteresting piece of rock. "I haven't found anything."

"You have to be patient. You can look and look and see nothing, and then the next moment the very thing you've been searching for is right in front of your eyes, where it has sat forever. It's a lot like life."

Like life? "You said everything we were searching for had died hundreds of thousands of years ago."

"Yes, but we can learn so much from the past."

"I don't understand. Da taught me lots of things, but he's not here anymore." Her voice wobbled and wretched tears sprang to her eyes. Cook said tears cured nothing and she'd tried so very hard not to cry for Da and now, here, at the very first moment she had felt totally happy . . . She knuckled the treacherous drops away.

Aunt Anthea's arm wrapped around her, but she shrugged her off. "Crying won't fix anything, I know."

"A good cry never hurt anyone. Come and sit down. This is my favorite spot to sit and think. It reminds me of Benjamin, and I sometimes sit here and cry."

Mellie sank down on the boulder.

"Move over. There's room for two."

She shuffled along and Aunt Anthea sat close, the warmth of her like a comfortable shawl. "Would you like to talk about your da?"

Would she? What would she say? It wasn't a pretty story. Not the sort of thing anyone would want to share.

"Start at the beginning. What's the first thing you remember?"

"The first thing?"

"Your earliest memory."

"Before Ma died. There was my brother, such a tiny little baby. I liked to hold him close." She rubbed her fingertips against the inside of her palm, remembering the soft, downy touch of his hair and his warm, milky smell. "Ma and baby John drowned." A day she'd never forget. The day everything changed. The terrible silence when she and Da returned home. The look on his face before he bolted down to the river bank. Too late, too late. Their blue, pinched faces; Ma's icy fingers still clutching baby John. She choked back a sob. "Then it was only Da and me."

Until the men had come to share their grog and their plans with Da and he went off every night. She'd tried to ignore the sly looks and finger-pointing when she went with him into town for supplies, but she'd known then where their money came from. Bloody Cogley and his bunch of ne'er-do-wells. Da had said only one more time, enough to get them settled, but one turned to four, then ten and more. "He got caught up with some bushrangers and someone got shot. They took Da to Newcastle. One of the men came back. He chased me, caught me—he wanted our stash . . ." Her voice choked and she dropped her head onto Aunt Anthea's shoulder. She couldn't talk about it, couldn't tell. "I don't know what happened. I don't know where Da is. Dr. Pearson took me away because of my chicken pox and burned all our things."

"Oh, my poor darling." Aunt Anthea wiped her hair back from her sodden face.

What had possessed her to tell Aunt Anthea? Least said, soonest mended, Mrs. Pearson had said. "Cook said I had bad blood and that's why I went sleepwalking—because the bunyip was calling me."

"Cook is a nasty old woman, and I don't want you ever to think such things again. You are not responsible for your father's sins, nor those of any man."

CHAPTER 10

1919
WOLLOMBI

The door flew wide open and PJ fell into a pair of outstretched arms.

"Penelope. You're home."

The scent of beeswax polish, lavender, and scones enveloped her. "Mrs. Canning." She bent her head to the shoulder of the woman who had nursed every one of her grazed knees and childhood sorrows.

"Let me look at you." Mrs. Canning held her away for a moment. "What happened to your beautiful hair?"

PJ ran her fingers through her shoulder-length hair. "I had to cut it short because of the lice. It's growing back."

Mrs. Canning wrinkled her nose. "And you've been in the sun. Look at those freckles." She shook her head, then pulled PJ into another hug. "We weren't expecting you for at least a week. Your telegram from Adelaide said you thought you might have to do a stint in quarantine once you reached Sydney."

"We were cleared first thing this morning."

"Dreadful Spanish flu, though I shouldn't complain. Wollombi was spared. We had barricades up for a month or so."

"Barricades?"

"No one in or out. There were cases in Kurri Kurri and Maitland, and Newcastle copped it. Fingers crossed it's over now. Oh, my dear, it's so good to see you home. And despite the freckles you look rosy, quite rosy, a bloom in your cheeks. It must be that young man of yours."

PJ disentangled herself. Where was Sam? He'd been right behind her. "Where's Pa?"

"Out visiting. He'll be back before long."

For a moment her heart missed a beat. "Pa's all right, isn't he?"

"He's fine, just fine. Not getting any younger, but still doing his rounds. Like I said, we weren't expecting you so soon. I want to meet this young man. Go and get him."

"Sam." She called out, running down the path. No sign of him in the garden. Sid languished askew in the driveway, so he couldn't have gone far. Shading her eyes from the afternoon sun, she squinted down the hill and spotted him leaning against the fence surrounding the cemetery, gazing out toward the hills. Looking, perhaps, for paddocks of grazing cattle and men in Stetsons. She should have described the house, explained that it sat on the outskirts of the village—it was not the vast pastoral property he'd imagined.

"*Cooee*, Sam."

He lifted his head, raised his hand, and made his way across the road toward her.

She met him halfway down the driveway. "Come and meet Mrs. Canning. Pa's out but he'll be home soon." Reaching for his hand, she led him back to the house.

Mrs. Canning appeared from the kitchen, brushing her hands

free of flour. "So this is the young man you mentioned in your letter."

"Mrs. Canning, may I introduce Captain Samuel Groves."

"Delighted to meet you, ma'am."

"Mrs. Canning is my second mother and our housekeeper since I was this high." She reached down and tapped the side of his leg. "We couldn't survive without her."

"Get away with you. Don't you believe everything Penelope tells you. She can be a right terror."

"I've got her number, don't you worry." Sam gave PJ's hand a squeeze. "I'll go and get our bags."

"Oh, my dear. It's so good to see you home. There were times when I feared we'd lose you too." Mrs. Canning dabbed at the corner of her eye with her apron, leaving a smudge of flour on her cheeks. "I thought for a while the news of Dan and Riley would break your pa. In a strange way this awful flu was a godsend. Gave him something else to think about. He took himself off to give a hand at Kurri Kurri and Maitland hospitals. Didn't see him for weeks on end. But you're home now. Home for good."

Not if Sam had his way, but now wasn't the time to discuss their plans. Let Pa and Mrs. Canning enjoy having them home.

"I've not lit the fires yet." Mrs. Canning's cheeks pinked. "And I'm sure you're hungry. Like I said, I wasn't expecting you this soon. But never you mind, I'll sort something."

"Sam will give you a hand with the fires. And there must be something I can do to help. I don't want to be a nuisance."

"What a load of rubbish. The sort of nuisance I've been waiting for. It's far too quiet around here. You go and get settled. Put Sam down the hall in the guest room."

With a crash and a wallop, Sam reappeared, a kit bag clutched in each hand and her haversack swinging from his shoulder.

"Anywhere special I should leave the car? I pulled it up outside the old shed."

"Sid will be fine there. Here, let me help." She took her bag. "Come on, I'll show you to your room."

"Next door to yours, I hope."

"I had strict instructions that I should put you in the guest room, which is at the other end of the house. I think Mrs. Canning's looking after me."

Every step of the way PJ gritted her teeth and tried to close her mind to the unnatural silence of a house that had always rung with noise and laughter. She threw open the door. "I hope you'll be comfortable."

He chucked his bag on the floor and bounced on the bed. "Luxury."

"What did you expect? A shearing shed?"

"Come on, sweetheart." He stretched out his hand. "What's the matter?"

She flopped down beside him. "It feels strange, that's all. I was so looking forward to coming home, but it's so quiet. I miss Dan and Riley." Her voice caught and tears sprang to her eyes.

He pulled her close. "'Course you do. Buck up. Your pa will never say yes if you're red-eyed and miserable. He'll think you don't like me."

She hadn't imagined coming home would be so hard. She scuffed her hand over her eyes. "I'll go and put my bags in my room. I told Mrs. Canning you'd help light the fires."

"Not sure we need a fire, do we? Look at that sunshine." He

gestured toward the French doors that opened onto the veranda, where a shaft of late-afternoon sunlight blazed through the glass.

"We will when the sun drops behind the hills. It's still winter."

"Vast improvement on Philly in winter. Maybe my plan wasn't such a bad one."

And it wasn't. As hard as it was to be home, she knew she couldn't have gone with him to America without seeing Pa first. "It's an excellent plan. Thank you for coming home with me."

PJ scooted out of the room and came to a halt outside the sleep-out, Dan and Riley's room; they'd always insisted on sharing. She stuck her head around the doorway. The metal-framed beds, separated only by Pa's old trunk, stood forlorn, and the air smelled unnaturally clean—the tang of sweaty bodies and soiled socks long gone.

She closed the door quietly behind her and made her way down the hallway.

"What's that machine doing sitting outside my shed?"

"Pa." She flew to the door and collapsed into his arms, inhaling the familiar mixture of wool, soap, and the underlying hint of carbolic.

After a moment, he disentangled himself. "So you managed to get home."

"I'm fine, Pa, just fine." Which was more than she could say for him. Always lean, he now appeared haggard, his shoulders stooped, his eyes dark from lack of sleep, his cheeks hollow, and his face pale and faded. "How are you?"

Without responding he made his way toward his study. "And where's this young man of yours?" he said, the words sounding like an afterthought.

"Mrs. Canning's got him laying the fire."

"I'd like to speak to you alone. Close the door and sit down." He gestured to the chair across from his desk. "Before I meet this

American, I want to know the nature of your relationship. That you haven't been bamboozled into some illicit liaison." Pa's eyes drilled into her as they'd done when she was a child.

Bamboozled? Illicit liaison? She squirmed on the chair more from habit than guilt. "No, there's nothing . . . Oh." Color flooded her cheeks. Did he think she'd become pregnant? It wasn't even possible. If Sam had tried to have his way on some of those warm, moonlit nights aboard ship, perhaps she might have encouraged him. But she'd spent every night in the shared cabin with five nurses while he slept on the upper promenade deck, as far away from the hammock he'd been issued as he could get.

"Well?"

She drew in a deep breath and took a gamble. "No, Pa. I haven't done anything foolish." The childish squirming sensation returned. "We're friends, mates. We've worked together for the last two years."

"*Harrumph.*" Pa reached for his pipe propped in the corner of his desk drawer and began to fill it from a leather pouch. A waft of dried apple and the sweetness of fresh tobacco filled the room. Knowing better than to disturb his ritual, her gaze roamed the familiar room. The toppling piles of books; the haphazard pictures, overcrowded, always crooked; the dangling skeleton parked in the corner, the subject of more of Dan and Riley's pranks than she could remember. It would disappear and reappear in the strangest of places, but when it ended up in the outside toilet, one clawed hand grasping the dunny seat, Pa had finally padlocked it to the stand.

Stifling a snort, she picked up the paperweight on his desk. "I've got something to tell you." The words tumbled out of her mouth. "While I was in London waiting for Sam, I went to the Natural History Museum and found some fossils from the Hunter. I didn't know there had been such significant finds . . ." Her words petered out as the look on Pa's face hardened. "One of the specimens came from Bow Wow Gorge." She lifted her shoulders. "Do you remember? Dan and Riley used to go camping there. They would be so excited. Sam and I are going to go and see what we can find out. They might have discovered—"

Pa's jaw clenched. "But for your encouragement, they might be here to enjoy it."

The venom lacing his voice doused her enthusiasm and she leaped to her feet. "Pa?" Surely he wasn't holding her responsible for Dan's and Riley's passing. She'd explained in her letters how surprised she'd been when she'd received the telegram saying they'd joined up and wanted to meet in London.

He heaved out of his chair, failing to mask a groan. "There's little point in discussing it. Your decision put ideas into their heads. You know perfectly well I never would have given them permission." And with that he gestured to the door—her dismissal.

Mind reeling, she staggered down the hallway. Images flickered of Dan and Riley whooping with excitement over an insert in the *Maitland Mercury* promising a free trip to Europe for all eligible young men and Pa's face much as it had looked a moment ago: cold, distant, and determined. He'd snatched up the poster and thrown it into the fire, then slammed his hand down on the table and told them in no uncertain terms that until they were of age they'd be staying home. He would not be signing any recruitment papers. Then came the long and familiar tirade about the sin of waging war.

She found Sam parked on the kitchen table, legs swinging, and Mrs. Canning with a girlish bloom in her cheeks. The moment Sam saw her he leaped off the table. "Come and sit before you fall down." He guided her to a chair. "What's the matter?"

She dropped her head into her hands and murmured, "Pa. He's blaming me because Dan and Riley didn't make it home."

A cup of tea appeared in front of her. "Been off on his usual rant about the evils of war, has he? Drink this and you'll feel better." Mrs. Canning peeled PJ's hands away from her face and wrapped her fingers around the cup.

She sipped, Sam's concerned face slowly coming into focus while Mrs. Canning explained Pa's unflinching belief that nothing, absolutely nothing, justified killing another human being.

Sam paced up and down the kitchen, his tension evident in every heavy step. "Someone needs to put him straight. How can he hold you responsible for your brothers' choices? I'll go and have a word with him. I thought he fought in the African War."

"Medical Corps. He didn't fight. Sam, please don't. You'll only make matters worse. He can't stay angry with me—"

"Dr. Martindale. It's a pleasure to meet you." Sam cut her off, stepping in front of her and holding out his hand.

Pa took it, gave it a brief shake. "How's the meal looking, Mrs. Canning? Time for a drink?"

Sam moved to her side. "You okay?" he murmured.

She nodded, unsure whether she was or wasn't. Nothing had gone as she expected. Instead, Pa's strange comments about her actions, his heated accusation, and now he seemed to be distant, closer to plain rude. Whatever would Sam think?

"I've got it all under control." Mrs. Canning's forced cheer only underscored the tension in the room. "Sam's lit the fire in the dining room, and the table's laid. Penelope, if you'd like to take the tray of glasses into the sitting room, there's a fire in there, too, and whiskey and sherry in the decanters. I'll let you know when everything's ready." Mrs. Canning brandished her wooden spoon and returned to her pots and pans.

PJ hovered for a moment, her hand on Sam's arm restraining him, while Pa wandered off toward the sitting room. "Don't say anything, Sam, please."

"Anything about what?"

"About us. About getting married. Pa's not his usual self. I don't know what's happening. He's different and he looks so frail. We can't talk about marriage when he's still mourning the boys and I can't tell him we're planning to go to America."

"We're not. We're not leaving, at least not for the time being."

"Please, Sam. Try to understand."

His mouth pulled down at the corners. "Then why am I here? How are you going to explain that?"

"The truth . . . just maybe not all of the truth to start with. You managed to secure a berth for us both to Australia and you brought me home." She offered a reassuring smile. "I started to tell him about Anthea Winstanley. When he's calmed down I'll explain more. Tell him you're here to help me." A sigh slipped between her lips. "Give him time. Time to get to know you and forgive me."

Sam picked up the tray, ignoring Mrs. Canning's quizzical look, and followed Pa into the sitting room.

"Please don't tell me I'm going to lose you too."

PJ closed her eyes, holding back the sudden rush of tears. "You're not going to lose me, Mrs. Canning. Why do you think that?"

"There's no mistaking the look of a man with romance on his mind, and you failed to mention anything about America."

"I told you, we're friends, good friends. We spent a long time working together and he's interested in Australia. We won't be leaving for ages." The words glued themselves to her tongue. More than good friends since Sam had proposed. She had to change the subject. "Sam's keen to explore Australia. While I was waiting for him in London I visited the Natural History Museum and I found some fossils from

Bow Wow Gorge. Sam's interested in paleontology." Not strictly the truth, but he hadn't complained about her ideas when she'd told him on the ship; in fact, he'd been enthusiastic.

Mrs. Canning propped her elbows on the kitchen table and studied her. "Bow Wow Gorge? The boys used to go there."

"I know. I was so surprised when I saw the name on a fossil in the museum in London. A paleontologist named Anthea Winstanley found it. She's buried in Lyme Regis, so while I was waiting for Sam I went down there and—"

"And why exactly are you so interested in this Winstanley woman?"

"It's not so much her, more that there could be important fossils right on our doorstep. Can you imagine how excited Dan and Riley would be? They always said they wanted to find a dinosaur . . ." Her words tapered off as she saw the look of pain cross Mrs. Canning's face. They couldn't keep ignoring the fact—Dan and Riley wouldn't be coming home no matter how any of them might wish otherwise.

"Do you think that's a good idea? It might make matters worse between you and your pa. Stir things up, all this talk about the boys."

Swallowing a gasp of exasperation, she plastered a smile on her face. "Sam and I might take a drive tomorrow and have a look around. See if we can find Bow Wow Gorge. A Digger from Kurri was on the boat; he knows the area."

"And do you think you should be dashing around the countryside alone with a man?"

"Mrs. Canning," she huffed. "I've spent the last two years dashing around France and Belgium with him and hundreds of other men. I hardly think—"

"Australia's not the Continent. Things are very much as they were. Not a lot has changed."

"We'll go for the day."

"I want nothing more than your happiness, Penelope. You know that."

"I'm going to go and dig out the boys' old fossil collection and leave Sam and Pa to get to know each other."

PJ spent the next half an hour sneezing and spluttering and rummaging in the corner cupboard outside Pa's study, searching for Dan and Riley's fossil collection. She found a series of bottles of tonic, a couple of old medical reference books, rolled bandages, a Bunsen burner, and a framed photograph. She tipped it to the light. A line of people, a family perhaps, in front of a rock wall; a group of girls in white dresses, a man and a woman standing on either side of a horse, and in the center an older man and a woman. Shrugging, she replaced it in the cupboard along with everything else and then remembered the old trunk between the boys' beds in the sleep-out.

The murmur of Pa's and Sam's voices and the *clink* of glasses drifted in the night air as she slipped into the sleep-out. She dropped onto her knees between the beds and ran her fingers over the faded name stenciled across the top of the trunk: *Dr. William Robert Martindale. NSW Medical Team.* Pa's trunk. It had surprised her when Dan and Riley dragged it down from the attic. She'd never seen any relic of his time in the African War. Ma always said his belief in pacifism stemmed from the atrocities he'd seen and he wanted no reminder. Dan and Riley had expected to find his uniform or mementos of his time in the army, and instead they had uncovered a collection of fossils. It was the beginning of their passion for all things prehistoric.

Rust pitted the metal clasps and hinges but there was no sign of a padlock. She spent a few moments wriggling the clips until they finally released, and when she opened the lid an agonizing pang shook her as she pictured Dan and Riley carefully unpacking and dusting all the bits and pieces. Who had stored them away? Pa? More likely

Mrs. Canning. Memories came flooding back as she picked up each one of the carefully labeled fossils arranged on the tray insert. *Dan Martindale. May 23rd 1914. Bow Wow Gorge; Riley Martindale. April 18th 1915. Bow Wow Gorge.* One after another she lifted them out and placed them on the bed, her hands trembling. The name Bow Wow Gorge had struck a chord when she'd first seen it written in London, but she hadn't known Dan and Riley had visited so often.

Lost in her painful reminiscing, she jumped when Sam pulled her back against him. "What're you up to?" He dropped a kiss on the back of her neck.

"I'm sorting out Dan and Riley's fossil collection."

"They collected all these?" He waved his hand over the single bed.

"This is only part of it." She tilted the tray on the top of the trunk. "There's more underneath. I hadn't realized how much. They were convinced if they pieced everything together it would form a dinosaur—it was one of the reasons we visited the Natural History Museum in London."

"Oh, come on, surely they didn't believe that. How old were they?"

"Twelve, maybe thirteen, when they first found the trunk." And only a few years later they'd enlisted, without Pa's permission, convinced they'd miss their chance and the war would be over if they waited any longer.

"Grown enough not to believe this was a collection of dinosaur bones." Sam wandered around the bed picking up bits and pieces, turning them over in his hand, and putting them back down. "How come some of them are labeled and some aren't?" He picked one up and turned it to the light. "Do you know what these fossils are? This one looks like a butterfly."

"That's a brachiopod of some sort, a lamp shell. I know that from the book I got at Foyles. I'm not sure about the others." Another

CHAPTER 11

—◆—

1847
Bow Wow

Anthea wrapped her arm around Mellie and gave her a hug. In so many ways Mellie reminded her of herself. Not that she'd suffered the way Mellie had, at the hands of an unscrupulous man, a grieving father, and a string of misadventures. Nothing could be further from the truth. More the awful sense of not belonging, of not knowing her place in the world. Benjamin had helped her understand with his patience and caring, guiding her with a loving but firm hand away from her family's overtly religious beliefs and irrational superstitions to the truth of science. Could she do the same for Mellie? "Dry your tears. I can hear the girls coming down the trail."

The poor child shot to her feet, scrubbing frantically at her eyes, her pale face luminous. Mellie's own account of her story had proved far more harrowing than Edna's brief words in her letter. And Lydia's comments about the continual emotional lashing Mellie received from Bea and Grace, fueled no doubt by Ella's sharp tongue and Edna's hoity-toity manner, couldn't have made it easier. No wonder Mellie was all at sixes and sevens. She would put a stop to it.

Almost as though to substantiate her thoughts, Bea and Grace's high-pitched *bawk-bawk* cry echoed down into the gorge. "Come with me, Mellie; let's set you up over here and no one will be any the wiser about our little chat."

As she stooped to pick up the spike, she caught sight of a small, jagged piece of rock that revealed a nice example of a brachiopod. She tucked it in the pocket of her breeches and wandered after Mellie. "I'd like you to continue working here. Remember what I said— slow, steady movements and let the rock and the soil fall. Check each piece once you have worked it free." She handed Mellie the spike.

With a frail smile Mellie turned her face to the wall and began to pick at the dirt. Anthea bent down and laid the brachiopod carefully on the ground. Hopefully Mellie would find it before too long.

"Girls, girls," she called. "Whatever took you so long? Mellie and I have been hard at work for ages."

"Ella didn't want to come again, but Nette said she couldn't stay at the house alone." Bea took a couple of steps toward Mellie, then hooted with laughter. "Lost your skirt, Bawk-bawk?"

Mellie had the good sense to ignore Bea's shriek and, as a gesture of solidarity, Anthea unbuttoned her coat and tossed it aside, revealing her own breeches. Bea's eyes widened in surprise and her mouth snapped closed.

"Come with me, Bea. I've got a job for you." She led her away from Mellie. "Grace, you come over here as well. Bring the brushes and the bellows. Lydia, if you'd return to your previous spot, and, Ella, would you give Nette and Jordan a hand setting up our picnic?

Mellie and I could both do with a drink, and perhaps some of Nette's oatmeal biscuits."

Anthea tossed back the glass of lemonade Nette handed her in a silent toast. She would handle these girls and make them accept Mellie. She was a delightful child and through no fault of her own had suffered the evil gossip that filtered from the servants' quarters at the doctor's house.

Squatting on her haunches, Mellie poked around in the crumbling soil. She would like a drink and a saint's mouth would water at the sight of the oatmeal cookies, but she couldn't bear to face Bea and Grace. She paused for a moment and flexed her gloved fingers, then she ran her hand down the leg of the breeches. No matter what the girls said she would wear them every time she came down to the gorge. They made her feel special—a dragon hunter just like Aunt Anthea and Mary Anning.

Straightening her shoulders, she hefted the marlin spike and jumped up on top of the round boulder where she and Anthea had sat. Let them come and attack her—she was ready. That delicious tingle traced her skin, the same as she'd felt when she stood above the gorge with Aunt Anthea staring down into the abyss. It was all she could think about—her dragon hunt. Like hunger in her belly, it consumed her; nothing else mattered.

With a burst of pleasure, she leaped down. Her ankle twisted, but her cry lodged in her throat. Right in front of her nose a rock, not much bigger than one of Nette's cookies, sat in the sand, its strange pattern catching the filtered light of the gorge.

Her fingers closed around the rock and she brought it close to her face. Butterfly shaped with evenly spaced lines spreading out from the center, the pattern was so perfect she knew she'd found something important.

Her whoop of triumph echoed back from the surrounding rock walls and everyone downed their tools.

Lydia reached her in less than a second. "Have you found something?" she whispered.

Mellie held out her hand and showed her the crusty-looking stone. "I don't know." She ran her index finger over the surface. "I saw it lying down here. I must have knocked it out when I was digging." It fit neatly in the palm of her hand and she closed her fingers and squeezed. "It's a dragon scale, like Aunt Anthea's."

"It's a lamp shell, a brachiopod." Lydia's dismissive sigh slashed an agonizing path to Mellie's heart.

How could Lydia sound so disappointed? Mellie traced the beautiful patterned wings, then scratched at the surface with her nail. She wet the tip of her finger on her tongue and rubbed hard.

The world silenced, nothing but the *thump* of her blood in her ears. No matter what Lydia wanted to call it, Mellie knew. "It's another dragon scale." A whole dragon scale, entire in its perfect beauty, safely encased in stone.

Anthea rushed to her side. "Oh, you clever, clever girl. Your first find." She hugged her tight. "I am so proud of you. It's not chipped or cracked—a lovely example of a brachiopod, perfectly symmetrical."

"Is that what dragon scales are called? Brach-o-pods?"

Bea jumped up, waggling her stupid head, making her blonde curls dance, and clutched her hand to her throat. "It's just an old oyster shell."

"No, it's not." She knew what oysters looked like. Da brought them home from Morpeth, not that she'd ever eaten one of the nasty lumps of gray snot. "Look at the pattern on its wings. It's perfect." In her heart of hearts, she knew. "It's a dragon scale."

"Bawk-bawk, it's an oyster. Nothing to do with a dragon."

Mellie's vision clouded and she clenched her teeth. "I've seen lots of oysters. They crush the shells for lime and use them to build houses." A horrid job that they saved for the worst of the convicts, the shell gangs. Which was exactly where she would like to send Bea right now.

"Girls, girls. Let's be a little more scientific about this. After all, that's why we're here. Gather around, everyone. Most of the fossils we find here are related to the shellfish we eat today. Oysters, clams, mussels. And up at the house I have some ammonites from England, which I will show to you. They're related to an octopus."

Mellie groaned. What did an octopus have to do with anything? Nasty sea monsters with eight long wavering legs that terrorized sailors and sucked sailing ships down into the depths of the ocean. She flexed the spike in her hand. Maybe Jordan had used it to fight them off.

She turned her dragon scale over. "It can't possibly be an oyster or the remains of an octopus." No chance. It was most definitely a dragon's scale. How she wished she could meet this Mary Anning and ask her what she thought.

Aunt Anthea ran her finger around her collar and pulled out her silver chain. "It will look like this once we've cleaned it up."

Mellie reached out and touched the pendant with the tip of her finger, her heart picking up the strange beat she'd felt the first time she'd seen it. "That truly is a dragon's scale." It made the one she'd found look like a lump of crumbled rock from the road the convicts had built through to Wollombi.

"We'll clean yours this afternoon when we get back. Your very first fossil. Now, girls, time for a break and a drink."

Mellie wandered away, her dragon scale clutched tight in her hand. Proof that dragons once inhabited this magical place and frolicked in the amber-colored water that gurgled over the boulders. She could imagine a whole flight of dragons circling above the treetops, their scales catching the sparkling sunlight.

"Here you are, Mellie. Have a drink and a biscuit or two. Dragon hunters need to keep up their strength." Lydia offered her the biscuit and a sympathetic smile.

"Thank you. I don't think I have ever been so happy. Aunt Anthea is so very kind to let me come and stay. You are so lucky to come here every year."

Lydia sank down on the rock. "Yes, we are, but this will be the last year Ella and I will visit."

Would that mean she couldn't come again? In fact, she never wanted to leave. "Why? Aunt Anthea will invite you again."

"Yes, she will, but we have to become ladies now, and searching for fossils is not something ladies do."

"Aunt Anthea is a lady."

"But she is not looking for a husband."

"Are you? You don't have to. I am going to be a famous dragon hunter like Mary Anning. I don't want a husband."

"Every girl must find a husband when she reaches a certain age and this"—she waved her hand around the gorge—"this searching for fossils is not a ladylike occupation. Not something of which a husband would approve."

"Well, I'm going to be like Mary Anning and discover everything there is to know about dragons."

"Oh, Mellie. You'll understand one day." Lydia stood and brushed off her hands. "Enjoy it while you can."

Mellie spent the remainder of the day crawling around on her hands and knees searching beneath the overhang. No other dragon scales presented themselves, but by the time Aunt Anthea called a halt she'd decided she was lucky, very lucky, because no one else had found a single piece worthy of attention.

They were simply looking in the wrong place. A dragon would tuck itself somewhere safe and secure, and curl up tightly out of the wind and the rain. Tomorrow she would explore the caves along the other side of the gorge. She'd ask Aunt Anthea about it when they got home. "My very first dragon scale." Mellie clasped it tight in the palm of her hand, then brought it to her lips. "I knew I'd find you," she whispered.

Cheeks flushed from the climb up the trail, Mellie wiped clean every one of the tools and left them on the bench to dry, closed the door to the workroom, and ambled up to the house.

Ella sat on the veranda in the afternoon sun, humming a tune, a notebook on her lap and a pencil in her hand. As Mellie passed her, she snapped the notebook shut and stuffed it into her pocket, then looked her up and down and let out a howl of laughter. "You can't wear those breeches all the time." She shook her head and rolled her eyes.

Mellie tossed her head and went inside. She didn't care what Ella thought, what any of them thought, except for Aunt Anthea. She'd found her dragon scale and they were going to polish it until it glowed, and then she'd wear it around her neck just like Aunt Anthea.

Lydia took no notice of her when she walked into the sitting room. Hunched in front of the unlit fire, a book on her lap, she sat staring into the nonexistent embers, while Bea and Grace huddled, their heads together, giggling over a drawing. Mellie edged closer. They slammed their hands down. "Mind your own business, Bawk-bawk."

She wouldn't look. She could guess what the drawing would be; she'd stumbled across several at Wollombi, carefully left for her to find. Chickens—chickens wearing her face, covered in spots, squawking and running around the millpond, their feathers covered by trailing nightgowns. They'd have to change their sketches now her spots had gone and she'd become a dragon hunter.

She wandered through into the dining room. A soft green cloth covered the top of the table and in the center sat three rectangular wooden boxes. Throwing a quick look over her shoulder, she slid open the lid of one. Just as she thought. Dominoes.

Carefully, so as not to disturb the peace, she tipped the box, smoothing her fingers over the perfect little stacks of ivory tiles. She stood the first one up, looked over her shoulder again. No one was watching. Then the next and the next, the way Da had shown her, curving the tiles across the table top in the shape of her dragon scale. She patted her pocket. Aunt Anthea had promised she'd help her clean away the rocky sediment, but ever since they'd returned, she'd been holed up in the kitchen talking to Jordan and Nette. Mellie hadn't hung around; she'd recognized the tone—not an argument, lots of what-to-dos. Money, more than likely. She'd listened to Da enough times to recognize one of those discussions.

She stood the last tile. A complete and perfect outline. With a sigh, she leaned back to admire her handiwork.

"Bawk-bawk, you can't play dominoes by yourself. You need a partner. Don't you know anything?" Bea barreled into the room and ground to a halt at the table. She raised her arm and her index finger hovered.

"No." Mellie spread her arms to protect the array of dominoes.

With a crow of triumph, Bea flicked her finger. "Too late." The first domino twisted and toppled, setting off a chain of clattering as the remainder fell, destroying Mellie's handiwork.

She reared up, fiery red flashes masking her vision, and launched across the room. Bea landed a spiteful kick to the back of her knee and caused her to stumble, sending the chair flying with an almighty crash.

"Mellie. What have you done now?" Ella stood in the doorway. "You'll be for it when Aunt Anthea sees this."

With a howl Bea burst into sobs, flapping her arms like the tormented chicken she accused Mellie of being. "She attacked me. She attacked me."

Grace and Ella rushed to Bea's side and eased her into the chair, fussing over her like a pair of maiden aunts.

"I did not. You kicked me and spoiled my game." Mellie hurled herself at Bea.

Strong arms pinned her. She kicked and bucked, thrashed and screamed. All in vain.

"Mellie. Mellie. Shh. Come away."

The red haze cleared. Aunt Anthea's face appeared. A frown of concern. "Come along, I need some help." Aunt Anthea's calm voice soothed the fraught atmosphere. "Lydia, would you see to the mess in here and settle the girls?"

Lydia eased Bea to her feet and guided her, limping and whining like a sissy, from the room.

"She attacked Bea, for no reason. We wanted to play dominoes with her," Grace moaned.

Lying toad. Turning, she threw an evil dragon glare at Grace, but before she could respond, Aunt Anthea had marched her through the door, under the covered walkway, and into the kitchen.

She'd tried so hard, but Bea and Grace, once they'd crawled out from under their mothers' skirts, had turned as evil as a pair of red-bellied black snakes and twice as poisonous. She was sick to death of them. Next time Bea uttered that *bawk-bawk* cry she'd . . . She clenched her fist . . . What she wanted to do was deliver one of those knuckle punches Da had taught her. It wasn't her fault she'd caught the chicken pox, and besides, she wasn't going to let their teasing bother her anymore—all the nasty scabs had gone.

Aunt Anthea nudged her down into the chair closest to the range. "Sit there and take some deep breaths, then you can explain to me exactly what happened."

Mellie stared down at the ground, willing it to open and swallow her. She couldn't drag enough air into her lungs to breathe, never mind speak. A surge of nausea coursed up her throat and she choked it down.

Anthea felt helpless—a poisonous mixture of anger and misery leached from every one of Mellie's pores. "We'll go and rescue your skirt from the workroom and then you can go to your room and wash your face and hands and change."

Mellie ground to a halt and wrenched her arm free. "No. You promised."

"Promised? What did I promise?"

"You promised we'd clean my dragon scale. Please don't tell me you were lying. Why does everyone lie to me?"

"It will take quite a while to clean your . . ." Anthea paused. It crossed every line she had ever drawn for herself, the difference between fact and fantasy, but poor Mellie needed her support. "Dragon scale," she finished.

"You do believe it too." A beautiful smile, one she'd never seen before, crossed Mellie's face and her eyes glowed with an almost religious fervor. "Can we go and do it now?"

Together they walked down the path to the workroom. Mellie threw open the door and dropped to her knees in front of the tool box. "I have to put the tools away."

"Let's leave that until later, shall we? The first thing we have to do is to wash your dragon scale with soapy water and see how much debris we can remove." She handed Mellie the enamel bowl she used for the job. "Go and fill this from the kettle in the kitchen. Not too full. I don't want you to burn yourself. Tell Nette I sent you."

Without a word, Mellie took the bowl and left. Anthea rummaged around until she found the soap and bristle brush she kept for cleaning her finds and set them out on the bench. At least if they made a start, Mellie might feel someone cared. The poor little mite made her heart bleed.

She hadn't cleaned the finds herself for years, preferring to send the best to Sydney. The crates beneath the benches contained years of work that still needed cataloging. The lure of the search consumed her. She'd believed when the girls arrived her dream of finding an Australia ichthyosaur might be fulfilled, but that would have to wait. Mellie's well-being was more important.

"Nette says we've got half an hour until it's time to eat and she says I can't come to the table dressed like a hoyden, so we have to hurry." Mellie kicked the door closed behind her.

"Does she indeed? Well, sometimes scientific discovery is more important than the correct attire. She should know that. Put the water here."

Mellie set the bowl on the bench.

"Right, now we need the soap. Swish that around and get a bit of lather up."

"Are you sure it won't break?" Mellie cradled the lamp shell in her hand as though it were made of glass.

"No, it won't. It's simply rock . . ." Anthea bit her tongue as Mellie's face fell. "Protecting the dragon scale," she amended. The child was as prickly as an echidna. Why not let her cling on to her belief if it provided the solace she needed? Who was she to interfere? It harmed no one; plenty of time for science later. "Put it in, right under the water, and we'll leave it there overnight. Some of the debris will loosen and then we'll paint it with a mixture of glue and sugar. Once that's dry we leave it to soak in vinegar to soften the rocky case and make it easier to clean."

With a great deal of reverence, Mellie lowered the brachiopod into the bowl, then stood staring down into the water.

"It won't disappear, I promise. While we're waiting, we must make a label for your find. Something all good paleontologists do. We record the date and place of the find and the name of the specimen." She pulled open the drawer of the table and brought out one of the triangular cardboard labels she favored for the purpose, as well as a piece of graphite. "Come over here." She held out the chair and waited for Mellie to sit. She had no idea if the child could write, but unless she was very much mistaken, the significance of marking her first find would live with her for a long time.

Mellie licked the stub of the graphite and glanced up, the excitement evident in her lively eyes. "Shall I write my name?"

"First we name the fossil."

"How do you write dragon scale?"

"We must use the correct name—*Spirifera* . . ."

Mellie's face fell. "But it's a dragon scale."

Anthea opened her mouth to argue, years of training warring with the pleading look in the child's eyes. "*D-R-A-G-O-N S-C-A-L-E.*"

Slowly and painstakingly, Mellie formed the letters.

"Now on a new line 'Found by Miss Mellie Vale' and the date."

"What is today's date?"

"Saturday, April the third."

With her tongue jammed between her teeth she formed the letters—*Satday apirl 3 1847*.

"Very good. Now the place. Bow Wow Gorge. *B-O-W*, finger space *W-O-W*, and Gorge is a little trickier. *G-O-R-G-E*. Very good. We will leave it here until we finish the cleaning and polishing. And now it is time for something to eat."

Mellie smoothed her finger over the label and offered the brightest smile. "I need to put the tools in the box."

"Neither your dragon scale nor the tools will come to any harm, trust me."

Once the girls had turned in for the evening and Nette and Jordan had left for their rooms over the stables, Anthea lay awake listening to the familiar night sounds. A faint scurrying, and the creak and groan of timbers as though the house were settling for the night, happy to have all its rooms filled once more, despite the girls' fractious natures.

And Mellie, dearest Mellie. Such a poor troubled child, yet her frail exterior masked a lively intelligence. Anthea could see herself at that age. Knowing she was different from the people around her; seeing it as a failing but unable to curb her innate curiosity. Dragons indeed.

Mellie's thinking was similar to Mary Anning's beliefs when she'd first discovered the strange jumble of bones with a long tail and wings that were believed to be those of the largest ever flying animals. That find had inspired Henry De la Beche to paint *Duria Antiquior*, the first pictorial representation of prehistoric life, and Thomas Hawkins to create his masterpiece, *The Book of the Great Sea-dragons*.

CHAPTER 12

1919
Wollombi

PJ wandered through the cemetery, her hand trailing across the tops of the weathered stones. So many people, so much history. She knelt and pulled at a clump of weeds spreading across Ma's headstone; at least she didn't have to suffer the agony of losing her sons. Three rows behind Ma lay the two Pearson girls, rosettes of lichen creeping over their headstones. As a child she'd brought flowers for them; it had eased the misery of Ma's passing to know she wasn't alone.

The bottom corner of the cemetery where the fence sagged and leaned out toward the millpond remained unoccupied. She climbed through and settled on a patch of grass, her back against the aged timber. Her favorite spot as a child, and since the fire that had destroyed the old mill, it had provided a tranquil refuge. Birds swooped from branch to branch of the scrubby trees at the edge of the water and a cluster of black cows grazed, lifting their heads occasionally to stare balefully at her.

Pa's terse reception rankled. She understood his disappointment and sorrow about the boys but couldn't fathom why he would hold her responsible. Her grief had subsided, tempered by the knowledge they weren't alone in their sorrow. So many boys and men had left full of dreams and hopes, and so few had returned. She'd known from the outset her decision to join the Ambulance Corps hadn't pleased Pa, but enlisting as the boys had done flew in the face of all his beliefs—lying about their age and breaking their promise the final straw. It would have been different if they had survived. Like all young boys they rarely thought of other people; selfish and self-centered, never considering anyone else. She'd been no less selfish, but she'd had nothing to do with them signing up; in fact, she'd told them they should listen to Pa before she'd left.

It was a conversation she and Pa would have to have, though one she believed she'd already addressed when she had written to him and told him the boys wouldn't be coming home. When Pa hadn't responded, her letters to him had slowed to a trickle. Finally she'd given up. Instead, Mrs. Canning's letters had kept her up-to-date.

She and Pa were as bad as each other. With a last glance at Ma's headstone, she rose and brushed down her skirt. She had to speak to Pa again. The longer the strange rift between them continued, the worse it would become. Not a conversation she would relish.

On her return to the house, PJ's courage deserted her when she found Pa in the kitchen, brooding over a cup of tea.

"Is there anything you'd like me to do today?" she asked.

He lifted his head. "I've got some calls to make. Mrs. Freeman is getting close to her time. With ten children, all boys, she's still hoping for a girl . . ." He heaved a sigh and downed the rest of his tea.

She couldn't help wonder what prompted the sigh. The sense that his disappointment lay with her hung heavy, but now was not the time. "Sam and I thought we'd go and see if we can find Bow Wow Gorge today. Do you have any idea where it is?"

"This is nothing more than another of your foolish schemes."

"I want to do it for the boys."

He gave an impolite snort. "Shame you didn't think more about them before you filled their heads with ideas of war."

PJ's blood boiled. "Pa, I . . . we need to talk about this . . ."

"Not now, Penelope." He pushed his teacup aside.

Why wouldn't he talk to her? His cold attitude made her more determined than before to forge some link to Dan and Riley through the fossils. It might encourage him to talk about them and give him something to remember them by. "I found Dan and Riley's fossil collection. I was right. They had visited Bow Wow Gorge. Can you remember anything about the original fossils, the ones in your trunk? Were they here when you and Ma bought the house?"

He shook his head and lifted a shoulder. "Your mother dealt with household matters, and you children. She sorted out all the rubbish we found in the house when we moved in. I had too much work to do. Wollombi hadn't had a doctor for so long I was working day and night." He hauled himself to his feet and picked up his bag. "I have calls to attend to."

She leaned in to give Pa a kiss, managed to miss his cheek and land it on his ear. "I'll ring if we're going to be late."

He stopped with his hand on the door and studied her for a moment. "Don't drive back after dark. The road's rough. The pub in Kurri has rooms and decent dining. I used it as a base during the flu epidemic."

The door banged behind him.

"Don't you worry yourself." Mrs. Canning's sympathetic tone soothed her heartache. "He'll come good. He needs time. Be different if we'd had a funeral. It's hard to believe, especially when you walked in the door with Sam in tow, hale and hearty. And your pa didn't even get a telegram."

"I wrote as soon as the telegrams found me." She'd known before she'd opened them what they would say. It wasn't until the initial shock had worn off that she questioned the reason the telegrams had come to her and not Pa. After following a long paper trail, she'd discovered that both Dan and Riley had listed her as their next of kin. But for Mrs. Canning, she wouldn't have known Pa had received her letter.

"It'll sort. You'll find the best way."

But that was the problem—she had no idea how.

Mrs. Canning sat down and steepled her hands, her index fingers touching the tip of her nose. "Do you want some breakfast? Or wait for that young man of yours to surface? No idea what time he got in last night."

PJ's head came up with a jerk. "What do you mean?"

"He went off for a wander after we'd eaten. You had your head buried in those rocks. Thought he'd mention it." Mrs. Canning cleared her throat. "Down to the hotel, I expect."

"Why would he go down there?"

"No idea. If you want to be back here before dark, you better not hang around. It's past ten."

How had that happened? She'd woken early and spent some more time sorting Dan and Riley's finds and then taken a walk to the mill-pond, but surely she hadn't wasted so much time. "I'll go and see if Sam's awake."

"And why don't you change into something nice? Might cheer

you up a bit. There's more than enough to choose from in your cupboard. And while you're doing that I'll pack you something for your lunch."

PJ brushed her hands down her trousers. She couldn't remember the last time she'd worn a dress. Sam wouldn't recognize her.

She slipped along the hallway to the guest bedroom and rapped on the door. Waking Sam was nothing new—for as long as she'd known him he'd been a night owl. A useful quirk when driving an ambulance, but annoying now the war was over. "Sam. Are you awake?" She pulled open the curtains and the winter sun streamed in.

He groaned and his tousled head appeared above the blankets.

"I told Pa we'd be going to Bow Wow today. Do you still want to?"

He scrubbed his hands over his face and gave her a bleary blink. "Why not?"

"What time did you go to bed last night?"

He shrugged. "Late. Chatting with the locals. Best way to get to know a place."

"You could have asked me. I've lived here all my life."

"Not the same." He shrugged into his shirt.

"I'll leave you to get dressed. See you outside."

She clattered along the hallway and threw open her bedroom door, fired with a sudden enthusiasm to get moving. Maybe she should take Mrs. Canning's advice and change. She opened the cupboard door and pulled out a dress and a cardigan, then threw her trousers and a shirt into her haversack, took a quick look in the mirror, and groaned. The atmosphere in the house weighed her down and Pa's distance made it all the more difficult. Perhaps if she could find something else to concentrate on, the fug in her head would clear.

PJ sat behind the wheel, drumming her fingers. The possibility of them finding Bow Wow Gorge and getting back to Wollombi before dark had become a long-lost dream. It would be at least two hours each way, and Pa hadn't sounded too confident about the condition of the road. At least if she made the decision to stay overnight no one would be concerned when they didn't return. She'd asked Mrs. Canning to tell Pa that they had taken his advice and would stay in Kurri Kurri at the hotel. Much to her horror, Mrs. Canning made her promise that they would take single rooms. It seemed everyone thought the worst of her.

PJ bit her lip as Sam slung his haversack and their packed lunch behind the seats, cranked the engine to life, and jumped in the passenger side.

"Is this the Australian you?" He cast an appreciative gaze over her dress. "The blue brings out the color of your eyes." He pulled a large piece of folded paper from the inside of his jacket.

"What's that?" she asked as they coasted down the driveway. He tilted the paper toward her and she snatched a glance. "Another map. Where did you get that?"

"That's what I was doing last night. Asking the locals about Bow Wow. Not sure how accurate the distances are; the time it takes will depend on the track."

"Did anyone know exactly where it is? I asked Pa but he dodged the question."

"Nope, but this map'll get us to Kurri Kurri. Great name that. Do you know what it means?"

No, she didn't. She studied Sam's smiling face. She'd misjudged him. He spent so much time talking to people that she sometimes became annoyed, but as usual it had paid off.

"In one of the local languages, the Awabakal language—I didn't know there were Indians in Australia—"

"They're not Indians; they're Aboriginal people. They were here long before Captain Cook stumbled across Australia."

"Same as our native people. Do you want to know what Kurri Kurri means or not? You're going to like it. I know you are."

"Go on, then. Tell me."

"It means 'The Beginning' or 'The First.' How's that? I reckon your Bow Wow Gorge might be that if the stuff you've read about Gondwanaland is anything to go by. Perhaps the Aboriginal people knew about these fossils."

"Maybe." PJ floored the accelerator pedal and Sid took off up over the rise, following the winding road toward Millfield.

"We're looking for the Rising Sun Inn on our right once we go over the creek and then about a hundred yards on there's a track." He tapped the map spread across his legs.

"No, the road carries straight on through Cessnock, then on to Kurri."

"This is the way I was told. Besides, it's supposed to be an adventure, isn't it?" He reached out and tucked a stray curl behind her ear. "Come on, lighten up."

She was being as difficult as Pa. What was the matter with her?

"Apparently it's a bit rough, but it takes us past a lagoon and then we follow our noses—nice expression that, I like it—and make a left at the end of the road. That'll get us to Kurri Kurri. About forty miles all up."

She really had misjudged Sam; he had made good use of his time down at the pub.

"I can't believe you've lived here all your life and not set foot outside Wollombi."

"That's not true. I went with Pa on his calls, and sometimes to Maitland . . ."

Her words dried. Sam was right; she knew very little about the area beyond Wollombi. She'd made the odd trip to Maitland and then Sydney to finish school, with a chance to attend the Women's College at the University of Sydney, until for want of anything better to do she'd found herself at St. Mark's in Darling Point learning how to drive. By the middle of 1916 she'd arrived in France. "If I'd had a vehicle and known how to drive when I lived at home it would have been completely different."

"Slow down—here's the Rising Sun. Turn right here."

They followed a winding track until they reached the top of an incline. PJ slammed her foot on the brake; the track disappeared from sight. The car skewed to the right and came to a shuddering halt.

Sam laughed. "It was worth coming this way. Look at that."

A wide expanse of water lay before them, populated by an array of waterfowl, swooping and diving.

"Pull off for a moment. We'll see what Mrs. Canning packed us for lunch. I missed out on breakfast. This is Ellalong Lagoon, better known as Catch-a-boy Swamp, if the locals are to be believed. The perfect place for a picnic." Sam crooked his finger. "If you hang around at twilight, a weird call echoes from those hills. It's the bunyip staking its claim."

"Oh, for goodness' sake. Who's been telling you that rubbish?"

"I'll have you know a young boy was taken while playing on the edge of the lagoon one night."

"Yeah, yeah. And the millpond back at home is supposed to be haunted too. A young girl who wanders the shores at dawn, summoning the creature from the dark."

Sam swung around to face her. "You didn't tell me that."

"Why would I? It's only a story parents tell to keep their children safe because the younger Pearson girl drowned in the millpond. Her tombstone is in the cemetery."

"You've completely shattered my belief in the local knowledge. How do you know it's not true?"

"I've never seen or heard anything and I've lived all my life opposite the millpond."

"You have no sense of romance, not one iota."

"Romance? What's it got to do with romance?"

Sam leaned over and slipped his hand around the back of her neck and planted a soft kiss on her lips. "Plenty."

A chill had entered the air by the time they drove past the small miners' cottages on the outskirts of Kurri Kurri.

"Considering we're supposed to be traveling over the richest coalfield in the Southern Hemisphere, you'd think the houses would be a bit more impressive."

"You have done your homework, haven't you?" PJ turned her head and smiled. She loved the way Sam had gone to such trouble to find out about the area—she'd never imagined the local hotel would be such a treasure trove of information.

"Forewarned is forearmed, and all that." He spun around. "Now that's more like it. Slow down. In fact, stop."

On the corner of the street overlooking a small park stood a majestic three-story building draped with ornate cast-iron lacework and brick arches, which wouldn't have looked amiss alongside the Natural History Museum. PJ gazed at the impressive hotel. "It's amazing. No wonder Pa liked staying here."

"It's a bit late to go exploring. What say we sort out a couple of rooms, find something to eat, and get to know the locals? Never know who we might bump into." Sam threw open the door and bounded out to greet a man making his way through the doors. "Ted!" Sam held out his hand.

The man pushed back his cloth cap and his eyes lit up. "Captain Groves. So you made it to Kurri." His blackened hand hovered for a moment halfway to a salute and then he grabbed Sam's outstretched hand and pumped it up and down. "Day shift's just finished. Going for a beer."

Sam was incredible. Here, right here in the middle of a country he'd only been in for a couple of days, he'd found someone he knew. She stepped up beside him.

The man dropped Sam's hand and wiped it down the back of his trousers. "And this'd be . . ."

Sam nudged her forward. "PJ, you remember?"

Ted's face broke into a smile. "Didn't recognize you out of uniform." He ran an appraising eye over her stockinged legs, making her wish she hadn't taken Mrs. Canning's advice to wear a dress.

"Gave you Captain Groves's message outside that big museum in London."

PJ studied the man's face, peeling away the layers of grime. "I remember. You gave me such a start when you told me Sam hadn't made it."

"You did what?" Sam's mouth gaped and Ted roared with laughter.

"Was so gobsmacked by such a beautiful sheila me words came out all wrong. I'm sorry, Captain."

"Why don't we drop the captain, Ted. I'm happily discharged from the army. Sam will do nicely. How about we go and have a drink?"

Ted cleared his throat and threw a look over his shoulder at the group of men standing on the veranda listening, beers clasped against their chests, watching every move they made.

Sam took a couple of steps toward the hotel. "Come on, PJ." His broad smile encompassed the audience.

"Ladies aren't allowed in the bar," someone piped up.

"Keep forgetting these Australian rules. Is there a garden out the back?"

The red tinge on Ted's cheeks dulled a little. "Take the car around and I'll bring the drinks out there. What would you like, miss?"

"Call me PJ, Ted." She swallowed, realizing how thirsty she was. "I'd like a ginger beer, please."

"Right you are. I'll see you around the back."

Before she knew it, Sam had followed Ted into the pub. Tossing back her hair, she slid in behind the wheel.

"Need a hand?" one of the men from the veranda called.

"I can manage." Thankfully the engine fired on the first go.

"Go to the corner, turn down the lane, and you'll see the garden behind the pub."

"Thank you." She raised a hand and edged down the dirt track, leading a procession of miners with their beers clutched in their hands and grins plastered over their coal-stained faces.

The back of the building opened onto a wide paddock with a view out over neatly fenced paddocks and a set of dual tracks cut through the dust that led to an iron shed housing a rusty old tractor.

Cursing Mrs. Canning and her ideas about dress code, PJ pulled down her skirt and clambered out, then made her way to a couple of bench seats. The men gathered around, waiting and watching, rather as though she were an exhibit in some museum.

"Strange-looking motor that." A young bloke, hardly more than a boy, broke the silence and flopped down on the bench beside her.

"It's a Wolseley, from England. Sam bought it and had it adapted in London, and it was used as an ambulance during the war."

"Don't see many motors around here, 'cepting tractors." He hitched a thumb at the rusting old machine in the shed.

"Old Dash has got a Model T van. Uses it for deliveries," someone said.

"And thinks he's God's gift because of it." The crowd of men edged closer.

"I'd like to drive. Where did you learn?" The young man let out a long moan as though he had given flight to one of his most treasured dreams.

"In Sydney, before I went to France. I drove ambulances."

The rest of the men settled, releasing a cloud of fine black dust from their clothes. "France, eh?"

"That's where I met Sam. He was a volunteer. He didn't join the army until the Americans entered the war in 1917."

Something in the air changed, and the remainder of the men found a perch or hunkered down in a semicircle at her feet.

"How did a pretty young lass like you end up in all that mess?" A grizzled older man plonked himself down.

"It's a long story." She didn't want to discuss the war, didn't want to run the risk of saying something that might cause upset or stir up grief.

"Leave the lass alone. She might not want to talk about the war. Tell us about the ambulance. We all saw a lot of nurses, but the drivers were usually men."

"You probably couldn't tell. Our uniforms weren't exactly flattering."

The younger man who'd said he'd like to learn to drive moved closer. "You said you learned in Sydney. How did that come about?"

Much safer ground. "I was going to go to university. I wanted to be a doctor like my father. I was invited to a"—not a reception, certainly not a reception for the governor general's wife; it would make her sound far too uppity—"a party. They'd just formed the Australian Red Cross and I heard about a St. John Ambulance course. I thought perhaps I could do something useful. I wanted to help, and knitting and fundraising are not my thing."

Suddenly she felt comfortable. How wonderful to be talking to a group of men who weren't maimed or injured, just the odd facial scar or finger missing here or there. "Dame Nellie Melba gave a concert at the Sydney Town Hall and raised so much money. I thought if she could use her talents to do something then there must be something I could do. I joined the VAD."

"And became a voluntary ambulance driver." The young bloke grinned.

"VAD is Voluntary Aid Detachment, you duffer." One of the blokes scuffed him across the head and he managed to grab his beer before he lost the lot.

"I wanted to drive a motor ambulance, and when the opportunity presented itself, I jumped at it. I'd done a first-aid course, and when the British Red Cross requested thirty women, I became one of them. We shipped out from Melbourne in September '16."

PJ barely registered the arm resting on her shoulder until a beaded glass of ginger beer appeared in front of her. She tipped her head back. Sam smiled down at her.

"Looks like you've made some friends."

"Yes, yes, I have. Though I've been doing all the talking."

"I've had a word with Ted. He seems to think some of the folks in there might know more than he does about Bow Wow. I'll go back inside. See what they have to say."

"No, stay, please—" Her words fell on Sam's retreating back and she tucked the half-empty glass down behind her feet with a sigh. "Do any of you know anything about the fossil beds in the area?" The sea of faces remained impassive except for the young man next to her. He jerked his head up and turned, bumping her elbow. "A place called Bow Wow Gorge. I believe it's not far from here," she added.

A bark of disparaging laughter greeted her words, beers were tossed back, and the men clambered to their feet and wandered off, leaving her alone with the young man on the bench. As she turned she noticed the crutch next to him on the ground and his rolled-up trouser leg. "Did I say something wrong? Is that why they left?"

"Maybe. People around here don't talk about the gorge."

"Whyever not? It's a significant fossil bed. There are specimens from around here in the Natural History Museum in London."

"It's private." The tips of his ears turned an interesting shade of pink and he ran his finger around and around the top of his empty glass.

Whatever was he talking about? "The place?"

"People don't talk about it." He put his glass down and stood up.

"You can't leave me sitting here all on my own." She reached for his arm. "Please."

"Not my place to tell you. It's a load of old rubbish. I've got to go, miss."

Rubbish didn't make grown men walk away. "I beg your pardon. I didn't ask your name."

His shoulders dropped and he let the crutch fall back to the ground. "Arthur, Arthur Blackman. Everyone calls me Artie."

"And have you lived all your life here in Kurri, Artie?"

"Since the mines opened. 'Cept for the stint in the army. That's how I got this." He flipped the folded end of his empty trouser leg as he settled back on the bench.

"I'm sorry."

He shrugged. "It's not that bad. Got used to it now and it keeps me out of the mines."

Only then did she notice that unlike the other grime-covered men, he was neatly shaven and had clipped fingernails without a trace of coal dust. "So what do you do?"

"Work in the office. Do the pay. I'm good with numbers."

Lucky. How many other men who'd returned with a disability ended up with a job? "You've done that since you came back?"

"Took over from my dad."

"Do you live at home?"

"With my mother. We lost Dad at Gallipoli."

"I'm sorry." She was going to have to stop saying sorry, stop asking so many questions.

"Why do you want to know about Bow Wow Gorge? It's not a place a nice lady like you wants to go."

"Whyever not?"

He flicked a look over his shoulder. "Told you." His voice lowered to a murmur. "Stories."

"What kind of stories?" Curiosity piqued, she turned to face him.

Artie chewed at his lip, took another look over his shoulder, then pulled in a deep breath. "The gorge . . . it has a bit of a reputation. Bad things have happened there."

"What kind of bad things?" For some unaccountable reason her voice dropped to a whisper.

"The gorge is part of the Bow Wow property. Big house on the top of the hill. It used to belong to the Winstanleys. The farmland's leased, but no one has lived there for donkey's years." Artie glanced around again, then sucked in a deep breath. "Mrs. Winstanley and a girl—some say more than one—disappeared, and the place has been empty ever since."

PJ sat bolt upright. "When?"

"Not quite sure. Eighteen fifties perhaps. My gran used to talk about it. None of us kids were allowed out that way. Strange noises at night. Howling and the like. Some said a bunyip. Mrs. Winstanley used to have these parties down there; she was a bit"—his face flushed an amazing shade of beetroot and his Adam's apple bobbed—"strange. Dressed like a man and took young girls down into the gorge. Then all of a sudden she disappeared." Artie shuddered and opened his mouth to say something more, then snapped it shut.

"Time for something to eat," Sam's voice boomed, "and we'll head out to Bow Wow tomorrow." He grasped her hand and pulled her to her feet, grinning at Artie. "Thanks for looking after my girl."

Artie took off faster than she imagined possible, crutch tucked neatly under his right armpit.

"Goodbye, Artie," she called after him. "See you again another day, I hope."

He turned, a quizzical look on his face, then made his way out around the back of the hotel.

CHAPTER 13

❈

1847
Bow Wow

Gray light tinted the sky behind the tree line. Mellie crawled from beneath the blankets and shrugged into her breeches and blouse, then laced her boots, ready for another day down at the gorge. Careful not to disturb Lydia, she closed the bedroom door behind her.

To avoid the kitchen and Nette's banging and crashing, she slipped through the front door and walked around the back of the house to the workroom. Ever since Aunt Anthea had shown her the collection, she'd managed to snatch a few minutes alone every day to explore, determined to see how many dragon scales she could find stored in the boxes. Most were cracked or chipped, but she was certain that over the years Aunt Anthea had lived at Bow Wow she would have amassed enough to clothe at least one dragon. What worried her most was the fact that Aunt Anthea had told her that, like Mary Anning, she sometimes sold some of her finds, mostly to women who wanted an original piece of jewelry to wear or to men who collected curiosities.

She lifted her dragon scale from the bench and ran her finger over the surface. She knew it had brought her luck.

The glow of the dragon scale had seeped into her life and made her world glitter. Bea and Grace's mocking no longer upset her; she could brush them away as easily as she cleared the soil around their finds in the gorge. Their hounding no longer stabbed at her heart; the dragon scale protected her, and besides, she had her own job now. Aunt Anthea had said she had a special touch and no one else could use the marlin spike.

Mellie lifted the lid of the tool box and, as she'd done every morning for the last week, took out each of the tools, upended the box, and shook out the loose soil. She then brushed each one and carefully replaced it in its spot. Aunt Anthea hadn't asked; she'd simply taken on the task. It gave her an excuse to spend time in the workroom.

By the time she'd finished, the sun slanted in through the shutters and she threw one open. The cool morning air circled inside the little hut and cleared her head. She had a few moments left, so she picked up her gloves, made sure the tools were all in order, and ducked back to the kitchen.

"Can you tell Aunt Anthea that I will meet her down at the gorge? I'd like to leave early."

Nette threw her a sideways glance. "Not without some food inside you, you won't."

"Oh, but I—"

Two large slices of bread wrapped around some bacon landed in her hand. "Eat that on your way down and I'll pass on the message. Take care."

Mellie took the secret path down to the gorge, exploring the various caves and nooks and crannies. She'd work for an hour or two alone until Aunt Anthea, Nette, Jordan, and the girls arrived.

Despite her best efforts, she didn't find any more perfectly formed dragon scales or any vertebrae, nothing but a mass of marine fossils and tiny icicle-like growths in the caves that Aunt Anthea called stalactites, and the imprints of leaves and ferns with wavy arms. Nothing that made her blood pound. Nevertheless, she relished her time alone as the gorge unveiled its hidden secrets, leaving her with a sense of peace and calm after the horrors of the past weeks.

"Good morning, Nette. Have you seen Mellie?"

"She's down to the gorge, left an hour or so ago."

Anthea nodded. It wasn't the first time Mellie had left early and taken the secret path. She said she loved to start the day that way—not only did she like to keep her eyes peeled for anything that could have been missed, but it made her feel special. "I finally capitulated and told Ella she could stay here today. I'm sure she won't come to any harm." She'd decided there was little point in continuing to argue with Ella. Truth be told, Anthea was tired of her continual complaints and the bickering.

"I can stay here with her if you'd like me to."

"No, that's not necessary. Not unless you'd like to."

Nette gave her a condescending look and continued to pack their picnic.

"I'm not serious." Nette relished the trips down to the gorge during the girls' visits. It gave her a break from the constant round of jobs she and Jordan took on and gave them time to spend together. "I'll go and chase up the girls. The barometer is falling. It may be a good idea to return a little early."

Benjamin's barometer, as always, proved correct, and not long after lunch they arrived back at the house to find the doors and shutters flung wide open and the sound of singing and piano music drifting in the cloying air.

"Looks like we've got a visitor." Jordan tilted the brim of his hat and squinted into the distance at the spot where a saddled horse grazed in the shade of one of the eucalypts lining the fence. "Horse hasn't got any water." Tutting and mumbling, he left the pack horse tied to the fence and strode across the paddock, hand outstretched.

"Go around the back, girls. Get yourselves cleaned up and I'll meet you for afternoon tea. Jordan will take care of everything." Anthea pulled Nette to one side. "Go with them. I wasn't expecting anyone. Keep your eyes open."

As soon as the girls disappeared around the back of the house, Anthea followed Jordan. By the time she'd reached the paddock he'd filled the trough and removed the horse's saddle and bridle and hung them on the fence.

"Don't recognize the horse. Do you?"

"No, but whoever was riding it either didn't plan to stay long or couldn't care less." She ran her hand down the poor animal's sweaty neck. "Ella's been alone . . ."

"If whoever it is had any rough ideas, they wouldn't have left the horse here for everyone to see. Expensive saddle too. Sure you weren't expecting a visitor?"

"Certain. I'll go and see who it is." The flicker of unease spread as Anthea made her way up to the house. The front door stood wide open—nothing unusual in that when someone was home, but the trickle of piano music and Ella's voice raised in song drifting in the air did little to ease her concern. Anthea could count on one hand the number of people who had turned up uninvited in the last twelve months. Steeling herself, she stepped into the sitting room.

Ella sat at the piano, eyes sparkling with laughter as she ran her fingers along the keys singing a rather racy rendition of "Robin Adair." Lounging against the piano was a man. A smallish man, sporting a very flamboyant waistcoat, his over-long black hair slicked back, straight and sleek above a domed forehead.

Anthea opened her mouth to speak, then stopped. Was this why Ella had nagged her into allowing her to stay home? Did she know the man would be visiting? Was he the Sydney beau she and Lydia had quarreled over? What was his name? George? The flicker of unease translated to pure annoyance, and she cleared her throat in a dramatic bid for attention.

Ella's fingers hovered above the keys and she turned her head. "Aunt Anthea. There you are." She stood, almost a head taller than the bow-legged man who offered an ingratiating smile. "This is Mr. Victor Baldwin."

He stepped forward, bobbing his head like a foraging duck. "Mrs. Winstanley."

Her vision blurred, black spots dancing in front of her eyes, and she reached for the back of the chair to steady herself.

"Please excuse my unexpected arrival, Mrs. Winstanley. Miss Ella has entertained me. She said you would be returning soon."

Breathing deeply, she schooled her face. Foolish to jump to conclusions. A common enough name. "I don't believe we've met, Mr. Baldwin." The name caught in her throat.

"No, indeed we haven't. I wish to offer my condolences."

Not at all what she expected. Benjamin had passed away nearly two years ago, although there wasn't a day without the most trivial event bringing an aching memory. "Thank you. Were you and Benjamin acquainted?"

"We were."

"I'm afraid I don't remember him mentioning your name." A blatant lie, but nothing she would admit until her suspicions were confirmed.

"I thought that might be the case. I haven't seen him since I was a child."

She bit back her next question; she had no intention of discussing Benjamin's earlier life in England with this man. Silence was her best approach.

"I come with a letter of introduction from Sir Thomas Mitchell." He rummaged in his inside pocket and produced a folded piece of paper. "I regret the intrusion, but Mitchell assured me you would do me the honor of speaking with me."

Thomas. How very strange, when she'd just been thinking of him earlier, impatient to hear more of his thoughts about the vertebra she'd sent. "Yes, certainly." In her own time, when she was ready to deal with this unexpected turn of events. She gestured toward the filthy coat masking her breeches. "I have just returned from a field trip. If you'll excuse me for a few moments . . ." She needed more than a few moments. Benjamin always feared this might happen, but as the years passed they'd both become complacent. "Ella, would you organize some refreshments for Mr. Baldwin?"

"Really, that's not necessary." He bestowed a radiant smile on Ella. "I have been very well looked after."

"And I shall continue to keep Mr. Baldwin entertained until you return, Aunt Anthea." The foolish girl simpered and took a step closer to him.

It was only then that Anthea noticed Baldwin's clasped right hand, where a chain dangled. Unless she was very much mistaken, he held her pendant. With a stab of annoyance, she realized Ella must have taken it into her head to remove it from her dresser and show it to him. "Are you interested in fossils, Mr. Baldwin?" She pointed to his hand and widened her eyes in question.

At least he had the grace to look embarrassed. He opened his palm and, as she expected, displayed her pendant. "I am most interested. Mitchell was telling me of his original discoveries, specimens of mollusks from a place called Harper's Hill and diprotodon bones from a cave somewhere westward. He was kind enough to show me some of his other finds. I also had the honor of hearing about the vertebra you sent him. An ichthyosaur, I believe."

Perhaps Mitchell had reached a conclusion. "That has yet to be confirmed." Her heart rate kicked up a beat and she stifled the smile that wanted to creep across her face. "Ella, would you be kind enough to go and see if the girls require any assistance? We all got a little mussy today in the heat." Hopefully his name was nothing more than an uncanny coincidence, but she had to be certain.

Ella hovered in the doorway, a look of curiosity on her face.

Anthea felt a flash of impatience. "Ella, please leave now. I would like to speak to Mr. Baldwin privately."

With a squinty-eyed grimace and a barely concealed moan, Ella left the room.

"Now, Mr. Baldwin, to what do we owe the pleasure of your company? People rarely find their way to Bow Wow without explicit directions. I presume Mitchell provided those. You said you had a letter of introduction?"

"Indeed I do." He unfolded the piece of paper and waved it in her general direction, but she had no intention of grasping for it like some tantalized beggar. "I'm recently arrived from England."

Which was more than blatantly obvious from his ostentatious waistcoat and pristine breeches.

"Benjamin's family also asked me to convey their condolences." His words brought her up short. Seventeen years since she and Benjamin had fled England. To the best of her knowledge, he'd severed all family connections unless . . . She shook the thought away, refusing to be rattled by the man's efforts to insinuate himself. "You're from Keswick?"

"My family hails from Keswick, yes, but I have only visited. I am a Londoner through and through."

Breathing had become difficult once more. What did Benjamin always say? *"Silence is a powerful ally."* She shifted her gaze to the window and waited.

"I'm very much hoping we might become neighbors."

So much for her good intentions. "Neighbors?" The word ended in an embarrassing squeak.

"Indeed. Mitchell led me to believe that you had a parcel of land you might be prepared to make available."

Mindless of her mud-splattered clothes, Anthea sank onto the nearest chair. She hadn't entertained the thought of subdividing the land since Benjamin passed. It had been his suggestion, as he wanted to spend more time in Sydney, and Mitchell, in his role as government surveyor, had endorsed the possibility. What a dreadful coincidence. Surely Mitchell didn't know of their connection with Victor Baldwin.

"I see." She didn't, but she could think of nothing else to say. What did "make available" entail? And why would he want it? Only a small part of the land was suitable for farming, the remainder rugged and barren in places, more rock than soil, and to add insult to injury, it would mean she had to relinquish a section of the gorge. Something she was not prepared to do, not now since her latest find. And besides, she didn't want any reminders of the past close to home. It was the very reason she and Benjamin had left England.

"I was hoping you'd permit me to view the lot."

"You'd like to look at the land?" For goodness' sake, she might as well have sheep fleece crammed between her ears, she could hardly grasp his meaning.

"Very much so."

The sun had sunk well below the hills and the sky taken on the gray-purple tinge. "It's too late this afternoon. It's a good ride." If she couldn't discourage the man now, she had no doubt his enthusiasm would wane once he saw the barren nature of the land. A far better way to deal with the situation.

"Perhaps tomorrow?"

"I'm afraid I can't offer you accommodation. I have the girls staying with me."

"I quite understand. The delightful Miss Ella explained their annual sojourn to me. That's how we ended up admiring your pendant."

She held out her hand, determined to retrieve her precious keepsake. The thought of him holding it made the hairs on her arms quiver more than his unheralded arrival. "I'll arrange for my man, Jordan, to show you the way to Mulbring. There's a tolerable inn there. It's not a difficult road."

"And you will be kind enough to allow me to view the land tomorrow?"

"Yes, yes." Or was that such a good arrangement? Maybe she should settle her suspicions. Benjamin's family could make no claim on what was rightfully hers. "Why don't you join us for a meal before you leave?"

With a beaming smile he deposited the pendant in the palm of her outstretched hand. "And perhaps I could also view the fossil beds tomorrow."

Mellie slipped into the seat next to Lydia, her gaze riveted on the stranger at the top of the table, his hair as oiled as his manner. Aunt Anthea had given him her seat and Ella sat on one side of him, simpering like a ninny and hanging on the man's every word. She wasn't alone. Bea and Grace were equally captivated, and surprisingly so was Lydia. So much so that she rose and moved her chair closer to the top of the table and gazed adoringly at the man.

"As I was telling Miss Ella . . ."

Miss Ella preened and patted her perfectly arranged hair.

"Oh, Mr. Baldwin, please share your secrets." Lydia's batting eyelashes almost blew out the candle. "I am so frightfully interested in all matters scientific."

What on earth was Lydia playing at?

"I had the privilege of attending the Australian Museum with Sir Thomas Mitchell—was one of the first in Sydney to view their new exhibit." Baldwin paused and adjusted his collar. "A bunyip skull. Proof absolute, irrevocable proof, that these creatures are no native legend."

Mellie shuddered as a sharp stab of pain invaded her chest. In a matter of moments the golden glow of the past days evaporated as Cook's threats and warnings about the creature haunting the millpond bounced around inside her head.

The man made her flesh crawl. His hooded eyes, the lazy way his gaze roamed Lydia's body, and his false good humor reminded her of the men Da used to bring home: their shifty looks telling a completely different story from the smarmy smiles plastered on their faces when she served them.

A creeping feeling worked its way up Mellie's spine and settled on her scalp.

"Mother says bunyips aren't real." Bea propped her elbows on the table and scowled. "Same as Mellie's dragons. They're legends, fairy tales."

"Bea, manners. If you are to eat with the adults, you will behave as an adult. Alternatively, you can go to your room."

"I beg your pardon, Aunt Anthea." Bea dropped her hands into her lap like a demure little princess. Served her right for saying dragons weren't real. Everyone knew they were. Why, even Aunt Anthea had agreed; otherwise, why would she have helped her label her find a dragon scale?

"Mr. Baldwin, pray continue."

Offering Lydia a smile that didn't reach his eyes, he rummaged in his inside pocket and brought out a folded piece of paper. "Since we are debating the subject, I might have something here that would interest you. Proof enough, I think you will agree." He handed the page to Lydia and bent close. "The skull is described as belonging to an amphibious creature that inhabits billabongs, swamps, lagoons, and various inland waterways."

Baldwin's lips curled in a crooked smile. "An illustration of the skull, believed to be a bunyip. Perhaps you'd like to pass it around the table, unless you feel it might be too intimidating for the *children*." He stared at Bea in much the same way that a man might eye a funnel-web spider crawling on his shirt. "The drawings appeared in the *Sydney Morning Herald* newspaper. As you can see, they show the side view of the upper half of the skull, an internal view, and the view from above and behind."

Ella reached across the table and attempted to pry the paper from Lydia's hand. Ignoring Ella's attempt, Lydia turned to Aunt Anthea. "Would you care to take a look?"

Ella's chair scraped across the floorboards and she flew to her feet. "Excuse me," she snarled and flounced from the room.

Aunt Anthea's mouth gaped for a moment, then she shook her head at Nette. "Now, where were we?" She pored over the picture, then placed it on the table. "All extremely interesting, Mr. Baldwin, but hardly conclusive proof of existence. It could be fictitious. I am sure you are familiar with the rubbish that was perpetuated about the Feejee mermaid. Nothing but the torso and head of a juvenile monkey sewn to the body of a fish."

"I doubt an establishment as reputable as the Australian Museum would display such an item unless it had clear proof of its authenticity."

Unable to stay still a moment longer, Mellie snatched up the paper; the pictures in Dr. Pearson's books loomed in front of her eyes. "What does this monster look like?" She clamped her teeth, trying to hide the wobble in her voice.

"This particular specimen was found in the vicinity of Melbourne. It's believed to be as big as a six-month-old calf, of a dark brown color, with a long neck, a pointed head, large ears, a thick mane of hair, and leathery skin—an amphibious animal, no doubt."

Did they live in millponds? That was what she wanted to know.

"Mr. Baldwin, I beg to differ." It was such a surprise to hear Nette speak that everyone at the table hushed their rumblings and Mr. Baldwin's paper lay forgotten. "I'm led to believe these creatures combine characteristics of a bird and an alligator. Its head is emu-like, and its body and legs those of an alligator. Many say it towers over the ancient gum trees and can rip them out by the roots. A veritable monster."

A sudden gust of wind swept open the door; the oil lamps and candles flickered. Caterwauling filled the room. Mellie jumped to her feet and wrestled the door closed, her heart hammering nineteen to the dozen. She slammed her back against the timber and spread her arms.

The candles flared and the darkness resolved, revealing the strange scene. Ella's vacant chair; Bea and Grace pinned to their seats, upright and white-faced; Lydia wide-eyed and rigid.

Aunt Anthea and Nette cupped their hands around the taper and relit the lamps. All the while Mr. Baldwin rested in his chair, a satisfied smirk curling his thin lips.

"Thank you, Mellie. That was very brave." Aunt Anthea straightened up and crossed the room, hands outstretched. "Are you all right?"

A shudder traced Mellie's shoulders. "The wind. Just the wind." She repeated the chant in her head until her shaking ceased.

Aunt Anthea guided her to her seat. "It appears the storm has reached us. Now let's clear up these plates, and I believe Nette has an apple crumble for us."

Mr. Baldwin rose, his shadow large and looming in the wavering light. "Thank you very much for your hospitality, Mrs. Winstanley. I fear I must forgo dessert. Time I was leaving."

As he spoke a flash of lightning illuminated the window and Mellie covered her ears as another clap of thunder shook the house.

"I think it's a little late." Aunt Anthea pointed to the rain pouring over the eaves. "I'm sure we can arrange a bed for you here, Mr. Baldwin. I can't send you out in this weather."

"I absolutely cannot put you to any trouble. A little bit of rain never hurt anyone. Thank you for your hospitality. I'm sure I can find my way to Mulbring, and, if the weather clears, I will see you tomorrow morning bright and early."

"Very well. If you insist. Nette, would you call Jordan? Ask him to escort Mr. Baldwin to the Mulbring road."

Offering little more than a grunt, Nette left the room.

"Good evening, ladies." Mr. Baldwin sketched a bandy-legged bow. "I look forward to tomorrow."

CHAPTER 14

———◦◦◦———

PJ crawled out of bed and lifted the curtain. The unexpected stillness of the town took her by surprise. Although she had spent a dreamless night, her first waking thought was of Artie's words. It was something to do with his quizzical look as he left, implying there was more to tell.

If nothing else, it proved they were on the right track. There couldn't be two women called Anthea Winstanley connected to Bow Wow Gorge. Impossible. Bending down, she pulled out her notebook and settled on the chair by the window. She flipped back through the pages until she found the spot where she'd made a few random notes and marked some dates. She'd noted the year 1847—the date on the vertebra from the museum—Anthea Winstanley's name, and Bow Wow Gorge. The second note also mentioned Anthea Winstanley, but at Lyme Regis in 1860. She must have left Australia and traveled to England. Did that have anything to do with the story Artie had told her? She hadn't disappeared; she'd simply left. But why would she do that without telling anyone? And he'd made no mention of a daughter.

What had Artie said? *"Bad things have happened there . . . Mrs. Winstanley and a girl—some say more than one—disappeared . . . The place has been empty ever since."*

Surely in the last seventy years someone else would have stumbled across the fossils in the gorge.

Perhaps Artie would call into the pub this morning; no, he'd be at work. Maybe this afternoon she would have another chance to speak to him. After they'd visited Bow Wow, and then she could ask him to clarify his story. There had to be more to it.

Pulling her coat over her nightdress, she picked up her washbag and towel and made her way to the bathroom. While she and Sam ate last night, the publican's wife had given them a complete run-down on the merits of the hotel. Her pride and joy, it seemed, were the thirty-four rooms and, most importantly, the flushing toilets. At one stage PJ almost exploded with laughter as Sam had demanded a complete explanation of their workings. Apparently the superior dunnies were the reason they'd secured the license in the first place. She could tell, simply from the look on Sam's face, that he'd filed that particular word away in his list of Australian expressions.

In a matter of minutes, having made use of the admittedly delightful bathroom, she was back in her room. Ignoring Mrs. Canning's recommendations about her clothing, she dug out her trousers and shirt. She would be prepared for whatever the day might bring.

Once dressed, she walked along the veranda overlooking the street and knocked on the French doors to Sam's room. Receiving no reply, she went in.

"Sam." She leaned over the bed and smoothed the hair back from his brow. "Sam, wake up. It's time to go to Bow Wow."

He lifted one eyelid, then propped himself up on his elbow, his other hand reaching for her. "It's too early." He yawned, his voice still thick with sleep. "Come here."

She relaxed against his warm chest and closed her eyes as he nuzzled her hair. The temptation to stretch out alongside him was overwhelming, but she'd promised Mrs. Canning nothing untoward would happen. Besides, they only served breakfast until nine o'clock and it was already past eight. "You need to get up." She rolled off the bed and threw down her trump card, though she doubted it would pay. "They might have coffee."

"You win." Sam struggled to his feet, full of groans and morning mumbles. "I'll see you down there."

Taking a deep breath, PJ pushed open the door of the bar and reeled, the stench of stale beer and smoke turning her stomach. A small, stocky man, with a checkered cloth hooked over his shoulder, eyed her with a belligerent stare. "No ladies in the bar."

"I wondered if we could get breakfast."

"In the dining room, but you'll have to be quick. Since you stayed the night it's on the house."

"Thank you. My friend will be along in a moment." There was no sign of Sam on the stairs so she turned back. "Do you know how to get to Bow Wow Gorge?"

The man gave the counter a final wipe, put down his cloth, and sank onto a nearby stool. "No one's lived there for years." His eyes narrowed. "Wouldn't want to go hanging around there; never know what might happen to a young girl like you." He gave a burst of macabre laughter.

PJ pushed her hands down into her pockets. "Is there anyone who might know about the family that lived there?"

"Hasn't been anyone there for decades. Nothing but rural properties around here until the mines took off."

Under his piercing gaze, PJ shifted her feet, suddenly self-conscious. "Can you give me directions?"

He scratched the top of his head. "If you're prepared to run the risk. Take the road out of Kurri toward Sydney and you'll see a turnoff marked Sandy Creek Road. It's about a mile and a half down there on the right. Take my advice and leave well alone. The missus will look after you in the dining room."

After a series of wrong turns on the outskirts of Kurri Kurri and around the coal mines, they finally found a rickety old sign dangling from a tree branch—*Sandy Creek Road*—the very track they had taken yesterday.

"I can't believe we drove right past. Didn't anyone in Wollombi tell you where the turnoff to Bow Wow was?"

Sam shrugged. "No one knew exactly."

"The publican said there's a track about a mile and a half down here, on the right."

Sam slowed to a crawl. "Hardly surprising we didn't see it. From the look of all this undergrowth it might be difficult to spot."

"Especially if the house has been empty for years . . ." She craned forward, fists clenched. "Do you think this is it?" She pointed to two lichen-blistered stone gateposts marking a dip in the track.

Sam drew the car to a halt and pulled on the hand brake.

An overgrown track curved up into the distance. "Look up there.

It might be an animal track, but I think I can see two rows of trees. I'll get out and walk." A flurry of excitement warmed her blood.

The track meandered into the heart of the scrub, then curved out of sight around a stand of acacia, the fluffy yellow blooms a splash of color against the silver-green trunks of the eucalypts. "I'm positive this is it."

"I won't get Sid up there. We'll have to stop here or find another way."

"No, look. Over there." The wind whipped through her hair, twirling it this way and that. "The tree line runs run right up to the crest of the hill. I'll go and have a look," she said over her shoulder as she strode up the hill.

Tiny birds calling to one another as they darted between the scrubby bushes, insects humming, and the occasional drone of native bees melded with her snatched breath. A creeping sensation made the hairs on the back of her neck stand up and she had the oddest sensation of being watched. Suddenly something much larger crashed through the undergrowth. She froze, her mouth dry.

From behind a scraggly geebung a pair of eyes shone.

For several seconds they stared at each other and then a rhythmic *thump-thump* sounded as a wallaby bounded out of sight. A little bemused by her panic, she laughed aloud. She'd been away from home for too long if a curious wallaby put the wind up her.

With a lighter heart, she stepped forward—the breeze blowing in her face, bringing with it the almond scent of the golden wattle flowers—up the steep incline, where the track narrowed and the wispy seeds on the clumps of kangaroo grass caught the light.

Moments later she crested the hill. A house rose out of the landscape. At first glance it seemed nothing more than a farmhouse, unlike the nineteenth-century sandstone homesteads all around the area and more like the farmhouses she'd passed on her trip down to Lyme. The walls, weathered to a soft honey color, huddled under a low, shingled roof almost hidden from sight by the encroaching bush.

Once she got closer, the remains of a dense, rambling garden became evident: introduced plants mingling with the native shrubs and wildflowers. Four ancient grass trees flanked the house, their needle-sharp leaves sprouting from gnarled, blackened stumps.

External shutters gave the building a disguised appearance, but she had the sense that the house stood watching—waiting and watching. Her palms grew sweaty and her insides clenched. She drew in an anguished breath. In her mind's eye, girls clad in delicate, white, lace-trimmed dresses flitted beneath the canopy, their chattering competing with the birds. In this moment she recognized that her curiosity about the past—this house, Bow Wow Gorge, its fossils, and Anthea Winstanley—had become a consuming passion. Who was the elusive woman, and what had made her leave this place?

A flagged veranda was clothed in glossy green leaves and a brilliant pink trumpet creeper spread the width of the house. Mesmerized, she stood for a moment, taking in the glorious display, then crept up the stone tread into the cooling gloom. All sounds of the bush faded, leaving an odd, still quietness.

Two hefty crossbeams barred a pair of heavy-hinged doors. She peeled back the intruding creeper and tugged on the rusting circular handles, then put her shoulder to the door. Not surprisingly, it wouldn't budge. Noticing the tremor in her hands, she turned away and returned to the overgrown gardens until the roar of Sid's engine heralded Sam's arrival.

"The house is locked." More than locked, firmly barricaded. Disappointment flooded over her.

"What did you expect, a welcoming party?"

She lifted her shoulders. "I don't know. It seems a bit of an anticlimax."

"We'll have a look around, but I thought you were interested in the gorge. Not the house."

"I . . ." She pulled her cardigan tighter around her shoulders. "Curiosity, I guess."

They crept along, hugging the wall of the house, the air redolent with the smell of moldy, disintegrating leaves. Fighting through the rampant creeper, they followed a series of flagged stones slippery with moss around the side of the house. Another veranda stretched along the back, mirroring the one at the front, the windows as shuttered as those on the other side.

Sam forced his way through the creeper to the back door. "It's barred." He bent down and ran his hand along the crossbeam. "Nailed shut, but there might be a keyhole underneath."

"I couldn't budge the front door." She turned away. A small two-story building stood behind the main house. "Come and look at this."

With a final tug Sam gave up the fight and followed her. "This door isn't nailed closed." He twisted the handle, put his shoulder against the timber, and shoved. It creaked and gave way, sending him staggering into the building. "It's the kitchen. Why isn't it in the house?"

"They didn't have kitchens inside back in those days. They were worried about fire. The one at home wasn't connected to the house when we bought it. Ma hated it so Pa had the veranda extended, added a bathroom, and joined it to the house."

Sam pointed to the back of the room. "Makes sense. This chimney's as far from the house as it can be."

A huge fireplace cradling a black range took up the back wall, the iron kettle still balanced on the hob as though waiting to boil. A scrubbed table with an assortment of mismatched chairs dominated the center of the room. A dusty dresser displayed a set of small cups, and alongside the stove hung an array of kitchen implements Mrs. Canning would envy. The range still held the remnants of a fire.

"Sam, do you notice anything strange?"

"Plenty. What specifically?"

"Look at the range. The kettle on the hob isn't dusty at all and there're the remains of a recent fire."

"What are you suggesting?"

"I don't think Artie and the publican are right. Someone has used this kitchen, and not too long ago."

Sam ran his finger over the thick dust on top of the mantelpiece. "I don't think their housekeeping's up to much."

"But someone's been here. This isn't a kitchen that has been locked up for decades. There's not enough dust or dirt and grime."

"I was chatting to a guy at the bar, after you'd gone to bed. He said it was a big property, a couple of thousand acres. A family called Lachlan has leased the farmland for years."

"And the house has remained empty?"

"Apparently."

On one side of the kitchen they found a series of small pantries containing nothing but empty jars and saucepans, a scullery, and attached to the wall a narrow flight of steep wooden steps to the next floor.

Sam stuck his head out of the door. "There's another outbuilding over there."

An overgrown rambling plot stood between the kitchen and a small slab hut. "I bet that was the vegetable garden." PJ ran outside and bent down. "Look, there's still parsley and rosemary growing here, and some sage and thyme." A pungent smell wafted in the air as she brushed against the sprawling plants. "And that's a lemon tree." She reached up and tore off a leaf, inhaling the citrus fragrance. "I think this is probably the gardener's shed."

She rattled the door. "Chain and padlock."

She tugged again at the door. "That's strange—why leave the kitchen open and lock the garden shed?"

"Maybe it's where they buried their treasure," Sam said with a spooky quaver, an amused smile tipping his lips. "Let's see, shall we?" He grasped one of the shutters. It refused to move. "Locked from the inside."

"Perhaps there's a caretaker. That would account for the state of the kitchen. They probably make themselves a cuppa when they've done the rounds."

Something nagged at her, didn't feel right, but she couldn't put her finger on it. "I've seen enough. Let's go and find this gorge." She strolled around the corner of the small shed and her heart lifted. A pool of sunlight and the fresh flurry of a eucalyptus-scented breeze welcomed her—a balm after the damp, oppressive atmosphere around the house.

She pushed her way through the scrub and found herself on top of a rocky shelf. The land dropped away into a deep gully, filled with swaying treetops.

"Gotcha!"

PJ's stomach rose to her throat as the ground swayed horribly, then Sam's grip tightened on her arms. "You scared the living daylights out of me."

"I don't want you to fall. It's a hell of a way."

"I'm sure that's the gorge down there. Do you think we can climb down?"

Sam released her and dropped down, legs dangling into the

tree-filled abyss. "Not without a decent rope. There's one in the back of the motor."

PJ sank down next to him and together they contemplated the treetops. As the seconds passed, the sound of running water gradually overpowered the cries of the bellbirds.

"And you're telling me that a Victorian woman in a long skirt clambered down there to forage for fossils? There's got to be another way down. We'll look tomorrow. It's going to take us a good couple of hours to get back to Wollombi. PJ? Are you listening to me?"

"Maybe Artie knows more than he's willing to tell."

"But why? This business about a woman and girls disappearing is no different from the rubbish about a bunyip in Ellalong Lagoon. Anthea Winstanley certainly didn't disappear, because you said she's buried in Lyme."

And then the breeze dropped and the sound of the water rose. "Come on, let's go."

"Just a minute. Dan and Riley's fossils were labeled Bow Wow. It's not true to say no one has been here for decades." She jumped to her feet. "I need to find Artie and talk to him. See if I can figure out the story."

"Then I guess it's another night at the Kurri Hotel."

Sam didn't sound very disappointed, and truth be told, she didn't want to leave now and face another evening of stilted conversation and Pa's condemning looks.

CHAPTER 15

1847
Bow Wow

The morning dawned clear with a touch of humidity after the storm. True to his word, Mr. Baldwin arrived on the doorstep long before the girls were ready.

Anthea smothered a groan. She'd spent the night mulling on her actions regarding the odious little man. She now wished she'd sent him on his way and not invited him to stay for dinner, but her curiosity had won out. Not that she'd learned very much, and his presence had caused another disagreement between Lydia and Ella, with Ella insisting he would be meeting her at the gorge after he had seen the parcel of land. That was the last thing she wanted. All his talk about bunyips hadn't fooled her. It was Mitchell's mention of her latest find that had aroused his interest.

"Mr. Baldwin's here." Bea rushed across the hallway, but Ella appeared on the veranda from the stranger's room.

"I'll go," she called.

"Ella's got a new beau." Bea shrieked with laughter, batted her eyelids, and clutched at her chest.

"Hurry up, everyone. Mr. Baldwin will be coming with us today as far as the gorge, then Jordan is going to take him to look over the property."

Although he had made a very overt suggestion that he would be interested in seeing the fossils, Anthea had no intention of encouraging him. Despite his very reputable letter of introduction from Mitchell, she couldn't take any chances. The man's name had put her guard up, and the opportunity to question his relationship with Benjamin hadn't eventuated. He'd made no further reference to Benjamin, and his flirtation with both Ella and Lydia had done nothing more than upset them both. The best thing to do would be to send him off with Jordan and hope that when he saw the rugged terrain he would lose interest. "It's time we left. Has anyone seen Mellie? Has she gone down to the gorge?"

"No. She's out in the workroom. Something about the tools. She took her porridge with her. I told her to wait and come with us this morning," Nette said.

Such a dear child. She blessed the day Edna had sent her. As each day passed Mellie became more confident. The haunted look had left her eyes, replaced by a blaze of curiosity and a wonderful streak of independence.

"Mellie's settled in well, hasn't she?" As much as she always enjoyed the girls' company, they did see the whole holiday as something of a jaunt, never pausing to consider how much work it entailed, for Nette especially.

"She's a delightful child."

"I'll go and find her. Girls, by the time I return I expect you all to be waiting on the front veranda, and please, Nette, make sure Ella is wearing decent shoes. She can't go clambering down to the gorge in those slippers she favors."

Mellie saved Anthea the trip to the workroom by appearing on the back doorstep, her plate and mug balanced on top of the tool kit and her muscles straining.

"Here, let me help." Anthea took the mug and plate and put it aside. "The box is too heavy for you to carry alone."

"I can manage. I'll take it out to Jordan and he can load it up. Is there anything else we need?"

"No. Bea and Grace can take care of the lunch hamper."

"Is Ella coming with us today?" Mellie asked over her shoulder and then came to a sudden halt. "Oh." The tool box fell to the ground with a resounding clatter and Mellie darted back into the kitchen.

"Good morning, ladies." Mr. Baldwin stood framed in the doorway.

"Mr. Baldwin's here." Bea shot through the door with a squeal. Anthea gritted her teeth. Bea's ludicrous singsong voice put her on edge. The girl was impossible.

"Nette, you'll have to help Grace with the hamper." Whatever had caused Mellie such distress? Her face had turned chalk white and she had her arms clasped around her body as though she'd fall apart if she didn't hold herself together. "What is it, dear?"

Mellie didn't respond, stayed rooted to the spot.

Nette's baffled expression mirrored her own thoughts. Something more than the simple change in routine had upset Mellie.

"Grace and I will take the hamper and we'll help Jordan load up."

"Thank you, Nette. Mellie and I will check the tool kit and we'll be right behind you."

Anthea eased Mellie down into the chair, crouched in front of her, and brushed her tangled hair back from her face. "If there's anything that's bothering you, you know you can tell me."

A frail smile drifted across the child's pale face and she shook her head. "I just got a shock. I'm sorry I dropped the tool kit." She struggled off the chair. "Mr. Baldwin surprised me."

"You met him last night."

"He made me jump. It's his boots."

"His boots?"

"Tall shiny boots, like Da's mates." Her entire body shuddered. "He wasn't wearing boots yesterday. I don't want him to go to the gorge."

"I expect they're his riding boots. He's going with Jordan to look at some land. They're just going to drop off the tools and our picnic. They won't stay at the gorge." Not if she had anything to say in the matter. "Now, give me a hand and we'll be on our way."

By the time they'd repacked the tools the girls had congregated outside. Baldwin sat astride his horse, reveling in the attention of the fluttering, gossiping group of wagtails surrounding him. The high-pitched giggles were enough to make Anthea's hair stand on end. The sooner Baldwin and Jordan were on their way, the better.

"You and Mr. Baldwin lead the way, Jordan. Just drop the hamper and tool kit at the end of the snig trail and go ahead. I must fetch something." She crooked her finger and stepped aside, hoping Jordan would understand her intention and follow her. "Tell the girls to wait with Nette. I don't want Baldwin down at the gorge when we arrive, so can you move on quickly?"

Jordan nodded and then led the pack horse toward the trail, Baldwin following.

"You come with me, Mellie. We need hats." Which they didn't because they never wore hats down at the gorge; the dappled sunlight of the trail and the gorge made it unnecessary, except in the height of summer.

Mellie grabbed the two cabbage-palm hats from the hook on the veranda, the color returning to her face.

"Right." Anthea clamped one down on her head and gestured to Mellie to do the same.

"Do I have to wear it?"

"No. I thought it would give us a moment to gather our thoughts. I want you to remember what I said to you—if there's anything bothering you, you must tell me."

Mellie swallowed. She didn't want to make Aunt Anthea angry, but how could she explain? Da had made her promise she'd protect their stash in the hills above the millpond. But someone had found out about it, otherwise why would the footsteps have dogged her every time she went out? Mr. Baldwin's knee-high riding boots had brought it all flooding back—those and the whiff of horse sweat and rifle oil at odds with his swanky waistcoat. She hadn't noticed his smell the day before.

By the time she and Aunt Anthea reached the bottom of the snig trail, there was no sign of Jordan or Mr. Baldwin, and Nette had all the girls organized. Even Ella was busy with her nose to the wall, brushing away the dust with a passion never seen before. Perhaps she was hoping to find a token for Mr. Baldwin.

A rash of goose bumps peppered Mellie's arms. She wouldn't think about him. Not anymore. She'd lock him up in that space in her head where she kept all the nasty things she didn't want to remember, buried deep in the layers of her memories, like the fossils.

As the remainder of the morning passed, Mellie settled into her usual routine, working with the marlin spike and poring over the loosened dirt and soil. Bea and Grace unearthed several bits of dragon scales, none of them perfect examples. Lydia found a very pretty sea lily with strange wavy arms, a crinoid, Aunt Anthea called it, but no complete dragon scales. Perhaps the collection Mellie had unearthed in Aunt Anthea's workroom was all that was in the gorge. Maybe the dragon had simply passed through. Did they shed their scales the same way snakes shed their skins?

Mellie laid down her spike and ambled over to the rock wall where Aunt Anthea crouched, carefully brushing away a fine layer of sand, still searching for more vertebrae. She pushed aside the curtain of ferns. "Do you think perhaps that vertebra belonged to another creature? I was wondering if dragons shed their scales like snakes and perhaps that's why we haven't found any more vertebrae. If the dragons are still alive, we won't find anything by digging because they couldn't be buried by the layers when the inland sea disappeared."

"Mellie, Mellie. Stop a moment. All these thoughts are chasing one another around in your head. Why don't we all have some lunch and we can discuss them? Nette has everything set up."

That was one of the things Mellie most liked about Aunt Anthea. She never told her to keep her thoughts to herself; she was always prepared to talk. She took off her gloves and slapped the dust from her hands, then splashed across the creek to the big tree where Nette always laid out the sandwiches. If she was lucky there might be a piece of delicious apple cake. "Can I help?"

Nette winked at her and handed her a large sandwich. "Eat this first, then you can have a piece of apple cake."

Mellie took the sandwich and perched on her favorite rock, the one that had just enough room for her to sit with Aunt Anthea. Although

Bea and Grace had pretty much given up on their teasing, she couldn't bring herself to discuss her new ideas in front of them. It would be asking for trouble. They seemed to have found someone else to heckle. The gorge rang with their annoying shrieks as they minced after Ella, imitating her outstretched arms and small delicate steps as she tried to cross the creek without getting her slippers wet. Fat chance of that. She should have listened to Nette and changed into her boots.

Munching her way through her sandwich, determined to finish before everyone else scoffed up all the cake, she turned her face up to the sky. A gust of cool wind teased her hair.

An eerie silence fell and thick gray clouds scudded across the sky. The sudden cackle of a kookaburra heralded a distant rumble.

Mellie jumped, her skin rippling. "Thunder." Great big fat raindrops as big as the holey dollars in Da's stash plopped down on her face—a few at first, then more and more until it threatened a torrent.

"Under the overhang, everyone, before you get saturated." Aunt Anthea and Nette, having grabbed hold of the picnic hamper, were slipping and sliding as they chased the squealing girls into the low cave.

Mellie turned her face up to the sky again. A bit of rain never hurt anyone. In fact, she liked it. Liked it a lot. She picked up the half-empty tool box and dragged it into the cave, placing it in the middle of the half circle the girls had formed.

One by one the girls handed over their tools. She wiped each one dry with the rag she kept in her back pocket and tucked them neatly in their allotted space. As soon as she'd finished she closed the lid and slid the box as far back into the cave as she could manage.

"Mellie, come and have some cake."

She flopped down and took the piece of cake Aunt Anthea offered. "I like the rain."

"So do I if I can stay dry, but I'm not sure I want to be caught out here in a storm."

"We're in for one." Another crash punctuated Nette's prediction, and a moment or two later a slash of lightning zigzagged its way through the gorge, followed by another thunderous boom right on its tail.

In the space of just a few moments the light dimmed and a green tinge lit the cave, making it almost impossible to see anyone's faces. Ella stood with her back against the wall and Bea and Grace sat huddled together, shrieking every time the clouds bumped. Lydia, Nette, and Aunt Anthea seemed quite content with their sandwiches and cake, watching the curtain of rain blocking the cave off from the world.

She picked up another slice of apple cake, licked the sugar from her fingers, and settled down to wait out the storm, cozy and safe beneath the shelter of the ancient rocks.

"I can just imagine a bunyip living here." Bea's shrill voice held a note of panic.

"Oh, don't be silly. Bunyips aren't real." Lydia glared at her younger sister.

"But they are," Ella announced with a degree of authority. "Mr. Baldwin told me he'd seen one with his own eyes."

"They're not real." Grace's voice quavered.

"They are. He told me all about them when he first arrived, while you were all at the gorge. He said men of science such as he and Mitchell and Macleay, even the public, are tremendously excited by the discovery of the skull. It's proof. Did you know bunyips never take men and boys, only girls and young women?" Ella planted her hands on her hips.

Mellie's throat constricted and she was back on the laundry floor listening to Cook's dire threats. The description of the ghastly, slimy half-man half-beast who lived in the murky millpond waters—the creature who'd chased her down and left her for dead. She shrank closer to Aunt Anthea.

"Not only that, hundreds of people have seen them. As big as a half-grown calf with a long neck and pointed head, large ears, and a mane of putrid black hair. Mr. Baldwin said one man saw six of them and he fired at them."

Mellie tried to swallow the terror clogging her throat. "Where are the bunyips' bodies, then?" She gulped the remains of the cake along with the traitorous tremor in her voice.

"He didn't manage to capture any. They ran off. The smallest was five feet tall, and the largest fifteen with a head the size of a bullock. And look at this." Ella opened her palm to reveal a series of cracked greenish-blue eggshells. "Bunyip eggs."

"Bunyip eggs. Bunyips don't lay eggs." Bea crawled closer, her eyes wide.

"Oh yes they do. Mr. Baldwin told me when he gave them to me."

"Is there anything Mr. Baldwin didn't tell you?" Lydia asked.

The barb flew right over Ella's head and she preened. "He shared all his scientific knowledge with me. He said he could see I was an intelligent young woman. Not like you, throwing yourself at him across the dinner table."

Lydia huffed and curled against the rock wall. "For goodness' sake, Ella. I thought you were in love with George Hudderson. You can't expect every man to fall at your feet."

Another flash of lightning illuminated the cave and revealed Ella lurching to her feet.

"The bunyip's bellowing cry strikes terror into hearts every-where." Her monstrous silhouette danced on the sandstone walls of the cave. "And it gobbles up young girls."

The great shadow loomed over Mellie, blocking out the strange green light. Her mouth dried; her hands shook. An uncontrollable trembling worked its way along her limbs until her whole body rattled.

"The bunyip hugs its victim tight, crushing the air from her lungs and breaking her bones."

Long arms wrapped around Mellie, squeezing every skerrick of air from her body. Black spots danced across her vision, and her ears filled with the sound of her pounding heartbeat. Her blood surging, she launched across the cave.

Anthea sat rooted to the spot, mouth gaping. Mellie flew at Ella with a primal scream and a string of indecipherable curses. She tossed Ella aside, eyes bulging and spittle spraying.

Anthea leaped up, wrapped both arms around Mellie to still her flaying fists. "It's all right. They're just silly stories."

With surprising strength Mellie wrenched free, sending Anthea flying. She landed with a spine-shuddering thump on the sandy floor of the cave, her bones rattling and flashes of light flickering behind her eyes.

Nette's soothing hands steadied her. "Are you hurt?"

"Give me a moment." Her bleary gaze roamed the small, dark space. Ella crouched, crumpled in the back corner. Lydia and Grace were immobile, and Bea was sobbing her heart out. "Where's Mellie?"

"She took off." Nette glanced outside, but the dripping ferns curtained the view.

Anthea struggled to her feet and gave her head a shake, shuffled her legs, and shook her arms.

"Not dizzy?"

"No." She stepped toward the opening of the cave. The walls of the overhang glittered in the strange green light. She smoothed the palm of her hand over the crumbling dirt. A ridge of bumps arched beneath her shaking fingers. She wasn't trembling from the shock of Mellie's outburst but with the realization that she had spotted more of the elusive vertebrae arcing their way across the roof of the overhang.

She closed her eyes for a moment and visualized the possibility of her discovery. The entire backbone of an ichthyosaur? Why now, after all this time? Shooing Nette away, she tested her stability, straightened her coat, and pondered her next move.

The curtain of slashing rain obliterated the view of the gorge toward Benjamin's steps, and there was no sign of Mellie, no Jordan, no pack horse, no help. The girls would never manage to carry the picnic baskets and tool kit up the track. Damn Baldwin and his ill-timed arrival, damn his posturing and dramatized stories, and damn Ella and Lydia for their ridiculous flirtation with him.

Poor dear Mellie. Scared out of her wits, alone in the storm. She squinted into the distance. What to do? She couldn't drag the girls through the bush looking for Mellie, nor could she leave Nette with the responsibility of seeing them to the house. Ella would whinge and carry on, stir up Grace and Bea and refuse to cooperate.

Only one thing for it. "We're going to pack up and leave everything down here for Jordan to collect later and go back up the snig trail to the house." With luck Mellie would find her own way home. After her morning rambles she was more familiar with the gorge than any of the others. "From the look of the clouds this is only going to get worse. The gorge is no place to be when night falls."

"We'll get saturated. My slippers will be ruined. Mother will be furious."

Ella's selfish statement made Anthea's temper snap. "You should have a lot more than slippers on your conscience. This debacle is of your making. If you hadn't behaved in such a foolish manner, Mellie wouldn't have run off."

Ella dropped her head and pouted. "I'm going to stay here until the rain stops. Mr. Baldwin said this morning he would see me here in the afternoon. He'll look after me."

"You will do no such thing. I have no intention of leaving you here alone." And if Jordan did as she'd asked, he would ensure Baldwin didn't return to the gorge.

"The bunyip will get you if you stay here." Bea waved her arms and lumbered around, her half-hearted howls echoing in the confined space.

"Stop that this instant. Enough. Follow me and stay on the track. Nette, will you bring up the rear, please? Make sure no one"—she glared at Ella—"dawdles."

CHAPTER 16

1919

KURRI KURRI

Sam slept on, oblivious of PJ's impatience. She had some vague memory of him calling good night from the veranda the night before and she'd woken to a bright beam of sunlight and a thrill of expectation. When they'd returned to the hotel there was no sign of Artie, but Sam had said he'd try to hunt him down. They'd managed to get through on the telephone to Mrs. Canning and she'd made a few inquiries about the sleeping arrangements, then assured PJ that she would let Pa know their plans. In a way PJ was pleased she hadn't spoken to him. Once she got to the bottom of Pa's displeasure and they spent some time together, hopefully they could sort out their differences.

When she couldn't stand it a moment longer, she raced along the veranda and into Sam's room. "Wakey, wakey. It's time to leave." She pulled back the sheets.

Sam groaned and dragged his eyes open. "Not without coffee, I'm not. Go and see what you can rustle up, sweetheart."

"I'll meet you downstairs." Picking up her bag, she closed the door behind her. It wasn't the first time he'd left her kicking her heels as morning approached afternoon. She stuck her head into the dining room where a woman was clearing away the remains of someone else's breakfast and resetting the tables. "Can I please order a cup of coffee?"

"Coffee." She gave a dramatic shudder. "Dreadful stuff. I can probably rustle up a pot of tea and some toast."

"Thank you." PJ sat down at the table. She could hear the clinking of glasses so she ambled into the bar. "Good morning. I was wondering if—"

"No ladies in the bar, I told you." He rolled his eyes and flicked his cloth.

It was positively archaic. "What time does the bar close?" she asked, feet firmly placed in the corridor, her head poking around the doorway.

"Six o'clock, same as everywhere."

"Can you get a drink anywhere else after six o'clock?"

He looked a little bemused. "Why are you asking?"

"Just curious."

"Might be a sly grog shop or two around the town. Nothing I know about. I've got work to do. Thought you and that fella of yours were off today."

"Yes, yes, we are. We found the house yesterday and today we're going to explore the gorge."

She turned to leave and slammed into Sam's broad chest. "Oops. Sorry. Are you ready?"

With a grunt he hefted his haversack onto his shoulder and headed out along the corridor to the back of the hotel. "Find any coffee?"

"No, but there's a pot of tea."

He grimaced. "Forget it." From the look on his face she might well have suggested bromide. "We've got water in the car. Is there anything left over from the sandwiches Mrs. Canning packed for us?"

"Some fruit cake and a couple of apples."

"That'll do." He headed for the door.

"Sam, this way. We have to walk around the hotel. The car's in the street behind."

"This way will work. Follow me."

Without a backward glance, he led the way past the dining room and along a dingy corridor, which hummed with last night's cooking, then out into a small yard ringed by a brick wall.

A few battered chairs were propped up against the wall and a square of stained carpet designated some sort of arena. "What happens out here?"

"Locals use it as a boxing ring."

Boxing. Now everything made sense. Sam had developed a passion for boxing on the ship when he'd discovered ten pairs of gloves among the sports equipment and taken it into his head to organize training sessions and weekly matches for the men. "So that's what you were up to last night."

He gave her a sheepish look and brought his finger to his lips before opening the gate in the side wall, bringing them into the garden where she'd first met Artie.

"Did you bump into Artie last night?"

"Nope, no sign of him, and everyone else was more interested in the match than talking about Bow Wow. Come on."

A couple of young boys with cloth caps and cheeky grins sat in the laneway guarding Sid.

"Been lookin' after the motor." The tallest one held out his hand and raised one eyebrow.

Sam reached into his pocket and flicked him sixpence. "Good job, boys."

While Sam cranked the engine, PJ slipped in behind the wheel; she had no intention of letting him drive—he still looked half asleep. The last thing she wanted was for them to run off the road, today of all days. She'd waited too long to visit the gorge. "I remember the way." Receiving nothing more than a grunt, she set off.

Armed with a rope, Sam and PJ skirted Bow Wow House and followed the same path as the day before to the rock platform.

A chilly moistness blew up from the abyss, dampening her skin. In the still morning the bewildering roar of the water and the strange wailing sound in the trees made the blood fizz in her ears and her limbs tremble. Sam's warm arms encircled her waist and he dipped his face to her neck. She turned and rested her chin on his shoulder and they stood swaying, listening to the call of the bellbirds until he pulled away, leaving her feeling strangely bereft.

"Come on, it won't be too difficult. I'll show you. We need to anchor the rope." He paced back into the scrub and found a solid gum, attached the rope, and unraveled it. "The rope goes between your legs, front to back, then around your right leg and across your chest." Sam wrapped it around his body. "Then it goes over your shoulder, and you hold the loose end." He grasped the end of the rope. "Reckon you'll be able to do the same? I'll go first. Watch how I do it." He gave a final tug, then backed to the edge.

By the time PJ had plucked up the courage to look down, he was on solid ground, sporting a wide grin. "Didn't need the rope. Reckon you could dangle your legs over and slip down." He scuffed the area at his feet, brushing away the dead leaves and twigs. "There's a shelf here we couldn't see. Haul the rope up and tie it around your waist in case you slip. We'll need it on the way back."

A twist of apprehension caught in her throat. She swallowed, loath to admit she found the prospect more daunting than anything she'd faced in France.

The drop-off seemed terrifying. Her vision blurred, and a sense of tilting disorientation swamped her. Letting out a long slow breath, she waited for the moment to pass. Exploring the gorge was something she wanted to do. Something she'd anticipated since her visit to the museum in London. And she certainly wasn't going to let Sam go without her.

Beneath her feet the shaded rock shelf seemed slippery from the morning dew, and the daunting prospect brought a cold sweat to her forehead.

Sam's head reappeared. "Leave the rope. Move along about ten yards. Seems we should have checked the area more carefully. It's a much easier drop over here."

The tension left her shoulders as the prospect of dangling from the end of a rope receded. She paced out ten long strides and then dropped to her bottom again.

Sam's smiling face shone up at her, his head level with her feet. "Ease yourself down and I'll catch you."

Sliding forward, she drew in a breath and with a false sense of bravado launched herself over the edge. Sam's hands slipped under her arms and two seconds later she stood firmly on both feet.

"Not too difficult, huh?"

"Fine." She straightened her jacket and ran her damp palms down her trousers.

"Come and see what I've found." Sam took hold of her hand and led her along the shelf. "See? Steps." Lichen-blistered stones wound down beneath tall stringy box and red gums draped with beards of mistletoe. "They look a bit irregular, but I reckon they lead right down to the bottom."

Picking their way down the track, they slipped and slid from tree to tree, the sound of the cascading water growing louder. Finally the bush thinned, leaving only a few remaining plants clinging with tenuous roots between the cracks in the hard-packed, rocky soil.

The next moment the stone steps ended and the area opened to reveal high sandstone cliffs framing a narrow gorge. The sun glanced off the surface of the water, throwing thousands of tiny sparks; ferns dripped with diamond droplets, and dragonflies hovered.

She ran her hand along the rock wall, every bump and indentation forming a map of the past. "Look at this." Layers of fossils lined the soaring sandstone walls, untouched for millions of years. More than she'd ever imagined. Delicate fan-shaped shells; fragile imprints of fernlike leaves and coral. She ran her fingers over the indentations. "We're standing at the bottom of an ocean. What was once an ocean. Fifty million years ago, maybe more." Her heart raced. "This is where Anthea Winstanley found the vertebra I saw at the Natural History Museum in London, and the other fossils Dan and Riley had in their collection were found here too."

And that's what she didn't understand. "Nothing makes any sense. Why would a paleontologist leave this treasure trove and go to the other side of the world, especially if she'd found something significant?"

"Seems odd." Sam echoed her thoughts. "What do you reckon they're worth?"

PJ shrugged, her fingers still playing across the indentations, her eyes darting from one spot to the next. "The Victorians collected them. There was so much they didn't understand about the earth, and their religious beliefs precluded all sorts of theories. How could God have made the earth in seven days if these were the relics of hundreds of thousands of years before man?"

"Well, Darwin put them right on that."

"And caused a huge uproar." Her hand stilled on one particularly exquisite, pleated fan-shaped fossil. "Have you got your knife?"

Sam slid his hand into his pocket and brought out his Swiss Army knife. He flipped it open and handed it to her. "Use the hoof pick. I reckon that'll work best."

A few delicate twists and the fossil fell into her hand.

"Do you know what it is?"

She smoothed the softened dirt from the edge. "I'm not sure. I need to check the books I got in London."

"So Ted was right?" Sam smirked. "He told me on the ship he had dinosaurs in his backyard."

"I'm not sure he has dinosaurs, but certainly fossils, maybe the remains of some marine mammals. These fossils were laid down hundreds of millions of years ago. A lot of work has been done in the area because of all the coal deposits. A man named Edgeworth David wrote a report. I think this is a brachiopod, a lamp shell. The Victorians thought it resembled an old-fashioned oil lamp. They used all sorts of names until they were classified—devil's toenails, thunderbolts, golden serpents, and snake stones." She slipped the lamp shell into her pocket.

Sam nudged her shoulder, his eyes twinkling. "Should you be taking that? Private property, even if the house isn't lived in."

Heat rushed to her cheeks and she pulled it back out again. "You're right. But we don't know if this area belongs to the house, do we?" She shuffled the fossil from hand to hand, not wanting to part with it.

"Go on, take it. I'm sure no one will mind. What's it worth?"

She shrugged. "No idea. Not a huge amount. Those days are long gone. The man at the museum told me someone paid over one hundred pounds for a complete skeleton in the 1800s, but then there were far more collectors, and museums were keen to build up their exhibits."

Sam whistled through his teeth. "One hundred pounds in those days would have been a lot of money."

"It's not about the money. It's more a question of history, understanding the past."

PJ felt suddenly, inexplicably happy and at peace. Her smile broadened as they walked along the stony floor of the gorge. "It's beautiful here, calm and peaceful." The silence of the bush, broken only by the occasional bird, was so far removed from the ceaseless, deafening roar of the motor lorries, ammunition wagons, and thundering trains of the war that her muscles relaxed and her bones slipped back into their accustomed places. Sand-colored rocks loomed above her, streaked with every color of the rainbow, the layers clearly visible; some formed stone arches weathered by millions of years of wind, rain, and waves.

"What was it Artie said to you at the pub about the property?"

PJ stilled in her tracks and ran her hand over the rich carpet of moss covering a decaying log. "That the Winstanleys owned the house and the original land grant of two thousand acres."

"And the farming land is leased and no one has lived here since."

"Anthea Winstanley disappeared."

"Well, she certainly didn't disappear if she's buried in England. She packed up and left."

"I'm sure Artie knows more."

"I reckon Winstanley found a fossil and took off to England to get it certified, if that's what they did in those days. And for some reason never came back."

PJ thought for a moment. What Sam said made sense to a degree, but then again . . . No. "Surely she wouldn't have left if she'd found something important. And why didn't she return? She would have wanted to see what else she could uncover. Make a name for herself."

"Come on, she was a woman. No one would have taken any notice of her."

"They took notice of Mary Anning in the end. And there was another fossil Winstanley found in Lyme, an ammonite, now in the museum in London. Mr. Ambrose said it was a fine example. She didn't give up fossil hunting, but she never came back here. Neither did her daughter. The question is why."

"Small-town gossip that's grown over the years. A load of local humbug because she didn't tell everyone she was leaving."

She couldn't argue with that. Knew it only too well having lived her life in Wollombi. "Then I think the best thing we can do is go back and find out some more about this gossip." She turned to Sam, who was sitting on a rock, his head tilted back to catch the rays of the sun through the trees, and noticed the look of amusement on his face. "What's funny?"

"Not funny. Just how involved you've become. You've really got the bit between your teeth, haven't you?"

"What do you mean?"

"Does it really matter what happened here? Ever since you went to the museum in London you've become obsessed by this Winstanley woman."

"You know why. It's the connection to Dan and Riley. They may have found something important."

"No—there's far more to it. Come on, sweetheart. What's all this about?" He shuffled along and patted the space on the rock next to him.

She sank down. "I don't know. Originally I wanted to come here because I thought I might find something to commemorate Dan and Riley, and I still do think that. But I feel there's something important beyond my grasp that I can't quite understand. Some unfinished business." The silence hung. Sam was right. Ever since she'd visited the museum in London and taken the trip down to Lyme, her curiosity had built, and now she was consumed. She'd even pushed Sam's proposal aside. Shuffling closer, she rested her head on his shoulder. "I should forget about it, shouldn't I?"

"That might be harder than you think. I know what you're like once you get an idea in your head. Why don't we have a bit more of a look around and then head back to Wollombi?" He dropped a kiss onto her head and ran his fingers down her spine. The delicious shiver sent her off the side of the rock and into the soft sand at the edge of the creek.

With a laugh she planted her hands flat to push herself upright. "Ouch." A stab of pain radiated up her arm.

Sam reached down, held out his hand. "Up you come. I didn't mean to hurt you."

"Hold on a minute." She smoothed the damp sand with the tips of her fingers and found the culprit. A small, irregular, whitish stone, the underside squared off and the surface concave. "Look." Her heart picked up a beat. "Do you think it's something important?" She held it out to Sam. Although smaller and much lighter in color, it was very similar to the one she'd held in London. An unbroken thread of connection danced over her, tying her to the place as though she'd brought something precious back into the light.

"Come on, hand it over."

She turned it in the shaft of sunlight. "It's like Winstanley's vertebra." There were no fractures, no cracks. Just the smooth, consistent surface, the only difference some strange wing-shaped protuberances.

"Did they say what it belonged to?"

"There was some sort of controversy. Winstanley had marked it as an ichthyosaur vertebra, but none had been found in Australia at that time. This is slightly different." She ran her finger over the wings.

"Perhaps they were wrong. Maybe we've hit pay dirt. Have they found any of these ichthyo . . . what were they called?"

"Ichthyosaurs. Edgeworth David found something similar in Sydney, but that was only about ten years ago. I saw that in the museum in London too."

Sam dropped down on his hands and knees and began to rake through the sand at her feet.

"Stop."

"Where there's one there could be many." He continued to scrabble in the damp sand.

"Sam, stop. Please. If we're going to look, we need to do it properly. We need tools and brushes and . . . they could be very fragile. And besides, we need permission from the owners. Have you forgotten we're trespassing?"

He rocked back on his heels. "We better get moving and find out who owns the land, then."

PJ's mind spiraled. "We already know. It's leased."

"That's the farming land, not the gorge. How does land ownership work in this country? Do you have some sort of central authority that keeps records? Someone must have inherited the place when Winstanley died."

"Mr. Woods, in Lyme, mentioned a daughter. I got the impression Artie thought Anthea might have indulged in something slightly . . . inappropriate."

"Inappropriate? What do you mean?"

"He said she had strange tastes and flouted convention. Liked to dress in men's clothes and invited girls down to the gorge. Artie made no mention of a daughter."

"You're falling for the local scuttlebutt, malicious rumors. I wouldn't expect that of you."

"I don't know. It all seems strange. In the nineteenth century people were far more conservative. Being a woman and interested in fossils would have created a stir."

"Come on. We could have stumbled on something important. Ted, Dan, and Riley might be right about their dinosaur. Stop standing there like a wet weekend. If you're worried about trespassing, we need to get permission."

"Who's obsessed now?"

Sam grunted and shaded his eyes from the sinking sun. "There has to be an easier way out of here than climbing back up that rock face." He pointed up to the sky. "That's west. It's way past midday. I reckon if we follow the creek, then cut up and across to the right, we'll end up at the front of the house." He strode off.

PJ took one last look at the dappled gorge and, tucking the fossil in her pocket, left behind the fascinating secrets of Bow Wow Gorge, regret prickling her skin.

CHAPTER 17

1847
Bow Wow

Lightning embroidered the treetops and the rumble of thunder rocked the sky. Needles of rain lashed Mellie's face as she splashed through the rising creek waters, not daring to look behind. The drum of her feet and howling of the wind mixed with her pounding heartbeat, blotting out any other sound.

Slippery fingers of fear twisted her stomach once she began to scramble up the steep incline, her back vulnerable to attack, her eyes blinded by the rain. Up and up she clambered, prickles and twigs scratching at her face and arms. Her fingers clawed around the marlin spike as she hauled herself higher and higher until she collapsed onto the rocky overhang.

Below her the creek twisted and swirled, swollen by the downpour. Easing onto her stomach, she hung over the rock shelf and searched the gorge for any sight or sound, a jumble of Cook's threats and Baldwin's description of a leathery-skinned, lumbering beast bouncing around in her head.

But there was nothing. Nothing but the thrashing waters and the plopping of raindrops from the canopy, and above her a sheer wall. Sucking in a long, slow breath, she straightened up. To her left the series of neatly placed slabs formed a winding pathway up the rock face. A familiar series of steps. Some wide and flat, others narrow and sloped, but a staircase nonetheless—Benjamin's steps.

In her mindless panic, she'd unknowingly followed the secret path back to the house. What had Aunt Anthea said? *"Benjamin and I used to keep a rope here for the return journey."*

With her back pressed firmly against the rock wall, she eased along the narrow shelf until she reached the platform, then pushed her hands into the straggly bushes. Her fingers closed around the knotted rope.

She hitched up her breeches, slipped the marlin spike into her waistband, and grasped the rope. Gingerly she placed one foot and then the other on either side of the lowest knot. Slippery but still firm. All she had to do was make her way to the top and over the platform and she'd be in spitting distance of Aunt Anthea's workroom.

The thought of the little slab hut filled her with a rush of warmth, loosening the hard lump of fear in her chest. Blinking the rain from her eyes, she clambered up the rope, hands burning against the rough hemp, hauling herself higher and higher.

No light shone from the house. She slipped inside the workroom and rammed the chair under the door handle. Bent double, her breath burning in her chest, she sucked in great gulps of air, then slumped down on the floor, pulled her knees up to her chest, and curled into a ball. As the lightning flashed and the rain poured down, the tears that had waited so long to escape found their release.

The sodden snig trail wound interminably up and up. Anthea pushed on. One faltering step, one stop for a breath, and she would never make it to the top. She risked a quick look over her shoulder. Bea and Grace followed close behind, heads down, shoulders cowed, doggedly placing one foot after another as Lydia shepherded them along. Farther back, Ella trailed along with Nette behind her, arms outstretched, refusing to allow her to slow her pace.

Bea grasped at the back of her coat. "Aunt Anthea, please can we stop, just for a moment to catch our breath."

"Yes, please." Grace staggered a couple of steps and flopped down in a muddy puddle, her breath spluttering and her face the color of Benjamin's favorite port.

Anthea didn't want to be out in the rain a moment longer than necessary, but Grace's high color and snatched gasps couldn't be ignored. "Just long enough for Ella to catch up."

"Up you get, Grace." Lydia slipped her hands under Grace's arms and tried to encourage her, but they both ended up sprawled in the mud.

"Mr. Baldwin can't be a gentleman. If he was he would come back for us."

Lydia hauled Grace to her feet. "You can't always rely on someone else. You have to look after yourself."

Ella staggered to a halt, bent double and wheezing. "Mr. Baldwin *is* a gentleman. He told me he'd come back for me. I should have waited down at the gorge. Then I wouldn't have had to walk. I could have ridden."

"Fat chance of that. You can't even stay on when the horse is walking. You couldn't have ridden up this slope."

"If Mellie hadn't run away we wouldn't be out here, drenched."

Anthea snapped and outright fury coursed through her blood. "Will you all be quiet?"

The stunned silence gave her a moment to realign. She let out a long, slow huff. All the way up the track she'd hoped they would find Mellie, find that she'd doubled back and not taken the shortcut. Benjamin's steps would be slippery and the rope might well be frayed. She had to get the girls home and then she would search for Mellie.

"We will be back at the house in another ten minutes." More like twenty, but sometimes lies were necessary. Mellie was fit and healthy, strong. Not weak and pampered like the other girls. She could well be home safe already. Anthea clenched her fists and offered a prayer to the God she'd so long ago dismissed. "Right. On your feet. We're not stopping again until we reach the house, and I don't want to hear another moan or groan." She stabbed her walking staff into the wet ground and dragged herself up the track.

How she wished Benjamin was beside her, his protective arm around her shoulder, guiding her up the path. He'd have made a joke, encouraged her on with the choice of port or brandy in front of a warm fire. Now was not the time for an attack of maudlin miseries— and she was more than capable of pouring herself a brandy, and one for Nette, too, once Mellie was found.

The clouds hung as heavy as burgeoning blisters, ready to deposit another onslaught. There'd be no light in the house and the fires would be cold. How ridiculous—it was months until winter took hold. A trickle of water traced its way down her neck and spread across her shoulders.

Never in her life had she felt so pleased to see the outline of her home. "Almost there, girls." She tried, and failed, to inject a note of enthusiasm into her voice. "Come along."

She reached the veranda well ahead of the others, pushed open the door, and staggered through into the kitchen. A small glimmer of light shone from the range, and once she added some kindling from the basket, the flames licked. The moment she picked up the sound of movement, she called, "Come straight into the kitchen. It's warm in here."

The bedraggled group staggered in, teeth chattering, and collapsed. Nette reached for the kettle and filled it.

"Right, girls. I want you to go straight to your rooms, take all your clothes off, and change. And I mean all." She glared at Grace, who frequently needed reminding about her undergarments. "Make sure you dry yourself well and put on your coats and gloves until the fire warms up. I don't want any chills. By the time you get back here, Nette will have a nice cup of tea for you all and something to eat."

With a succession of mumbles and grumbles the girls trooped off.

"A glass of brandy for both of us, I think, and then I'll go back out and look for Mellie."

"You can't go out in this." As Nette spoke, another massive clap of thunder shook the walls. "We made it back just in time. There's going to be another downpour."

"Get yourself changed and look after the girls. I won't be going far." She tossed back the brandy, then pulled off her sopping coat and replaced it with Benjamin's oilskin. The rest would have to wait. "I won't be long."

If she had guessed correctly, Mellie would have returned earlier than they had, providing she hadn't slipped or become paralyzed by fear. And she doubted either. The girl had more courage and a far greater survival instinct than anyone appreciated.

No light showed through the windows of the workroom, but then would Mellie have lit a lamp? Did she even know where to find the waxed matches? Generally, she visited the workroom in the early hours, when the morning light slanted through the shutters.

Her heart sank when she tried the door. She ran her hands along the timber, searching for the crossbeam. Why hadn't she brought a lantern with her? She cocked her hip against the door and pushed. It gave a little, then held firm. "Mellie, are you in there?"

In the next flash of lightning she spotted the crossbeam propped against the wall and the weight on her shoulders lifted. Mellie must be inside. "Mellie. Mellie." Relief snatched at her throat and her words caught on a cough. She forced her fingers around the gap between the door and the frame.

With a slam the door closed, catching her fingers. "Ow." She put her shoulder against the door and wrenched her hand free, hugging her squashed fingers. "Mellie. Open up."

Silence. Nothing but the *drip, drip* of the rain from the leafy canopy. She couldn't leave Mellie. She must be terrified. She stuck her throbbing fingers under her arm, clasped them tight, and leaned against the door again. "Mellie, it's Aunt Anthea. Come along. Come into the house. We're all home."

Stamping her feet to keep her blood flowing and ease the pain in her fingers, she waited. How much longer? Should she force open the door? Surely the child couldn't be terrified of the thunderstorm, otherwise she wouldn't have run off into it. The climb up the path in the teeming rain would have tested the pluckiest. Ella's ridiculous display must have terrified her.

She lifted her hand to rap again but the door opened a crack and she jammed her foot over the threshold. Mellie's face, wide-eyed and pale, appeared from the darkness.

"Oh, Mellie." She forced the door open, stepped into the workroom. "Come here, child. You're safe now."

Mellie stood horribly silent, her mouth slightly open, drenched hair hanging in strings over her bleached face, her eyes unfocused and tears pouring down her cheeks.

Anthea scanned her body for injury. She wasn't favoring either leg; her arms, though hanging loose, didn't appear injured.

"I'm going to light the lamp." Slowly she moved toward the table, opened the small drawer where she kept her nibs and pens, and drew out Benjamin's silver matchbox. Reaching for the lamp, she lifted the glass chimney, wound the wick, and struck the wax match. It flickered, then caught, filling the small space with the fishy stench of whale oil.

Mellie remained still, her back against the wall but her eyes now focused, following Anthea's every move, a ghoulish grimace on her face.

Hands out, fingers spread, as though approaching a frightened animal, Anthea took a step forward and then another. "You're safe now," she crooned as she reached for Mellie's icy hands. She lifted them and chafed her dirty fingers and torn nails.

Mellie flinched, then her body slackened.

"That's it. Come and sit down." Anthea eased her down onto the chair and crouched at her feet. "I was worried about you." She bit her tongue, held back the desire to ask, no demand, why she had run off. "You're safe now," she repeated. "Such a brave girl. Did you come up Benjamin's steps? You must have climbed the rope."

Mellie's lips twitched, as though she might speak. Anthea waited and waited in vain.

"Nette has a fire going in the kitchen and some lovely warm milk on the stove. Will you come up to the house?"

Blinking, Mellie unhooked the marlin spike from her waistband and surveyed the room.

"We had to leave the tools and the picnic hamper down in the gorge. We'll get them when Jordan returns. The storm's almost over." Gritting her teeth, Anthea held out her hand for the marlin spike, the memory of Mellie's lunge at her down in the gorge foremost in her mind. "Give it to me. We'll leave it here on the table until the morning."

After an agonizing moment, Mellie lowered the spike to the table and wrapped her arms around her waist.

"That's a girl. Come on." Anthea drew her close, tucked her under Benjamin's oilskin, and guided her across the room.

When they reached the door, Mellie froze.

"We'll check outside." Anthea opened the door and made a pantomime of looking first left and then right. "The rain has stopped and no one's about. Come along. I can't wait to get in front of the fire."

It took an age to guide Mellie up the path because of her continual backward glances, but by the time they'd reached the house she was all but catatonic, eyes glazed again, placing one foot in front of the other without any understanding of where she trod.

A single ray of light illuminated the back veranda as Anthea half carried, half dragged the trembling child toward the door. "Home now." The blast of warmth fanned her face and the delicious smell of comfort and normality embraced her. "A nice cup of warm milk and a rest and it will all be better." The lie slipped from between her lips with such ease it made her wonder which part of her befuddled brain had created it.

Nette sat in front of the range, the door open, toasting her bare feet. She leaped up, her eyebrows raised in question. "I've sent the girls to their rooms with warm milk and bread. There's more in the pan. You sit down too."

What would she do without this woman? For the hundredth time, Anthea blessed Benjamin and the day he'd insisted they should find her a convict maid. Over the last fifteen years, Nette had become far more than that; she was a friend who had stayed beside her through the best and worst of times.

"Here, take this." Nette handed her a tin mug.

She wrapped her hands around it and inhaled the warm milk and the underlying sticky sweetness of brandy.

"What about Mellie?" Nette asked.

Anthea took a sip of the milk, felt the warmth ease down her throat. "I don't know. She hasn't spoken, not since—" Her breath caught.

"We need to get her into bed."

And disturb Lydia and possibly the other girls? "No, we need to keep her here. It's warmer and I don't want the girls to upset her."

"I'll be back in a moment, then."

Anthea reached out to stop Nette from leaving but she slipped away into the darkness. She pulled the blanket closer around Mellie's small, limp frame. "Take a sip of this." She lifted the cup to Mellie's blue lips. A dribble of milk traced a path down her chin.

A moment later the door opened with a whisper and Nette stood with her arms full of blankets and a clean nightgown. "We'll make her a bed down here on the floor next to the range." She formed a pallet on the floor and fluffed up the pillow. "Come and sit down here, close to the fire." Nette patted the makeshift bed.

Anthea reached for Mellie's arm. She reared away, her eyes flickering frantically.

"Come on, Mellie. You need to rest."

The girl struggled, pushed her aside, and ran for the door, knocking over a chair in her frantic flight.

"We have to settle her."

"This, then." Nette pulled a small blue bottle from her apron pocket. "I'll put some in the milk. It will make her sleep."

"Laudanum?"

"It won't do her any harm. Can you sit her down?"

Anthea guided Mellie back to the chair, crouched beside her, one arm wrapped tight around her shoulders, while Nette eased the spoon between her lips. The first drop dribbled down her chin like the milk had done, and then her lips parted.

"Good girl. And another one."

"We have to get her out of these wet clothes."

As gently as she could, Anthea unbuttoned Mellie's blouse and lifted off her chemise, murmuring meaningless words of comfort as the laudanum worked its magic, then slipped on her nightgown over her head.

With little or no argument, Mellie settled onto the pallet. Nette unbuttoned her boots and took off her breeches, then tucked the blankets around her and turned to Anthea. "Drink the rest of your milk. The brandy will warm you and you can tell me what happened."

"Is Mellie asleep?"

Nette ran a hand over the child's forehead. Mellie let out a small sigh and snuggled down beneath the blanket. "That dose would have knocked out a horse. She's not going anywhere."

"What I'm about to tell you must not be spoken of in the girls' hearing."

Nette didn't deign to answer, simply rolled her eyes and took another sip of her milk and brandy.

"Lydia brought a letter with her from Edna, explaining Mellie's circumstances. Her father was hanged for murder. He was involved with a gang of bushrangers."

A gasp slipped from between Nette's lips and she covered her mouth with her hand. "The poor child. Does she know?"

"I don't believe so. It also appears that she had an unpleasant experience with a member of the gang. I haven't questioned her, and I have no intention of doing so, but it happened around the millpond in Wollombi. Then, to add insult, Edna's foolish cook and scullery maid told her she would be attacked by a bunyip if she wandered. I believe Mellie has somehow, during her illness and subsequent distress, confused the events and thinks she is being chased by a bunyip."

Nette stared at her, eyes wide. "And then Baldwin turned up with his chatter about bunyips. And my foolish comments. I'm so sorry." She bent down and smoothed Mellie's hair back from her forehead. "And then Ella's nonsense down in the gorge made her take off."

"That's my conclusion."

"What are we going to do?"

"I don't rightly know. She has to know what has happened to her father. I'll have to tell her. The rest . . ." Anthea let out a slow breath, trying to make her muscles relax and her heart rate slow. "What time is it?"

"Almost evening." Nette shrugged. "Mellie will sleep well into the morning."

"Is Jordan back?"

"I expect he'll have stayed overnight in Mulbring because of the storm. Sensible thing to do."

Anthea wished he hadn't. She missed his comforting presence.

The whole episode had left her insecure and confused.

CHAPTER 18

1919

WOLLOMBI

PJ and Sam arrived back in front of Bow Wow House, breath rasping from the fierce pace they'd maintained.

"We can be back in Wollombi before it gets too late. The road's nowhere near as bad as the locals said." PJ had no concerns about their ability to handle the road, even in the dark. Compared to some of the mud-strewn tracks they'd managed in the past—driving through the stinking, smoky darkness to the front lines to retrieve the wounded— it would be a picnic.

"I'll drive," said Sam. "You picked up everything from the hotel, didn't you?"

"My stuff. Have you got yours?" PJ cast a look over her shoulder and had the question answered by the pile of clothes strewn across the stretchers in the back. She sat cradling the fossil while Sam eased the car down the track and back onto the road, her fingers compulsively stroking the surface. With its thumb-sized indentation on either side, the vertebra was uncannily like the specimen she'd accidentally taken from the museum. It was the top where there was an almost crown-shaped appendage that was different.

If only she hadn't returned Winstanley's fossil to the museum. The thought sent her upright in her seat.

"Are you okay?" Sam asked as he hit the headlights, illuminating the junction where the track met the winding road leading back to Ellalong.

"I'm trying to remember the vertebra I took from the museum."

"You did what?" He turned and stared at her. The car lurched and he tightened his grasp on the wheel. "Damn potholes." He sighed and concentrated on the road. "Have you still got it?"

"No, of course not. I took it back the next morning. I didn't realize that I had it in my pocket until I left and the museum was closed."

"What did they say?"

"Nothing much. Mr. Ambrose understood."

"Mr. Ambrose? I thought it was Mr. Woods."

"Mr. Ambrose in London and Mr. Woods in Lyme Regis."

"Should I be jealous?"

"I shouldn't think so; they were both fossils in their own right. You don't suppose this is part of the same creature, the ichthyosaur, Anthea thought she'd found?" PJ stared down at the specimen in her hand. "Maybe Dan and Riley have some in their collection. A lot of the specimens are unlabeled." *Ichthyosaurus martindalii*. Her original purpose flickered to life, fanned by her discovery.

"Your pa might have some idea."

If she could get Pa to talk. "I'll ask him when we get back. At least this proves I wasn't off on an entirely ridiculous crusade." She slipped farther down in her seat and closed her eyes, the vertebra nestled in the palm of her hand.

"Be about another hour or so. There's Ellalong Lagoon on your left. I wonder if the same bunyip roams the gorge."

Her eyes snapped open. "For goodness' sake, I keep telling you bunyips aren't real. It's the sort of thing they tell kids to keep them away from trouble." She leaned over the seat and pulled the blanket around her shoulders. "Are you warm enough? Do you want your jacket?"

"I'm fine."

PJ snuggled down under the blanket as the miles rolled away and the track improved when they turned onto the Wollombi road. Maybe she slept, maybe not, but the next thing she knew Sam had cut the engine.

"Hope Mrs. Canning's got something on the stove," he said. "I'm famished. I thought the days of missed meals were over."

Heaving herself out of the car, PJ made her way up to the house. "Pa, Mrs. Canning. We're home." She pushed open the kitchen door, reveling in the warmth and familiar smells.

Pa sat at the table, a mug of steaming tea in front of him and an empty plate set to one side. He lifted his head and pushed his spectacles up onto his forehead. "I didn't expect you back tonight. It's late."

"Sam drove." As she spoke Sam appeared at her shoulder. "Evening, sir."

Pa nodded a greeting. "Mrs. Canning's gone home, but there's a stew and some bread."

PJ slipped the vertebra into her pocket. More than anything else she wanted to show Pa, but she feared it might change his mood. "You sit down, Sam. I'll get us something to eat."

Sam pulled out a chair and sat down opposite Pa. "Somewhere along the line I missed out on breakfast and lunch."

"They do a good meal at the Kurri Hotel. I spent several weeks there while we were dealing with the flu epidemic. I expect you know all about that."

"We saw quite a bit of it, especially after the Armistice. Took its toll."

"We're clear of it now. The Hunter escaped lightly."

PJ let their voices waft over her as she dealt with the food, her heart lightening as she listened to Sam and Pa chatting. It was much more as she'd expected things would be from the outset, when she and Sam had first arrived in Wollombi. She placed a plate of lamb stew—*"Mrs. Canning's dinosaur stew,"* as Dan and Riley had christened it—on the table in front of Sam. Her brothers had always tried to piece together the bones that flavored the slow-cooked meat. Her heart wrenched. How they would have enjoyed the last few days. She couldn't have kept them away. She dragged her gaze from the two empty chairs and put her plate next to Sam's and sat down.

Silence descended while both she and Sam ate their meals, and much to her surprise, Pa stayed with his tea and his newspaper. She wiped the last bit of gravy with a piece of bread and pushed back her chair.

"You stay there." Sam collected the plates. "I'll make us a drink—coffee?"

"Mrs. Canning has some of that essence. I'd rather have tea."

"I've got a feeling I better learn to like tea a whole lot more. Why don't I make it? How many spoons in the pot?"

"One for each person and one for the pot."

Pa raised his head. "I'll have another cup if you're making fresh." At last, Pa sounded like his usual self. Determined to keep him talking, she leaned forward. "Sam's interested in our early life in Wollombi." She ignored Sam's quizzical look and waited, hoping to keep the conversation going.

Pa put the newspaper aside. "When I came back from the African War, I wanted a quieter life with my family. I saw an advertisement in the Sydney papers and decided we'd come and have a look. The place was furnished but had been empty for a while and Wollombi needed a doctor." His eyes took on a distant look. "Some of the happiest days of my life—when Penelope and the boys were young, before my Alice passed."

"What about the fossil collection?" She led him away from the past as quickly as she could.

He shrugged. "There was all sorts of rubbish left behind in the attic. You know as well as I do."

Before she realized what she'd done, her discovery sat in the middle of the table. "I found this today at Bow Wow Gorge."

Pa picked up the fossil and turned it over in his palm a few times, held it up to the light, then wrinkled his nose and placed it back on the table. "What do you think it is?"

"A vertebra perhaps? I was going to compare it to the pieces in the old collection. It's like one I saw in the Natural History Museum in London."

"Saw or pinched?" Sam murmured in her ear as he put down the teapot. She shot him her most ferocious frown.

Pa turned it this way and that, hooked his spectacles over his ears, and examined it more closely, then got up and took it closer to the brighter light over the stove. PJ knew better than to interrupt. She recognized the expression on his face and his mutterings and mumblings.

After a few moments he returned to the table. "You found it at Bow Wow Gorge?"

"Yes, that's right. This afternoon, in the sandy soil on the edge of the creek bed."

"And it's like one you saw in the Natural History Museum?"

"Similar . . ." She paused, trying to remember the exact shape and size of the bone from the museum. "The bit on the top . . . here." She pointed to the crown-shaped protuberance. "The one from the museum was smooth all the way around. More like a small bowl. And this feels different. Chalkier, not dense."

"And what do you think this is?"

Hope might be a better word than *think*. She felt as though she was on a quest. She had this need to solve the question of Bow Wow Gorge, but the only problem was that she didn't know truly what answers she was searching for.

"A vertebra—a fossil perhaps, from an ichthyosaur, a sea-dragon." She traced a pattern with her finger in the crumbs on the table. Anthea's premise hadn't been proven and this wasn't identical but perhaps . . .

Pa's *humph* made her look up. His features had softened and in the half-light he looked more as she remembered him instead of the gruff, disappointed man she'd encountered since she'd returned. "I'm not sure . . . I think I can answer your question, but I don't believe you're going to be happy. Follow me."

He led the way into his study, reached high on the shelves, and brought down a leather-bound tome. "Sit down." He gestured to the two ladder-back chairs, usually occupied by patients waiting for a diagnosis, on the other side of the desk. He tossed aside his stethoscope, stacked some letters out of the way, and placed the vertebra in front of them.

Sam's chair scraped as he pulled it closer.

Pa wiped the cover of the book. *Gray's Anatomy*. She'd seen him refer to it a hundred times. He flicked through the pages. PJ shifted forward and rested her elbows on the desk. If only he would hurry up.

With a snap he closed the book and looked up. "So what makes you think this is a fossil?"

"Because we found it at Bow Wow Gorge. There are hundreds of them; they litter the walls and the floor of the gorge."

The corner of his mouth lifted. "Still jumping to conclusions?"

PJ opened her mouth to respond, then thought better of it and bit her lip.

"So, sir . . ." Sam spoke for the first time since they'd left the kitchen. "Can you identify it?"

"I believe I can." The lift of Pa's lips showed the first semblance of a smile PJ had seen for a long while. It was almost as though he had all the time in the world for Sam but none for her. She batted down the curl of jealousy. "Penelope is correct. This is a vertebra." An audible gasp escaped her lips. Where there was one there had to be others. Her mind slipped to Mary Anning's display in the museum, and for a moment she saw *Ichthyosaurus martindalii* neatly inscribed on a brass plate alongside it. "However, I don't believe it is a fossil."

"How do you—"

Pa raised his hand, making her swallow her words. As always, he surprised her with the breadth of his knowledge. He picked up the vertebra. "It could possibly belong to an animal—a kangaroo, wallaby perhaps—but unless I'm very much mistaken, it's human."

"Human?"

"You were correct about the irregular shape at the top." He ran his fingers over the lumpy crown she'd pointed out to Sam when she'd found it. "These are the remnants of the transverse and spinous processes. On each vertebra, there are two transverse processes and one spinous process." His index finger touched each in turn. "The back muscles and ligaments attach to them."

"So what you're saying is that we've stumbled upon a human body." Sam rocked back in his chair and dragged his fingers through his already disheveled hair.

"I don't believe we can classify it as a body. Part of a human skeleton."

"Mrs. Winstanley and a girl—some say more than one—disappeared."

A shiver tiptoed along her spine, the picture of lifeless bodies left to rot in the pristine waters of the gorge foremost in her mind. "And how long do you think this body—skeleton—has been there, Pa?" She couldn't control the quiver in her voice.

"Difficult to say. A body decomposes at a different rate depending on the place, temperature, moisture and the like, cause of death, whether it has been disturbed by animals. You're jumping to conclusions that the whole skeleton is there. One vertebra. The rest of it may be elsewhere. Scavengers could well have played a part—goannas, monitors, birds of one sort or another. I don't think this could be called a fossil. I'd hazard a guess it's fifty to a hundred years old." Pa pushed back his chair and stood. "Fossils form in sedimentary rock. The sediment quickly covers the body and it, and the bones, gradually turn into rock." He pulled a wry grin. "I'll leave you two to mull on your find. Kurri police must be notified. They have a very good doctor, Mavis Elliot, who has an interest in pathology, attached to the hospital. We worked together during the flu epidemic. She will no doubt be better able to answer your questions. Good night." And with that he closed the door behind him.

Neither Sam nor PJ spoke. Sam stared at the vertebra on the desk while PJ's mind swirled and twisted. Fifty, a hundred years. It couldn't be Anthea—she was buried in Lyme Regis. What about her husband? Could it be one of the girls Artie spoke of? She leaped to her feet and made for the door.

"Where are you going?" Sam dropped his hands from his head, leaving his hair standing on end.

"I need to look at Dan and Riley's collection."

"I'm pretty sure your pa knows what he's talking about."

"Of course he does," she snapped and flew to the sleep-out, only to realize there was no light. She darted back into the study. "Sam, can you help me, please?"

He pushed to his feet and followed her into the boys' bedroom. "I want to move the trunk. Take it somewhere where there's some light." She grabbed the handle of the trunk and tugged. It caught on the irregular floorboards.

"Here, let me." Sam grasped her shoulders and eased her out of the way. "Where would you like it? In the study?"

"No. Not in there. Pa uses it for his consultations."

"Are you sure this can't wait until morning?"

"No, it can't. Take it into the kitchen. It's freezing everywhere else."

Easing himself sideways, Sam edged through the door and made his way through to the kitchen, where he plonked the trunk down at the end of the table. "Are you going to tell me what this is all about?"

"Yes." She pushed her hair back from her face, her hands shaking in anticipation. "In a minute. I'm not sure what I'm looking for. Can you clear the table?"

"Wash up too?"

"I'll do it later." She opened the trunk and lifted out the tray, placing it carefully on the table, and then bent to take out the remaining fossils. As fast as she laid them down, Sam moved them to another spot.

PJ stretched and studied the array of rocks and fossils. Sam had done an amazing job. All the unlabeled rocks were at one end of the table. The center contained haphazardly marked rocks—Dan's and Riley's penmanship, or lack of it, obvious—and the pieces of paper carrying the labels were tied with random bits of string and baling twine. She ran her hands over them and then lifted her eyes to the far end of the table. A slow smile spread across her face. She picked up a small white object from the table, then searched through the others until she found two similar ones, not much more than an inch or two long, with nubs at either end. The label informed her that Dan had found all three of them at Bow Wow, as she'd expected, but they weren't fossils. Of that she was certain. Her heart beat faster. "What do these remind you of?"

Sam picked up one, turned it over. "It's chalky, like the vertebra. I think they're bones. All three of them."

PJ rested one alongside her index finger.

"You think these are phalanges, finger bones?"

She nodded. "Dan's written 'bryozoan,' with a question mark."

"Which is?"

"I need to check, but I think they're coral-like creatures. They have a mouth at one end and an anus at the other."

Sam turned the bone over and over. "Nothing like that. These nubs are more like knuckle bones."

PJ flopped down in the chair. "And they were found in the gorge."

"I recognize that look on your face. You want to go back and have a look for more, don't you?"

She nodded. Most definitely. She slipped the vertebra into her pocket. "We're going to have to report it to the police."

"You're jumping the gun. Three more bones still don't preclude scavengers. The body could be anywhere."

"Or bodies. We must have another look, and we're going to have to put everything else back in the trunk. Mrs. Canning will have heart failure if she finds these all over her kitchen table when she arrives in the morning. Can you pass them down to me?" PJ squatted down next to the trunk. "Wait a minute."

At the bottom of the trunk lay a yellowing newspaper, covered in dust and fragments. "I'll empty the dust outside." She picked up either side of the paper and then dropped it, scattering a fine, chalky dust all over the floor.

"What did you do that for?"

"Look." Littered at the base of the trunk lay a collection of small triangular pieces of cartridge paper, each carrying a name and a date and, most importantly, a location; although the handwriting varied, every single one of them read *Bow Wow Gorge*.

Carefully she withdrew one. The ink had faded, but the writing was still visible.

Brachiopod, lamp shell
Found by Lydia Pearson
At Bow Wow Gorge
March, 1845

She sank to her knees, picked up another—*Bea Pearson*—and then another found by Lydia, and another. "These must belong to those unmarked fossils. I don't remember any of these labels being attached to the fossils. Dan and Riley must have taken them all off. The Pearson sisters, who lived here, must have visited Bow Wow Gorge quite regularly."

"The doctor's daughters who lived in the house before your pa bought it?"

She grunted and reached for a handful of the labels, then dropped them onto the table.

Sam leafed through the labels. "Then who are Ella and Grace Ketteringham? These labels put them at Bow Wow Gorge too."

"I don't know." What was it about Artie's mention of girls that kept bringing her back? Lydia and Bea Pearson, the two girls in the cemetery, and then Ella and Grace Ketteringham, another pair of sisters, if the names were anything to go by. At Bow Wow Gorge seventy years before Dan and Riley's trips.

"So we know that these four girls went fossil hunting in Bow Wow Gorge and brought their finds home."

"We don't know if Ella and Grace lived here. I don't remember seeing their names in the cemetery or hearing of them before." PJ hauled herself to her feet and worked her way through the fossils Sam had neatly lined up. "I can't see anything that looks like the vertebra I saw in London."

"Maybe they didn't find any vertebrae, just these sea shells, mollusks. And besides, didn't you say the museum couldn't decide whether Anthea's fossil belonged to an . . . what was it called?"

"Ichthyosaur. You're right."

"Nothing with Anthea Winstanley's name here."

"That makes sense. I think this was a private collection, and if you look at these dates, regardless of the year, they're all the same time—March and April." She drifted to the other end of the table. "I wonder how often Dan and Riley went to Bow Wow."

"A bit of a hike. It took us a good few hours in the car."

"They had bikes. They were forever going off adventuring. They used to camp. They'd converted their old billy cart into a trailer for one of the bikes." Her words caught in her throat and turned into a splutter of laughter. "They were dreadful. Always getting into strife and always managing to talk their way out of it." She turned over a smooth, round ball of sandstone and read the scrap torn from a buff-colored envelope, attached with what looked remarkably like a strip of bandage and a blob of gum. *Dan Martindale, September 1915, Wollombi Brook* and, added in a different scrawl, *(and Riley)*. Was this how they'd spent their weekends while she'd been in Sydney? "Larrikins—that's what Mrs. Canning called them, though she never could bring herself to stay angry for long. Always bailed them out when Pa went on the rampage."

"What made them join up?"

She shrugged her shoulders, not wanting to give voice to the guilt she carried. "Boys being boys." She couldn't have this conversation until she'd sorted it out with Pa. It would be a betrayal. "I don't want to report our find to the police. I'd like to go back and have another look around first."

"You think Dan and Riley might be involved?"

"No. I'm sure they weren't. Pa said fifty to a hundred years ago." She paused for a moment to control the grin tipping her lips. "Unless meat ants got hold of the body."

"Meat ants?" Sam's broad shoulders shuddered.

"Don't you have meat ants in America?"

"Not in Philadelphia."

"Amazing things. I've seen them strip a snake down to a skeleton in a couple of days, not an inch of flesh left on the bones."

Sam's eyes widened. "You're kidding, right?"

"Nope. Farmers dump animal carcasses on meat-ant mounds as a method of disposing of them. Takes a bit longer for them to be eaten than a snake. A couple of weeks. You want to watch out—we've got some nasty animals in Australia."

Sam swallowed, straightened his shoulders. "The gorge is a great place to hide a body, but I'm in favor of the scavenger theory. There's one thing you've forgotten."

"What's that?"

"One vertebra and three finger bones does not a skeleton make."

PJ plonked down on the chair. "You're right. Maybe I am jumping to conclusions." But still, she couldn't rid herself of Artie's words.

"Mrs. Winstanley and a girl—some say more than one—disappeared." "I still want to go and have another look."

"Fair enough. We'll get a decent night's sleep. Then go back to the gorge tomorrow."

CHAPTER 19

—◦•◦—

1847
Bow Wow

Anthea lifted her head from the table and squinted out of the window. The sky remained overcast, but the worst of the rain had passed. What was she doing in the kitchen? Had she slept the whole night slumped over the table? And then she remembered.

No sign of Nette or Mellie, and only a crumpled heap of blankets and a pillow on the floor.

Hauling herself to her feet, every muscle in her body screaming, she peeled the blanket from her shoulders and pulled on Benjamin's oilskin, for warmth and comfort more than any need for protection from the rain, and opened the back door. She was getting too old to clamber up and down tracks in the pouring rain. And where was Nette and, more importantly, Mellie?

A mist hovered over the garden, blanketing the tree line in a hazy blur. Anthea headed toward her workroom, but before she reached the lemon tree she noticed a movement in the scrub.

The shadowy outlines shimmered and took form.

A sound rose, animalistic, painful in its intensity—a yowl of torment. Anthea raced closer. Nette stepped from behind a trunk, lifted her finger to her lips, and then beckoned.

The moment she reached the rock platform, her stomach turned over and her knees buckled. Mellie teetered on the edge of the gully, one arm raised, the marlin spike held high.

Nette's hand clasped Anthea's outstretched arm and brought her to a sudden halt. "She's sleepwalking."

A wave of terror flooded her body. "She'll fall."

"I don't think so. She's sure-footed, and I don't believe she wants to go down there. It's as though she's standing guard. Her eyes are open and she hasn't moved any closer to the edge."

"You said the laudanum would make her sleep for hours."

"I expected her to. It was a huge dose for someone her size."

"Have you spoken to her? Did she respond?"

"I called her name when I heard her leaving the kitchen but she didn't answer."

Guilt streaked through Anthea. "Why didn't you wake me?" How could she have slept through? "What should we do?"

As the words left Anthea's lips, Mellie dropped her arm, the marlin spike hanging loosely at her side. She then turned and made her way back along the track, her gait sure and steady, arms stiff, still staring ahead, not even a blink.

"I think she's going to put the spike back," Nette whispered.

Anthea nodded. "We'll follow and see what she does."

Like a wraith, Mellie glided across the grass until she reached the workroom. Anthea and Nette hovered, watching as she carefully wiped the spike on her nightgown and placed it back on the table. She then raked her hair back from her face and lowered herself into the chair. Slowly her head came up and she stared at the open door.

"Can she see us?"

"I don't know. Why don't you step inside and speak to her?"

Was that the right thing to do? She couldn't leave Mellie sitting there in the freezing cold, wearing nothing but a sopping nightgown. She needed to be inside, in the kitchen in front of the fire.

Gingerly, Anthea stepped into the workroom and crossed the floor. "Mellie, are you awake?"

Mellie's flat eyes stared through her, fixed on some distant spot, no flash of wonder, no lively spark.

"Sweetheart, wake up. You're safe."

Mellie's eyes flickered and then she jumped. She pressed her hands under her armpits, hugging herself tight.

Better not to make a fuss. "Nothing to worry about." Anthea peeled off her oilskin and wrapped it around Mellie's shoulders, covering her nightgown. "Let's get you inside and we'll have a cup of tea." Before the girls woke up, with any luck. None of them had managed to arrive in the kitchen early any other morning.

By the time they'd crossed the garden, Nette had Mellie's blankets tidied away, the range stoked, the kettle boiling cheerfully on the hob, Mellie's clothes warming, and everything much as it always appeared, even down to the porridge waiting for Mellie to stir.

Normality, that's what Mellie needed. "Let's get you dressed and then perhaps you can help Nette with the porridge."

Anthea shook out Mellie's chemise, blouse, and breeches and held them up. Mellie's face crumpled and she opened her eyes wide, tears trickling down her cheeks. At a total loss, Anthea opened her arms. A great shuddering yowl racked Mellie's body and the girl fell into her embrace.

Holding her tight, Anthea hummed a long-forgotten lullaby until Mellie calmed. "Time to get dressed. Let me help." She reached for the crumpled pile of clothes.

Mellie took her breeches, slipped them on under her wet nightgown, then turned her back and pulled it over her head, replacing it with her chemise and blouse. She bundled her nightgown under her arm.

What to do now? One wrong move and Mellie might flee. Nette leaped to her rescue. "Just drop your gown by the door. I'll sort it out." She handed Mellie the wooden spoon and gestured to the pan. "I'm hungry, and I bet you are too. Can you stir the porridge?"

Mellie took the spoon, her lips pinched tight and her face an expressionless mask.

Anthea winced as a streak of despair laced her as she recalled Mellie's dreadful primeval screech when she stood above the gorge, the marlin spike raised.

The bubbles broke the surface of the porridge with a sound like sticky mud. Mellie's belly cramped as the memory washed over her. The crashing steps tracking her, the darkness and the horrible stench of rancid sweat and grog. The weight of him as he pinned her against the tree. The air whistling from her as she hit the ground. The rough grass cutting her cheek.

"No." She threw down the spoon, the porridge hissing and spitting as it splattered on the hob. Arms wrapped around her, the smell of lavender, soap, and damp wool replacing the stench of him.

"Shh. You're safe. Everything is fine."

Her body crumpled, then the tightness in her chest eased and her legs went to jelly.

"Why don't you take your porridge down to the workroom? I can look after the girls." Nette's words broke through the last remnants of her panic.

"What a lovely idea. We'll light a fire down there, have a picnic. What do you think, Mellie?"

Aunt Anthea's words came from a great distance, made no sense. She wanted sleep to come, to blot out the frantic dreams and her shivering terror. Too exhausted to speak, she sank down, let her head fall and her cheek rest on the scrubbed table top.

"We can spend the day in the workroom, just you and me."

A long, low moan slipped from her lips. Safe, she wanted to be safe. She loved the gorge, loved searching among the rocks for the dragon scales, but not if the bunyip was there. How had he tracked her? Ella's open hands cradling the blue eggshells flashed in front of her eyes. The towering shadow looming over her—the bunyip had followed her to the gorge.

"Why don't I go and light the fire in the workroom. Anthea, you and Mellie make up a tray. The kettle's warm—make a pot of tea. There's cream and butter for the porridge just the way Mellie likes it." The door banged as Nette hurried out.

"Come along, Mellie. I need help." Aunt Anthea bustled around, collecting this, that, and the other. "Butter, cream, sugar. Some of this lovely bread." Mindless babble as she ticked the things off on her fingers, but it scattered the flickering images in Mellie's head. "And we'll take some of the bacon. We can cook it on the fire. Benjamin and I used to have picnics in my workroom all the time. You'd like that, wouldn't you, Mellie?"

Yes, she would. Perhaps in the safety of the workroom her mind would clear and she could get rid of the shadows that kept escaping from behind the barricade she'd built. She thought she'd managed that, put it all away, protected by the dragon scale. Why now? How had the bunyip found her?

"Come on, Mellie. I need some help. Wrap that blanket around your shoulders. It'll be a bit cold until the fire gets going."

Aunt Anthea's soothing words seeped into her mind. She picked up the blanket and draped it around her neck.

"You take this tray and I'll bring the hot water. We don't want any accidents. I'll be right behind you."

Clutching the tray, Mellie stepped outside. No sign in the garden of any lurking shapes. No broken plants or disturbed soil. No heaving breaths or heavy footsteps. She tilted her face up to the sky. Patches of blue shone between the scuttling clouds, bringing the promise of sunshine.

Inside the workroom a cheerful fire and Nette's smile greeted her. "I've opened the shutters—the sun and the fire will have the place warm in no time. Is Anthea on her way?"

A finger of panic traced her spine and she glanced over her shoulder. True to her word, Aunt Anthea had closed the kitchen door and followed her down the path and into the workroom.

"Thank you, Nette. This looks lovely. Mellie and I will have a cozy picnic and then we're going to clean her dragon scale. The girls are stirring. Can you organize them? Tell them we won't be going down to the gorge today. The snig trail will be much too slippery. It's their last day before they return home. They need to get organized."

Mellie's head came up with a snap as Aunt Anthea's words sank in. The last day at Bow Wow? She couldn't go, couldn't leave Aunt Anthea alone.

She licked her lips, cleared her throat. Why wouldn't the words come? She had to stay; once the girls went home, who would protect

Aunt Anthea from the bunyip? Her fingers closed around the marlin spike.

"Put it down, Mellie."

She let the marlin spike clatter to the desk, then straightened up, glanced across the room through the open door, to the line of trees wavering in the breeze masking the way to the secret path. Was he still there? Waiting, waiting? She shot across the room.

"No. Stand still." Aunt Anthea slammed the door shut and led her across the room. "Come and have something to eat." She sank down to her knees and patted the folded blanket spread in front of the fire. "Some porridge, then a bacon sandwich. It's my favorite. Here you are."

Mellie took the bowl thrust in front of her and checked the room one more time before lifting the spoon to her mouth.

"And here's a cup of tea." Aunt Anthea settled a tin mug on the floor next to her. "Two teaspoons of sugar. Just what you need."

The warmth and the food settled her; they eased the knots in her shoulders, made her body limp and her eyes drowsy.

Aunt Anthea took her empty plate. "I love this little house. It's where Benjamin and I lived when we first came to the property, over seventeen years ago. It holds so many memories. We visited Mitchell in Sydney and he'd taken us to meet some people who lived in Parramatta. I fell in love with their property, such a beautiful house. Just like the English farmhouse I'd lived in as a child. I couldn't imagine we could have a slice of England in the Hunter, but Benjamin was determined. In those days we had a lot of help. The right to convict labor came with the land grant. We had to sleep in a tent at first, the same as the convicts, and then they built this little place in no time at all. Twelve months later we moved into the big house, and I even had a maid-of-all-work. We added the kitchen and the stables, and finally

Nette and Jordan's room above. They were the only two who stayed after Benjamin died."

Aunt Anthea's words flowed around her like the bedtime stories Ma used to tell. Mellie's eyes grew heavy and her head sank to her chest. The flickering flames of the fire lulled her and she curled up, warm and safe, sinking down and down . . .

"He said what?" Aunt Anthea's outraged voice cut a path through Mellie's dreaminess. She struggled from the tangled blanket.

"Full of bullshit, that man," Jordan said. "We trailed all over the place yesterday, followed the creek for miles. Got caught in the storm. He said I should return to the inn at Mulbring, make sure he had a room for another night or two and wait for him there. Said he wanted to get to know the area. No idea what he did or where he went. By the time he got back late into the night I'd taken up the offer of a bed in the stables."

"And a meal and a couple of jugs of ale, unless you've changed your habits."

"That too. You know me. Just as well I did. Bloody awful thunderstorm. Stable boy said Baldwin was holding court until the early hours. Hope to Christ he doesn't make you an offer you can't refuse."

"I simply won't accept it."

"Says he's already put down an option to buy."

"Before he saw the property or discussed it with me?" Aunt Anthea's voice wavered. "Don't be ridiculous."

"They're all like that, these new chums, more money than sense. Showed me a map of Bow Wow with a section marked *Baldwin's Lot*, said it was a copy from the surveyor's office. Asked him what he was going to run and he hadn't made up his mind. Cows, sheep, horses—sounds like he's planning a menagerie. He reckons he's going to spend some time in the local area. Big-noting himself more 'n like, talking about family connections. Kept bellyaching about where the lot started and finished. He's not the sort of neighbor we want."

Mellie pushed aside the blanket and stretched. Her movement caused Aunt Anthea to glance around. She rested a hand on Jordan's arm and closed the door behind them. What was she going to say to him? Something she didn't want Mellie to overhear? Baldwin gave her the collywobbles. He was up to no good. Jordan was right. The bunyip hadn't found her until Baldwin turned up. She pushed herself to her feet and, ducking below the open shutter, tiptoed to the door.

"The girls are due to go home tomorrow. Ella and Grace are to be dropped off at Mulbring and they'll wait there for the Maitland coach. The others are to be returned to Wollombi. I'm afraid it will be a bit of a roundabout trip."

"I'll collect your tools and the hamper later today, then after I drop off all the girls, we'll stop in Wollombi for a night or two and pick up some supplies. Be back in a day or two . . ." Jordan's words faded.

And then Aunt Anthea called, "Don't worry about it."

Mellie scooted back to her place in front of the fire. Don't worry about what? How long had she slept? Time had tangled. The sun slanted low across the floor, marking it well into the afternoon. She cast a look around the homely room. She didn't want to leave. Didn't want to return to Wollombi and put up with Cook's and Fanny's blathering. She scrubbed at her eyes, wiping away the tears. Crying. She never cried. Not when Ma and the baby went, not when they took Da away, not when the bunyip found her. She sniffed, scuffed her hand under her nose—blubbing for the second time in as many days.

"What is it, Mellie?" Aunt Anthea appeared by her side.

"I don't want to leave." The words tumbled out of her mouth, caught on a sob.

Aunt Anthea enveloped her in a warm hug. "Shh. You're not leaving. You can stay as long as you like. Would that make you happy?"

Her muscles unwound and her blood warmed. Stay at Bow Wow with Aunt Anthea, keep up the search for dragon scales? A pang of pure joy worked its way into her heart; no Bea, no Grace, no taunts or scalding looks. Perhaps the bunyip would go back to Wollombi. But what about Da?

"I can't."

"Whyever not? Of course you can."

"Da might not be able to find me."

A strange look wafted across Aunt Anthea's face and then she settled on the floor and put her arm around Mellie's shoulders, pulling her tight. "He's not coming back, sweetheart."

That wasn't right. "He promised." He'd told her he'd explain to the magistrate what had happened, that he hadn't meant to shoot the man, and while he was gone, she should stay and keep an eye on their stash up behind the millpond because it was their money, their stake in the future.

"Sometimes we make promises we can't keep, no matter how much we want to." Aunt Anthea sighed, her fingers soothing as they brushed Mellie's hair back from her face. "There's no way to make this any easier. I'm sorry."

A shiver ran down Mellie's back and goose bumps flecked her skin. She burrowed deeper into Aunt Anthea's shoulder.

"Your da was found guilty of murder. They hanged him at Newcastle Gaol."

A great howl built in Mellie's chest; it gathered until she couldn't restrain it a moment longer. The sound filled the little hut, bounced off the walls, ricocheted from the ceiling, and shattered her soul, reducing her to nothing more than an empty shell.

How long she sat, Aunt Anthea holding her close, rocking her gently to and fro, she didn't know, but gradually her world steadied and she dragged in a shuddering breath. "That's why the bunyip came. He wanted Da's stash. He ran me down." The stench came again and filled her nostrils: leathery hands, big shiny boots.

She jumped to her feet and backed up against the door, searching for his shadow.

"Mellie, Mellie. You're safe."

Warmth, lavender, and soap . . . Aunt Anthea's face drifted into focus. "I will keep you safe as Benjamin kept me. Stay here. It'll be just the two of us, dragon hunters."

Too scared to spoil Aunt Anthea's promise, she nodded.

"Is that a yes? I need to hear it from your own lips."

"Yes," she murmured. "I don't want to leave, not ever. Promise I can stay?"

"It is my solemn promise." Aunt Anthea tipped her chin up and their eyes met, sealing their bond.

Anthea sat with the girls, cataloging and discussing their finds and their plans for the remainder of the year. While they chattered, the implications of the promise she'd made to Mellie the day before sank in. In the blackest part of the night she'd railed against Edna, blamed her for not telling Mellie the truth about her father, but as the dawn broke, she'd found a certain solace in the knowledge that, with love and care, Mellie would come through. Her reaction to Baldwin and the nonsense about the bunyips now made perfect sense. Only time and education would help heal her wounds, and she would provide both of those to the child—the only question was how.

Other than the few days a year when the girls came to visit, she had no experience of children, no knowledge of the necessary education, formal or social. She cast a look down the workbench where Lydia and Ella sat at either end, heads bent, studiously ignoring each other; Bea and Grace were between them bickering over the ownership of various specimens and haphazardly scratching their names onto the small triangular pieces of card she'd provided. Mellie chose to remove herself, as far away as she could possibly manage. She sat cross-legged on the floor in the corner, poring over Thomas Hawkins's *The Book of the Great Sea-dragons*. The plates were enough to give lesser mortal nightmares, but Anthea was not concerned: Mellie's terrors stemmed from something much closer to home.

Anthea knew she would simply have to come to terms with the responsibility. She couldn't change her mind, go back on her promise, but what exactly would she do with Mellie? There wasn't a school within spitting distance of Bow Wow and she hadn't the skills, or the patience, to become a governess. She could teach her about fossils, and basic reading and writing, and Mellie could certainly do with some help in that department, but Nette would have to step in and cover the domestic skills.

What a load of nonsense. Mellie had a lively mind and keen intelligence—she'd make a perfect student of paleontology. That was where her interests lay. She already had more than adequate skills as far as domestic matters were concerned.

"Come along, girls. Time to pack the crate. There's plenty of straw to bed down your specimens and keep them safe."

Ella groaned and massaged her temples. "Mellie, dear. Would you pack mine for me? I need to rest my eyes."

Anthea's spine stiffened. "Mellie will do no such thing." Lazy, underhanded, conniving little princess. "You are responsible for your own specimens. You know that very well."

"I have to go and pack." Ella smoothed her fingernails. "I have to prepare. Mr. Baldwin will still be at Mulbring."

The thought made the hairs on the back of her neck rise. Jordan had said Baldwin intended to acquaint himself with the local area. She must make certain Jordan didn't leave Ella and Grace until their coach arrived to take them to Maitland.

"You'll do it, won't you, Mellie?" Ella simpered.

Mellie lifted her head from the book, lips tipped in a sickly sweet smile. "Of course I will. I'll do everyone's. I don't have to pack my clothes, do I, Aunt Anthea?"

She'd intended to tell the girls later that Mellie would be staying at Bow Wow, but it seemed Mellie had taken matters into her own hands. "No. No need at all."

The four girls turned as one, identical, incredulous, questioning glances plastered on their faces.

Anthea bit back a smile. "Mellie will be staying here, with me, at Bow Wow."

A communal intake of breath filled the workroom.

"But school starts next week."

"That's not fair."

"I want to stay too."

Anthea raised her hand to silence Bea and Grace. "The matter is not for discussion. Thank Mellie for her offer."

"Thank you, Mellie," the girls chorused, their faces still bright with curiosity.

Silently congratulating Mellie for her pluck, she gave a short, sharp clap of her hands. "Off you go. Pack your belongings and Mellie and I will see you in the dining room. Lydia, could you spare me a moment?"

Ella, Bea, and Grace trooped off, heads together, mumbling no doubt about the turn of events. Never had she invited any of her visitors to stay beyond the prescribed ten days. She folded the letter she'd written and closed it, using Benjamin's brass seal. No opportunity for any tampering.

"Lydia, if you would be kind enough to give this to your mother. I've outlined my reasons for asking Mellie to stay. I can't see that she will object." Which wasn't strictly true. She had no doubt that Edna would be quite outraged by the lambasting she had given her. However, she had no intention of letting the poor child return to Wollombi, and she had told Edna so. Mellie was thoroughly traumatized when she arrived; she needed safety and security, not rumors, gossip, and innuendo. All Baldwin's ridiculous talk of bunyips had set her back. If she had the misfortune to cross paths with the man again, she'd give him a piece of her mind. And what's more, she wouldn't put it past Bea to stir the pot, never mind the ghastly women Edna employed who put the idea of the bunyip into poor Mellie's head in the first place. It was a travesty, and she intended to ensure Edna knew what she thought of her guardianship skills. If she couldn't keep her servants' viperous tongues under control, then she shouldn't have taken Mellie on. It'd be a shame to spoil their relationship, but it wasn't one she'd instigated. Benjamin and Dr. Pearson had struck up a friendship, and she and Edna became acquainted as a result. However, she had no doubt Benjamin would have approved of her decision. Mellie's well-being came first.

Lydia dropped her gaze and swallowed audibly. "When will Mellie be coming back to Wollombi?"

"That will be up to Mellie to decide. Now, off you go."

It wasn't until Lydia closed the door that she turned to Mellie. "Are you quite sure you'd like to stay here with me?"

"How else can I learn to be a dragon hunter?" Mellie picked up the book and smoothed the cover with reverence. "Hawkins's picture of the battling sea-saurians made me think. If you found vertebrae, then I'm certain ichthyosaurs lived in the gorge, not dragons." She rubbed her hands together, her eyes lively with interest. "I'm going to begin an ordered search. The cave under the overhang is the best place to start."

A girl after her own heart. Perhaps fate had smiled upon her. Quite why she was worrying about Mellie's education, she had no idea. Once the other girls left they could go down to the gorge and investigate the ridge of bumps she'd noticed on the afternoon of the thunderstorm. Mellie would be a wonderful fossil hunter—she had an inherent curiosity and a desire to seek solutions.

"It's an interesting hypothesis."

CHAPTER 20

1919
Bow Wow

Armed with a series of tools—a shovel, crowbar, rake, and brushes purloined from the garden shed—PJ and Sam made the trip back to the gorge. They debated a flurry of ideas and plans, but none left PJ with any sense of certainty. Sam stuck to his scavenger theory, and she remained convinced they'd find traces of at least one of the fossil-hunting girls.

Sam pulled to a halt outside the house and reached for the tools. "Still fancy yourself as a fossil hunter?"

Overnight, all thoughts of finding proof that ichthyosaurs once inhabited the gorge had evaporated, leaving behind the firm and solid belief that they would find proof of Artie's tale of the disappearing girls. "We must be careful not to disturb anything."

"Well, you have to admit there is a whiff of possibility we might have stumbled on something prehistoric. We might just have to get Andrew Carnegie involved."

"Carnegie?"

"Oh, come on, I thought you knew all about the diplodocus. Isn't that why you went to the Natural History Museum in London?" Sam said. "A man called William Harlow Reed found a large thigh bone in a sheep paddock in Wyoming, twenty-odd years ago. Turned out that didn't belong to the diplodocus, but on a return trip financed by Carnegie, Reed found the first part of the skeleton—just a toe bone—and the rest, as they say, is history. They uncovered the entire skeleton. I thought that's what you wanted—to find one of these sea-dragons."

PJ scrambled down the embankment and waited for Sam to pass down the tools. "Right now I'm more interested in finding out whether the rest of this human skeleton is here or not."

"You don't honestly believe Artie's rubbish, do you?"

PJ bit back a stinging rebuke and tried for a change of subject. "I wonder if there's any way of accurately dating bones."

Sam jumped down beside her. "No idea, but I'm sure we can find out. Come on, let's get started. Sit back on that rock like before and I'll give you a shove, and that'll give us a place to start."

PJ lowered herself onto the rock and stared into the gorge. The familiar image of the girls in their white dresses danced in her peripheral vision. To think that something might have happened to one of the girls whose fossils lay in the trunk sent a pang of despondency through her. Imagine lying for decades, no one to care, no one to mourn for you. It'd be as terrible as the poor Diggers who were left where they'd fallen in France. She shook the wave of sorrow away and slid off the rock, trying to replicate her previous fall.

She landed with a thud on her backside, hands splayed. "Right, don't move."

She stared at Sam's booted feet. "Don't start digging. We need to comb through the sand and dirt carefully. Anything we find could be brittle and break easily. We have to be scientific about this." A thrill shot through PJ as her fingers raked the soft sand and she crawled on her hands and knees over the area, Sam alongside her.

After a while Sam stood up and stretched. "We're not getting anywhere. I'm convinced the vertebra was just a fluke. I wish we knew the exact spot where Dan and Riley found the finger bones. The scavenger theory is the only one that makes sense to me."

"I guess we ought to call the police, as Pa said. Get it over and done with, then we can explore the rest of the gorge with a clear conscience."

Sam winced as though her words caused him physical pain. "They'll think we're deranged." He rocked back on his heels and crouched, working his way closer to the overhang, away from the narrow stream of water at the base of the gorge. "Pass me the shovel, can you?" he muttered over his shoulder before disappearing into the shadows.

"Use the brush. The vertebra wasn't buried. Anything else might be near the surface."

Several hot and sweaty hours later Sam threw down the shovel and wiped his face on the tail of his shirt. "I've had enough. There's nothing here. Let's forget about it."

"Maybe it's time to stop and get the police."

"I really didn't want to say this, PJ, but I want you to think twice about this compulsion to involve the police."

"Why? You heard what Pa said."

"There's something you've forgotten."

Whatever was he talking about? "There's no way Dan and Riley could be implicated. Pa thought the bone was between fifty and a hundred years old. Oh. You mean trespassing?"

Sam nodded. "We've proved there's nothing else here." He gestured toward the mess they'd made of the creek bed and the surrounding banks. "It has to be scavengers. The bones could have come from anywhere."

"But what if—"

"What if nothing. Come on. Pack up. I'm not looking forward to the climb back up the hill and I could do with a beer."

"Sam . . ." Her plaintive cry stopped him in his tracks. "You don't understand. I have to do this."

"For goodness' sake, why?"

"I have to know what happened. I'm going to keep looking."

Across the creek she stepped through a curtain of ferns and found that they obscured the entrance to a small cave worn into the walls of the gorge by the rising and falling of the water. Parting the fronds, she ducked inside. Waiting for her eyes to adjust to the filtered light, she crouched down, relishing the cool, shady retreat while the shadows took shape and the depth of the cave became obvious.

Crawling on her hands and knees, she made her way forward. Above her, the roof sloped upward. Hands over her head, she raised herself to her feet, ready to duck to avoid hitting her head. But much to her surprise, she was able to stand upright. A long shelf stretched the width of the cave. Step by step she approached, her heart hammering as the shadows dissipated. A domed skull and two hollow eye sockets filled her vision.

"Sam!" Her screech bounced from the walls and echoed back at her. "Sam!"

A loud *thump* reverberated.

"Ouch! Why didn't you warn me?" Sam knelt, cradling his head, moaning softly.

"I've found her."

"Who?" His voice sounded vague and confused.

"One of the Ketteringham girls. I'm certain." Her voice, frayed with emotion, echoed in the cave. The skeleton lay as though sleeping peacefully. One hand cradled under her cheek, knees tucked up, feet neatly aligned. "I think it's the older one, Ella."

He groaned again and rubbed his head. "How can you know that?"

"From the size of the skeleton. Ella was the elder. You can tell from the handwriting on the fossil labels. It's far more sophisticated. This skeleton is too tall for a young girl."

He wiped his hand over his head and grimaced at his palm. "I suppose you've got a point."

"You're bleeding."

"It's nothing." He rubbed his hand across his face, leaving a streak of blood on his cheek.

"I'm so sorry. I should have warned you."

"It takes more than this to fell a Philadelphian." He threw her a wry grin. "Come on, then. Show me Miss Ella Ketteringham."

She grasped his hand. "Duck your head. You should be able to stand upright after a few more steps. Come on." She tugged at his hand, and together they edged toward the skeleton at the back of the cave.

"She looks peaceful." PJ reached out her hand to the dome of her skull.

"Don't touch." He leaned forward and studied the collection of bones. "Looks as though we both might be correct." He pointed to the curved spine. "See, there are several vertebrae missing. And the pelvis is crushed."

"Scavengers, definitely. That would account for the vertebra, and the finger bones Dan and Riley found. Look at her left hand."

"I'd say so."

PJ let out a sigh. "I am determined Ella will have a proper burial."

"PJ, you can't keep jumping to conclusions. You have no proof that Artie's story is any more than scuttlebutt."

"Then how did she get here?"

"What's the matter with you? You're usually so precise, sensible. Think about the alternatives. We have no idea how long it's been here, how it got here, whether an animal dragged it here . . ."

"You'll be spinning some tale about a bunyip next. Only a person would be able to arrange a body so carefully. I know it's Ella Ketteringham."

"Right, that's it." He grabbed her arm to lead her away. "We're going now. And I don't want to hear another word."

The trip back to Kurri passed in total silence. Sam sat in the passenger seat, his eyes closed and his handkerchief held against his head. She had a perfectly good first-aid kit in the back, but he'd refused any help, just told her to drive. Despite his words to the contrary, he had to have a headache; she could tell from his pained expression and the periodic groans he let slip.

She bypassed the pub and pulled up outside the hospital. Sam opened one eye. "What are we doing here?"

"You need to get your head checked. It might need stitches."

"I'm quite capable of making my own diagnosis, and you're quite capable of stitching my head together should it need it, which I seriously doubt."

"Then I'll call into the police station and report Ella's death."

Sam sat bolt upright, anger flaring in his eyes. "You will do no such thing. It's highly unlikely they'll go rushing down there now. They're more likely to lock you up. They'll think you're stark staring mad. 'Ella's death.'" He let out a splutter.

"I know . . ."

"You know nothing, and we're not going to discuss it until the morning when I've got shot of this headache. Another night or two isn't going to make any difference to her."

"There, see? You said 'her.' You agree with me."

Sam growled a series of indecipherable syllables. "Stop here. I want a drink."

"I'll park around the back and we can discuss our plans for tomorrow."

"Drop me here."

She slammed her foot on the brake. Sam staggered off through the doors and into the bar. She knew he wouldn't be gone for long—from the look of the sky it was almost six o'clock, closing time.

PJ sat on her bed in the hotel, reading through her notebook, the sandwich she'd managed to beg from the dining room uneaten on the plate and the pot of tea now cold. The more she looked at her notes, the more convinced she became that it was Ella Ketteringham lying like some fairy-tale princess in her ferny bower. It all made perfect sense. The two Pearson girls were buried in Wollombi, so it couldn't be them, and what she had said to Sam about the handwriting on the tag on the fossils made perfect sense.

First thing tomorrow morning she would go down and report their find to the police. Surely they would be able to date the skeleton. Pa had said there was a pathologist working at the hospital; she must be able to prove that the skeleton was female.

Throwing open the French doors, she wandered out onto the veranda. An oily stillness hung in the air—no raucous sounds from the bar that had closed hours ago after the six o'clock swill—and lengthening shadows were thrown into the main street by the odd light in an upstairs window. Where was Sam? She cupped her hands and peered into his room—no light, no sign of him sprawled across the bed.

She leaned out over the veranda. The town was so quiet and still, strangely like the evenings on the ship coming home, but without the continual vibration of the engines. With a sigh, she turned back. Sam would be in his room in the morning, tousle-headed and grumbling for coffee.

A sudden shout stopped her in her tracks. It built to a roar and then she heard the raucous bark of laughter and applause. She'd left Sid parked behind the hotel, and the noise seemed to be coming from that direction. Without a second thought she closed the door behind her and made her way down the stairs. One hand on the wall to guide her in the half-light, she followed the corridor out to the back of the hotel and across the garden to the spot behind the old tractor shed. There was nothing much anyone would want to steal from Sid, but a foolish prank could mean days spent repairing tires or replacing engine parts.

With only half the distance covered, another roar of laughter, louder this time, echoed from behind the wall enclosing the garden at the back. The door Sam had led her through when he'd shown her the shortcut stood slightly ajar. A beam of light drew her forward.

She pushed the wooden door open and stopped.

A group of men stood in a dense, bunched circle, the stench of alcohol thick in the sweaty air. Then a thud, an exhaled breath, and the crowd stepped back to reveal a man spreadeagled on the canvas mat and another, clenched hand raised above his head, acknowledging the roars of the crowd.

She stepped closer and picked out Sam's mop of dark hair across the other side of the ring. She waved.

Her movement must have attracted him because he lifted his head, his eyes locking with hers, and a moment later he stood beside her. "I thought you'd gone to bed."

"I did but I couldn't sleep. What's going on?"

"I told you. There's a bit of a boxing club."

The waft of alcohol lingered. "I thought the bar closed at six."

"It does. Come along. This is no place for a lady."

No place for a lady. Next he'd be offering her smelling salts. "Sam, listen to me. We must go first thing tomorrow morning to the police and tell them about Ella."

He let out a tiresome sigh. "Let it rest, will you? Go to bed."

"Ted and Artie are over there. Let me go and ask them what they think. I want to hear Artie's story again."

"Not now, PJ. Go and get some sleep. I'll speak to Ted and Artie. We need to find out who owns the place. It's not going to look good if we were there without permission. Go on, off you go." He dropped a kiss on her cheek and turned back to the tightly packed group around the canvas.

Resisting the temptation to barge through the crowd and follow him, she paused. Nothing she could do tonight. It wouldn't be a bad idea if Sam did try to find out who owned the property. Chances were, he'd do better without her.

PJ woke with the sun, turned over, shot out of bed, and tiptoed along the veranda in her pajamas, hugging the wall. The open curtains and Sam's undisturbed bedcover proved he hadn't slept the night there, but at the end of the bed was a piece of paper. She picked it up.

Got a plan. Back in a day or two. Look after Sid. Love you.

Back in a day or two? What was he thinking? What about Ella? Where had he gone? She flopped down onto the bed and studied the room. His haversack rested limp and discarded in the corner, the contents scattered. He couldn't have intended to go far without his papers. She rummaged through the contents. No papers and no money belt. He hadn't taken a walk down the road. He'd gone farther afield. What did he expect her to do? Sit twiddling her thumbs until he returned *in a day or two*?

She stormed back into her room, threw on her clothes, and clattered down the stairs. There were times when Sam's impulsiveness infuriated her. This was one of them, especially after sending her off to bed last night while he cavorted around with a bunch of larrikins betting on boxing matches and drinking sly grog. No, she couldn't accuse him of that. He wouldn't be lying in the gutter having drunk too much. One or two beers were his limit; she'd rarely seen him drink more—the odd brandy, perhaps—and he never smoked. Coffee was his vice, and there was nowhere in Kurri that served the kind of coffee Sam liked.

Damn him. Well, she wasn't going to hang around for *a day or two* waiting until he'd sorted out his plan. What if he'd gone to try and find the owners of the property? What if they knew the skeleton was there? Had in some way been involved? Ella deserved a decent resting place. There was only one thing to do. She would go and talk to the police. Besides, Pa would ask what they'd done when they got back to Wollombi, and the last thing she wanted was another reason to argue with him.

She had no idea where the police station was, but it wouldn't take long to find, judging by the neatly laid-out streets. She'd put money on it being near the telegraph office, just as it was in Wollombi. When she rounded the corner behind the hotel, she found two boys sitting in the gutter tossing rocks at a pile of tin cans stacked against the tractor shed and, more importantly, Sid parked just where she'd left him.

The boys jumped to their feet, hopeful grins on their grubby faces.

"Morning, boys." She slipped her hand into her pocket, searching for a sixpence. It came out empty. "Have you seen Sam, Captain Groves?"

They shook their heads in unison and scuffed their feet.

Tricky. She didn't want to tell the world that he'd upped and disappeared, but maybe these two boys could find out. "If you see him, tell him he owes you sixpence for looking after Sid. I'm afraid I haven't got any money on me. And that I'll be back here this afternoon."

"Right you are, miss." They nodded at each other and took off like rockets around the corner.

Pleased with her plan, she lifted the hood and checked the water, oil, and spark plugs. It was a job that had to be done daily during the war, but Sam had seen to it when they were in Wollombi and they hadn't covered enough miles to warrant a full check. Finding everything satisfactory, she cranked the engine, then slipped behind the wheel. The boys would track Sam down long before she did, and by then she would have reported Ella's skeleton to the police.

Ten minutes later she pulled up in front of a small weatherboard building proclaiming itself to be the police station. She scraped back her hair, rammed her hat onto her head, and marched up the flagged path. It wasn't until she was halfway to the door that she stopped. What was she going to say? That she wanted to report a murder? That she'd found a skeleton while exploring Bow Wow Gorge? Perhaps Sam was right. She stood biting her lip, looking up and down the street. He was an indescribable nuisance. Why couldn't he have come with her, or at least told her what he planned? Wherever had he gone? Before she could change her mind, she strode up the rest of the path.

The door squeaked open. "Morning, miss. Anything I can do for you? Seen you standing here looking uncertain."

She smiled, the decision made for her. She could hardly ignore the young man and walk away. "I wondered if I could have a word with someone in authority."

"No worries. Come inside." He stood back from the doorway. "Nice vehicle you've got there. Could do with a bit of work, though. My uncle's a carriage maker by trade—he might be able to give you a hand, if you've got a problem, that is."

"No, no problem with Sid."

He frowned.

"Sid Wolseley. That's what we call the motor."

The young policeman scratched his head and she realized it was probably better not to go into the details at that moment.

He showed her into a small front office. "Sit down. Can I get you anything? A cuppa?"

"No, thank you. I wanted to speak to the sergeant-in-charge."

"That'd be me. Sergeant Wallis." He sat down opposite her, his boyish grin making the color rise in her cheeks. He didn't look old enough to be out of short pants.

In for a penny . . . PJ dragged in a deep breath. "My name is Penelope Jane Martindale. My"—why complicate things—"my friend Sam and I have found a body."

"I see." He sat up a little straighter. "A body, you say."

"Not exactly a body. A skeleton."

His mouth dropped open. "Right. And where did you find this . . ."—he cleared his throat—"skeleton?"

"A human skeleton."

He rocked back in his chair, drummed his fingers on the armrest. He didn't believe her. She could see that. She shoved her hand deep into her pocket, closed her fingers around the vertebra, wishing she hadn't left the finger bones at home. It was too late now to change her mind. If she got up and left, he'd think, as Sam suggested, she was deranged. And she could hardly say she'd wait until Sam got back from wherever he was. She hadn't thought this through. She plonked the vertebra down on the table. "At Bow Wow Gorge. I think this is part of it."

"Bow Wow Gorge." He poked at the vertebra with his index finger, nudging it across the table, as though loath to touch it. "What makes you think it's human? It could be a roo or some other animal."

"My father, Dr. Martindale, was in no doubt when I showed it to him. Sam and I went back for another look, to see what else we could find, and discovered the skeleton in a cave underneath an overhang." She clamped her lips tight, mindful of Sam's reaction when she mentioned Ella. That could wait.

"Could I ask what you were doing down at the gorge, Miss Martindale? It's private property."

For goodness' sake—no one paid any attention to things like that. People continually used the path through the back of the garden in Wollombi as a shortcut. "Do you know who owns the property?"

He cleared his throat. "The land is leased, has been for years."

That seemed to be all anyone could tell her. "I was wondering about the house. It's all locked up."

"Had a good look around, did you?"

She squirmed in her seat, a flush of guilt tainting her cheeks. Why hadn't she listened to Sam? They'd done nothing wrong. Not really. Hadn't hidden what they were doing, even asked for directions. "We asked the way. The publican told us and we went and had a look. I saw a fossil found at Bow Wow by an Anthea Winstanley in the museum in London and my curiosity was aroused. My brothers . . ."—no, don't bring Dan and Riley into this; it would just make the whole thing seem even more far-fetched—"my brothers and I are interested in fossils."

"Ah." The word whistled out between his teeth. "Anthea Winstanley. I see. And I suppose you heard the local rumblings. Mad woman and her fossil-hunting parties. Young girls disappearing . . ."

"Anthea Winstanley didn't disappear. At least I don't believe she disappeared. She's buried in England at a place called Lyme Regis."

"And how do you know that?"

"I've seen her grave." Not strictly true, but she had no reason to doubt Mr. Woods.

"I dare say there's more than one Anthea Winstanley in the world."

Suddenly her temper flared. "Highly unlikely that there should be two Anthea Winstanleys who were interested in fossils and had connections with Bow Wow Gorge."

The sergeant let out a long, slow breath and pushed himself to his feet. "Let me see if I've got this right. The skeleton you found in Bow Wow Gorge cannot be Anthea Winstanley, but you believe it's human."

"Not only that, I believe I know who it is." She slapped her palms down on the desk and rose, looking the foolish little upstart in the eye. "Her name is Ella Ketteringham, and she visited the gorge several times in the 1840s."

"And I suppose you're one of those spiritualist people and you're going to tell me this Ella Ketteringham has come back and asked you to free her."

What poppycock. "No. I'm not a spiritualist."

"I'll tell you what, Miss . . ."—he looked down at the piece of paper where he'd originally made a few notes, before he'd decided she was some sort of crazed medium—"Martindale, why don't I take you down to the hospital."

"Hospital? I don't need to go to the hospital."

He raised his palm. "To make an appointment for you to meet Mavis Elliot to discuss what you've found at the gorge. She's the local doctor and acts as pathologist if we have any need. She might be able to shed some light on this skeleton of yours. And I'd like a word with your friend. Get him to call in as soon as he can."

PJ cruised to a halt outside the hotel and unpeeled her fingers from the steering wheel, still smarting over the sergeant's attitude. Although he must have believed part of her story, otherwise why else would he have suggested the pathologist?

The driver's door swung open and the two larrikins grinned at her. "We couldn't find Sam, but Artie's over there. He might know where he is." One of them hitched his thumb toward a wooden seat in the park opposite the pub where Artie sat under a large tree, throwing crumbs from a brown paper bag to a chattering group of noisy miner birds.

The very person. She walked over and sat down next to him. "Hello, Artie. I thought you'd be at work."

He threw the last handful at the birds, screwed up the bag, and put it in his pocket. "Half day, Saturday. Wages are all done. I've got to pick up a few bits and pieces for Mum."

"Can you spare me a moment? I called in to the police station."

His head came up with a jerk and he turned to face her. "The police station? Everything all right? The boys said you were looking for Sam. I haven't seen him."

"It's not about Sam. Well, not really. He had a couple of things to do. It's about the gorge. Sam and I went down there."

Unless she was very much mistaken, a shiver crossed Artie's shoulders.

"To the gorge?" His clear-eyed gaze roamed her face.

"I'd rather you kept this to yourself. We found a skeleton."

"A skeleton? One of the girls?"

The first person not to jump to the conclusion it was Anthea Winstanley. "What makes you say that?"

He shrugged and chewed on his lower lip. After a moment or two he mumbled, "I talked to Mum, about Gran."

PJ sat for a moment, casting her mind back to the first time she'd spoken to Artie. She remembered him saying his gran used to talk about strange noises in the gorge and made mention of a bunyip.

"She worked up there."

The silence hung, broken only by the repetitive *pwee, pwee, pwee* of the noisy miners.

"At Bow Wow House?" PJ asked.

"She was the maid-of-all-work when Mr. Benjamin was alive. After he died, Mrs. Winstanley let all the staff go except for a couple of ex-convicts."

Maybe that was where the rumors began. A young girl upset because she'd lost her job. "Artie, why did you think the skeleton would be one of the girls? Why not Mrs. Winstanley?" He couldn't possibly know she was buried in Lyme.

Just like the first time they'd spoken about Anthea, Artie's face turned beetroot red and his Adam's apple bobbed. "Gran said Mrs. Winstanley changed after Mr. Benjamin died. No more Easter parties, just a few girls, and then all of a sudden she upped and left. Gran reckoned something bad happened down there to the girl."

PJ dropped her head into her hands. Artie hadn't solved any problems; he'd just made matters worse. "Can I talk to your gran?"

Artie shook his head. "Nah. She died in the flu epidemic, not long after I got home. Never got over losing Dad, but she got me back together before she went. Made me look ahead, stopped me feeling sorry for myself, and sorted out the job for me. Told the mine they owed me. That's why I got the job in the office. I miss her." He scuffed his hand over his eyes. "The birds have gone. Time I got moving."

Every family was broken in some way by the war, not only those from countries in the front line; even here, thousands of miles from the fighting, people were hurt, left to pick up the pieces of their shattered lives. "I'm sorry, Artie. You must have been very fond of her."

CHAPTER 21

1847
Bow Wow

"Come on, love. Give us a hand. Can't let these sweet young things get their Sunday best dirty." Jordan spat on his hands and hefted the end of the specimen crate.

Not to be outdone, Mellie wiped her hands down her breeches and grabbed the rope handle at the other end. Already seated, Lydia and Ella glared at each other from opposite sides of the carriage while Bea and Grace chased each other around, spooking the poor horse. Mellie could hardly wait to see the back of them. She'd lain awake half the night trying to come up with a way of searching for the sea-saurians. As the sun rose, she landed on the perfect plan, but it would require some equipment from Jordan. She wanted to ask him before he left. She planned to divide the area into squares and track backward and forward until she'd searched every inch. And she'd start just as soon as the girls left. If Nette and Jordan were going to spend time in Wollombi, it would just be her and Aunt Anthea. She couldn't wait.

"Bea, where are you going?" Grace hovered, half in, half out of the carriage, as though she couldn't make up her mind about anything without Bea's say-so.

"I've left something in the workroom. I won't be a minute." Bea smirked and took off down the path.

The back of Mellie's neck itched. No matter how hard she tried, and she had tried mightily since she'd known she wouldn't have to put up with Bea after today, she didn't trust her. Not one inch. She craned her neck, trying to see past Jordan's bulk, and caught sight of Bea disappearing around the house.

"Hey, stop fidgeting or we'll drop this." Jordan wrangled his end of the specimen crate onto the back of the carriage. "Heave ho."

Mellie sucked in a great breath, flexed her muscles, and gave one last shove, and the crate slipped into the space next to Ella's trunk as neatly as a jigsaw piece.

"There we go. Now all I've got to do is round up the rest of them and we'll be off."

Mellie dusted off her hands. "Jordan, have you got any rope I can use?"

"What do you want rope for?" Jordan grabbed Grace's wrist as she tried to slip past him. "You, get in."

"I've got to go and get Bea."

"Oh no you haven't, Grace. Mellie will do that. I'm not losing you too."

"Can I use the rope in the stable?" Receiving a nod from Jordan, Mellie took off around the back of the house and arrived outside the kitchen, just in time to see Bea glancing over her shoulder before slipping into the workroom.

Mellie crossed to the path and crouched beneath the lemon tree.

Seconds later Bea pranced around the corner. "Mellie." Her face turned the color of stewed rhubarb. "You made me jump."

"Everybody's waiting for you. What were you doing in there?"

"None of your beeswax, Bawk-bawk." And with that she hitched up her skirt and took off squawking.

Mellie spun around, checked the door on the workroom, fastened it just as Aunt Anthea liked, then galloped after Bea. She got to the front of the house as Bea flopped down onto the seat opposite Grace in the carriage and leaned in to whisper in her ear.

"Goodbye, goodbye," Lydia called, her handkerchief fluttering high above her head.

Jordan flicked his switch and the carriage took off down the driveway, leaving Aunt Anthea waving madly and Mellie barely able to contain the mixture of relief and excitement blossoming in her chest.

"Can we go down to the gorge this afternoon? I can't wait to get started. Jordan said there's some rope in the stables that I can use to make my digging grid."

"Not today. We've got chores to do. With Nette away there's bread to bake and meals to prepare, never mind the mess in my workroom." Aunt Anthea sighed and slipped her arm around Mellie's shoulders, drew her close, and gave her a squeeze. "I'm pleased you're staying. I'd be lonely without you."

A warm wave of happiness spread from Mellie's toes to the very top of her head. "I can bake the bread, make some pies and soup. I did the cooking for Da and me, and the other men."

"Other men?"

"Pa's friends." The nice warm feeling drained from her body. She didn't want to think about them. Not now when she was feeling so happy.

Aunt Anthea threw her a sympathetic look and her lips twitched as though she was about to ask a question. She must have thought better of it and gave her another squeeze instead. "Come along, then. Let's go and see what's left in the kitchen and you can give me a cooking lesson."

Anthea stood back and surveyed the kitchen. Mellie hadn't exaggerated when she'd said she could cook. Two beautiful balls of dough stood proofing under a damp cloth and the aroma of chicken soup wafted through the kitchen. Mellie had relegated her to the role of kitchen hand and sent her off to the garden with instructions to dig up a variety of vegetables, which she had added to the soup. Then Mellie had whipped up some pastry and created two perfect little chicken pies and assured her that the soup would be ready for their evening meal. And now they had the afternoon free.

Mellie covered her mouth with her hand and let out a loud yawn. "I don't know why I'm tired. It must be because it's warm in the kitchen."

"And you've had a busy few days. Why don't we go down to my workroom? I have some letters to write and I want to record the finds we made. You might like to read some more about sea-dragons."

"I would, and I'd like to finish cleaning my dragon scale."

They ambled down the path, the lunchtime sun warm on their backs. Anthea threw open the shutters and the doors and stared despondently at the mess. Chunks of rock containing specimens the girls had rejected littered the bench tops and a fine dust covered everything. The girls' indiscriminate collecting always infuriated her, and she'd forgotten to oversee their tidying up, having been far too concerned about Mellie. Next year she would have to make sure she encouraged them to contain themselves to entire and identifiable specimens.

Mellie stood over the bench, pushing bits and pieces around and creating even more mess. "I can't find my dragon scale," she wailed, her poor face a picture of abject misery.

"We left it soaking, remember?"

Mellie turned, the empty metal basin clutched loosely in her hand. "It's gone."

"I doubt it very strongly. No one could find anything among this mess." She waved her hand around the room. "It'll turn up. And if it doesn't we'll find another. In all honesty, it wasn't a very good specimen. We can do much better than that. And then we'll send it down to get it polished like this one." Anthea ran her fingers around her neck searching for her chain, but her hand came away empty. "How very strange. I don't seem to have my pendant. I must have left it on my dresser."

"Shall I go and get it?"

She shook her head. "You settle down with your book and I'll attend to my paperwork. You deserve a rest after all your hard work in the kitchen. I can fetch it later."

Anthea pulled out her ledger and listed the dates of the girls' visit and the appearance of Victor Baldwin. She intended to write to Mitchell and find out exactly what Baldwin had said to him. The fact that he'd acted in such a peremptory fashion and, if Jordan was correct, and she had no reason to doubt him, attached his name to a section of her land made her blood boil. Mellie's reaction to the man wasn't as far-fetched as she'd first thought. His behavior had been quite odd and totally audacious. Nevertheless, it would give her the opportunity to contact Mitchell again. She wanted to inquire about the vertebra. Perhaps she was being impatient; it was highly unlikely he would have received confirmation from England yet, but if her latest discovery bore fruit she'd need his further opinion.

Sometime later she pushed back her chair and stretched. Considering the events of the last couple of days and the early morning, she felt quite invigorated. The prospect, no doubt, of the ridge of bumps she'd spotted during the storm waiting to be uncovered.

She glanced down at Mellie, opened her mouth to suggest they should, after all, go down to the gorge, and swallowed her words. The child lay fast asleep on the rag rug, the heavy book open on her chest. She tiptoed across the room and moved it. Mellie didn't stir, so she tucked a blanket around her and stood for a moment watching the slow, peaceful rise and fall of Mellie's chest. She couldn't wake her.

Curiosity about the ridge on the roof of the cave burned a hole in her mind. How long would it take her to pop down to the gorge and have a look? Mellie lay sleeping peacefully. Why disturb her? Picking up her nib she scrawled a note—*Gone down to the gorge to collect something.* (Hardly a lie.) *Stay here. I will be back soon. Anthea.*

Mellie felt safe in the workroom; she wouldn't come to any harm or be scared if she woke up. As she closed the ledger, the corner snagged; beneath it lay her pendant. How odd. She never took it off in the workroom. Still, no harm done. She slipped it over her head and placed the note on the floor next to Mellie, then picked up a lantern. If Mellie woke she'd see the note and know she hadn't deserted her. With a quiet smile at her own whimsy, she locked the door behind her and left.

Anthea loosened her hair, reveling in the warm breeze and the late-afternoon sun dancing in and out of the clouds. In the aftermath of the storm, every leaf and blade of grass glistened. Each step of the way was as familiar as the lines on her palm, leaving her plenty of opportunity to muse on the possibility of her find. In the poor light of the thunderstorm, she could have made a mistake. Unlikely. What were the chances of half a dozen similarly shaped, dark-colored rocks lying in a delicate curve? The rain may have loosened some more of the surrounding soil.

Her heart began to pitter-patter as the thrill of a discovery mounted. Many of her best finds in the gorge occurred after rain had flushed the surface. She hitched the hem of her skirt into her waistband, then ran the last hundred yards down the trail to the swollen creek bed. Before long the sun would drop behind the hills and there would be even less light than during the thunderstorm.

She picked her way across the creek, scrutinizing the entrance to the small cave, trying to pinpoint the exact spot. She offered a silent prayer to whatever god inhabited the ancient landscape that her eyes hadn't deceived her. Seventeen years she had waited for this moment—the image of Mary's drawings danced in front of her eyes. An ichthyosaur, maybe a plesiosaur? She'd take either, and so would Mellie. The thought of having someone to share her elation spurred her on and she jumped the last yard onto the sandy bank of the creek.

Her hands came down to steady her and her breath snatched. In the damp sand was the impression of footsteps.

A neat line leading away from the creek toward the cave. Too small for Jordan and his great, clumping sea-boots. Any prints belonging to the girls would have washed away in the storm, and besides, they were leading to the cave under the overhang, not away from it.

She lined up her boot against the print. Not much bigger than her own.

A spider-like crawl of anxiety inched its way down her spine.

Shadows danced against the wall. Mellie let her eyelids fall. Not morning, not yet. She snuggled farther down under the blanket and rolled onto her side, her hip bone grating hard against the floor.

Against the floor? Why wasn't she in her bed? She lurched upright. Where was she?

Throwing off the blanket, she sprang to her feet.

The workroom. The silhouette of the benches, the crates and specimens, the desk, but no Aunt Anthea. She ran for the door, tugged at the handle.

Locked tight.

Stretching on her tiptoes, she looked through the shutters. Out. She had to get out.

She dragged the chair across the floor, wedged it under the window, unlocked the shutters, and stuck her head outside. Not too big a drop. Hands outstretched, she wriggled her body through the opening. A bolt of pain shot up her arms as she hit the ground, twisted, and found her feet. Back pressed flat against the wall, she eased her way to the door, the sound of blood pounding in her ears adding to her frantic confusion.

Barred from the outside.

She reached to her waistband for the marlin spike. No. Not there. On the bench.

Mind racing, she sucked in a faltering breath, let it seep out between her lips.

Think. She had to think.

Aunt Anthea was gone. Had she locked her in the workroom? Why?

She lifted the crossbeam and slipped back inside. The outline of the marlin spike glistened on the bench. Her fingers closed around the cool metal and her heartbeat slowed.

Hawkins's book lay on the rug, next to the screwed-up blanket she'd tossed aside. The scene slipped back into her muddled head. Aunt Anthea at the desk, the pictures in the book—an ichthyosaur and a plesiosaur, necks entangled, muscles tensed, the gray of the sky and the slippery sheen of the water.

She edged around the rug. Had she been dreaming?

Next to the open book a piece of paper glinted in the fading light. Squiggly scribbles blurred across the page. Tilting the paper toward the window, she squinted at the scrawl. Only one word made any sense—*Anthea*.

What was Aunt Anthea telling her? Her mind raced as she stared at the writing. Aunt Anthea's name, but what else did it say? Letter by letter she sounded out the words: *G-on d-ow-n to the . . . G-or . . .* Gorge. She'd gone to the gorge and left her alone, asleep. And locked her inside the workroom.

Why?

Two seconds later she was back outside, the marlin spike tucked into the waistband of her breeches and the note a crumpled mess in her balled fist. Why would Aunt Anthea go to the gorge so late in the day?

The shortcut beckoned, then sense took hold. Not in the twilight. Climbing back up the track in the thunderstorm had been difficult enough. She took off, skirting the house, and thundered down the snig trail.

Time lost all meaning, nothing but the rhythmic thump in her chest echoing the beat of her thudding feet and her deafening pulse until she ground to a halt overlooking the gorge. Dappled shadows swirled and the leaves rustled with each eddying gust. And no other sound but the rushing water. Not even the cry of a bird.

Creeping along the snig trail, with the marlin spike clasped tight in her fist, she searched for any movement, any sign of Aunt Anthea. Where was she? She'd said time and time again that the gorge was no place to be once darkness fell.

A cold breath of wind touched the back of her neck as her eyes adjusted to the gloom. Above the tree line, the clouds swelled and curled against the deepening darkness. She stopped, snatched a rasping breath, and moved forward again, step by step, afraid she would lose the track.

Below her the creek snaked between the cliffs. Crouching low, she peered over the edge. No sign of Aunt Anthea, but a glow of light under the overhang and the sound of stones slipping and then settling in the creek.

"Aunt Anthea." Mellie's voice echoed, hollow and distant, from the towering sandstone walls.

A movement caught her eye. A shadow drifting along the creek. She wormed her way closer to the edge, her cheek pressed into the damp earth.

A hunched silhouette, long arms dangling, the *slap, slap* of its steps sending waves of water up the bank.

The rattle of dislodged rocks became louder as the shadow inched toward the light.

The murmur of a voice—not one, two voices. One low and growling, the other high-pitched.

Throwing caution aside, she scrambled down the bank and leaped from boulder to boulder across the creek.

A mournful cow-like sound reverberated, then another bellow.

Teeth clenched, she inched closer.

A dark body crouching in the lea of the overhang detached itself. Its shadow swelled and darkened, rearing up the wall, and hung, waiting, towering over the once tranquil spot.

"Aunt Anthea."

The bellow came again and the insistent wheeze of labored snorts, twisting her insides into a rock-hard knot. The bunyip turned, paused, head tilted, then moved on, its shadow looming large before it vanished into the cave with another husky gasp. The frail spot of light flickered and died.

She tightened her sweat-slicked grip on the marlin spike. Bending low, she ducked under the curtain of dripping ferns.

An arm snaked around her neck; a stinking, leathery hand clamped over her mouth and threw her back against the rock wall. Unable to pull enough air into her lungs to shout a warning, desperation lent her strength and she lurched sideways, raising the marlin spike high—twisting, turning, trying to break free. Its grip faltered; the stranglehold lessened. She tasted a moment of freedom until the splayed claws reclaimed her in a grotesque embrace, sending her marlin spike skittering across the ground.

Tears burned her eyes, distorting her sight. Shimmering shadows danced. Icy horror numbed her. She struggled upright. The hold on her throat slackened. Sucking in a breath, she kicked out. Her booted foot found home.

In a violent tangle of limbs, growled curses, and an outraged howl, the bunyip toppled backward.

Her head slammed against the rock wall.

Pain exploded, her vision blurred, then doubled. The bunyip's bellow filled every crevice of her mind. Darkness descended.

CHAPTER 22

⸻ ◈ ⸻

1919
Bow Wow

PJ arrived at the gorge as arranged by the sergeant to find a serious-looking woman leaning against the rock wall, a dark-blue cotton coat covering her clothes, sleeves rolled to the elbows. She might have been in her late thirties, maybe older; her hair was tied back in a messy knot, the escaping strands framing her face.

She stuck out her hand. "Mavis Elliot. I'm sorry I wasn't available yesterday."

PJ took her cool hand, felt the firm grip. "Penelope Jane Martindale. Everyone calls me PJ."

"The doctor's daughter. Back at last from Europe, then."

PJ shot her a perplexed glance.

"He mentioned you, often." Dr. Elliot answered her unasked question. "We closed the isolation hospital at the beginning of the month and the children are all back in school now."

No wonder Pa looked drained. Too tied up in her own problems, she hadn't thought to ask about the details of the flu epidemic. No wonder he was angry with her.

"We arrived back in Australia earlier than expected. We didn't have to do any time in quarantine. They just handed out masks and told us to wear them in Sydney." A wave of guilt rocked her. "They're not necessary here, are they?"

"No. It seems we've pulled through. The advantage of being outside the big population areas. You said *we* arrived?"

"Samuel Groves. We both drove ambulances at the front. We came back together. We—" She clamped her lips—she'd almost told this woman of Sam's proposal. She could hardly do that before he'd spoken to Pa.

"I heard your brothers didn't make it. I'm sorry."

No nonsense about this woman, just facts. And she obviously knew Pa better than she'd imagined if he'd spoken of the boys. A shudder traced her shoulders. She couldn't imagine working as a pathologist. Bad enough transporting the wounded, never mind attending to the deceased. She took a breath, pushed down the sudden flash of memories.

When she turned, Dr. Elliot stood, a heavy torch held high, head cocked to one side surveying the cave.

"You have to keep your head down; it opens up once you're inside. I'll show you." PJ ducked down, shoulders hunched, and shuffled forward until the air became fresher, then she straightened up. "You can stand now."

Light flooded the cave. Dr. Elliot held the torch upright and stepped toward the rock shelf. "Can you hold this for me?"

PJ took the torch and directed the pool of yellow light onto Ella's skeleton.

Dr. Elliot let out a breath of surprise and stepped closer, poking the loose dirt with an implement that resembled a large scalpel, then pulled a brush from the pocket of her coat and began gently clearing the area around the bones. "Good job you didn't interfere any further. You're quite right. It's a human skeleton."

"How long do you think it's been here?"

"Difficult to tell."

"Maybe the bunyip got her."

Both PJ and Dr. Elliot jumped as the gravelly tones of the sergeant filled the small space.

"What a load of rubbish." Dr. Elliot recovered first. "I would have expected better of you, Sergeant Wallis."

"Lot of truth in those old tales." He frowned unhappily. "Some say they take only females. No interest in men."

PJ bristled. "You'd think the cave would be littered with bodies, then." Whatever was she saying? Maybe it was. A sudden whisper of air lifted the strands of hair on the back of her neck.

"One step at a time. If you'd go back outside, Sergeant Wallis, and give me some room. I'm going to try and keep the skeleton as intact as possible while I uncover it." Dr. Elliot bent to her work and Wallis retreated.

Gradually the entire skeleton became visible. The bones seemed slender and fragile, the legs slightly bowed and the teeth intact.

PJ crawled closer and sank to her knees. "It's almost as if she's sleeping."

"She? What makes you say that?"

PJ rocked back on her heels, unwilling to voice her conclusions. "It's not terribly big and it's curled up as a girl would sleep." She crawled closer again, her initial horror abating. "What's that?" She pointed to a tarnished chain that lay among the collapsed pile of ribs. She reached out.

"Don't touch it." Mavis leaned forward and hooked up the chain with the scalpel. "A piece of jewelry, by the looks of it." A butterfly-shaped pendant dangled from a silver bail.

PJ's heartbeat grew, loud enough to drown out the doctor's words—the sight of the collapsed ribs and the hollow spaces suddenly brought to life by a piece of jewelry. "Whatever happened to the poor girl? It's so sad. No gravestone, nothing to mark the spot, hidden forever, forgotten. I don't understand how I managed to find one vertebra. It was a chance in a million."

"I'm surprised the skeleton is as intact as it is." Dr. Elliot dusted off more of the soil and debris. "I suspect insects, meat ants more than likely, stripped the flesh fairly quickly. Then perhaps other scavengers, but once there was no flesh left they would have lost interest. Where did you say you found the original vertebra?"

PJ dragged her gaze away from the poor girl and with a long, drawn-out sigh indicated over her shoulder. "Outside. I'll show you."

Dr. Elliot took the torch and flicked it off and they ducked out of the cave into the bright sunshine.

"Next to that rock. Sam nudged me and I slipped. I put out my hand to save myself."

"What an amazing coincidence." She fixed PJ with a steely stare. "Why didn't you dig further? Surely your curiosity . . ."

"We did. All around here. We thought perhaps an animal, a bird, had dropped it." Her cheeks flushed. This brittle, efficient, knowledgeable woman would laugh if she told the truth. She sucked in a breath. Why lie? She had nothing to hide. "Originally I thought I'd found something prehistoric. Pa put me straight."

"Prehistoric?"

"Yes. A fossil. In London I was shown a vertebra that was thought to belong to an ichthyosaur. It was found here at Bow Wow in the middle of the last century. I had high hopes . . ." The more she said, the more foolish she sounded. "I took the vertebra we found home and showed it to my father. He wasn't in any doubt it was human."

Dr. Elliot let out a huge laugh. "I wouldn't have pegged you for a treasure hunter."

"I'm not. Well, not usually. It's a long story."

"I hope you have time to tell me one day. It sounds fascinating. It'll take me some time to extricate the bones, then I need to get them back to the hospital for examination."

"I'd like to help."

"That's not possible. No matter how old this skeleton is, it's a police investigation."

Her cheeks heated as the woman's gaze slid over her, then she smiled, her mouth wide. "Come to the hospital tomorrow around eleven and I should have something for you then."

PJ arrived at the hospital long before the appointed hour. She wandered around until she found the main entrance and approached the woman sitting at the desk. "Good morning. I have an appointment with Dr. Elliot."

"I'm not sure she's in yet. What time was your appointment?"

PJ looked up at the clock behind the woman. "First thing this morning," she said with what she hoped was a winning smile.

"Down the stairs over there. Turn to your right and you'll see the sign on the door."

"Thank you." PJ turned and scooted off. The odor of antiseptic and chloroform turned her stomach, a smell she'd hoped she'd never inhale again. By the time she reached the bottom of the stairs with her handkerchief held tight to her nose, she didn't dare take a deep breath. The last thing she wanted was to lose the contents of her stomach in the middle of the hospital.

Once she rounded the corner, she found the sign and knocked on the glass-paneled door.

"Come in." Dr. Elliot stood with her backside against the desk and her legs stretched out in front of her, surveying the cleaned, reassembled skeleton lying on the slab. "You're early. I haven't written up my report."

"Eager. My curiosity is killing me."

Beside the skeleton was a collection of bone fragments and the chain and pendant.

"Do you think it's one of the girls who came fossil hunting with Anthea Winstanley?"

"What makes you say that? Why one of the girls? Why not Mrs. Winstanley?"

PJ ran her tongue over her lips, felt the heat rise to her face. "It can't be Anthea Winstanley. She's buried in England. She died in 1870."

"Interesting. How do you know that? The local hearsay is she disappeared, but nothing more."

PJ lifted her shoulders. "I've seen her grave and have firsthand information that she was a paleontologist of some renown who spent time in Australia and then returned to England."

Dr. Elliot studied her, a slight grin tipping her lips. "Then we can probably cross her off the list."

"Have you got another theory?"

"Possibly. I'm interested in the legs." Dr. Elliot ran her hand over the leg bones. "See the curvature? I'd hazard a guess that our mystery person suffered from rickets."

"Rickets?"

"A common complaint in England—it's not seen very frequently in Australia. Mostly during the Victorian era among children in cities like London because of the smog and lack of exposure to sunlight."

"So this"—PJ waved her hand over the bones—"person was English?"

"Not necessarily, but unlikely they were born in Australia. It's not a common complaint here. Now look closely at the teeth."

The last thing PJ wanted to do. She craned over the table and followed Dr. Elliot's finger as it bumped along the ridge of teeth. "In very poor condition, weak tooth enamel and several cavities. And these teeth here, the third molars. They're the last to erupt. Can be as early as twelve to thirteen, but I'm leaning toward an adult."

"So it couldn't be a young girl?"

"Why are you set on a young girl?"

PJ let out a long huff; she didn't want to appear foolish, but she had to clear it up. "You know the local rumors." She bit her lips together. "I believe that two of the fossil-hunting girls used to live in our house in Wollombi, Lydia and Bea Pearson. They both died in 1847, around the same time Anthea Winstanley disappeared. They're buried in the Wollombi cemetery but there were two other girls, Grace and Ella Ketteringham, who also visited the gorge with them and I don't know what happened to them. Based on the size of the skeleton I came to the conclusion it was the older of the Ketteringham girls."

"How do you know their names?"

"My brothers found a fossil collection in our attic and their names were on some of the labels."

"And I presume this is the long story you mentioned yesterday."

PJ nodded, feeling more and more foolish as each second ticked by, waiting for Dr. Elliot to debunk her theory.

"Let's worry about that in a moment. Let me tell you what else I know about our skeleton."

"Can you tell for certain that it is female?"

"Unfortunately, no. The pelvic bone is shattered and sections are missing."

"I'm sorry, I don't understand."

"The pelvis is the most accurate way of determining whether we are looking at a male or female skeleton. In a female the pelvic bone is open and circular. Women are built for child bearing—broader hips, more outwardly flared, unless it's a very young child, which you've quite rightly discounted because of height. The differences appear at puberty."

"And in a male?"

"The pelvic bone would be narrower and heart-shaped. I suspect the scavengers who dislodged the vertebra you found have been at work here too." Dr. Elliot waved her palm over the hip area. "I'm out of my depth. I'm going to refer the matter to Mr. Brown, the district coroner. The pathologist in Newcastle has an interest in forensic science. I expect Mr. Brown will see what he has to say."

"Can I pick this up?" PJ's fingers reached for the pendant.

"Yes, go ahead. It's quite interesting. A complicated setting." She dropped the pendant into PJ's outstretched hand.

"It's a fossil, a lamp shell." She picked up the chain. The butterfly-shaped fossil dangling from an intricate silver bail spun slowly. "I think it's something a woman would wear."

"We can't presume the victim was wearing it. It could have fallen onto the body."

"So the person wearing it might have . . ." She swallowed the remainder of her words; she couldn't jump to conclusions, be swayed by Artie's half-told stories.

"The death could be from natural causes, though that doesn't seem to fit. Despite the scavengers, the position of the skeleton indicates the body was deliberately placed."

Sam's theory bit the dust. PJ dangled the pendant. The polished lamp shell caught the rays of sun slanting through the high window. "So the person wearing this was somehow involved?"

"Possible. Simple conjecture, really. Nothing I can prove. The chain appears to be broken."

"How do you think she died?" Her previous distaste forgotten, PJ brushed her fingers gently over the brow bone.

Dr. Elliot pointed to the ribs on the left-hand side of the skeleton. "I suspect this rib was fractured when a blade went into the heart. Most likely from behind."

"Stabbed?"

"The edges of the break aren't as I would expect. A sharp implement, but not a knife. It's the most likely cause of death. I'll wait for Mr. Brown to confirm."

"Gossip aside, I can't fathom how Anthea Winstanley and a group of young girls would be involved."

Dr. Elliot shot her a look of disdain.

"It's more of that long story . . ."

"Perhaps one you'd better tell me." Dr. Elliot removed her white coat. "It's about time we had a break. I must call in on a patient, a friend, not far from where I live. She might have something to add to the local stories."

"What will happen to the skeleton?"

"I'll have to write up a report for the coroner and ask his opinion. I'd appreciate it if you would keep my revelations to yourself. If the identity is not found or if there are no descendants to pay for a funeral, then the bones will probably lie in a cardboard box in an archive somewhere."

"They won't bury them?"

"Highly unlikely. You might have stumbled on a Victorian murder mystery."

CHAPTER 23

"And so Sam and I came to Australia together." PJ had no idea what had made her go into such detail about the way she and Sam had met, but it was too late to take it back now and Dr. Elliot had seemed interested. "He was humoring me. I'd seen an Australian fossil from Bow Wow in the Natural History Museum in London. My brothers fancied themselves as fossil hunters, and when I saw the name Bow Wow, I remembered it from their collection. I had dreams of finding an Australian dinosaur and having it named for them." Certainly not an unidentified skeleton.

"Not much farther now." Dr. Elliot hitched her bag a little higher on her shoulder as they left the neat rows of miners' cottages and turned onto a track that wound up the hill. "Miss Baldwin's getting on a bit. She's still hale and hearty, with an enthusiasm for life I sometimes envy. She had an accident a few years ago so I make a habit of calling on her regularly. She lives alone now. She used to have a woman who came in three or four times a week, did some cooking and cleaning, but they had a falling out and Miss Baldwin refused to employ anyone else. So now we all keep an eye on her, call in and do a bit of work for her: tend the vegetable garden, make sure she's got wood chopped in winter, and drop off supplies to save her going into town. Otherwise, she insists on driving her old dogcart—she's a bit of a liability now there are so many motorcars."

"I could have driven us here. I'm sorry, I didn't think."

"The fresh air and exercise are good for me. I spend too much time indoors."

The track doubled back on itself and the scrubby bushland cleared, revealing a squat house sitting proudly between two massive fig trees.

Dr. Elliot bounded up the steps, knocked on the door, and went straight in. "Miss Baldwin. It's Mavis Elliot."

PJ waited, not quite sure whether to follow or not.

"I've brought someone to meet you." A door banged, then the low murmur of voices. "Come in, PJ," Dr. Elliot called. "Down the hallway to the end. We're on the back veranda."

PJ's boots squeaked on the polished floorboards as she walked past a ticking grandfather clock, a variety of chairs, and an occasional table tucked against walls hung with drawings and paintings in matching frames. Finally, the hallway widened and opened into a bright room overlooking a vast panorama of a large dam and the surrounding farmland.

"Miss Baldwin, I'd like to introduce you to Penelope Jane Martindale." Dr. Elliot spoke very loudly and beckoned PJ closer.

She stepped from the shadows and stood in front of the small woman sitting in a cane chair.

"Penelope has just come back from France."

"Hello, Miss Baldwin." PJ held out her hand and smiled into a bright pair of eyes, their lively interest belying the crosshatched wrinkles covering her face.

"A visitor. How lovely. I'll put the kettle on." She bounced to her feet, her fashionable dropped-waist silk dress rustling, and disappeared inside.

"Let me help . . ."

"She won't hear you. She's very deaf, lip-reads most of the time. Just make sure she can see your face."

"Oh, how awful."

"Not really. She's perfectly fine otherwise. And sufficiently vain to refuse to use any kind of hearing device."

"Should I go and see if I can help?"

Dr. Elliot shook her head. "No. It's a waste of time. She won't let you. She spent years traveling the Continent and insists on brewing *proper* coffee, as she likes to call it. If we're lucky it'll come with biscotti." She stretched out her legs. "It's a wonderful view, isn't it?"

"Beautiful. There's not another house in sight and the dam is perfect. Is that a black swan I can see?"

"Yes. They have a huge nest in the shallow water. Last time I looked there was a clutch of eggs, a pale greenish-blue color. The male and the female take turns sitting on the nest."

"Just as it should be. When will the cygnets hatch?"

"Difficult to tell. They're highly aggressive defending their nest. They chase you off, beating their wings. Not for the fainthearted." Dr. Elliot gave a dramatic shudder.

"So you're fine with skeletons but not swans?"

"Skeletons don't beat you off."

The scent of coffee drifted from the kitchen. PJ inhaled the aroma. Sam would be in seventh heaven. "Sam loves coffee. He's always complaining that he can't get a decent cup anywhere, ever since we left France."

"And where is this mystery man?"

"I'm not sure."

Dr. Elliot's head whipped around, her green-eyed stare intimidating.

PJ swallowed the knot of embarrassment clogging her throat. She'd asked at the hotel last night, and the publican had shrugged and said he'd keep the room for another couple of nights. "He left a note saying he'd be back in a few days."

"And when was this?" Dr. Elliot shot back. "I thought he was with you when you found the skeleton."

"He was. We spent the night at the Kurri Hotel, and when I woke up he'd gone."

"Have you told the sergeant?"

"Not in so many words."

"Don't you think it's a little strange?"

PJ squirmed in the chair. "Not really strange, just Sam. He does that sort of thing. He's impetuous—once he gets an idea in his head he won't rest." Saved from saying any more by Miss Baldwin's timely return, PJ jumped to her feet. "Let me take the tray for you." Without waiting for a response, she placed it on the small table between the chairs. "Freshly brewed coffee. How wonderful."

"If you spent time on the Continent I'm sure you'll appreciate it. Coffee is not something Australians do well. Hopefully one day that might change." She poured out three tiny cups of rich espresso from a small metal coffee pot and handed one to each of them. "Biscotti? Quite authentic. I learned to make them in Tuscany."

PJ sipped at the coffee, searching for something to say. She hadn't given much thought to the reason for Sam's disappearance; she'd been too caught up waiting for Dr. Elliot's report. And besides, it wasn't the first time he'd taken off on a whim. It had happened more than once in France, all part of his impulsiveness, and he'd always had a perfectly plausible reason. "How long have you lived here, Miss Baldwin?"

"Oh, let me see. I arrived in Australia in the seventies and had the house built. Long before Kurri was a town, before any of the coal mines."

PJ slumped down in the chair. Miss Baldwin couldn't have known Anthea Winstanley. She masked her sigh with another sip of coffee.

"The view from here hasn't changed since I built the house."

How strange. No mention of a husband or children. Unusual for a woman to have a house built. "What made you settle in Australia?" That was rude. "I beg your pardon."

"No, no. A perfectly valid question. The country fascinates me, and I no longer had any ties in Europe. Were you born in Australia, my dear?"

"My father and mother settled in Wollombi after the African War."

Dr. Elliot put down her cup. "Penelope's father is the doctor in Wollombi. We worked together during the flu epidemic."

"Such a dreadful time. We lost so many friends. Poor Mavis was run off her feet. Still, it seems as though we've got on top of it." Miss Baldwin patted her lips with a fine lawn handkerchief and settled her cup back in the saucer. "Wollombi, you say. A pretty little town."

"I brought PJ along to meet you because she has some questions about this area in the early days. I thought maybe you could help her."

PJ washed the remains of her biscotti down. She was certain Miss Baldwin wouldn't be able to shine any light on Anthea Winstanley or the skeleton, not if she'd come to the area in the 1870s, but she could hardly stop the conversation now. She wasn't sure whether she should speak of the skeleton. Was there some sort of protocol that had to be followed—police procedure that prevented Dr. Elliot from talking about the case? She'd asked her not to discuss it. "I wondered if you knew anything of an Anthea Winstanley."

Miss Baldwin's forehead creased. "Winstanley, you say? The name sounds familiar. Does she live in the area?"

"I believe she might have, some time ago." PJ trapped her lip between her teeth. "She was a paleontologist."

"The study of life on earth as it existed many, many years ago. I remember the publication of Darwin's *The Origin of Species*. It caused such an uproar. The mere idea that God hadn't created the world in seven days. How times change." Miss Baldwin stood, as straight and upright as a woman half her age. "Right, my dears, I have matters to attend to. Thank you for checking up on me." She threw Dr. Elliot a wry smile. "I am, as you can see, perfectly fine. Call in again. Coffee is better shared."

PJ followed Dr. Elliot and Miss Baldwin down the long hallway, her eyes drawn to a dark and sinister etching of strange fighting beasts, entangled necks and tense muscles silhouetted against the gray of the sky and the slippery sheen of the water. She stepped closer to read the small plaque attached to the frame. *Duria Antiquior by Henry De la Beche. 1830.*

"Goodbye, my dear." Miss Baldwin's bony hand came down on her arm, breaking her contemplation. "Thank you again for visiting."

PJ dragged her stare from the fascinating picture. "Thank you for the coffee, Miss Baldwin. It was delightful."

"See you soon," Dr. Elliot called as they clattered down the steps. She came to a halt and turned back to the door as it closed, then she puckered her lips and sighed. "That was strange. She's usually much more talkative. I have trouble getting out of the place."

"Perhaps she didn't take too kindly to me being there. Interrupting your chat."

"I doubt that very strongly. Anyway, there doesn't seem to be much wrong with her. I only hope I'm as healthy as she is when I reach my eighties."

"Eighties. Goodness, she's very spry."

"And the blood pressure of a woman a third of her age, which is strange because she doesn't get very much exercise."

They walked along a little farther down the tree-lined driveway in silence, and then Dr. Elliot stopped. "Do you think you can find your own way back? I have a couple more calls to make, and I suspect you'd like to track down that fellow of yours. I won't mention anything to the police, but I do think it would be a good idea if he was on hand to answer any questions, should they ask."

Good heavens. Had she understood correctly? It hadn't occurred to her that either she or Sam would be in any sort of trouble. They could hardly be responsible for stumbling across a skeleton. "I'm sure I can, Dr. Elliot. Let me give you our telephone number. I'm on my way back to Wollombi."

"Mavis, call me Mavis, and I've already got your father's number." With a wave of her hand, Mavis turned down another driveway and left her on the outskirts of town.

PJ ambled back along the road, a vague sense of disappointment lurking. When Mavis had suggested talking to Miss Baldwin, she'd imagined finding out all about Anthea Winstanley. Not the local gossip, but at least a version of the truth.

Lost in her thoughts, she soon found herself outside the hotel. She propped her backside on Sid's hood and pulled Sam's note from her pocket with a huff of irritation. *Got a plan. Back in a day or two.* He'd done something similar once before. She'd helped one of the injured into the triage tent, left Sam with Sid checking the water, spark plugs, and oil, and when she'd returned he'd gone. One of the nurses had handed her a note with a smirk and a shrug. *Be back soon. Don't worry.* Turned out he'd heard about a couple more soldiers who'd had to wait at the dressing station because there wasn't room in the transports for them. And he didn't want them to spend another night on the front line. What he hadn't anticipated was destruction to the road—he'd had to take a huge detour and his return took over twenty-four hours.

What on earth could he be up to this time? And what did he expect her to do? Hang around in Kurri chewing her nails and waiting?

She had no intention of doing that, and if the police wanted to ask more questions, she certainly couldn't go poking around down at the gorge; it would look most suspicious. Besides, she didn't want to upset Pa anymore, especially not when he had thawed a little discussing the vertebra. The best thing would be to go back to Wollombi, bring Pa up-to-date, and hopefully spend some time with him.

Pushing the side door of the pub open, she slipped through and headed for the dining room. Surely an establishment this size would serve lunch. In her enthusiasm to get to the hospital she'd forgone breakfast, and Miss Baldwin's coffee and biscotti, delicious as it was, hadn't filled the gap.

"Hello." She stuck her head through the little window.

After a few moments a voice said, "What can I get you?"

"I was after some lunch. Is the dining room open?"

"Nope, don't serve lunch during the week. Only bar food."

Well, that wasn't much use to her since she wasn't allowed into the bar.

"Missus has made some pies. You can have one of those in the Ladies' Lounge if it takes your fancy."

"Thank you, that would be lovely. And a glass of ginger beer, please."

Obviously lunch in the pub was not something the ladies of Kurri had embraced because she had the small sitting room all to herself. She chose a table close to the window and sat, chin cupped in her hand, staring out.

It was time to go home. She'd leave a note for Sam at the bar.

CHAPTER 24

"Like a bit of company?" Sam's deep voice broke PJ's musing. "I was hoping I'd find you here—that I wouldn't have to beg a ride to Wollombi."

How could he swan in with a big cheesy grin on his face? He'd have to do better than that. "Where have you been?"

"What's for lunch?" Sam ignored her question and scrutinized the room as though expecting food to materialize.

"Meat pie. You have to order it from the bar."

He ambled off without another word. A little harsh perhaps. She'd missed him. But how could he behave as though he'd been by her side for the past two days? He'd left her to deal with the whole situation and then hadn't even asked how she'd managed.

"Here we go. Two meat pies and a ginger beer for you. Ale for me." He threw himself down opposite her.

"Are men allowed in the Ladies' Lounge?"

He lifted his shoulders, mouth full of steaming pie, eyes full of intensity. He had something to tell her and she was damned if she was going to ask.

"Don't you think it's a little unfair?"

He frowned. "What, no women in the bar? Least we haven't got the threat of Prohibition to deal with. I'm getting to like Australia."

"Why didn't you tell me where you were going?" The words flew out of her mouth, taking her intentions to appear disinterested with them.

"I didn't want to get your hopes up."

She blinked twice. Whatever was he talking about? "Where did you go?"

"Sydney."

"Sydney?" It was the last thing she'd imagined; she rather expected him to be off somewhere with Ted, immersed in something that involved boxing.

He swallowed a mouthful of pie and wiped his mouth. "Delicious. While you eat yours I'll tell you my news."

She blew on the pastry crust and took a bite. She had news, too, but she had no intention of sharing it until he told her what he'd done in Sydney. She chewed in stony silence while he drank his ale, until she could wait no longer. "I could have been accused of murder."

"Don't be ridiculous. It's a skeleton, a vintage skeleton. The murder, if there was a murder, happened before you were even a twinkle in your pa's eye. It's highly unlikely the perpetrator is alive."

Right at that very moment she wasn't remotely interested in the skeleton. She was much more interested in what he'd been up to. "Why did you go to Sydney?"

"Ted's idea. We jumped the milk train."

She had known all along Ted would be involved somehow. "Why take Ted?"

"He knows his way around."

"I know my way around Sydney. I lived at the Women's College before I left for London." Her voice caught. "And besides, I had to deal with the police." Damn, she hadn't meant to mention her visit to the police station just yet.

"So you went to see them. What happened?" His warm, reassuring hand grasped hers. Still annoyed and determined not to respond, she turned back to the window. "The doctor, Mavis Elliot, has examined the skeleton. She's going to get the coroner's opinion and the police want to speak to you."

He threaded his fingers through hers. "Why?"

"There has to be an inquiry."

"There's nothing to explain."

"They're interested in your whereabouts and want to know what we were doing down at the gorge. As you pointed out, we were trespassing." Not strictly true, but she still hadn't forgiven him for disappearing.

"But not anymore." He pulled a large bundle from his pocket and dangled a bunch of decorative brass keys in the air. "These are the reason I went down to Sydney—the keys to Bow Wow House."

PJ snapped her mouth shut. How on earth had he managed that?

"Ted and I went to the Land Titles Office. Just like the locals say, the property belongs to an A. Winstanley."

"Anthea?"

"Maybe."

"Unlikely it would be in a woman's name in those days, especially if she was married."

Sam nodded. "She could have inherited it on her husband's death. They wouldn't tell me any more but said they'd review their records."

"Did they know who inherited when she died?"

"The owner is still listed as A. Winstanley. Maybe they don't know she died."

"But that's ridiculous."

"Grinstead & Gilmour Solicitors in Elizabeth Street were marked as the contact so I called in to see them. They recommended that I should chat with the people at the University of Sydney's Department of Geology if I was interested in the fossils. The solicitors seemed to think they might have some knowledge of Bow Wow Gorge. Other than that, they weren't dreadfully forthcoming. The company has managed the property since the nineteenth century. And as everyone has said, the farmland is leased out. Only thing of interest they let drop was the fact a forty-acre lot was marked for possible sale sometime in the middle of last century. It included the gorge and part of the creek. The deeds were drawn up, but the sale was never finalized. And as we know, no one lives in the house."

"Someone has been there; maybe not in the house, but in the kitchen for certain. It hasn't stood empty for that long."

He jangled the keys. "And that's why I have these and a map of the property. I told them I was interested in making an offer."

"You did what?" How on earth could he be so brazen?

"Let's go and have another look. No trespassing this time."

PJ pushed her plate aside and stood. "First we have to go and see the police, let them know you're back."

"There's one other thing I haven't mentioned." She sank back down.

"I left Ted kicking his heels while I was talking to the solicitor the second time. He got bored and went to the Geological Society. I've got the name of a person he spoke to." He rummaged in his pockets and pulled out a handful of bits and pieces, then pounced on the stub of a tram ticket. "Here it is. Matthew Morane. They thought the name Winstanley sounded familiar, that she might have contributed to what he called 'their little magazine.'"

"A current contributor?"

"He seemed to think so, although he wasn't certain; said he'd investigate and I was to contact him the next time I was in Sydney. So that's that."

"I had another chat with Artie after I went to the police station. He told me his grandmother worked up at Bow Wow House. Anthea dismissed her after her husband died. I wondered if she might be responsible for the rumors—a case of sour grapes."

"Rumors have to start somewhere. Let's go and see what your sergeant has to say."

"Sergeant Wallis, please." PJ approached the counter.

"Good afternoon, sir." The constable looked straight through her to Sam. It was as though she hadn't spoken.

"We have an appointment." PJ inserted herself between the counter and Sam. "He asked me to call when I spoke to him yesterday."

"Would you have any idea what this is about, sir?"

PJ sucked in a breath and gritted her teeth. Funny how men in the trenches cared little about whether their ambulance driver was male or female, but back here in Australia she was invisible.

"Miss Martindale, thank you for coming along." Sergeant Wallis appeared through one of the back doors. "I take it this is Captain Groves." He held out his hand to Sam.

Unable to resist, she threw a patronizing smile at the constable behind the desk and turned her back on him.

"Come this way. I've a few questions I'd like to clear up." Wallis led them through into a small room down the corridor.

"As you know, the skeleton has been removed to the hospital. Dr. Elliot has concluded her assessment. And I'm sorry to say we are none the wiser. The matter will now be referred to the coroner." He turned to Sam. "I'd like to know what you were doing at the gorge."

Sam let out a sigh and rested his elbows on the table. "I'm interested in buying the property. Our visit was somewhat premature, but I've since contacted the owner and have permission to view both the house and the property." He brought out the bunch of keys.

Wallis rocked back in his chair. "The owner? No one has lived there for years."

"Is that information necessary for your inquiry? I've answered your questions. I can't believe that you think either Miss Martindale or I are in any way involved."

Blood rushed to the sergeant's face. "Absolutely not," he spluttered.

Sam rose to his feet. "I presume we're free to go."

"I'd think twice about buying Bow Wow. Are you aware of the local rumors?"

"Local rumors?" The corner of Sam's mouth twitched and he sat down with a *thump*, looking for all the world as if he had suffered some sort of a shock.

And then PJ understood. Sam wanted confirmation of Artie's story.

"Mostly gossip, of course. Nothing that can be proven, although this discovery does add to the claims. I would appreciate it if you could keep our discussion to yourselves." The sergeant scratched his head and shifted in the chair. "It doesn't do to stir up old rumors. However, under the circumstances . . ."

"Why don't you start at the beginning?" Suddenly the tables were turned and Sam was interviewing the sergeant. It was a side of him PJ had never seen. He'd made mention of his father wanting him to study law despite his interest in medicine, but this was the first time she'd seen his aptitude for it.

"The property was one of the first grants in the area, two thousand acres all up. Benjamin Winstanley brought his wife from England and built a house for her in the 1830s. They spent a lot of time poking around in the gorge. Sending fossils to various museums and collectors and hosting interested visitors."

Nothing new in any of that. "Until . . . ," Sam prompted.

"After Mr. Winstanley passed away, his wife became a little strange."

Sam shot her a look and the corner of his mouth quirked. It was beginning to sound remarkably similar to the story told by Artie's gran.

"Strange? What do you mean strange?"

"The nature of those visits changed." Wallis cleared his throat and looked down at his clasped hands, refusing to make eye contact. "Some say she lured young girls down there. Took them into that gorge. There was talk of unusual rites and unseemly behavior, that her husband's death had unhinged her, and that her personal tastes became strange, exotic even." He wiped his face with a large checkered handkerchief and stuffed it back in his pocket. "Then just like that. Poof." He snapped his fingers. "She vanished."

PJ opened her mouth to correct him, to tell him that Anthea had gone to England with her daughter, but a long stare from Sam silenced her. "What do you think happened?" Sam asked.

"That's where the gossip comes in. Stories of"—the tips of his ears pinked—"bunyips inhabiting the gorge." He cleared his throat. "It's just old-fashioned mumbo jumbo." His lips twitched and he glanced over his shoulder. "But they do say bunyips prefer female victims, and there're many who have heard the strange cries echoing from the gorge. Ellalong Lagoon is another well-known haunt."

"You can't be serious?" Sam stared at Wallis, a look of incredulity on his face. "You think a bunyip might be responsible for the skeleton?"

"We can't preclude any theory at this stage."

PJ stood under the tall grass trees flanking Bow Wow House—beneath the sprawling canopy a perfect spot for picnic rugs, a game of croquet, and a flurry of young girls playing hide-and-seek. She blinked away the recurring image. "Let's go and look at the house. I can't wait to go inside."

Sam jangled the keys. "Why don't we try the back door? It looked as though it might be easier than the front."

Once Sam had removed the crossbeam, he inserted one of the heavy keys in the lock. Despite his efforts it refused to turn.

"Try one of the others." PJ hung over his shoulder, bouncing on her toes, unable to keep still.

Sam picked the heaviest and it slipped into the lock but scraped as he jiggled it, refusing to turn.

"Let me try." She slid in front of him and wrapped her fingers around the intricate brass fitting and twisted it to the left with both hands. With a grinding *click* the lock released.

Sam put his shoulder against the timber. The door grated against the flagstones as he forced it open.

The smell hit her first. An all-engulfing stench of wood rot and decay tainted the air. A pale, reluctant light, tinged the color of cold tea, filtered in, revealing the outlines of furniture furred with dust.

She took several tiny steps, her feet making a soft, hollow sound on the wooden floor. Neatly arranged chairs upholstered in heavy brocade were grouped around occasional tables as if waiting for visitors to settle and take afternoon tea. Framed pictures, festooned in spiraling cobwebs, covered the walls, and a colorless carpet lay in the center of the room. Two doors led off to the left and the right.

PJ grasped Sam's hand and made for the door to the right. It opened with barely a squeak onto a sitting room. After much rattling and banging, Sam wrenched the shutters open and shafts of sunlight streamed in, revealing dust mites dancing lazily in the stale air. Sofas and soft chairs were clustered around a large fireplace, the cushions still dented as though the occupants had only recently left, and under the window stood a well-worn upright piano.

Her nose twitched and her explosive sneeze rebounded from walls that had suffered no sound for decades. "Don't you think it's odd that the furniture wasn't covered in sheets when the house was closed up?" She brought her hand down on the back of the largest sofa and instantly regretted it when a cloud of dust billowed. Another fit of sneezing overcame her.

Sam coughed and spluttered in sympathy. "You're right about the kitchen, though. Someone's using it. Compared to this it is positively pristine." He nudged a thick wodge of velvet-like dust from the surface of a small table.

"It's almost as though they left in a rush."

"They?"

She shrugged her shoulders. "I don't know if it was a 'they,' but it feels as though the house was once full of people. And Mr. Woods claimed Anthea had a daughter, although Artie and the sergeant said she lived here alone after her husband died."

"Except for the girls she invited down to the gorge."

"Yes, but if the dates on the fossils are right, they only visited at Easter."

Sam tucked a loose curl behind her ear and dropped a kiss on her cheek. "You're overthinking it. I'll go through and open as many windows as I can. See if we can get rid of the smell and the swirling dust. Might be better not to touch anything else."

PJ followed, handkerchief held close to her nose. The sitting room led to a largish bedroom furnished with a four-poster brass bed swathed in fine curtains and beyond it a smaller room with a single bed. "This must have been Anthea's room."

"How can you tell?"

"It stands to reason she was the lady of the house, and the smaller bedroom must be the dressing room." She pointed to a large brimmed hat crowned with spiderwebs lying on the top of a dresser.

PJ rubbed the heel of her hand over the window and gazed out at the sandy driveway, the clumps of rambling flannel flowers with fat velvety leaves blurring the edges. "There has to be a basis of truth in Artie's story."

"Some, perhaps. A widow who tried to fill her empty life, then returned to the country of her birth when it all became too much. Nothing odd in that. Perhaps she took a fall or became ill. I just can't imagine why she never sold the place."

"None of that accounts for the gorge. There's something sad about it, a miasma."

Sam wrapped his arm around her shoulders. "That's not like you. You're usually all practicality and evidence."

"There's a strange feeling down there."

"What do you mean?" Sam cupped her face in his hands and stared into her eyes.

"I don't know."

"Can you describe it?"

"As though something's trapped, the past caught up, as though it's wrinkled and wants to be smoothed—there's something unfinished."

"Are you sure you're not just getting caught up in memories of your brothers?" He dropped a kiss on her cheek.

She shrugged. "It's not Dan and Riley, it's something else—the skeleton and the gorge. I don't get the same feeling here, in the house.

It's as though the past, the skeleton, has been neglected, yet the house is full of love." She shrugged, pushing aside a twinge of unease, unsure where the words had come from.

"Let's see if we can open the front doors." Sam drew back the thick velvet curtains, releasing another flurry of dust.

Leaving him to his task, PJ turned to her right, her feet scuffing on the floorboards, each one almost the width of one of the spotted gums lining the driveway. A door opened into a room dominated by a large, plain cedar table and matching chairs—the dining room. Beyond, she discovered two more bedrooms, the first furnished with two brass beds, an armchair, a dressing chest with jug and bowl, and a large wardrobe. PJ swung open the door to reveal a worn pair of boots and a disintegrating cabbage-palm hat. A pang of sorrow snatched her breath. "Sam!"

His strides rang on the timber floor and his head appeared around the corner. "What is it? You sounded panicked."

Placing her palm over her heart, she tracked the uptake in the beat. "I'm fine. I've no idea what made me call out like that. I felt so alone."

"I wasn't far away. There're two extra bedrooms with doors that open on to the front veranda, not into the house."

"They'll be the stranger's rooms. Lots of old Australian houses have them so accommodation could be offered to passing travelers without the fear of having them in the house."

"Neat idea. I like it. Better than staying at the pub." He held out his hand. "The house is quite small, really, but I guess with the kitchen out at the back it's about all that's needed."

"It must have been built around the same time as ours in Wollombi."

"The sergeant said the 1830s, remember?"

"It's a beautiful house, and it has a nice feel to it. As though the people have just popped out for a while and will come tumbling through the doors at any moment."

"That doesn't tie in with Sergeant Wallis's story. I would have expected the house to be in a much worse state, closed up for all this time." Sam dangled the keys in front of her nose. "Want to check out the rest or have you seen enough? I've got three unaccounted keys."

She took the keys from his hands. "We know the kitchen's open, but one of the keys might belong there, then there'll be one for the stable block. I wonder what the other one is for?"

"Maybe the garden shed."

They walked out through the back doors and Sam ground to a halt, sniffing the air like a dog.

"What is it?"

"Can't you smell it?"

PJ inhaled deeply. "No, nothing, but I've been sneezing like crazy. It's hardly surprising."

Sam nudged the kitchen door wide and stuck his head inside. "Coffee. I tell you I can smell coffee."

After the chill of the main house, the kitchen seemed warm. A small metal pot stood on the hob and the remains of a fire glowed underneath. "Someone's here." Her voice dropped to a whisper.

"Hello?" Sam's voice boomed in the small space. Nothing.

Everything was very much as it had been the first time they had come into the room. "It definitely doesn't seem dirty enough, does it? Not seventy years dirty and dusty."

"Do you know what seventy years dusty looks like?"

"After seeing the house, I do." She turned around to find Sam tipping the little pot and pouring the dregs of the coffee into a small cup. He closed his eyes and sighed as he inhaled the contents. "Espresso."

"Put it down. We shouldn't be in here."

"We have every right. We have permission from the solicitors. I've got the keys. Remember?"

"But we might take them by surprise. Frighten them."

He tipped the cup and drank the remains. "Whoever it is we're going to frighten makes a good coffee."

"But where are they?"

"Sitting somewhere enjoying a cup of excellent coffee. Not in the house."

"I'm going to go and see if I can find them."

CHAPTER 25

———◆———

"I'll have a look around the stable block." Sam didn't wait, simply took off.

"I'd like to have a look around the garden and then go down to the gorge again," PJ called after him.

"Don't go down that way without me. I don't want to find you splattered at the bottom." His words floated in the vacant space behind him.

PJ wandered off, choosing not to dwell on the proprietorial note in Sam's voice. Bow Wow House had seeped into her soul. The way the light played through the trees, the sense of peace and tranquillity that pervaded the air.

Ever since Sam had returned from Sydney with the keys, he'd talked about the place as though he owned it. She choked back a laugh. What hope had Sam of owning a place like Bow Wow? Chance would be a fine thing.

It wasn't until she rounded the corner of the path toward the track that she stopped trying to place the sense that something had changed. No sound of bellbirds or the breeze in the casuarina leaves, an overwhelming silence but for a rapid and rhythmical *tap, tap, tap-tap, tap*.

The shutters on the garden shed were open. She stepped up to the window, rubbed the heel of her hand on the glass. And stopped. Glass? Who put glass in the windows of a garden shed? She stretched up on tiptoes.

A small, hunched figure sat, pecking at the keys of an ancient typewriter, the feather on her hat bobbing like a frustrated cockatoo.

PJ edged toward the door. Unlike on her previous visit, it was no longer barred. A large rock, the pattern of an intricate sea lily clearly visible on the upper edge, held the door ajar.

She cleared her throat. "Hello?"

The woman's head encased in the velvet cloche continued to bob in time to the movement of her hands on the keys.

"Excuse me." PJ raised her voice. "I hope I'm not disturbing you."

The woman didn't acknowledge her presence. PJ covered the space between them in two long strides and stood in front of the desk.

The tip-tapping of the keys stopped and the woman looked up, over her spectacles.

PJ's heart gave a thud of surprise. "Miss Baldwin?" What on earth was she doing here?

"Ah, Penelope, isn't it? Mavis's friend. I won't be a moment. Just let me finish this before the thoughts fly away. The curse of age." Miss Baldwin bent her head to the typewriter once more and her fingers flew across the keys.

Never mind the curse of age—every coherent thought whipped away from PJ's mind; her mouth gaped, and her gaze landed on the sheets of paper piled on the side of the desk. *The Geological Society . . . a dissertation on the origins of Bow Wow Gorge.* She rammed her hands into her pockets to prevent herself reaching out and snatching them up.

Miss Baldwin thumped a final key and released the paper from the typewriter with a satisfied grunt. "There. Finished." She laid it on the top of the pile.

PJ's eyes raced to the type. No doubt the cover sheet had come from the same typewriter. Overuse had smudged the center of the *a* and *e*.

Before she could study the papers any further, Miss Baldwin collected them up, tapped them into alignment, then placed them facedown on the desk. "What can I do for you, my dear?" She spoke as though it was nothing out of the ordinary for her to be sitting at a typewriter in the middle of a slab hut on a deserted property surrounded by dusty old boxes and crates. "I rarely have visitors when I am here."

PJ's mind still swirled. To cover her confusion and blatant nosiness she studied the remainder of the room. Not all the boxes and crates were sealed. The contents of some spilled onto the floor and the benches at the back of the room. "You have an amazing collection of fossils."

"Indeed. Many, many years' work. I doubt I will finalize the cataloging in my lifetime."

"Do they all come from the gorge?" What was she doing standing here making polite conversation when all she wanted to do was screech, *What are you doing here?*

"Indeed they do." Miss Baldwin pushed herself to her feet and buttoned her rather smart belted jacket before adjusting her hat. "I seem to remember you enjoyed my coffee. Shall we go and make a pot? You look as though you could do with a cup." Without waiting for an answer, she turned on the heel of her boots and strode—no other word for it—through the door and along the path to the kitchen.

PJ scampered after her, the scent of rosemary and lavender pungent as Miss Baldwin's skirt brushed the sprawling plants.

"Could you bring in a handful of kindling from the pile around the corner? The fire will need a helping hand."

Inhaling deeply, PJ ducked around the corner, trying to gather her scattered thoughts. What was Miss Baldwin doing here? More to the point, how had she gotten here? She appeared very sprightly, but Bow Wow was miles from her house on the outskirts of Kurri and Mavis had commented on her lack of exercise. PJ picked up an armful of neatly split wood from the stack against the wall. Someone kept Miss Baldwin well supplied. What else had Mavis said? *We all keep an eye on her, call in and do a bit of work.* She shook her head, trying to make sense of the unexpected turn of events . . . Perhaps a neighbor brought Miss Baldwin here and then came back to collect her. "Where would you like this?"

"That's far more than we need." Miss Baldwin took several pieces of the kindling from her arms. "Put the rest down inside the door. It will do for next time."

Next time. So this wasn't a one-off visit; it was something she did regularly. PJ stared around the kitchen. The reason why the kitchen had seemed used and the remnants of the fire recent now made perfect sense.

"You'll know when the coffee is ready—it makes an appetizing little hissing and bubbling sound. A pleasure I have had to forgo." Miss Baldwin tapped her right ear, closed her eyes, and gave an appreciative sniff. "Now, what brought you to Bow Wow?" She skewered PJ with a piercing gaze. Her eyes had lost their slightly myopic squint and blazed with intensity.

"Sam, my fiancé," she stuttered, for want of any better description, "got the keys from the solicitor in Sydney."

"Did he indeed?"

"He's interested in buying the property." What claptrap. Sam could never afford to buy Bow Wow.

"I wasn't aware the property was for sale."

"Coffee . . ." Sam rescued her, throwing himself through the door with a groan of pleasure. "How on earth did you manage . . ." His words faded and his eyes widened.

"Miss Baldwin, this is Samuel Groves, my fiancé."

"Pleased to meet you, ma'am." Sam inclined his head, then threw PJ a quizzical glance.

"Miss Baldwin and I met yesterday. She lives just outside Kurri and is a friend of Mavis Elliot, the doctor."

Sam took no notice of her; instead, his eyes locked on the little metal coffee pot hissing on the stove and a low, contented sigh wisped past his lips.

"I take it you are a coffee drinker," Miss Baldwin said with a smile.

"Indeed I am. And from the sound of it, it's ready." He pulled down his sleeve to cover his hand and lifted the little pot from the stove and flipped it. "Cups?"

"In the cupboard above the sink." Miss Baldwin waved her hand over her shoulder. "Penelope, would you get them, please?"

PJ opened the door and brought down three small, mismatched porcelain cups and placed them on the table.

"And you'll find a jar of biscotti somewhere up there."

Sam poured the thick brew into the cups, then stood sipping his with his eyes closed and a look of pure delight on his face.

"Penelope tells me you're interested in the property." Miss Baldwin toyed with her cup.

A hint of color stained the top of Sam's ears and he glared at PJ. "I wanted to have a closer look."

"And how did you manage to find the owner?"

"I haven't done that yet. I went to the Land Titles Office and they gave me the name of a firm of solicitors, who released a set of keys."

"Very resourceful." Miss Baldwin pursed her lips. "And do you like what you see?"

"It's a beautiful property," PJ interrupted. "The house is in remarkable condition." It was on the tip of her tongue to say something about the gorge, but the memory of the papers beside the typewriter prevented her.

"Do you know the owners? I'd very much like to speak to them." There was something in the way Sam asked Miss Baldwin the question that made PJ think he knew more than he'd told her.

Without acknowledging Sam, Miss Baldwin put down her half-finished coffee and rose. "It's time I was going."

"Perhaps we can give you a lift?" Ever the gentleman, Sam stepped to her side.

"No, no, thank you. I can make my own way back."

How ever did Miss Baldwin get here? Even though she was remarkably spry, PJ couldn't imagine her covering the distance before nightfall, and there was no sign of anyone coming to collect her. "It's a dreadfully long walk to Kurri."

"Indeed it is, but it is a pleasant ride in my dogcart. Perhaps you'd like to tidy up for me, dear. If I delay my departure any longer, I won't be home before the sun goes down." Miss Baldwin replaced her hat and straightened her jacket. "Make sure the door is closed tight. The possums can be a nuisance."

Sam offered his arm. "Allow me, ma'am."

Miss Baldwin slipped her hand into the crook of his elbow and without a backward glance he escorted her outside.

The air shimmered above the treetops and the first almond scents of spring drifted in on the breeze. Far below, the secrets of the gorge remained undisturbed. Miss Baldwin tightened her grip on the young man's arm, batting back a sudden wave of dizziness. An age had passed since she'd willingly held a man's arm, yet her eighty-four years of life seemed nothing more than a mere hiccup compared to the history of the gorge.

How she'd love to wander down the snig trail and embrace the cool stillness. She took a step closer to the edge and examined the rock platform.

"Hold tight, ma'am. We don't want you falling." The young man—what was his name? Sam, that was it—guided her away, his tone gentle, compassionate.

She pulled back and stared into his handsome face. The corner of his lips tilted in the semblance of a smile; his eyes were bright with a lively intelligence. "It's nothing more than a goat track, horribly steep."

"Yes, ma'am. PJ and I—"

"PJ?"

"Penelope."

"Ah, yes. Mavis's friend, the girl in my workroom." The girl who had quite taken her by surprise when she'd found her standing there. A nice enough girl, kind, she could see that. But it was this young man she was interested in—not like those two young boys buoyed by foolish rumors and bravado she'd stumbled across in the gorge. How long ago had that been?

It had crossed her mind in some far-flung fantasy that they might, under guidance, have been the ones to pursue the secrets of the gorge. She'd sat watching them, hiding out of sight, under the overhang, willing them to make the find that had eluded her. She'd seen their extraction of the fossils, their high-spirited laughter belying the care they took, been surprised by their knowledge. About to reveal herself, she'd taken the first tentative steps. Hadn't expected their cry, the gunshot, and the sudden flurry of falling rocks.

By the time she had come to in the hospital they'd vanished. She'd hoped one day they might return, but they hadn't. No one until now. Until the girl with the strange faraway look in her sky-blue eyes and this brash, coffee-drinking American. Slick and smooth with his polished manners.

Time encroached, each year blurring into rapid confusion; soon she would have to make a decision. She'd put it off for far too long. "You said you'd explored the gorge?"

"We climbed down the other day. It's a beautiful spot. Lots to see." His eyes sparkled as he spoke. "Penelope has an interest in fossils." He bit his lip rather as though he was going to say more but had thought better of it.

She wouldn't give him the opportunity—she didn't want to discuss the gorge. "My dogcart is along here." She moved away from the drop-off and started down the path. "There's a small enclosure beyond these trees. The horse is happy enough. Perhaps you'll give me a hand getting him into the traces." Not that she needed any help. The dear old thing knew the routine as well as she did. Could probably climb into the harness unaided. Nevertheless, it made a pleasant change to have a young man's arm to guide her. "I'll be interested to know if you decide to make an offer on the property. My land backs onto Bow Wow. It's known locally as Baldwin's Lot." Not named for her, as most presumed, but for another. An irony that gave her perverse pleasure.

There was much to be said for the stamina and agility of youth; within moments Sam had the dogcart hitched and handed her up. "Before you go, ma'am . . ."

She considered his upturned face while she slipped on her calfskin gloves.

"Could I ask why you come here? You seem very familiar with the property."

Damn. Not such a nice young man. What had happened to personal privacy and etiquette? That time when no one questioned a lady's motives. "It's a longstanding arrangement. I, too, have an interest in fossils." She fastened the buttons on her gloves. "I hope you enjoyed the coffee."

At the click of her tongue, the horse moved off. She lifted her hand in farewell but couldn't turn back, terrified he might see the heat in her cheeks. The ability to lie was yet another skill that diminished with age.

The drive to and from Bow Wow always afforded her a great deal of pleasure. At first she'd seen the dogcart as a blatant sign of her advancing years, but she'd come to embrace it. For many years, the two-hour walk was a way of reliving the past. She'd pack some lunch and visit the gorge, collect a few samples, always looking for that elusive discovery that would prove Anthea's theory. But after the strange and terrifying experience with the two boys, her enthusiasm had waned. A gurgle of laughter rose in her throat. The look of horror on their faces as the gun exploded was the last thing she remembered of them. Lucky they were such a dreadful shot. She brought her fingers to her brow and felt the scar in her hairline. Lucky, too, that it was a dislodged rock and not the bullet that had found her temple.

With a sigh she pulled the dogcart to a halt and sat admiring the vista. A magical array of pinks and lilac painted the rolling hills and the meandering creek weaving down to the gorge, the place where so many secrets lay hidden by the towering cliffs and encroaching bush.

"There you are. I was beginning to worry." Mavis Elliot appeared from behind the stables, dragging her from her daydream. "It's getting late. I thought you'd be home by now."

She bit back a sharp retort. Barely a day went past that Mavis didn't call in, but twice in one day was a little more than necessary. *"Just to see if you need anything."* What a load of hogwash. Checking to see if she'd survived another day. More often than not, she enjoyed Mavis's company, but she'd had a surfeit of people today. Not only Penelope and the American, but the crowded memories. Some days the past shone crystal clear whereas her activities of a matter of hours ago slipped into a vacant, blind mishmash. That's why she liked to visit Bow Wow. It settled her thoughts and anchored her.

"Out for another drive? You only went a couple of days ago."

Meddlesome girl. Though she was hardly a girl. Not like Penelope, with her mass of pretty blonde curls, so unlike the shingle haircuts girls favored nowadays. "I can smell spring in the air. I wanted to feel the sun on my face."

"Let me sort out the horse. You go up to the house. I've brought some pies from the hotel. I thought we could eat early. I wanted to ask for your help."

Smothering another sigh, she shunned Mavis's proffered hand and eased down from the dogcart. What on earth would Mavis want help with? She was more than competent, more than any of the other doctors she'd come across over the years.

The aroma of meat pies and a pleasing warmth greeted her as she wandered into the kitchen to find the table set for two and the kettle cheerfully whistling on the hob.

She unpinned her hat. Such a frivolous little nonsense. She hadn't been able to resist it when she'd seen it in the David Jones catalog. A far cry from the dreadful cabbage-palm hat she'd worn as a child. Smoothing the ruffled ostrich feather, she placed it aside and closed her eyes, only for a moment or two before Mavis came back and disturbed the peace.

"Are you all right?"

Mavis's face drifted into focus. "Just resting my eyes."

"Good, I thought for a moment you were unwell. You're very pale."

"A little weary, nothing more." She batted Mavis's hand away from her forehead. "The meat pies smell delicious."

"They'll be ready in a few moments." Mavis sat and propped her elbows on the table. "Like I said, I was hoping you might be able to help me."

"I doubt it but fire away. I often find the problem is resolved once it is spoken aloud."

"It's about a case I'm working on."

"A case? I thought there was something about doctor-patient privilege that prevented you from discussing cases."

"In this instance I don't believe it applies. The police called me in. Someone uncovered a skeleton. We're trying to discover who it might be." Mavis twisted the tea towel in her hands and then stood up from the table and looked out over the view. "Down there." She pointed beyond the hills. "Along Bow Wow Creek, down in the gorge."

Her heart gave one thunderous thump, paused, then thankfully resumed beating. "And why do you think I might be able to help?" She cleared her throat, trying to dislodge the quaver in her voice.

"You've lived in the area longer than anyone else. You must know something of the local gossip."

"Let's eat these pies before they get cold. I'm famished." And she needed a moment, more than a moment, to recover her equilibrium.

Mavis brought the two steaming pies to the table. "Be careful, they're very hot."

"I can see that." How could Mavis one moment ask for her opinion, her help, and the next treat her as a half-witted child? "Gossip, you said?"

"Yes. I know you're aware of the stories of the gorge."

"I've never paid very much attention. Old rumors get blown up out of all proportion." She licked her dry lips. "Can you tell how old a skeleton is?"

"The body was probably laid out somewhere between fifty and a hundred years ago. As far as I can ascertain, Anthea Winstanley left Bow Wow around the late 1840s. I believe she died in England. It's unlikely to be her."

And how would Mavis know that?

"She used to host fossil parties."

Fossil parties. A ridiculous description.

"And there's also some rumors about mythical creatures—bunyips."

The air sucked from her lungs and a piece of pastry caught. She clutched at her throat, her head spinning as she gasped for air.

Mavis dragged her upright and dealt a heavy thump to her back. With a gut-wrenching cough, the offending piece of pastry flew from her mouth, her vision cleared, and she sucked in a welcome breath.

"That's it. Sit down now. Sip this." Mavis placed a glass in her hand.

Bunyips. She coughed again, expelling a spray of water. Oh, but her back hurt. She dropped her head toward her lap.

"Sit up." The irksome woman forced her hands under her armpits and dragged her upright. "Breathe. That's it. You'll be fine in a minute."

Would she? Every breath she took made the spot between her shoulder blades scream, and every time she closed her eyes a black shadow loomed. She had to regain control. She inhaled. Long, slow breaths. In and out. In and out.

"Goodness me. You quite frightened me for a moment. Just sit quietly." Mavis picked at the crust of her pie and then pushed her plate away. "I'm afraid you might be a little bruised. I had to give you a hefty whack."

That was the least of her worries. How could this be happening? Seventy years. No one else had set foot in the gorge for over seventy years. And then Mavis's muttering and mumbling faded, leaving only the tattoo of her heartbeat and the realization that people had set foot in the gorge more recently—the two boys.

She took another sip of water, felt her heart rate steady. Calm. She had to be calm. And think. Today—the girl, the girl and the American. He said they'd visited the gorge. "Who found it?"

"I'm sorry?" Mavis reached for her wrist and felt for a pulse. "That's better."

"Who found it? The skeleton."

"We can discuss that later. When you're feeling better."

Later. No. She didn't want that. The matter had to be laid to rest. She gave a snort. Poor joke. "I'm quite fine. Tell me. It'll take my mind off . . ." She gave a feeble cough.

"If you're sure."

She wrangled her lips into a smile. "I'm sure."

"Penelope Martindale, the Wollombi doctor's daughter, and her young man. Remember I brought her to meet you? Dr. Martindale worked with me during the epidemic. They were exploring the gorge."

Yet they'd made no mention of any skeleton. How had they found the cave? The entrance was hardly visible, just a narrow aperture beneath the overhang. The American, Sam, he'd said the girl was interested in fossils. Surely there were enough in the exposed walls to keep her occupied.

"She found a vertebra on the creek bank, thought it belonged to some prehistoric creature. Took it home to her father and he put her straight. Obviously a human vertebra because of the spinal processes."

She opened her mouth to ask more and then thought better of it. Let Mavis do the talking.

"When I reassembled the skeleton back at the hospital I discovered large sections of the pelvis missing. Scavengers most probably, which would put pay to any of the local rumors about bunyips. I've sent it to the coroner for a second opinion."

Her throat dried. Slow breaths. Keep calm. The thundering in her chest would ease.

"I wondered if you have any knowledge of the people who own Bow Wow. After all, they are your neighbors."

The second person today to question her knowledge of Bow Wow. She must be getting careless. "It was empty when I built this house. No one's lived there since I moved here." No lie in that.

"Someone must own it because the Lachlan family has leased the farmland for years. They must pay fees to someone."

"It could be some sort of in-perpetuity arrangement." Too much information. But the last thing she wanted was for Mavis, or the coroner—always officious little men—to go poking around and finding Messrs. Grinstead and Gilmour in Sydney. But the American had, and the insufferable Grinstead or Gilmour—she never could tell them apart—had given him a key. Their grandfathers would never have made such a slipup. She dropped her head into her hands.

"I think it might be a good idea if you had an early night. You still look peaky. Why don't I make you a cup of tea?"

She shuddered. "No tea, thank you. Will you be able to find out who this . . . skeleton . . . belongs to?"

"Highly unlikely."

She drew in a deep breath and her shoulders dropped. "What will happen to it?"

"The bones will be bundled up and put in some archive box to gather dust. I always find it disheartening."

A satisfactory outcome. Poor Anthea never fully recovered.

CHAPTER 26

PJ studied the papers still lying on the desk in the workroom. She picked up the pile and leafed through it. *Bow Wow Creek Gorge is rich in geological and botanical species . . .* Her eyes raced down the pages covered in detailed drawings of fossils, the date collected, their possible origin, all neatly typed between the illustrations.

"Well, that was interesting." Sam's face appeared around the corner of the door.

"So is this. I couldn't tell you before, but when I came in here I found Miss Baldwin sitting at the typewriter. She was working on this." She held out the sheaf of papers.

"Not that strange." He glanced down at the cover page. "She told me she uses the place for her work. Maybe she's editing something, completing it. She said she had an interest in fossils."

"Something feels off." She rubbed her hands up and down her arms, attempting to rid herself of the prickling sensation. "Why work here?"

"Her property backs onto this one—it's close to the gorge." Sam foraged in his inside pocket and brought out a map, elbowed aside a series of neatly laid out fossils on one of the benches, and unfolded it. "This is the original Bow Wow grant. Two thousand acres. A big chunk of land." He traced his finger around a large area on the map, then paused and bent his head closer. "And this is Baldwin's Lot. It appears to be part of the Bow Wow property, according to this map, but Miss Baldwin said *her* property backed onto Bow Wow, not that it was part of Bow Wow."

PJ moved closer to the map. "Well, it does back onto Bow Wow." She circled the area marked Baldwin's Lot with her finger. It ran in a horseshoe shape, taking in a large section of the gorge and the creek.

"The solicitor said an option to buy the lot was taken out in the mid-nineteenth century, but it had never eventuated."

PJ shrugged. "I expect it's called Baldwin's Lot because she lives there. It happens a lot in Australia. Wollombi House is known as The Doctor's House."

"You could be right." He scratched his head. "And Miss Baldwin asked if we'd explored the gorge. I told her we had and that you had an interest in fossils."

"What did she say?"

"Not a lot. The conversation came to an abrupt halt and she left. I think it's time we made a move too. We can come back tomorrow."

"We should tell Pa what happened, and I'd like to have another look at Dan and Riley's collection. Perhaps Miss Baldwin would like some of their fossils for her research, the paper she's working on. Her drawings are incredible."

"Anything about skeletons?"

"Don't be ridiculous. Why would there be?"

"Someone had to have dumped it there."

PJ sat with her head balanced in one hand, half-heartedly sorting through Dan and Riley's fossils. Every time she picked up a specimen she could see their faces and hear their voices. Her entire idea, spun in the halls of the museum in London, was to commemorate their lives, pay tribute to two lovely young men who hadn't made it home. Except for Pa's somewhat enthusiastic identification of the vertebra, he'd shown no interest in her venture, in fact no interest in her. As though he begrudged her survival.

Quite why she felt the need to return the fossils to Bow Wow, she had no idea. The sight of Miss Baldwin's meticulous drawings and notes? The need to have Dan's and Riley's names alongside Anthea Winstanley's?

She lifted the top tray out of the trunk, bent down, and reached into the bottom.

The story of the uncovered skeleton hadn't sparked Pa's curiosity as she hoped it might. He seemed to be more interested in Sam. The two of them had spent the previous evening in his study poring over the chessboard. Unable to control her whirring mind, she'd given up and taken herself off to bed, trying in vain to pinpoint what it was that continued to nag at her. Returning the fossils from Dan and Riley's collection to Miss Baldwin would be the perfect way to continue their conversation and perhaps appease her curiosity.

Shaking away her sense of disquiet, she returned to the fossils. She was no authority, but anything unlabeled, which appeared to be nothing more than an unidentified rock, she put to one side.

She ran her finger over the scrawl on the labels. Neither Dan nor Riley could be described as good students; their handwriting, like their education, had been madcap and spontaneous. Always jumping into some sort of scrape without thinking. Full of dreams and far-fetched plans, they'd left school at twelve and try as Pa might, he wasn't able to get them back there. Big strapping lads always searching for adventure, their deep voices and muscular bodies belying their age. Yet these fossils meticulously cleaned and labeled showed a side of her brothers she hadn't appreciated.

If Dan and Riley's discoveries were to be recognized, then those belonging to the Pearson and Ketteringham girls should as well. She took out one of the beautiful fern-like fossils, its intricate fronds delicate and detailed. She turned the label. *Sea Lily*. The neat cursive handwriting looped across and finished with a swirl. Holding it under the lamp, she squinted at the fading words. She bent closer to the trunk and brought out more fossils, laying them on the top of Dan's counterpane. Once she'd removed the entire contents, she rocked back on her heels and started flicking through the labels and lining them up in date order. Lydia, Bea, Ella and Grace Ketteringham, and one more, the handwriting juvenile and badly formed. *Dragon Scale*. A dragon scale? Hardly.

Even she recognized it as a lamp shell.

Fownd by Miss Mellie Vale.
Satday apirl 3 1847.
BOW WOW GORGE.

Another girl who had searched for fossils at the gorge. And the date 1847, the year Anthea Winstanley had sent the vertebra to the museum in London, but nothing after that until Dan and Riley's finds.

As she arranged the fossils in the crate to take to Miss Baldwin, another date caught her eye—June 30, 1917. Dan and Riley must have visited the gorge only days before they joined up. Maybe this was the opportunity to engage Pa. She leaped to her feet, bolted along the veranda and through the kitchen door. "Mrs. Canning? Mrs. Canning, where are you?"

"Calm down. Calm down. It can't be that bad."

"Where's Pa?"

"Sam's taken him over to Millfield. Some sort of emergency at Sweetman's sawmill."

"Can you remember the exact date Dan and Riley joined up?"

Mrs. Canning took a maddening age to wipe her hands before sitting down. "The last time I saw them was the morning of the day they left for Bow Wow. All packed up, that billy cart hooked up to Dan's bicycle. Full of gear. They'd been there the weekend before and wanted to go back. Said they'd leave when they knocked off work on Friday and then go straight to work from there on the Monday. I wasn't expecting to see them until Monday afternoon; I'd even cooked a roast chook for them . . . The sixth of July, I saw them last." Her face crumpled and she pulled her apron up to blot her eyes. "They must have had it all planned. Why didn't they tell me?" She exhaled a long painful sigh. "Not that I was surprised. From the moment you left they wouldn't stop talking about going. I remember it clear as day, the argument you had when you came home and told your pa you'd done the St. John Ambulance course and were off to London. I was right proud of you."

How could she forget it? Pa red with rage, flailing his arms about, saying they were contravening every principle he had. He'd eventually accepted the role she intended to play, not with particularly good grace, but he'd agreed she'd be saving lives, not taking them. There was little he could do—she was over twenty-one. It was to the boys he'd simply said no. No son of his would carry a gun. And until they were of age, they'd have to toe the line. They couldn't enlist without his permission, and he wouldn't be giving it.

"I always thought they'd accepted it. You left. Life went on. Taking off to Bow Wow, nothing they hadn't done a hundred times before. Except they didn't come home. Telegraphed from Sydney. They'd joined up and were shipping out after training, sometime toward the end of July."

"How could they? They needed Pa's signature."

"Lied, I guess, same as lots of others. Both of them big strong boys. They would have met the physical requirements. Can't understand why they put you down as next of kin, though. They must have known I'd tell their father they'd signed up. Your pa and I went into Kurri, talked to the recruiting depot. He rang Sydney, gave the poor officer what for, but there was nothing anyone could do. I let you know as soon as the boys' telegram arrived to say they were shipping out."

How could Pa blame her, and more to the point, how could Dan and Riley tell such a whopping lie? "They told me they'd badgered Pa until he agreed."

PJ dropped her head into her hands. "Why won't Pa listen to me, let me explain? If you've remembered the date correctly, I was already in Flanders. How could I have had anything to do with them enlisting?"

Mrs. Canning shrugged, then pulled PJ into a fierce hug. "He needs time. He's his own worst enemy."

CHAPTER 27

Miss Baldwin sat on the veranda, a thick mohair blanket covering her nightgown as the moon rose large and full over the ridge, painting the landscape with an ethereal glow, illuminating the secret she'd kept hidden. She couldn't keep circling the past. She had to face it. Put it to rest. She was running out of time.

She wriggled deeper into the blanket, an aching weariness invading her bones. The treasures of the gorge belonged to future generations. Anthea had always insisted she'd one day marry and her children would inherit, but never once had she overcome that nothingness, the blank darkness, that swamped her if any man got too close. It was an inbuilt fear she couldn't conquer. A shadow, shrouded in the past. In a past before she'd come to the gorge.

So long ago. Her lids closed and her mind drifted . . .

"What are you doing out here?"

She started, looked down at her bare feet. The water lapping her toes, the shimmering outline of her ghostly self reflected in the inky water of the dam, the cold morning mist seeping into her bones. What was she doing? Her feet were numb and her nightgown drenched.

"You'll freeze. Come along." An arm grasped her.

A deep black pit of fear opened in her chest, threatening to twist her inside out. She wrestled away. And suddenly she was running, her breath rasping, branches slashing her face, crashing stomps dogging her. Her feet went from under her and a foul stench invaded her nostrils, making her retch. Damp and rancid, a malodorous miasma of rotting vegetation.

Covering her head with her hands, she braced herself against the crushing weight.

"Miss Baldwin. It's me. Mavis. Let me help you up. You've had a fall."

Fragmented reality realigned and she blinked into the sunrise and sniffed. No stench. No slimy hands, no leathery skin blackened with water weed.

"Can you stand?"

Mavis's strong arm supported her and lifted her onto her useless legs. Her knees buckled; she sucked in a breath, gritted her teeth.

"One step, then another and we'll be back at the house in no time. I'll make you a cup of tea. I need to look you over, make sure you're not bloodied."

Bloodied. Bloodied.

She reefed away, the word pummelling her brain. Plucking at her clinging nightgown, she studied her shriveled feet, clawlike toes gripping the mud. Her vision tunneled, the angry rush filled her ears. The stink of horse sweat, the guttural bellow, the rasp of labored breath. Groping leathery hands pinning her against the old spotted gum. The whispered threats before he'd thrown her aside and left.

She raised her face to the sun. No sign of Cook's bloated red face, nor of the old white horse translucent in the mist, just the rolling hills and the lightening sky. She blinked away the memories and hobbled as fast as her legs would carry her to the safety of the house.

Determined to be on her way to Miss Baldwin's before she had to explain her motives, PJ sorted through the fossil samples, placing only the best into one of Mrs. Canning's small vegetable crates; she nestled each one between layers of Dan's and Riley's flannel shirts to ensure no harm would come to them. In all truthfulness, she felt left out last night when Sam had returned late with Pa, full of praise for the way Sam had assisted him after the accident at the sawmill, and with schemes to convince the hospital board in Kurri to acquire an ambulance that could serve the area.

She might as well have been a fly on the wall for all the notice either of them had taken of her. She'd served the meal Mrs. Canning had prepared before she'd left for the day and then had Pa's study door shut firmly in her face as he and Sam continued their discussion long into the night.

Childish she might be, but if they weren't interested in her news, her plans to return the fossil collection to Miss Baldwin, then so be it. She would take matters into her own hands.

Praying she wouldn't bump into Mrs. Canning arriving on her bicycle, she crept past the kitchen. She settled the crate onto the stretcher in the back and, thankful for Sam's habit of always turning Sid in the right direction for a fast getaway, slipped behind the wheel, released the brake, and coasted down the driveway onto the road.

Well before the sun had breached the surrounding hills, she passed through Millfield. She had no idea how Miss Baldwin spent her days, but she intended to arrive in time to offer her a lift to Bow Wow. Quite how she'd broach the subject of the fossils, she wasn't sure. Surely Miss Baldwin would be interested in the boys' collection. There might be something there she could add to her paper.

In just under two hours she arrived at the gates of Baldwin House. Against every instinct to hurry she crawled up the drive and pulled to a halt outside the stables. At the sight of the dogcart and the old pony grazing in the adjoining paddock, her heart lifted.

Leaving the crate in the back of the ambulance, she walked up the path to the front door and raised her fist to knock. Before she had the chance, the door flew open and Mavis's startled face appeared.

"Is everything all right?"

Mavis pushed a bedraggled lock of hair back from her pinched face and slammed her finger against her lips. Dark shadows underscored her tired eyes.

"Miss Baldwin . . . is she . . ." Her words dried in her throat.

Mavis closed the door behind her and guided PJ back down the steps. "She had a difficult night and I had to give her something to help her sleep." Her brow furrowed and she caught her lower lip between her teeth. "Why are you here?"

"I wanted to show something to Miss Baldwin. I thought she'd be interested," she whispered.

"Now might not be the moment. I was about to see to the horse. Why don't you come with me and you can tell me all about it?"

Not exactly what she had envisioned. She'd rather intended Miss Baldwin to be the first to see the collection. "I'll come back later. It's not important."

Mavis heaved a sigh. "I hardly think you'd arrive here before eight o'clock in the morning if it wasn't important. It's a good two-hour drive from Wollombi."

How would Mavis know she had driven from Wollombi? She could have spent the night in Kurri. An embarrassed flush rose to her cheeks. "It is important, but it can wait if Miss Baldwin is indisposed."

"She'll be fine when she wakes. A few cuts and bruises, but nothing life-threatening."

"She had an accident?"

"We both have tales to tell. Let's sort this horse out and discuss it over a cup of tea. I'm not expecting Miss Baldwin to wake for at least another hour or two. You're not in a hurry, are you?"

"No, I'm not. Do you have to be at the hospital?"

"I've got a couple of days off, as long as there are no more emergencies. That's why I called in early. Did your father and Sam get back all right?" Mavis gave a laugh. "They must have, otherwise you wouldn't have driven here. Sam might well have missed his vocation. Not only is he a great driver, he's got the makings of a fine doctor. Nothing like learning on the job."

So that was how Mavis knew she'd returned to Wollombi. "You're not the first to say that. There are plenty who owe their lives and their limbs to Sam's quick thinking." It had never crossed her mind to wonder if he'd like to train to become a doctor. After seeing him grill Sergeant Wallis at the police station, she had imagined him returning to his father's business, seen him brandishing a gavel, not a stethoscope. But now she wasn't so sure. "Will the man from the sawmill recover?"

"He's not out of the woods yet. Got to watch out for infection but, as I say, his chances are good, thanks to Sam's experience. Sam's exactly what we need in this area. His quick thinking and his ambulance. Some of the accidents in the mines can be dreadful, never mind the sawmill and farm mishaps. Too much time is wasted getting the patient to the hospital."

PJ swung open the stable door and slipped a bridle onto the horse. "Where does he go?"

"Through the gate over there. I'll bring him some food. Once you let him go, check he's got some water and then we can find that cup of tea. I'm spitting feathers."

PJ licked her lips. She'd grabbed a glass of water from the carafe beside her bed before she'd left, but the dusty drive had left her throat scratchy and her mouth dry.

"We'll go into the house through the back door. That way we won't disturb Miss Baldwin. Her bedroom is at the front of the house."

"Lucky I didn't knock, then."

"Miss Baldwin's had quite a lot of luck this morning. I don't usually turn up this early. Sleepwalking, I think. In the midst of some terrible dream."

Was that why Mavis called in regularly? "Does she often—"

"No. Nothing I've ever seen before. Obviously, she's getting frailer. No one reaches their eighties without a few things breaking down. I hadn't expected it to be her mind." Mavis clapped her hand over her mouth. "Forget I said that. Quite appalling, discussing a patient's symptoms. She hasn't any family and I—"

"Please don't upset yourself. I know what Pa is like. He bottles everything up and I can see it eating away at him. He's horribly tight-lipped."

"As I should be. Sit down, and while I make the tea you can tell me why you're here. I can sense your underlying excitement."

Soothed by Mavis's obvious care for Miss Baldwin and the revelation that she had no family, PJ decided to tell all. Surely Mavis would know if the fossil collection would upset Miss Baldwin. It was the last thing she wanted to do.

"It's all a bit confusing. What I didn't tell you was that Sam proposed to me in London." The memory of his enthusiastic and totally unexpected drop to one knee in the forecourt of the Natural History Museum brought a smile to her face. "He had this old-fashioned idea that he had to ask Pa for my hand in marriage."

"And I'm sure he agreed."

Heat flew to PJ's cheeks and she dropped her head. Whatever had made her tell Mavis about Sam's proposal? She didn't want to explain anything about Pa's strange behavior, especially not to Mavis, not to the doctor who had worked side by side with him.

"Have you and Sam had a falling out?"

"No, not at all." For goodness' sake, this was ridiculous. "He hasn't asked Pa yet."

"Whyever not?"

She needed to say it and get it out of the way. "I asked him not to. Pa and I haven't been getting along very well since I got back." She was no better than Pa. Bottling things up. She huffed out a breath, forced the tightness in her belly to ease. "He holds me responsible for my brothers' deaths."

Mavis turned the teapot three times. "That's ridiculous. Why would he do that?"

"Pa didn't want any of us going to war. Something happened during the African War, I have no idea what, but he is violently opposed to any form of combat. He says it's in direct conflict with the oath he took when he became a doctor."

"'Do no harm.' He has a point."

"I went to England with some others after I completed a driving course. I intended from the outset to be an ambulance driver. Pa wasn't happy, but I was of age . . . there was little he could do and he finally accepted it. Dan and Riley, my younger brothers, had only just turned sixteen, and Pa refused to sign their enlistment papers. He thinks I did."

"Did you?"

"No. I was already in Flanders with the Red Cross. We had over a thousand men to evacuate from Sanctuary Wood." Thirty motors running continuously only a hundred yards from the German lines. Four hundred thousand lives lost in three months. PJ wrapped her hands around her arms to steady her shaking and drew in a deep breath. "Dan and Riley lied about their age and listed me as their next of kin. Pa didn't even know they'd joined up until after they'd left the country. They were killed within seven months of arriving in France." She clamped her back teeth, swallowed to clear the scratching in the back of her throat. Now that her story was out in the open, it sounded weak, pathetic. What was it about Mavis that made her bare her soul?

Mavis stirred two teaspoons of sugar into the tea and pushed a cup and saucer toward her. "Drink your tea."

"I don't take sugar."

"Drink it. Doctor's orders."

PJ sipped the tea. Felt the sugar work its magic.

"Would you like me to speak to your father?"

"You?" God, that sounded rude. "I'm sorry. That came out all wrong."

"Don't worry. I must ask one question, though. I can't understand why you feel the need to tell Miss Baldwin."

"Oh, no, I don't. That's just the beginning. I was leading up to my reason for being here to see Miss Baldwin. I told you about my brothers' collection. It contains other fossils collected by the girls who used to live in our house back in the 1840s."

"Girls?"

"Yes, collected by Dr. Pearson's daughters and three other girls, friends, I presume. My mother found them in the attic when we moved into the house in Wollombi. Their names were on the fossils."

"And then you were sucked in by the local gossip."

PJ gave an embarrassed nod. "And the fact that I hadn't realized how serious the boys had become about their fossicking."

"So that's how you came to visit Bow Wow Gorge."

She nodded. "I thought maybe Miss Baldwin might like to add to her collection up at the house."

Mavis rocked back on her chair. "Her collection up at which house?"

"Bow Wow. Miss Baldwin's working on a paper, I found her there, typing . . ."

A shadow fell across the table and PJ looked up.

Damn the girl. Miss Baldwin reached for the back of the chair. Now her duplicity was out in the open and Mavis wasn't one to let things lie.

"You're awake. Come and sit down. I'll make a fresh pot of tea."

She eased into the chair. "Good morning, Penelope."

"Good morning, Miss Baldwin." Two bright pink spots highlighted the girl's face and she failed to meet her eyes.

"To what do I owe the pleasure of this visit?"

Penelope flashed a look at Mavis and received an encouraging nod in response. "I brought something for you. A collection of fossils I thought you might like. They're from Bow Wow Gorge."

Top marks for honesty. Penelope didn't appear to be hiding anything. She was the one with the secrets, and now it seemed they might come out. "Interesting. Did you and the American find them?"

"No. They belonged to my brothers. Shall I go and fetch the fossils?"

Mavis placed a cup of tea on the table, sat down opposite her, and narrowed her eyes. "I didn't know you went up to Bow Wow House."

"You recommended gentle exercise. I like to take the dogcart out." She sipped the tea.

"The track is impassable."

"No, it is not. Penelope and the American got that machine of theirs through without any trouble." She had no intention of revealing the fact that she had another route to the house that cut through the back of the property. And she most certainly didn't want a troop of fossil hunters stomping through the gorge—worse, a group of ghouls and gossips pandering to the local rumors. She intended to follow through and complete her submission to the Geological Society and have the Messrs. Grinstead and Gilmour create some sort of covenant that would prevent any disturbance. Then, and only then, would she consider her next move.

A clatter and a thump brought her from her musings. Penelope shouldered open the door and deposited a wooden crate on the floor. More evidence for her submission, maybe. Her blood surged. "Goodness me, young lady. I expected a shoebox or something similar, not a crate. Wherever did you find these specimens?"

Penelope swiped back her hair and sat down at the table. "As I said, the collection belonged to my brothers. They found some of the fossils in the attic at our home in Wollombi and added to it."

She blinked and straightened her back. She must concentrate. "Wollombi, you said. Of course, I'd forgotten your father. You must live in The Doctor's House, opposite the millpond." For a second the darkness shimmered on the edge of her vision. She squeezed her eyes tightly shut and forced the image aside. "Well, open up the crate."

Unless she was mistaken, the fossils would be those the girls had collected all those years ago. Smarmy, grinning faces flickered, making her fists clench. *Bawk-bawk*. She hadn't thought of them for more years than she could remember.

Penelope placed two crinoids on the table. Not particularly well prepared. Then a series of brachiopods, very nice examples of *Spirifera convolute*, *Merismopteria macroptera*, and *Trachypora wilkinsoni*. All labeled. She reached into her pocket for her spectacles. Her hand came away empty. For goodness' sake, she was still wearing her nightgown. How had that happened? "I need my spectacles."

Mavis jumped up. "Let me get them for you."

"No. I shall sort out the matter."

By the time she returned to the kitchen, suitably attired, the table was strewn with fossils and Mavis appeared to have left. "Where's Mavis?"

"She asked me to stay until she returns." The corners of Penelope's mouth twitched. "And she said no coffee. Would you like me to make you something to eat?"

"Thank you. I would, if you'll join me. There are some eggs in the pantry. Mavis sees I'm kept supplied."

Despite several attempts over the years, she'd never managed to overcome her fear of the diseases chickens carried—all that scratching and shitting—although she was happy to eat their eggs, as long as someone else prepared them. "And yesterday's bread." She turned back to the fossils. "A large collection."

"I only brought the ones that were labeled and looked as though they might be important. There are others in the trunk at home."

She lowered herself to the chair and picked up the closest fossil. *Dan Martindale. Bow Wow Gorge. June 1916.* She placed it to one side, reached for another. *Riley Martindale. Bow Wow Gorge. May 1917.*

With increasing interest, she checked the names and the dates, then sat back with a sense of satisfaction. At long last the boys in the gorge had names. "Your brothers, you said."

"Yes."

Too bemused by the next fossil her eyes had lit upon, she failed to respond. She reached out, let it settle in her palm.

Home at last.

She hooked her spectacles over her ears and brought the label closer. No doubt in her mind, but she still needed confirmation. A curl of anger clutched at her stomach. She'd hunted high and low for it after the girls had left. That dreadful *bawk-bawk* creature must have taken it to spite her. She smoothed the writing:

Dragon Scale.
Fownd by Miss Mellie Vale.
Satday apirl 3 1847.
BOW WOW GORGE.

Her dragon scale. It nestled in the palm of her hand and she ran her finger over the wings, letting her mind drift back to the day in the gorge. The memory of the clutch of exhilaration as she picked it up stirred her sluggish blood despite the intervening years. It was the very beginning of a lifelong passion.

A plate of scrambled eggs appeared in front of her and two thick slices of toasted bread. She stroked the dragon scale one more time and laid it carefully on the table before checking the eggs were well cooked and forking up a mouthful.

Penelope sat down opposite her and picked it up. "I only found one fossil belonging to Mellie Vale."

She started. Strange to hear that name spoken aloud. "I'm sorry?"

"It's the only one I found with Mellie Vale's name on it, but the date is the same as some of the others found by the Pearson girls and another pair of sisters, Ella and . . ."

She reached for another fossil. "Grace Ketteringham." The name popped out of her mouth, no longer trapped in the mists of time.

"You knew them?"

A foolish mistake. "The name is here." She tapped the little triangular tag. "Now what about these other ones? You said your brothers used to visit the gorge."

"I thought perhaps you might like their collection." Penelope's face flushed again and she put down her fork. "I noticed the paper you were writing for the Geological Society and I thought there might be some specimens that would be of value."

So she hadn't been mistaken in the workroom. She'd noticed Penelope's attention to the paper, hadn't thought very much about it at the time. Could the girl be after money? Surely not. Nothing in her previous behavior had marked her as a gold digger.

"I never paid very much attention to my brothers' interest. I regret that now. They died in France."

"I'm sorry." What a shame. Another door closed. So much for her idea of trying to find them to see if they would be interested in maintaining the gorge. By the sound of it, Penelope was interested in laying her own demons to rest. "Thank you for thinking of me. Perhaps you'd like to accompany me to the workroom at Bow Wow and we could take the fossils."

Penelope's face brightened. "I'd like that very much. When you're feeling better," she added, a touch of disappointment lacing her voice.

"I am feeling perfectly well. Especially after my delicious breakfast."

"What will Mavis say?"

"Contrary to Mavis's opinion, she is not my keeper. I noticed a vehicle outside."

"Of course. I'll drive you."

CHAPTER 28

PJ took the driveway to Bow Wow House slowly, although Miss Baldwin seemed quite at ease staring through the windshield, a look of anticipation on her face.

"It's a long time since I entered the property from this direction. There's a track that cuts across from my back boundary that is quicker, but I doubt it would be suitable for a vehicle of this nature."

"You'd be surprised the terrain we've coped with. Sam and I both drove ambulances in France. That's how we met."

"How very brave of you. Dreadful business. Sending all those poor boys off to defend a country they'd never even seen."

Miss Baldwin and Pa would get on well. Not a discussion she intended to become embroiled in this morning, however. "Here we are." PJ pulled to a halt as close to the house as she could and raced around to open the passenger door.

"Thank you, my dear. Delightful, just delightful. I'll go and unlock the workroom if you can manage the crate." And without a backward glance, she skirted the veranda and headed around the corner of the house.

PJ stopped for a moment and rested her buttocks against the

hood. Miss Baldwin appeared very familiar with the house and the surroundings, but she'd made a point of saying the track she used ran from her back boundary. At odds with the map Sam had procured from the solicitors, and she hadn't noticed a track marked either.

"Oh." Whatever was the matter with her? So tied up in Dan and Riley it hadn't occurred to her to wonder how Miss Baldwin knew the property. And she'd spoken the name Grace Ketteringham almost as though she was familiar with it.

How ridiculous. The fossils were dated over seventy years ago. What had Mavis said? *"You don't reach your eighties without"* . . . Miss Baldwin would have been a mere child. The hair on her arms rose and her skin broke out into a rash of goose bumps. Had Miss Baldwin known Anthea Winstanley? Impossible. She said she hadn't come to Kurri until the 1870s.

Only one way to confirm her suspicions. She grabbed the crate and took off at a run, whipping around the back of the house. The aroma of coffee greeted her.

"There you are." Miss Baldwin appeared at the door of the kitchen. "Put the crate down and come and have a cup of coffee. I've got the fire going; the water will heat in no time."

"Mavis said—"

"What Mavis doesn't know won't hurt her." Miss Baldwin threw her a conspiratorial wink. "I'm sure you'd like a cup."

PJ smiled. "Thank you." She'd hoped that the fossils might cement their friendship. It seemed coffee would seal it.

She sat down at the table and reached for the small cup and inhaled.

"It's lovely to meet someone who appreciates real coffee."

"Something Sam introduced me to."

"During the war, I presume."

"If we were lucky. Otherwise, it was chicory and acorns." PJ took a sip, hoping to still her fidgeting leg.

"I acquired the habit long ago in Italy. I spent many years on the Continent. It always seemed monstrously unfair that young men should have their European tour but young women were rarely afforded such a privilege. I intended to visit every site where an ichthyosaur had been uncovered."

"Have you ever found any evidence of ichthyosaurs in the gorge? I saw a fossil in the Natural History Museum that Anthea Winstanley found. They thought it might belong to an ichthyosaur."

The tiny cup rattled as Miss Baldwin replaced it in its saucer. "No, I haven't. Probably just more of the rumors that abound." As though the sun had slipped behind a cloud, a shadow flitted across her face.

"Do you think there's any truth in the local rumors about a bunyip in the gorge?" PJ asked.

Well, that had to come out, didn't it?

Miss Baldwin removed her hat and placed it on the table, then pushed her chair back a little and sat with her hands neatly in her lap. Though hardly surprising that the rumors would resurface after Penelope's discovery of the skeleton. Maybe she should agree. Although she had long ago researched everything she could find about bunyips and the foolish episode, proving beyond a shadow of a doubt the falsehood. A useful falsehood, however. The stories created a wonderful barrier to snoopers and prank-filled children, and it had worked remarkably well until the boys—she must stop referring to them in that way now she knew who they were—Dan and Riley had thrown caution aside in their search for fossils. Truth be told, she hadn't only intended to protect the fossils. "Stories such as these abound all over the world, not just in Australia."

Penelope gave a tight smile. "I wouldn't have expected you to believe all that tittle-tattle about a bunyip. I'll accept that something happened that gave rise to the rumor in the first place. Most likely the fact that everyone believes Anthea Winstanley vanished. But she didn't. She went to England and died in 1870. She's buried in Lyme Regis."

Something she hadn't anticipated. "Lyme Regis?"

"I was sure you would have heard of it. I visited before I came home to Australia. It's very famous for its fossils, particularly those found by Mary Anning: the ichthyosaur and plesiosaur."

"Of course. How foolish of me. Everyone knows of Mary Anning's work. Quite something of a pioneer in her day. Now, why don't we take these into the workroom and have a good look at them. I have a magnifying glass and reference books." Mentally wiping her forehead, she responded to Penelope's quizzical expression by leading the way.

Time to accept that she wouldn't live forever and she needed someone to continue her work, Anthea's legacy.

Right at this moment she couldn't think of a better candidate than Penelope.

"Let me give you a hand with that."

"Sam. What are you doing here?" The swirl of joy caught PJ by surprise.

"I might ask you the same question."

"I wanted to talk to Miss Baldwin about Dan and Riley's collection. I thought you'd be busy with Pa." Her face crumpled.

"Come here, sweetheart." Sam pulled her into his arms and hugged her tight. She inhaled his warm, comforting, overtly sweaty aroma. "I've missed you too, but I did have a legitimate excuse."

"I know," she murmured into his shoulder. "Mavis told me about the amazing job that you did at the sawmill, saving that man's life. I'm just being foolish." Lifting her face for a kiss, she let her mind empty and her heart fill. She could hardly complain. She was obsessed by the whole Anthea Winstanley story and Sam had been nothing but supportive despite being thrown headfirst into her family problems. "I'm so pleased you're here."

"Next time leave me a note or tell someone where you've gone." He pulled away from her. "I was worried sick."

"I'm sorry, I didn't think. Miss Baldwin is in the workroom waiting for me. I'm taking the fossils around there."

"Is there any coffee left?" He picked up the little metal pot, unscrewed the lid. "Just enough. Hang on a minute."

"You can't drink it like that."

"Watch me." He tossed back the remains of the coffee. "Perhaps there'll be time for another before we leave."

She bent down and hefted the box.

"Give it to me. There must be something I'm good for."

"Plenty." She punched him lightly on the arm. "How did you get here?"

"Mrs. Canning's bicycle. And I won't be doing it again—it took me hours. The hills are ferocious. Sid's looking after it. I've thrown it in the back with the stretchers."

"I've got a lot to tell you, but it is going to have to wait. Miss Baldwin is very interested in Dan and Riley's discoveries, and I'm certain she wants to include some of them in her paper. And I think I am finally going to get to the bottom of the story about Anthea

Winstanley and the girls. I'm convinced Miss Baldwin knows more than she's letting on."

They found Miss Baldwin, pencil jammed behind her ear, poring over a large ledger. Sam put the crate down with a thud, and she closed the book with a determined snap before turning to face them. "These brothers of yours, how old were they when they went to war?"

"They'd just turned sixteen. Why?" PJ asked, the familiar mixture of dread and responsibility weighing on her shoulders.

"Curiosity. I haven't any siblings, or children. I wondered about your relationship with them."

"They were six years younger than me. They lied about their age, enlisted, and followed me to Europe."

"So you were very close?"

"No, not really. To be honest, I was surprised when I found out they'd enlisted. Pa is opposed to war. He refused to give them permission or sign their papers, but one day they just took it into their heads to go to Sydney and join up. They didn't tell Pa. Just took their bicycles and went. I didn't know until I received a letter saying they'd be in London before being deployed to France and they wanted to meet up."

"They were at the gorge in June 1917 because you have fossils there with that date." Miss Baldwin gestured toward the crate. "The blastoid on the right."

"I beg your pardon, ma'am?" Poor Sam stared in confusion at the array of rocks.

"This one here." Miss Baldwin indicated to an uncleaned but tagged specimen, proving her long-distance vision more than adequate despite the spectacles she usually wore. "And I know for a fact they were at the gorge on the seventh of July, 1917."

"How?" PJ's mind raced.

"Because I have it notated in my ledger."

"I don't understand. Why didn't you tell me when we first met or this morning when I showed you their fossils?"

"Because, my dear, I didn't know their names or who they were. I wanted to confirm my suspicions." She tapped the ledger. "Two boys visited the gorge on several occasions. I presumed initially they were interested in the local rumors about bunyips, and I made a point of keeping an eye on them. On that day, I stepped forward, intent on making myself known, and they fired at me."

PJ snapped her gaping mouth shut. Dan and Riley would never shoot anyone. They didn't own a gun and wouldn't have known how to use it. Pa strictly forbade any arms in the house. Didn't even allow them to go rabbit shooting. "I'm sure you must be mistaken."

"No. No mistake." Miss Baldwin slipped off the stool and walked to the bench. "Sam, could you please pull out those two crates?"

Sam was by her side in an instant, curiosity evident on his face. He dropped to his knees and eased out the first of the crates. PJ clamped her hands by her sides, forcing back the urge to cover her face. The second crate squeaked as it scratched across the floor.

"If you can crawl under there, I think you'll find what we're looking for."

Before PJ could ask what, Sam appeared from under the bench, a revolver cradled in his hands.

"Why are you making up this ridiculous tale? That didn't belong to the boys."

Sam turned it over a few times. "It's old." He ran his fingers over the casing, almost caressing it. "A revolver. Webley, Mark IV." He snapped open the breech and checked for shot.

"It's not loaded, not anymore. I made sure of that."

A moan slipped between PJ's lips. What had she done? More to the point, what had the boys done? Why churn up old issues? Dan and Riley were dead. Wasn't that enough? She slumped down onto the stool in the middle of the room.

"I think you should tell us what this is all about." Sam's voice held a steely note as he glared at Miss Baldwin.

"Yes, I should, and I will, but there was little point in my recounting the story without any proof."

Proof? How could a revolver, older than Dan or Riley, be proof of anything?

"As I said, I was down at the gorge intending to make myself known. I stepped from the shadow of the overhang and all I remember is a dreadful noise and a cloud of acrid smoke. When I came to—"

"They wouldn't have fired at you."

"In my general direction and missed. A piece of falling rock struck me." She swept back her white hair to reveal a scar. "I woke in the hospital. Mavis is the one to tell the full tale."

"But why would they shoot you?"

"I suspect the stories about bunyips got the better of them and I'd frightened them."

"But they left the revolver?"

"I didn't find it until after I recovered. I went back down to the gorge looking for them. They'd built some sort of rough shelter. I found the revolver in there along with some food supplies, a crosscut saw, and a few other implements. I wanted to thank them."

"For shooting you?"

"For taking me to the hospital. If they'd fled I could well have died down there. We tried to find them, but they had simply disappeared. No one knew who they were."

PJ stood speechless as the scene played out in front of her eyes. Another hare-brained scheme, but with far more consequences than any of Dan and Riley's previous scrapes.

Sam's reassuring arm pulled her close. "And this happened on the seventh of July?"

"I believe my records are accurate. Apart from knowing the date I was admitted to hospital, I made a record of the find some days later—*Martiniopsis subradiata*. I found it at the same time I found the revolver. No doubt loosened by the bullet."

Only a couple of days before they'd signed up. "I don't understand where they would have gotten the gun or how they knew how to fire it." She rubbed her numb hands together. "Can I look at it, please?"

Sam handed her the revolver. It was cold and heavy—PJ supported the weight in the palm of her hand and ran a finger over the brass plate on the barrel. An uncontrollable shudder swept her body. "It belongs to Pa. It's his gun."

Both Sam and Miss Baldwin turned to her, their eyes wide.

"I don't think you should jump to conclusions, my dear. You've already said your father doesn't approve of guns. I expect they borrowed it from a neighbor. A foolish prank . . ."

"It is Pa's." She traced the words *NSW Medical Team* and the initials *W.R.M.*—William Robert Martindale. The same as his trunk. The trunk Dan and Riley had found in the attic with the fossils. "There's no doubt."

Oh God. What should she do? It would crucify Pa to think that the boys had even touched his gun, never mind fired it. And running away. She wouldn't have expected that of them: larrikins, troublemakers always, but never cowards. They would have stood up and taken their punishment. "There must be some mistake." Her legs refused to support her and she sank down onto the stool again, cradling her head in her hands.

Sam gave her another hug. "I think it's time we got you home, Miss Baldwin. I'll go and hitch up your dogcart."

"Penelope drove me. If you'd be kind enough to give me a ride home . . . Are you all right, my dear? You look a little pale."

PJ wiped her hair back from her face and swallowed the bile burning her throat. "I'm sorry. I'm . . ." A sense of utter helplessness swamped her.

"Quite understandable. Come along, young man, you have two ladies to account for. If you would lock up, Penelope and I will wait for you at the front of the house." Miss Baldwin reached for her arm and guided her outside.

Fine clouds covered the sun and a hint of chill in the air brushed PJ's cheeks. "Pa's already angry with me. This will just make everything worse. I don't know what to do."

"Perhaps nothing for the moment. Think about it, my dear, although, if I may offer some advice, keeping secrets can be more difficult than facing the truth." Miss Baldwin stopped for a moment and turned back to the house. "I remember the first time I came here. Such a long, long time ago." Her voice quavered for a moment. "You're very lucky with Sam. Don't let that love slip through your fingers. You may never find such closeness again."

CHAPTER 29

Within half an hour they'd arrived back at Miss Baldwin's house. PJ eased around Mrs. Canning's bicycle and climbed out of the back of Sid. Before she had time to speak, the front door flew open to reveal Mavis, hair standing on end and her face harrowed with concern. Sam whisked around the car and helped Miss Baldwin from the front seat, then led her inside.

The thought of having to explain the events to Mavis was more than PJ could bear. She opened the passenger door and slipped into the seat, rested her head back, and closed her eyes. Such a far-fetched string of coincidences from Mr. Ambrose at the museum in London, down all the winding paths to Dan and Riley, and now to Pa. She had to face Pa, try and make him understand that she wasn't responsible for Dan and Riley joining up. They had made their own decision. He couldn't have prevented them from going forever.

"Here you are." Sam's voice shook her from her reverie. "I thought you were coming inside. I think you'd like to hear what Mavis has to say. She has far better recall of the events than Miss Baldwin." Sam took her arm and helped her to her feet. "Don't look so miserable. It might not be as bad as you think."

How could he say that? She pulled away from him. "I can't think of anything worse than discovering your brothers attempted to murder a defenseless old woman."

"Miss Baldwin told you she believed they were shooting at a bunyip. Come inside and listen to Mavis."

Shrugging away from his outstretched arm, PJ marched into the hallway, resisting the temptation to slam the door behind her. She couldn't decide who had annoyed her more. Sam, Dan and Riley, Pa or, heaven forbid, herself. And there was nothing Mavis could possibly say that could change anything.

She threw herself down in the chair, propped her elbows on the table, and glared.

Sam offered a sympathetic smile, an infuriatingly attractive tilt of his lips, which simply made her angrier. A small cup of coffee appeared in front of her and she pushed it away to the center of the table. "Sam seems to think you have something I should hear, Mavis." Her tone sent Mavis's eyebrows scuttling up her forehead and a wave of contrition surged through her. "I'm sorry. I'm all at sixes and sevens."

"Apology accepted. Let's get this over with and Sam can take you home." Mavis stood with her hands behind her back at the head of the table as though about to address a class of unruly children. "I'm sure my recollections will be clearer than Miss Baldwin's, and it's an event I remember well because it was the start of our friendship." She beamed down the table at Miss Baldwin.

"The start of your mollycoddling." Miss Baldwin threw her a defiant stare and sipped at her coffee.

"I was coming off duty at the hospital after a long day; there'd been an accident in the mines. A young man threw his bicycle down at my feet and grabbed hold of my arm. My immediate thought was that there was another problem at the mine. Bent double and gasping

for breath, he pointed behind him. Out of the darkness came a second bicycle, the rider standing, forcing the pedals down as fast as
he could, shouting, 'Shooting accident!' The bicycle towed a wooden
contraption more like a billy cart than anything else."

PJ's stomach performed a neat somersault and her mouth filled
with saliva. She didn't need any further confirmation. Dan's billy cart.
He'd turned it into a trailer by adding a set of bicycle wheels he'd
swapped for two days' work at the sawmill. They would tow their gear
behind them. Whatever they needed for the jobs they did on the local
farms. Their two-man crosscut saw, crowbars, shovels, and spades.
She let out a groan.

Sam drew her close, anchoring her. "Listen."

"There was a body in the trailer. Out cold, covered in blood. Head
wound, though I didn't know it then, bleeding like the blazes. We got
her inside and I sent one of the nurses to give the boys strict instructions to stay where they were because I needed further information.
By the time she got outside they'd gone. Vanished."

PJ opened her mouth to ask what happened next.

Mavis didn't give her the opportunity. "Their diagnosis proved in-
correct. It wasn't a gunshot wound. A falling rock had hit her and
knocked her unconscious. She suffered nothing but a head wound,
which some stitches fixed."

"And a mighty headache," Miss Baldwin added.

"Back home the next day."

"And the mollycoddling began."

"In someone of your age, one cannot be too careful."

"I'll thank you not to discuss my age."

The conversation faded as the scene played out in PJ's mind, then
the tension leached out of her and her thoughts darted back to the
past. Dan and Riley's obsession with the story about the monstrous

beast that lurked in Ellalong Lagoon—the story used to reinforce the dangers of the swamp. It had become a rite of passage for the local boys to swim in the lagoon. Not very different from the story of the millpond—the girl who would wander the shores at dawn summoning the creature from the dark. How many nights had Dan and Riley camped out there hoping to prove the story?

"So what are we going to do about the revolver?" Sam's question brought PJ back to the present.

"I don't know. I have no doubt Dan and Riley were responsible. I just can't understand why they ran away. Pa would have understood if they'd explained what had happened."

"Would he?"

Another of those questions that she wasn't sure she wanted to answer.

"As someone who was once a foolish teenager, I think I'm best qualified to put myself in their shoes. They might have been big and strong, but they were boys. Not men. They'd already argued with your pa about enlisting and they would have been terrified about confronting him and saying they'd killed a woman with a revolver they'd stolen. To make matters worse, his revolver. You said they signed up in Sydney. I reckon they got on their bicycles and hot-tailed it down to the city rather than face the consequences."

What a ridiculous mess. But Sam's account made perfect sense. They'd had no intention of going against Pa's wishes, just a foolish set of circumstances and no one to talk to led them to their fate. If only they'd waited, hadn't taken off.

"I reckon"—Sam turned to Miss Baldwin—"with your permission, ma'am, PJ should take the revolver and show it to her father."

"I have a better idea." Miss Baldwin pushed back her chair. "If you agree, Mavis, I think we should all pay a visit to Dr. Martindale."

PJ clutched the back of the seat, trying in vain to keep her balance as Sid bucked and rocked over the potholes on the driveway. Mrs. Canning's bicycle took up most of the space, leaving her body slumped in the burlap sling, legs dangling, and the revolver, wrapped in her cardigan, sitting in her lap. Unlike Mavis, who'd sprawled out on the other stretcher like a corpse, her hands neatly folded on her chest, eyes closed, and a look of serenity on her face. Pa always said the art of catnapping whenever the opportunity presented was a most useful trick for a doctor. Mavis had certainly mastered the art.

PJ wrapped her arms around her body. She had no idea how to approach Pa, what she'd say. When Miss Baldwin and Mavis insisted on coming, she'd wanted to refuse. She had to talk to him first, alone, before everyone else. Or did she? A pulse flickered a warning in her throat. It would be a coward's way out to let someone else tell Dan and Riley's story.

The engine clunked to a standstill. Mavis hauled herself up on her elbows, brushed a hand across her eyes, and pushed back her tangled hair. The handbrake groaned and Sam flung open the door and came around to the back. He dropped the tailboard and handed Mavis down, then reached in and pulled the bicycle out before offering PJ a hand. "Ready for this?"

"As ready as I'll ever be. I hope Pa's home." She slipped her legs over the edge of the tailboard and jumped down.

"Why don't you go up first? I'll stall Mavis and Miss Baldwin for a moment or two."

She had no idea why she ever doubted Sam. "Maybe Mrs. Canning will do tea on the veranda."

"Chin up, sweetheart. It'll work out."

"Thanks." She threw Sam a sad smile, took his advice, straightened her shoulders, and lifted her chin. At this time of day Pa should be in this study, hopefully alone, with no patients waiting. Clutching the revolver in its cardigan-wrap she walked, one agonizing step at a time, up to the house.

She didn't even make it to the back veranda before Mrs. Canning emerged from the kitchen wiping her hands on her apron. "There you are. I thought I was going to have to do a ring around and track you down. Where's Sam? Did he find you? Has he brought my bicycle back?"

"He's out the front, with your bicycle. We've got visitors, Dr. Elliot from Kurri and Miss Baldwin. Could you take them some tea? I want to have a word with Pa."

"You sound flustered."

"I just need a word with Pa." And now the moment had come she couldn't wait to speak to him. She'd procrastinated far too long. Old habits. *"Don't disturb your father. He's got more important things to think about."*

"Off you go, then. He's in his study. I'll rustle up some cake and a pot of tea."

PJ raised her knuckles to the half-open door, rapped, and walked in. "Pa, can you spare me a moment?" Why ask? She intended to say what had to be said and not be put off. "I need to speak to you."

He took off his spectacles and lifted his head. "I'm busy, Penelope."

"Now, Pa. I need to speak to you now."

With a sigh, he pushed back his chair, the fingers of one hand drumming an irritated tattoo on the armrest, his pen in the other hand and his gaze glued to the papers on the desk, refusing to make eye contact with her.

"I have to talk to you about Dan and Riley." She searched the wall behind him, seeking the security of Pa's favorite picture—the three of them in the treehouse peeking through the branches, grinning like fools, Christmas hats balanced on their heads.

It was gone, and in its place was a patch she hadn't noticed before, where the wallpaper pattern showed its long-forgotten colors.

"For goodness' sake, Penelope. I've told you. We have nothing to discuss."

"I have something to tell you." She put her bundled cardigan on the chair next to the desk and perched in front of it, taking the weight off her feet before she fell. "I didn't sign Dan's and Riley's enlistment papers. I didn't go against your wishes. I didn't even know they had joined up. I was in Flanders." She hit the desk with her finger, punctuating each sentence. She'd never dared speak to him in that way, to be so bold.

Another weary sigh drifted in the air.

"Look at me, Pa." She reached for his hand, but he snatched it away.

"Penelope, there is little point in having this discussion. What's done is done. The boys won't be coming back."

"There is every point. You hold me responsible, and I'm not. It was their choice."

He lifted his shoulders. "Is that all? I've got work to do."

"No, it's not. This is important." She slid to her knees and reached again for his hand. "I want it to be as it was between us before I left. I miss you, Pa." Her voice caught and she swallowed a bitter rush of misery. "I've found out what happened, why Dan and Riley enlisted."

"You can paint the picture whichever way you choose. Nothing is going to change my mind. You know my beliefs, and you knew my wishes."

Stubborn, pig-headed . . .

PJ swallowed the string of words and pushed to her feet. "I had

nothing to do with their decision. They thought they had shot someone and they ran away. They went to Sydney and enlisted to escape
punishment." She unwrapped the revolver and slammed it down on
the desk. "Perhaps this will change your mind."

The color leached from Pa's face. His hand hovered over the
revolver. "Where did you get this?" His finger traced the brass plate.

"From the woman they believed they'd shot. Miss Baldwin. She's
waiting outside with Dr. Elliot. If you won't believe me, then perhaps
you'll believe her."

"Mavis Elliot? What's she doing here?"

"She wants to speak to you. She was the last person to see Dan
and Riley before they left for Sydney. She and Miss Baldwin thought
you might like to know the full story."

Pa dropped his head into his hands. The kitchen door banged and
Mrs. Canning's tread echoed on the veranda, then faded. The lace
curtain on the window billowed in the breeze, bringing with it the
scent of citrus and a waft of something sweet from the kitchen, and
still Pa didn't move. "Alice promised me she'd dealt with everything.
'No reminders,' she'd said."

PJ leaned forward, trying to make sense of his muffled words.
"Ma?"

Pa lifted his head, his eyes fixed on the small photograph on his
desk as if willing Ma to speak for him. "They sent me to work in the
British camps, thousands of women and children in appalling conditions." He bowed his head. "The things I saw, things I never want
to see again: mangled bodies, starving babies, barely any food, and
widespread disease—diphtheria, whooping cough, dysentery, measles,
typhoid. Hollow, sunken eyes pleading, and nothing I could do." Pa
reefed off his spectacles, rubbed at the edge of his eye, and wiped away
an invisible irritation. "I wanted no more to do with the British and

their wars. That's why we came here, away from the city, away from the pain. But for Alice I . . ."

PJ licked her dry lips and reached out. Pa didn't pull away this time. She wrapped her fingers around his hand to still the shaking. So much more to his story than the brief statements he'd made in the past. Without Ma, he'd had no one who understood his torment, no one to share his pain. The invisible scars of war.

He opened the bottom drawer of his desk, slipped the revolver inside, and locked it. "It's all in the past now. A long time ago. Give me a few moments. I'd like to speak to Mavis." He offered a frail smile.

Without another word she slipped through the door and down the hallway to her bedroom. The hum of voices drifted from the veranda—Mrs. Canning fussing over the tea and offering slices of cake.

Her pale face stared back at her from the bedroom mirror. She pulled the brush through her mussed hair, straightened her blouse, then sat on the bed and focused on the garden. So much she hadn't known, so much she hadn't understood.

Much to her surprise, when she walked through the front door she found Pa standing, teacup and saucer in hand, chatting with Mavis while Sam tucked into a huge slice of cake, Mrs. Canning hovering over him with a look of satisfaction on her face. Miss Baldwin, though, had disappeared.

She squinted into the distance. The trees had grown, the vast expanse of the millpond reduced to nothing more than glistening glimpses. No sign of the flour mill or the old white horse who'd spent his days walking in patient circles powering the capstan.

And buildings, many, many more than she remembered. A tall gabled roof atop a solid sandstone building to her left, and as she stood trying to guess its purpose a bell rang, a cacophony erupted, and a flurry of children tumbled out onto the grass.

Her feet chose a path of their own, leading her ever closer, her line of sight fixed on the shimmering glow until she stood at the water's edge. The ruffle of a breeze stippled the surface and water lapped her toes. The outline of her ghostly self reflected in the inky water, the damp seeping into her bones.

A foul stench, damp and rancid, the underlying stink of stagnant water. Leathery hands grabbing, earth tilting, long shiny boots. Sweat, rifle oil, and grog.

The air punched out of her lungs as she hit the ground.

"Miss Baldwin, Miss Baldwin."

She kicked out. Crouched, ready to flee, she came eye to eye with a concerned expression. Not Cook's florid complexion, jowls quivering in outrage; not Fanny with her sneering, snooty airs. She shook her head to clear her vision. It had to stop, these exhausting lurches into the past.

"It's Penelope. I've come to take you back to the house. You must be parched after the drive. Here, let me help you."

The girl. Yes, Penelope. Lovely girl, with the American boy. "The house?"

"Wollombi House, The Doctor's House."

"Dr. Pearson." Her feet crunched on the stony surface as Penelope led her across the road behind a gaggle of children herded by two weary women and a mangy dog.

"Dr. Martindale. My father. Remember, we all came together from Kurri. Mavis and Sam and I. You rode in the front of the motor."

Quickly glancing over her shoulder as they took the path to the house, she saw nothing but the fading light on the millpond. Her breath was now ragged gasps, her skirt damp and heavy. Penelope's hand tightened on her arm. She shrugged her off.

"This way."

She veered to the right, pushed aside the bare branches of the wisteria, and stepped up into the sleep-out. Two iron bedsteads, not one. Her knees buckled and she sank down into the dip of the mattress, her feet swinging. All sense of balance deserted her and she toppled.

Penelope's frowning face peered down at her. "Miss Baldwin, can I get you anything?"

Head on the pillow. Eyelids heavy. A hand on her brow, cool, cooling the fever.

"It's the drive. It was too much for you. Let me go and get Pa."

Nestled in the cocoon of the mattress, her eyelids fluttered closed and blocked out the past.

PJ skidded to a halt at the corner of the veranda. "Pa, Mavis. It's Miss Baldwin. I found her down at the millpond. I think she's taken a turn."

"Where is she?"

"In the sleep-out, on Dan's bed."

"Follow me." Sam took off along the veranda, Mavis hardly a step behind him.

"Come with me, Penelope."

She galloped after Pa through the front door and down the hallway to his study. She didn't need to wait for instructions; he'd get his medical bag while she arranged the other necessities.

"Bring a blanket, something to keep her warm," he called over his shoulder.

By the time she'd grabbed the eiderdown from her bed and returned to the sleep-out, Pa was crouched beside Miss Baldwin, stethoscope planted in his ears. And Mavis was holding her wrist, two fingers on her pulse, while Sam paced the small space at the end of the beds.

Pa pulled off his stethoscope, inhaled, and stood. "Doesn't seem to be much wrong. No elevated pulse. Heart rate's excellent. She appears to be sleeping." The even rise and fall of Miss Baldwin's chest seemed to confirm Pa's diagnosis.

Mavis smoothed back Miss Baldwin's hair and nodded. "She's done this once before. She woke naturally, no underlying symptoms."

"Let's give her half an hour." Pa picked up his bag and left the room, followed by Sam.

"I'll stay with her." PJ sat down on the opposite bed, rested her elbows on her knees, and cupped her chin in her hands.

"I doubt there's any need for you to stay. I expect the drive and then the walk exhausted her. Your father's right, let her sleep," Mavis reassured her before wandering out.

PJ's breath caught. Curled on her side, legs bent, one hand tucked beneath her cheek, Miss Baldwin lay in the very same pose as the skeleton in the gorge. Pushing the morbid thought away, she tucked the eiderdown around her and crept away, back into the house.

The sound of voices, Pa's and Mavis's, drifted from behind the sitting-room door. PJ trailed through the house and back to the front veranda where she found Sam tucking into another slice of Mrs. Canning's cake and regaling the woman with some far-fetched story about the Moulin Rouge.

PJ sat down onto the bench, her mind racing. Without a doubt Miss Baldwin knew Wollombi House, given the shortcut through the wisteria to the sleep-out and, most of all, her reference to Dr. Pearson. "Mrs. Canning?"

"Yes, dear."

"What else do you know about the Pearsons, the doctor and his family who used to live in Wollombi House? They had two daughters, I know that—they're buried in the cemetery."

"Yes, that's right." She scratched at her head. "Long before my time. I remember your father and mother arriving, after the African War. You were such a pretty little thing with your sunshine curls and snub nose, and your poor dear ma, in the early stages she was, but suffering badly; your pa, not the man he is today. The war took its toll."

She'd heard the story more times than she could count, although she'd never truly understood Mrs. Canning's meaning until now. It made a little more sense after everything Pa had said about the camps. Right now she wanted to hear about the Pearsons.

Mrs. Canning sighed. "Those were the good days, happy days, once you'd all settled in. Have you sorted out your differences with your pa? There's only the two of you left now. You can't be at loggerheads."

"I tried. I hope so."

"It'll sort. Mavis told us about the boys while you were off fetching Miss Baldwin. Give him time. Where is he by the way?"

"He and Mavis are in the sitting room, the doors closed. I didn't want to interrupt."

"There was a telephone call. Now, what was it you were asking?" Mrs. Canning perched on the edge of the seat.

Sam put down his empty plate, gave a satisfied sigh, and stretched out his long legs. "About the Pearson family, who lived here. There were two daughters, Lydia and Bea, but there were also two other girls, Ella and Grace Ketter-something—"

"Ketteringham. And it's three other girls. You're forgetting Mellie Vale," PJ interjected.

344

"Ketteringham, you say. Why does that sound familiar? Let me think while I clear this mess up and I'll look in on Miss Baldwin when I've done the washing up. Why don't you show Sam the garden? Tell him about the treehouse you and the boys had."

The treehouse . . . "Do you know what happened to the photograph Pa had on the wall in his study? The one of the boys and me in the treehouse with Christmas hats? It isn't there anymore."

Mrs. Canning's face pinked. "I don't want you taking offense. It was a bad time . . ."

"And?"

"Your father threw it out in a rage when your letter came about the boys. I rescued it—it's at home. I'll bring it back tomorrow. You'd like it in your bedroom, I expect."

Pa's favorite photograph. He'd invited the photographer, Mr. Kedwell, to call on his way to Sydney and he'd arrived just two days before Christmas. He'd taken the photograph, along with pictures of the house and gardens. Pa'd framed them all and shown them to anyone and everyone. He must have been heartbroken to throw it away.

While PJ helped collect up the plates and cups and saucers and loaded up the tray for Mrs. Canning, Sam lolled on the bench seat, fingers laced behind his head, soaking up the sun. "Sky's never this blue at home." Their eyes met and the physical tug caught her unaware, the same as the very first time they'd met when the shell had fallen directly in front of her ambulance.

It wasn't until Mrs. Canning left that she sat down next to him. He took her hand in his and turned to her, his face so close she could see the flecks in his toffee eyes.

"How did your pa take the story about Dan and Riley?"

"The revolver took him by surprise. He recognized it as soon as he saw it." It wasn't her place to tell Sam about Pa's experiences, though he'd more than understand. "He thought Ma had disposed of it. The boys had no idea how to use it."

"Which probably saved them from a gaol sentence when they took a potshot at Miss Baldwin. I remember someone telling me you had a better chance of throwing a Webley at your enemy than firing. A revolver like that packs a punch, dreadful kickback—lucky they didn't blow their own heads off. Leastways they did the right thing getting her to the hospital."

"I wish they'd come home and told Pa what had happened."

"And run the risk of getting in trouble for stealing his revolver? Never mind firing it. Not sure I'd be that brave. He'll come around— he'd better because I don't think I can wait much longer." He wrapped his arms around her and pulled her close, his lips warm as they came down on hers in a long, slow kiss. "Still want to marry me?"

She nodded, nestling closer in his arms. "When Pa's forgiven me."

"I'm sure he has. And if he hasn't, then let me talk to him man-to-man. It's all a foolish misunderstanding."

CHAPTER 30

The last of the sun slanted through the louvers and the tangled branches of the wisteria made dancing patterns across the bed. Soon the weather would warm and the heavy purple flowers would create a perfumed cave. Miss Baldwin lifted her hands above her head and stretched. Memories from long ago jumped to the forefront, pushing back the here and now. Being at The Doctor's House made her a tad bewildered.

The breeze ruffled her hair, cooler now the sun had set. Not much longer for this chill, though. In a month or two spring would arrive, and orchids would bloom along the snig trail and the dappled gorge would offer the peace she longed for. She needed to be there among the ferns and fossils. She'd ask the boy to take her back.

Her heels beat a familiar tattoo on the timber boards along the veranda, words drifting in the air. She paused and tilted her head, trying to snatch at the fragments of sound . . . "Broken rib bone . . . Cause of death . . . Reconstructed pelvis." Then silence, a deep, menacing silence that did not bode well. Mavis must have received the coroner's report.

She rounded the corner, cleared her throat. Every eye lifted; gazes fixed on her: Mavis and Martindale side by side on the bench seat; Penelope, legs tucked under her; and Sam standing behind her, his hands resting on her shoulders. They made a lovely couple.

Mavis recovered first, bounded to her feet. "Are you feeling better?" She plumped the cushions on a wicker chair. "Come and sit down."

For over seventy years she'd waited for this moment, imagined facing a bewigged judge and a sea of jurors, not those she'd come to care for. She licked her dry lips, took a long, slow breath—a vain attempt to still her thundering heart—and lowered herself into the chair.

PJ clutched at Sam's hand as a thousand questions fell like embers around her feet. Now that Mavis had spoken to the coroner on the telephone, there was no doubt. A stab from a sharp implement was the cause of death. She'd known from the very beginning Mavis suspected foul play.

Mavis took several steps away from the wicker chair where Miss Baldwin sat, nesting like a bird among the cushions, eyes closed and the corners of her mouth tilted in a smile, perhaps a grimace. "Ah, Mrs. Canning, come and sit down. I'm sure you'll be interested."

Mavis rested back against the veranda rail and waited until Mrs. Canning had settled, then smiled briefly. "I'll start from the beginning again. I've just received a call from the coroner, Mr. Brown. He's examined the skeleton, and with the assistance of the pathologist at the Royal Newcastle Hospital, has reached several interesting conclusions. He agrees the bones cannot be more accurately dated."

PJ felt Sam's body tense.

"There's not enough evidence to proceed formally. He has, however, confirmed my findings. A stab wound to the heart by a sharp implement is the most likely cause of death. One of the ribs is fractured."

"A knife?" Sam asked.

"Possibly, but more likely some sort of spiked implement. We simply don't know. We have no murder weapon, no witnesses, no suspects, and we are unable to accurately date the bones."

PJ squeezed Sam's hand, a strange mix of excitement and sorrow coiling in her stomach. "I know I'm right. It has to be Ella Ketteringham."

"Penelope," Pa barked. "Mavis hasn't finished. Would you please give her the opportunity to speak?"

She bowed her head in apology. "Please, go on, Mavis."

"I'm certain these bones do not belong to one of the fossil girls."

"How can you be sure?" PJ clapped her hand over her mouth and buttoned her lips.

"They reconstructed the pelvis at the Royal Newcastle. There is no doubt the skeleton is that of a man. A small man, but a man nonetheless."

Mavis couldn't be right. There had to be some mistake. "But—"

"The skeleton is definitely male," Mavis repeated.

PJ leaned forward, ready to argue, and caught Sam's movement as he turned a concerned gaze on Miss Baldwin's chalky face. "So there is no possibility that it could be a young woman?"

"Why are you so set on it being a woman?" Pa asked. "You can't argue with science."

"I'm certain it's the elder Ketteringham girl. We can discount the Pearson girls and Anthea Winstanley because we know where they are buried."

Mavis shook her head. "I'm sorry, there's no doubt about it. The skeleton is a male. Other than that, and the possible cause of death, I'm afraid I have no other information or answers."

"Think, Penelope." Pa's tone took her scuttling back to her childhood. "Any number of people could have discovered the gorge. The boys managed to find their way down there."

Miss Baldwin covered her mouth, masking a yawn, and Mavis rose on cue. "Sam, I think it's time we returned to Kurri. Would you drive us?"

PJ curbed a groan. She still had hundreds of unanswered questions. Miss Baldwin had to know more about the fossil girls. It was obvious that she knew the house. "It's far too late to return to Kurri. We have ample room for visitors, haven't we, Pa?"

He gave her a long, thoughtful look, rather as though he suspected she had something planned but couldn't quite work out what she intended.

More unbridled curiosity rather than any kind of plan. "Miss Baldwin could take my room and, Mavis, if you wouldn't mind, we could share the boys' room, the sleep-out."

Mavis tipped her head to one side in question and received a nod of approval from Miss Baldwin, which brought Pa to his feet. "Very good, very good. Sam, will you see to the fires? I have something to do in my study." With a beaming smile, the first she had seen since she returned, Pa ambled off down the hallway.

"And I have a nice shepherd's pie ready for the oven, which I'm sure will be ample." Mrs. Canning eased to her feet. "I might need a little bit of a hand, Penelope. Beds to change and tables to set. Show Miss Baldwin and Dr. Elliot the amenities and then come and help me in the kitchen."

Having completed her tasks, PJ left everyone chatting in the sitting room and went into the kitchen to find Mrs. Canning sitting at the table, head in her hands. She lifted her tear-stained face. "Oh, it's you." She gave a rueful smile. "I popped home and picked up the picture of you and the boys. Do you want it in your room or shall I hang it back on the wall in the study if you and your pa have made up your differences?"

"Why don't I go and hang it up?" She held out her hand. "Could we have some drinks? I think maybe whiskey might go down well after Mavis's news. My theory about the skeleton being Ella Ketteringham has gone up in smoke."

"Of course it's not Ella Ketteringham. I couldn't for the life of me remember where I heard the name, then it came to me in a flash while I was cycling down the road. Not really sure why I ever forgot."

"Forgot?"

"Famous she was, really famous. She ran a music shop with her husband, the piano teacher George Hudderson, and her sister in Pitt Street in Sydney. A singer, she was. Performed to packed houses at the Royal Victoria Theatre. Mr. Canning took me to Sydney to hear her when we first started stepping out."

And so that is what had happened to the Ketteringham girls. She squeezed her eyes shut, recreating the first moment when she had seen the skeleton. She was so convinced that Ella had died in the gorge. "Why didn't you tell me? Their names are all over the fossils."

"I haven't got time to waste poring over those stinky old rocks, what with everything going on around here. Now what about helping with the drinks while I finish the pie?"

Exhaling slowly, PJ stood. She had no one to blame but herself. She'd jumped to a conclusion with no real evidence, swayed by Artie's story and the local scuttlebutt. Pa was right, she couldn't argue with science. "I'll go and get the decanters." PJ wandered along the hallway, gazing down at the photograph and the ludicrous grins on Dan's and Riley's faces. She would always miss them, but she knew they'd rest more peacefully now their story had been told.

She pushed open the door to the study and reached up and reinstated the Christmas photograph in its usual place. Dan's and Riley's voices rang in her ears, full of laughter and praise, happy to be home where they belonged. She kissed the tips of her fingers and pressed them to their lips.

"I'm sorry if I upset you by taking the picture of you and the boys." Mrs. Canning stood in the doorway with a drinks trolley, mopping at the corner of her eyes with her apron.

Poor Mrs. Canning. All this upheaval. "No. You didn't. Here, let me take the trolley."

"You do that and I'll go and sort the rest of dinner. It's good to have a full house again."

The candles on the table flickered, reminding PJ of old times; all the seats filled, the hum of conversation batted across the table. Sam reached out beneath the tablecloth and rested his hand on her thigh. "More as you imagined your homecoming?"

"Better than I could have imagined," she murmured.

"I still want to know about these bunyips."

"Local rumors. You heard what Miss Baldwin said."

"I bet your pa has something to say on the matter, and Mavis. Aren't you interested?"

Before she had time to respond, Miss Baldwin met her eye. "All rumors are based on fact, and science always holds the answer."

A flush of color heated PJ's cheeks. Miss Baldwin might be hard of hearing, but she had truly mastered the ability to lip-read.

"There's a kernel of truth in all these local stories," Miss Baldwin said. "It wasn't until I discovered science that I realized I'd allowed my overactive imagination to swamp my senses. A little logic often provides answers." She paused, looked from one face to the next, almost as though she wanted to ensure she had everyone's attention. "Shall we take these *stories* one at a time?"

Without waiting for everyone's agreement, she continued. "The bunyip is a creature from Australian Aboriginal legend. I made a point of investigating as much as I could some years ago, more for my own benefit than anyone else's. The word was largely used in Victoria. It wasn't until the middle of the last century that the stories spread, fueled by an exhibit at the Australian Museum purported to be a bunyip skull. It caused an uproar, but in a matter of weeks the idea was debunked. Sir Richard Owen, a controversial figure and an English paleontologist of some repute, confirmed it was a hydrocephalic skull of a foal or calf, and the belief it was a bunyip was as mythical as Alice's Jabberwock."

Pa's bark of laughter came as such a surprise. "If I remember correctly there were many people who tried to debunk our Australian fauna, the platypus being the most contentious. The Royal Society maintained it was the bill of a duck sewn onto the body of a beaver."

"Ah, yes, and in the case of the bunyip, Dr. Martindale, Sir Richard was correct and we adopted a wonderful word into our vocabulary, a Sydney synonym for *imposter* or *pretender*. Idle men with plenty of loose time and spare cash."

"Indeed, the bunyip aristocracy." Pa rocked back in his chair, his fingers interlocked, hands resting on his stomach. His eyes twinkled and an amused smile tugged at his lips, an expression PJ hadn't seen for longer than she could remember. Light-headed with relief, she blinked away a tear.

"Just a moment." Sam held up his hand and she turned to him. "You've lost me here. What exactly is a platypus?"

Surely Sam had heard of a platypus. "An Australian animal." As a child, she had spent hours watching their antics down at the brook.

"A duck, with fur, not feathers? You'll be telling me next it lays eggs."

"It does," everyone chorused and burst into laughter.

Sam threw up his hands. "PJ, help me out here."

"I'll take you for a walk tomorrow, if you're up early enough, and show you."

Sam turned to Miss Baldwin. "Are there any of these platypuses in the gorge?"

"In the deeper waters of the creek, indeed there are." Miss Baldwin nodded emphatically. "And I can assure you, Sam, they do lay their eggs, in burrows."

"But no bunyips?"

"I've never found any reference to bunyips whatsoever in relation to the gorge. My belief is it's simply an extension of the story surrounding Ellalong Lagoon put about by someone for an alternative reason." Miss Baldwin schooled her face, as though suppressing a smile.

A tap on her shoulder made PJ turn from the table. "Penelope, can you give me a hand clearing the plates?" Mrs. Canning stood by the door with the trolley.

"Of course." She pushed back her chair. How could she have forgotten? "Mrs. Canning has solved the mystery of the Ketteringham girls. Shall I tell everyone, Mrs. Canning, or will you?"

"You go ahead. I can manage the plates."

PJ sat down again. "Apparently the Ketteringham girls ended up in Sydney. Ella married and became a well-known singer, and she and her sister ran a music shop. So that just leaves one person unaccounted for—Mellie Vale."

PJ blinked. She wasn't mistaken. Miss Baldwin could hardly control the smile on her face. "There was a fossil belonging to her in Dan and Riley's collection." She bit her lip. Whatever had made her bring the conversation back to the sensitive topic of Dan and Riley? For the first time since she'd arrived home, Pa was his old self, eyes bright behind his spectacles, offering titbits of information from his vast store of knowledge. She shot a glance in his direction, seeing his head bent toward Mavis; they appeared deep in a conversation of their own. Perhaps he hadn't heard her. Mellie Vale and an unknown murder victim—the coil of curiosity she'd nursed since she'd seen Anthea Winstanley's name in London unraveled, replaced by the image that had haunted her since she and Sam had first arrived at Bow Wow: the girls in white dresses against a backdrop of sandstone rocks and draping ferns.

A sense of warmth spread through her body. "Excuse me just one moment."

She flew down the hallway and opened the door of the corner cupboard. She ran her hand along the back of the shelf and brought out the framed picture she'd found when she first came home and was searching for Dan and Riley's fossils.

Behind the glass, the gray images flickered into shape: the girls as she remembered, and also the older man and woman in the center, and on the right a laden pack horse flanked by two people, another man and another woman, and the background of rocks and ferns—the gorge, unless she was mistaken. Unlike any other early photographs she'd seen. No formal poses, aspidistras, and frozen faces. Almost like a bleached, discolored painting. An intense yearning swept over her. She hadn't imagined the scene.

Hugging the heavy picture tight to her body, she returned to the dining room and stood at the head of the table, ensuring Miss Baldwin could see her lips; she didn't want her to miss anything. "I have something I'd like to show you all." She plastered a hopeful smile on her face and held up the picture. "I believe this was originally stored in the trunk with the fossils from Bow Wow. Miss Baldwin, I'm certain it's the gorge, and I wondered if you recognized any of the people."

Miss Baldwin pulled her wire-framed spectacles from her pocket and hooked them over her ears. "May I have a closer look?"

PJ handed her the picture, her throat suddenly dry.

"You're quite correct. It is the gorge. It's more overgrown now."

PJ's pulse picked up. "And the people. Do you know who they might be?"

"The fossil girls." Miss Baldwin gave a sharp laugh.

The fossil girls. Artie's story blossomed and took shape once again. It didn't answer the question about the strange happenings, though. A trickle of perspiration worked its way between her breasts.

Miss Baldwin squinted at her over the top of her spectacles. "That's Lydia Pearson and her sister, Bea—the doctor's daughters. This one, the pouty girl with the parasol, would be Ella Ketteringham."

PJ's breath caught in her throat. She clearly remembered Miss Baldwin saying she hadn't arrived in Australia until the seventies. "What about Mellie Vale?"

"She isn't there." And neither was Ella's sister, Grace. Probably chasing chickens. *Bawk-bawk.* Miss Baldwin clamped her lips together to prevent the squawk escaping.

"Do you recognize anyone else?" Penelope asked, narrowing her eyes suspiciously.

"The two with the horse might be the people who worked for Anthea, Nette and Jordan."

"Nette and Jordan?" Mrs. Canning chipped in as she clattered the last plate onto the trolley. "Nette and Jordan Simpson? They're buried in the cemetery, died in the coaching accident on the rise at Ellalong Lagoon along with the older Pearson girl."

Much to her horror, tears sprang to her eyes. They'd been so kind to her, and that simple fact answered so many questions. She and Anthea had left Bow Wow in such a rush, a passage booked to London within days, expecting Nette and Jordan to return to the house after they'd dropped the Pearson girls at Wollombi. Anthea had written on many occasions. Several years later the letters came back marked *Return to Sender*. Anthea had presumed they'd moved on—a fact Miss Baldwin thought she'd confirmed when she finally returned to Bow Wow and found the house as they had left it.

Mavis pressed a handkerchief into her hand. "Enough for one day?"

Perhaps it was. When Penelope handed her the daguerreotype, she hadn't imagined the heartache it would cause. "I'm perfectly fine, just a little dust in my eyes." She made a fine show of removing her spectacles, dabbing at her eyes. "I don't know any of the other girls." No one she'd ever seen before. The man beside Anthea? She didn't recognize him, although only one person would be permitted such a proprietorial arm at Anthea's elbow. It had to be Benjamin. "When was this picture taken?" She handed it to Sam.

He placed it in his lap and turned it over. "There's nothing on the back. May I take it out of the frame, sir?"

"Go ahead." Dr. Martindale's voice made her start. She'd almost forgotten he was there.

Sam rummaged in his pocket and brought out a strange contraption. He flicked a metal arm out; it was a knife of some sort with a collection of other blades and implements. What an interesting tool, far more compact than a marlin spike, probably not long enough to kill a man, though. She clutched at her knees to still their trembling.

The knife scored the back of the frame, and with a neat flick of his wrists Sam removed the leather-backed daguerreotype, neatly encased in a copper surround. "It has a signature on the back. 'George Goodman, 1845.' I didn't know they took photographs in those days."

"Goodman opened the first professional studio in George Street in Sydney in 1842. Mostly portraiture, but he'd done some work in Tasmania—street scenes. He traveled to regional areas in New South Wales to take photographs of prominent local families at their homes. Charming work and surprisingly informal for the time." Martindale gave a slightly apologetic smile. "I've always had a fascination for the photographic process. Can you make a guess at anyone else, Miss Baldwin?"

"That's Anthea Winstanley, and the man next to her must be Benjamin Winstanley." No lie in that, but the full story was better kept in the past. During the passage to England, Anthea had admitted to her that she and Benjamin had never married; that in fact he had a wife. They'd left England on the same ship, as Anthea Winstanley and Benjamin Baldwin, and arrived in Australia as Mr. and Mrs. Winstanley. Anthea's inheritance had allowed them to take up the land grant at Bow Wow Gorge. Unable to divorce his wife, Benjamin had left her the family fortune and simply disappeared—he never returned to England.

She masked a smile, remembering her outrage, until Anthea explained that it was his wife's decision that they should lead separate lives. Their marriage was nothing more than a convenience. He hadn't, however, anticipated the greed his nephew, Victor, would display, attempting to make a claim on Bow Wow when he learned of Benjamin's death.

As for herself, she'd adopted the Baldwin name when she'd arrived back in Sydney and discovered Mitchell had marked part of the Bow Wow property with Victor Baldwin's name. She thought it would save any unfortunate inquiries that might arise—it meant people wouldn't question her right to the land.

"What about Mellie Vale?" PJ asked. "You said she wasn't in the photograph."

A chill brushed the back of her neck. She'd rather hoped that little slip had passed unnoticed. The time had come. She and Anthea shared the secret of what had happened in the gorge, and she had no intention of ever revealing it. And if Mavis was to be believed, it could not be proven one way or another. It was a bond that forever tied them, but the rest could be shared. "When Anthea left Bow Wow and returned to England, her daughter was with her."

"Her daughter?"

"Her adopted daughter—Amelia Winstanley."

"A. Winstanley?"

The delight and satisfaction on Penelope's face made her revelation far sweeter than she'd anticipated. "Perhaps it is easier if you call me Mellie."

CHAPTER 31

Much to PJ's amazement, in a totally unexpected move, Sam woke her before dawn, determined to see the platypus down at the brook. She'd had no difficulty finding the spot, and sure enough, as the sun rose, a bull's-eye pattern rippled across the top of the glassy water. The slightest splash echoed in the hollow near the bank, and a glistening shape glided through the water, arched its back, and launched downward.

"Just wait, watch for the pattern on the water. It'll resurface downstream."

The concentric circles spread outward and then a hind foot appeared and the platypus gave a leisurely scratch before diving again.

"There, you've seen your first platypus."

"Strange little critter. And they lay their eggs in burrows?"

"Yes, and the mother feeds her young."

"So they're mammals."

"Monotremes. Egg-laying mammals. There's only two, the platypus and the echidna."

"Echidnas?"

"Spiny anteaters."

"And have you got one of those around here?" Sam looked around as though he expected another strange animal to stroll into the clearing.

"They're shy creatures. There used to be one up in the bush behind the house. I'll ask Pa if he's seen it lately."

"I'd heard about kangaroos—it's a whole new world out here. Have you got anything else to show me?"

"Lots, but not right now. We should be getting back to the house. Mrs. Canning will want some help with breakfast."

"Ah, but I have something for us first." He reached into his haversack and pulled out a thermos flask and two cups. "Coffee?"

"Coffee? Where did you get that?"

"A place called the Emporium Coffee Palace in the Haymarket."

"Don't tell me. Ted found it. Just as well you took him and not me."

"Next time we'll go together. I bought enough coffee to stock Wollombi House for the foreseeable future. I showed Mrs. Canning how to use the pot so Miss Baldwin won't have to miss out on her morning coffee. There's a lot I'd like to explore in Australia. I didn't realize just how much the country had to offer."

"But not yet. I'm not ready to go anywhere yet, but I want you to stay." PJ leaned her cheek against Sam's chest.

"Too many unanswered questions?" He ran his fingers through her hair. "I'm so pleased you've let it grow again."

"Far too many unanswered questions. Every time I go back over last night I see how clever Miss Baldwin—"

"Mellie."

"Mellie . . . was with her answers. She might be old, but her mind is as sharp as someone half her age."

"When did you realize she knew more than she was letting on?"

"I had my suspicions, but I couldn't work out which of the girls she might be. It wasn't until I found Mellie's dragon scale that I realized another girl had visited Bow Wow that year. She had ample opportunity to tell me who she was when I showed it to her, but she didn't. Then when we arrived here and I found her down at the millpond, she mentioned Dr. Pearson's name and she seemed so familiar with the house. I can't help wondering what else she's hiding. I think she's behind all the rumors."

"Why would she be? If she and Anthea were mates—great word, so great I'm going to adopt it—then why drag her name through the mud? And why does she call herself Miss Baldwin, and why doesn't she live at Bow Wow? Why keep it a secret from everyone that she's going there? Even Mavis didn't know."

"Think back to last night in the dining room . . ."

"The conversation about Australia's weird and wonderful animals?"

"About the bunyips. Mellie said she couldn't find any reference to bunyips in the gorge, that it was an extension of the Ellalong story."

"I remember. I thought it was interesting because you'd insisted from the very beginning that the stories were just to keep children away from danger."

"Yes, but after that. She said the stories were put about for an alternative reason. I was so centered on finding out about the other girls in the daguerreotype, it slipped my mind. Did you see that sneaky little smile when we asked if there were bunyips in the gorge? I'm certain she's behind those rumors too." She reached down and grabbed Sam's hand. "We've got to go home. I want to talk to her before she leaves."

"Slow down, slow down. They won't be going anywhere just yet. I said last night I'd give them a lift home after breakfast."

Mellie sat in the wicker chair, cup of coffee in hand, and let out a long, satisfied sigh. Early, before the sun rose, she'd heard PJ and Sam leave on their platypus hunt. She lay on the bed watching the sunrise with an unnatural sense of peace and calm pervading her entire body.

Nothing remained of the room to remind her of the past. Bea and Grace had shared the large bed when she'd first come to The Doctor's House, and she hadn't set foot inside the room, hadn't dared, only peeked through the window when no one was about. Her finger reached for the dent in the center of her forehead, all that remained of the dreadful chicken pox. Not as dreadful as it had seemed because without it, she never would have come to Wollombi, nor to Bow Wow, where her life had truly begun.

The certain symmetry of it all appealed, like the shining ammonite Anthea found on the beach at Lyme, a flawless specimen. A perfect spiral. Deep down inside she was still the same person, but thanks to Anthea she'd grown, moved further and further away from the past, yet never lost the central attachment, and now she'd traced that path back. Soon it would be time to step aside, but before that could happen, she had one more thing to do, and in the frail light of the morning she'd made her decision.

She stretched out her legs and circled her feet. It would be wonderful to feel the grass between her toes. Leaving her coffee cup, she slipped out of her shoes and with a quick glance over her shoulder, stepped off the veranda and made her way across the cool grass and beneath the tangled branches into the wisteria cave where someone had placed a bench seat among the limbs. She sat down and inhaled the sweet scent of the first wisteria flowers carried on the morning breeze.

An unexpected touch on her shoulder made her start.

She flinched and whipped around, heart thumping. Penelope and Sam. She hadn't heard them approach.

"Miss Baldwin, may I ask you something?" Penelope, hair swinging like a splash of sunshine and her face flushed, beamed at her. "Last night you said the stories about the gorge were put about for an alternative reason. What did you mean?"

Such an astute girl. "Why don't you sit down? The wisteria is coming into bloom; its lovely subtle fragrance should be enjoyed."

Sam dropped to the ground and crossed his legs, and PJ took the spot beside her on the bench.

"As you have rightly surmised, Penelope, the stories of the gorge are nothing but rumor, albeit a rumor I fostered."

"But why?" Penelope's sunny disposition disappeared in an instant. "Why spread rumors of a bunyip and why, for goodness' sake, take the name Baldwin and allow Anthea's name and reputation to be tarnished? All that scuttlebutt about girls disappearing and her strange and exotic tastes. She considered you her daughter, and left you everything."

And a responsibility for the preservation of the treasures of the gorge. "I chose to take the name Baldwin because the area where I built my house was known as Baldwin's Lot. I couldn't use the name Winstanley if I was to foster the rumors about the gorge and thus keep its treasures safe."

Those rumors took on a life of their own, with a little help from Anthea's one-time maid-of-all-work, who in a fit of spite had initiated the story.

She'd reacted at first with shock, outraged that Anthea's memory should be tainted in such a way, and then had come to realize the story provided not only protection of the gorge but also ensured Victor Baldwin's remains lay undisturbed. That is, until PJ and Sam discovered the skeleton and she'd had visions of having to take responsibility for Baldwin's murder and spend the remainder of her life behind bars.

She could never betray Anthea. A close escape and one she shouldn't dwell upon. "I simply wanted to protect the gorge. I'm sure you agree it should be preserved. I noticed the first time we met at Bow Wow your interest in the paper I was writing."

PJ's cheeks colored and she opened her mouth to speak.

Mellie didn't give her the opportunity. "I intend to submit the paper to the Geological Society, providing they'll deign to accept something from a woman."

"I'm sure they'll be happy to receive it, ma'am. You deserve to have your work recognized."

"That is not my reason, Sam. I'm more interested in the preservation of the area. It's a unique geological marvel. I'm hoping for their support. Anthea always presumed I would one day pass the property on, but marriage and children never eventuated." She couldn't repress the shudder that passed through her, nor the waver in her voice. "I intend to place a covenant on the area that will prevent any future disturbance. It should be preserved as a living museum. And I would like your help, both of you."

"Of course, anything." Penelope covered her hand and patted it gently, making her feel every one of her eighty-four years. "Perhaps the boys' fossils might be of some use. I'd love to help you catalog them. I'm no authority but—"

"I would be more than happy to do anything I can to help." Sam leaned toward her, his chin resting on his clasped hands. "My father has some connections that may assist with the Geological Society."

"He has?" Penelope's face paled. More interestingly, the tips of Sam's ears turned red, a sure sign in a man that he had something to reveal.

"Father is a longtime supporter of the Carnegie Museum of Natural History in Pittsburgh. He and Andrew—"

"Andrew Carnegie, the man who unearthed the fossils of the diplodocus?" Penelope asked, a look of incredulity on her face.

"I don't think he exactly dug it up. He and Father go back a long way . . ."

"It's named after him. *Diplodocus carnegii*. You told me he played a role. Not that he was a family friend."

Sam shrugged. "Father and I haven't seen eye to eye since I left for France. I didn't want to disappoint you, lead you to imagine he might offer some kind of assistance."

"Then why bring it up now?"

"Seeing the problems between you and your pa made me realize how foolishly I've behaved. I sent him a telegram, just to let him know where I was and our plans. I got a response far sooner than I expected—within a couple of days. He and Mother can't wait to meet you."

"Sam, Penelope . . . Thank you for your offer of Carnegie's assistance, but I would rather not involve additional people. I feel it's a responsibility I have to Anthea's memory to sort out the matter myself."

"We'll help however we can, though, won't we, PJ?"

Still smarting from her surprise at Sam's revelation, no doubt, Penelope didn't respond—she continued to glare at the poor boy.

"What a coincidence that you stumbled on Anthea's Bow Wow ichthyosaur vertebra in London."

Penelope's face brightened. "Yes. And I remembered Bow Wow Gorge from the boys' collection." Her eyes dropped and she plucked at her sleeve. "I had a foolish idea that perhaps they, too, had found remains of an ichthyosaur. I imagined their names commemorated— *Ichthyosaurus martindalii*."

"Not as far-fetched as you might believe. Anthea and I left Australia intent on discovering everything we could about ichthyosaurs and plesiosaurs, the sea-dragons. Fascinating creatures, dolphin-like marine reptiles, thought to have died out long before the dinosaurs. We spent many years on the Continent, our Grand Tour, Anthea called it, researching the great sea-dragons. It wasn't until after I returned to Australia that the first was found in Queensland."

"So there could still be evidence hidden in the gorge?" Penelope's eyes sparked and a pink glow warmed her cheeks.

Unless she was very much mistaken, the bug had well and truly bitten this passionate young woman. Just as she'd hoped. A worthy successor. And now there was no reason for the quest not to continue. "I have something I think you would enjoy. Hawkins's *The Book of the Great Sea-dragons*."

EPILOGUE

CHRISTMAS 1919
Bow Wow

"Is everyone ready?" PJ pulled the door to Bow Wow House closed. It had taken weeks to peel away the layers of the past, but now the old house glistened and gleamed. They'd cut back the creepers covering the veranda, the dappled shade revealing its simple beauty; the shutters were opened and new glass installed in all the windows; the mold-spotted walls scrubbed and the rotten floorboards replaced. But for Ted and Artie and the team of men from the mines who had devoted every Sunday to helping, she and Sam never would have managed to complete everything before Christmas.

"I think that's it." Sam hefted the picnic hamper onto the dogcart. "Come on, Mellie. Your chariot awaits." He patted the cushion on the seat.

"I have absolutely no intention of riding down the snig trail. I never have and I never will. Back up the hill possibly. We shall see." She tossed her head and opened her new bright orange sun umbrella with a flourish.

PJ had discovered Mellie's Achilles' heel when a large parcel had arrived only a few days earlier from David Jones in Sydney. Full of day dresses, sun umbrellas, and even shirts, ties, and hats for Pa and Sam. Early Christmas presents Mellie had insisted, with strict instructions, that they should all wear their new clothes for the Christmas Day picnic. It would be the beginning of a new tradition.

The cavalcade made its way down the snig trail. Pa, looking exceptionally jaunty in a straw boater, and Mavis, in a very smart navy-blue dress with a white collar taking the lead, arm in arm. In the past weeks their friendship, forged during the flu epidemic, had blossomed into something more—quite what, PJ wasn't sure, but it brought a smile to both of their faces and there had been many discussions with Sam about the new ambulance service they hoped to introduce to the area. Artie and Ted were right behind them, taking great care of Mrs. Canning, who still looked a little flustered from her exertions in the kitchen.

"Are you going to ride with me?" Sam tilted his new Akubra back from his face and picked up the reins.

"Mellie and I will walk."

"I'll bring up the rear. Let me know if you get tired and want to ride."

Darling Sam, her rock, as solid and strong as the ancient cliffs protecting the gorge, and soon to be her husband. Quite how she would have managed without him in the last months she refused to imagine.

The very evening after Mellie and Mavis had left Wollombi, he'd disappeared into Pa's study, she'd presumed for another game of chess, but Sam must have let Mrs. Canning in on the secret because within ten minutes they'd reappeared with huge smiles, congratulations, and a bottle of the new Hunter Valley sparkling wine. And that's when they had all agreed that it would be a far better idea to invite Sam's parents to Australia for the wedding than to travel to America, because both she and Sam had commitments in Australia. So, while they awaited the arrival of the luxury liner, the RMS *Aquitania*, from New York, Mellie had made the decision to prepare Bow Wow House for occupation once more.

In a moment of retrospection PJ had written, as she'd promised, to Mr. Ambrose and Mr. Woods, telling them the story of Anthea Winstanley. Mr. Ambrose had replied, saying he would be happy to receive any other specimens they might be prepared to part with, and if they found more evidence of ichthyosaurs in Bow Wow Gorge, he would support an application to the museum. Mellie hadn't reacted with quite the enthusiasm she'd imagined when PJ had shown her Mr. Ambrose's letter. She said she still didn't want to draw attention to the gorge, but PJ was not convinced. Time would tell.

The grass covering the snig trail, still green beneath the canopy of trees despite the increasing heat, blew in the gentle breeze as they worked their way down to the gorge, their journey punctuated by the overwhelming racket of cicadas.

Mellie drew to a halt and stepped to one side. "Does this remind you of anything?"

PJ's gaze roamed the track from Sam in the dogcart to Pa and Mavis meandering down toward the creek, and her heart jolted. "The daguerreotype. It's almost the same, even down to our parasols."

"Everyone seems very happy." Mellie rummaged in the small bag she had insisted on carrying. "I have another present."

"Mellie, you shouldn't. You must stop . . ."

"Allow an old lady to enjoy her weaknesses." She handed PJ a small but heavy rectangular package. "I thought you would like this. Go on, open it now. You may want to use it."

PJ closed her umbrella and rested it against a tree before pulling off the paper wrapping. "It's a camera."

"Not any camera. The very latest Eastman Kodak Brownie." Mellie ticked its attributes off on her fingers. "It's ugly but practical, light and portable, aluminium case, not cardboard. I shall expect you to keep a record, not only of today, but of all our cataloging. Much more accurate than my drawings."

"Is everything all right there?" Sam slowed the dogcart to a crawl. "Sure you don't want a ride?"

"Yes, we're fine. Go ahead." PJ turned the camera this way and that, unsure how it worked.

"I believe you hold it at waist height. It has a window on the front, and at the top and inside there is an angled mirror. It works in the same way as your eye. I'm sure you won't find it too difficult. Just look through the window, compose the picture, and depress the shutter, the lever."

PJ brought the camera closer, moved it slowly from one side to the other, looking through the small window as the image formed. With a quick flick of her wrist, she captured the moment. Maybe one day it would help fill in events that might otherwise be lost to future generations.

"Now come along. I don't intend to miss out on this picnic." Mellie strode ahead, leaving PJ to gambol after her.

Although Mellie hated to admit it, the walk had taken more out of her than she anticipated. She leaned back against the iron bark, comfortable on the blanket and pile of cushions Sam had provided and unable to curb the smile of satisfaction. Everything she'd dreamed had come to pass and the demons that had plagued her life had finally been laid to rest.

"Happy?" Mavis slipped down beside her on the rug.

"Happier than I ever imagined, and I can feel Anthea's spirit—she's here with us still." At peace at last, her secret safe and her reputation assured. "Her gorge will be preserved. A living museum. It's a wonderful expression."

"I thought you might like this." Mavis held out her clenched fist and slowly opened her palm.

Every skerrick of breath left Mellie's body. She blinked twice. Anthea's pendant. The winged brachiopod, the perfect dragon scale, its polished surface catching the sunlight filtering through the trees, the decorative silver bail gleaming as it had the first time she saw it.

"I believe this belonged to Anthea Winstanley."

Mellie pushed back against the trunk, the knobbled bark anchoring her, and managed to restrain the nod of her head. Not now. Not after Mavis had said the coroner had closed the case. "Why would you think that?"

"Do you remember the daguerreotype Penelope showed us?"

Of course she did. She nodded, didn't dare speak. That was the moment she'd made her first slip, named the fossil girls, and said Mellie Vale wasn't in the picture. It had led to her confession. No, not a confession. She had nothing to confess. She had Anthea's reputation to protect.

"William—"

"William?" Did she notice a hint of color in Mavis's usually pale cheeks?

"Dr. Martindale. He has an interest in photography. He wanted to replace the frame on the daguerreotype that Sam removed when we were having dinner. It's vitally important that the backing remains sealed, otherwise the image deteriorates."

Mellie licked her dry lips. Why was Mavis sitting here chatting as though this was insignificant? And more importantly, why hadn't *she* thought to wonder whether Anthea's pendant had been found in the cave? When she returned to Bow Wow, she'd searched and searched but had never come across it. It must have been with Victor Baldwin's body.

"Mellie?" Mavis's green-eyed gaze studied her with concern. "Are you thirsty? Shall I get you a drink?"

"No. Please continue. It would be such a shame if the daguerreotype was lost." A lie. Better if it had never come to light.

"We were examining the depth of detail in the picture. So remarkable at such an early period in the process. William handed me his magnifying glass, and that was when I recognized it."

She had to know. "You recognized it?"

"Yes, I found it in the chest cavity of the skeleton. Penelope was with me."

And yet neither of them had mentioned it. Undone by a magnifying glass. It was almost laughable.

"However, it's of no consequence now. The coroner has reached his verdict, and besides, it's nothing more than circumstantial evidence."

Mellie couldn't restrain the sigh of relief that whistled out between her lips, and she raised her eyes to the heavens. Was Anthea up there watching on? Waiting to see if the troubled child, prone to flights of fantasy, whom she'd rescued from a life of misery, would keep their pact?

She still didn't truly know what had happened that day in the cave. She remembered the looming shadow, the leathery grasp throwing her against the wall, and the bunyip's yowl filling her head as her world turned to darkness, but no matter how hard she'd tried over the years, Anthea refused to discuss the details.

When she'd regained consciousness, Baldwin was dead, the marlin spike impaled in his back. Anthea had pulled it free and they'd laid out his body in the cave and made their panic-stricken escape across the seas to the Continent, Anthea terrified that someone would come searching for Baldwin. Finally news came of Thomas Mitchell's death, the one person of consequence who had known of Baldwin's interest in Bow Wow Gorge. Only then had they felt safe to return to England. Anthea couldn't entertain the thought of returning to Australia; however, the days in Lyme held some of her happiest memories and Anthea's remains, but she had promised she would return and take care of the gorge.

A spark of sunlight glistened in the corner of her vision, bringing her out of her reverie. The pendant dangled in front of her, directing the rays of sunlight onto her face.

"I thought you might like to keep it." Mavis lifted Anthea's pendant and dropped the silver chain over her head. "A fitting reminder of the past."

HISTORICAL NOTE

Bow Wow Gorge does exist. It is listed on the Register of the National Estate held by the National Trust and preserved under a Voluntary Conservation Agreement with National Parks and Wildlife, and visits are not encouraged. I was, however, fortunate enough to receive an invitation and the memory of its beautiful, undisturbed tranquillity stayed with me throughout my writing.

Wollombi House was built in the 1860s for the magistrate of the day. He sold it to the major businessman of the town, a Mr. Chapman. In 1888, Dr. Bapty moved to Wollombi and bought the house. He served as Wollombi's much-loved doctor from 1888 until the 1930s. (The two doctors in the story are in no way based on Dr. Bapty.) The house has been beautifully restored by the current owners. It overlooks both the millpond and the cemetery, the resting place of many pioneers of the district. (I did indulge in a little bit of poetic license—I'm not sure anyone would be able to get a cricket ball into the millpond from the garden.) A flour mill, used to grind locally grown wheat, originally stood on the far side of the millpond, opposite the cemetery. The mill was powered by horses turning a capstan and later replaced by a steam engine. It burned down in 1904.

All references to the 1919 Spanish flu pandemic are, hopefully, accurate. HMT *Norman* arrived in Australia in August 1919, and I couldn't resist including the lovely comment about wearing masks on your face and not your pocket that I found on the Australian War Memorial website, while reading the diary of one of the repatriated Diggers. As I write this it seems that one hundred years later not much has changed in the management of pandemics. TROVE (Australia's free online research portal) provided all the references to the pandemic in the Hunter region, and thankfully by August 1919, the worst was over in the area.

Kurri Kurri Hotel is still in business and is majestic in every way—a wonderful example of Australian pub architecture. Licensed for business on April 7, 1904, the grand thirty-four-room hotel was built at a cost of about $5,500 and was given the nod by the magistrates to proceed with a conditional license over other applications, because of the superior dunnies.

And so to the other side of the world . . . I have an ongoing love affair with museums and old artifacts. London's Natural History Museum was my introduction at a very early age to museums, and I can still remember the overwhelming awe I experienced when I first stood in front of the giant diplodocus, Dippy, constructed entirely by human hand, a giant jigsaw sent across the Atlantic Ocean in thirty crates and assembled in the museum.

I spent a summer holiday or two in Lyme Regis as a child, galloping out onto The Cob in a howling gale, searching for fossils and mackerel fishing with the locals. Mary Anning, Elizabeth Philpot, and many other characters and works referred to in passing are, I hope, true to life. I highly recommend the book by Christopher McGowan, *The Dragon Seekers—How an Extraordinary Circle of Fossilists Discovered the Dinosaurs and Paved the Way for Darwin*.

And finally to bunyips. The Australian Museum in Sydney did exhibit a "bunyip skull" in 1847. Its authenticity was questioned and quickly debunked. I believe it is, at the time of writing, on exhibition at the University of Sydney. The "story" about Ellalong Lagoon is a local myth, and if you drive the road through Paxton to Ellalong, it takes little imagination to envisage an accident, or, when the moon is high, a bunyip!

The story is purely fictional. The Winstanleys, the Pearsons, the Ketteringhams, the Martindale family, and Victor Baldwin, are all figments of my imagination. Bow Wow Gorge has a fine array of fossils, but, as far as I know, no human or ichthyosaur remains have been discovered to date!

ACKNOWLEDGMENTS

I would like to acknowledge the Wonnarua, Awabakal, and Darkinjung people as the traditional owners of the land where this story is set and pay my respect to Elders past, present, and emerging.

There are a host of people I wish to thank:

Colin and Pamela Fitzsimons, for sharing their wealth of information about Bow Wow Gorge and for allowing me the privilege of visiting their glorious property. Camilla and David, the current owners of Wollombi House, for their time and wine, and all sorts of snippets of information and bits of furniture that made their way into the story. The Coalfields Local History Association, and most especially Lynette Hamer, for her help with the history of Kurri Kurri and the hospital. Dr. Victoria Francis and Barton Lowe, for their knowledge of all things skeletal (all errors are my own). And finally, Kes Harper, Studio Gleaned, Wollombi, for her description of Anthea's necklace.

As always—chief researcher, Charles; chief historian, Carl Hoipo; chief engineer, Denis Brown; critique partners Sarah Barrie and Paula J Beavan; and my wonderful publisher, Jo Mackay, and her team at HQ. Annabel Blay, Jo Butler, and Chrysoula Aiello, for their assistance in turning my manuscript into a book. The marvelous designer Darren

Acknowledgments

Holt of HarperCollins Design Studio, for yet another wonderful cover, and Natika Palka and the HarperCollins sales team, who take my stories out into the world. And in the US, my thanks to Amanda Bostic, Julie Monroe, and every member of the Harper Muse team. Your skill, unflagging patience, and encouragement know no bounds.

And most importantly to Penelope Jane Wallis (PJ), for the loan of her name—sometimes finding the right name for a character is one of the hardest tasks!

Finally, to my wonderful readers: thank you. Without your reviews, emails, support, and enthusiasm my stories would remain buried!

DISCUSSION QUESTIONS

1. Legends and their influence play an important role in this book. What did you think of the legend of the bunyip? Were you told any legends as a child, or perhaps even as an adult?

2. In what ways does the story shed light on how women were treated in the second half of the 1800s and during the World War I years?

3. The author gives vibrant, brilliant descriptions of Australia—the sights and sounds, the animals, the legends, the people. Were there any that particularly stood out to you?

4. Why do you think PJ's father blamed her for Dan's and Riley's deaths? He said PJ's decision to join up "put ideas into their heads," but could there be another reason he blames her? Do you think the beginning of a reconciliation between father and daughter was visible at the end of the book?

5. What did you think of the surprise connection between Mellie (Ms. Baldwin) and PJ's twin brothers, and their subsequent enlistment in the army?

6. Mellie commented that it was "time to accept that she

wouldn't live forever" and "needed someone to continue her work, Anthea's legacy." What do you think of Mellie's choice?

7. Discuss the impact Anthea had on Mellie's life—from her support of Mellie's "dragon hunting," to allowing her to stay with her when the other fossil girls returned home, to her eventual, though unofficial, adoption of Mellie.

8. What do you think happened in the cave between Mr. Baldwin, Mellie, and Anthea? Even Mellie says she does not know all the details. How did Mr. Baldwin's death impact Mellie's and Anthea's lives?

9. Discuss what you think the future holds for PJ and Sam.

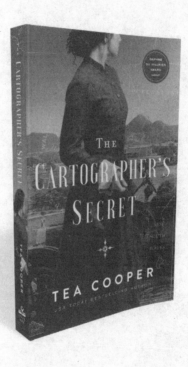

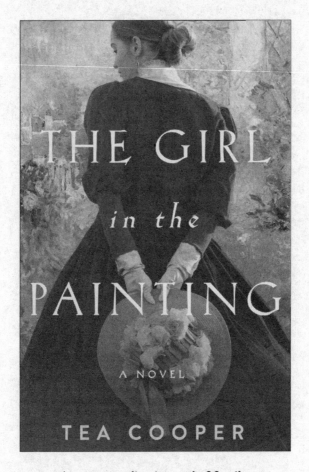

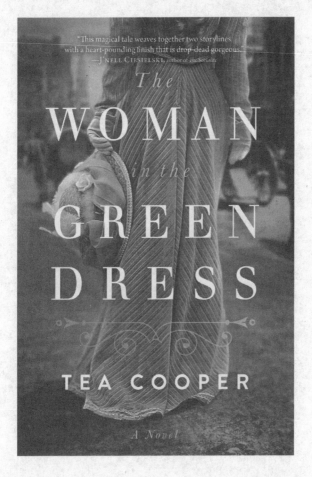

ABOUT THE AUTHOR

Copyright © Katy Clymo

Tea Cooper is an established Australian author of historical fiction. In a past life she was a teacher, a journalist, and a farmer. These days she haunts museums and indulges her passion for storytelling. She is the winner of two Daphne du Maurier Awards and the bestselling author of several novels, including *The Horse Thief*, *The Cedar Cutter*, *The Currency Lass*, and *The Naturalist's Daughter*.

teacooperauthor.com
Instagram: @tea_cooper
Twitter: @TeaCooper1
Facebook: @TeaCooper
Pinterest: @teacooperauthor